THE CURSE OF THE HOUSE ON CYPRESS LANE

JAMES HUNT

D1520135

❀ Created with Vellum

*M*oonlight penetrated the branches of the old cypress trees that sprouted from the swamp. The black water was still and reflected the night sky. Cicadas buzzed and frogs croaked. A hot breeze blew the dangling strands of Spanish moss that hung from branches. They wiggled like fingers and moved shadows in the dark, breathing life into monsters that didn't exist, and concealing the ones that did.

Sharon's bare feet smacked against the thick Louisiana mud on her serpentine sprint through the swamp. She swatted at the Spanish moss dangling from the branches, catching on her hair and arms, tickling her body with scratchy fibers. Her wet, soiled tank top clung to her body like a second skin, and her jeans with the holes in the knees were heavy with water.

The skin around her eyes twitched as she stole a glance behind her on the run, the shadowed figures still in pursuit, and she tripped over an unearthed root. She thrust out her hands to help break the fall, but the deep mud swallowed them whole, slapping her face and chest against the muck.

Sharon struggled to lift herself out of the earth sucking her deeper into the ground. Her hands and knees slid awkwardly in the mud that kept her on all fours, desperately clawing, driving forward. She blinked and wiped away the mask of crud from her eyes, tasting the gritty flecks of Cajun sludge on her lips.

"I think I see something over there!"

The voice was distant but growing closer. Desperation, and the instinct of survival, propelled Sharon to her feet. Slabs of mud fell from her stomach, legs, and arms and then plunked to the ground.

The quicksand-like mud eventually gave way to water that rose to her ankles, and with each noisy splash, she gave away her position to the crazies chasing her.

A cramp bit at her left hamstring and Sharon slowed to a hobbled limp. Her lungs burned and her chest tightened as she waded into warm, waist-high water, the mud dissolving into the black water. She ducked behind a tree, praying that the ripples from her wake calmed before the men saw.

Sharon shivered and hugged her stomach. An adrenaline-laced fear gnawed at her innards. She pictured the bodies back at the house, her family torn apart by that... that... thing. She couldn't rid herself of that rattling noise, those bones, the screams. She saw the teeth, claws, and black eyes. How could it even see with eyes so black? Part of her believed that it wasn't real. It couldn't be. But the proof was in the fresh blood oozing from the bite marks on her arms.

Feet splashed quickly in shallow water, then slowed and transformed into a heavy swoosh as the legs submerged deeper into the swamp. The movements sent ripples around the tree where Sharon squatted. She covered her mouth and passed silent breaths through her nose, which filled her nostrils with the hot stink of the swamp. The swooshing ended and the water grew still.

"It's no use, sweetheart. It's either death by bullet or claws. I would think a bullet is kinder." The voice was thick with a Louisiana drawl. What had been charming Southern flattery when she first arrived to the town was now evil and ominous. "You don't have nowhere else to go, darlin'."

More water rippled to her left, and Sharon shivered in the dark, covered in blood and mud, and stinking of a young woman fearful of death's open, waiting arms. Tears squeezed through the corners of her eyes and trickled down her cheeks. She slowly submerged herself deeper until the water reached her upper lip.

A knee appeared to her left along with the end of a rifle, and Sharon shut her eyes tighter, her head and neck vibrating from the effort it took to remain still. The man took another step forward and ripples from the movement sent water up her nose.

"Fine," he said, exasperated. "Have it your way, bitch."

Water swooshed again, the noise drifting away from her, then grew into softer, fading splashes. Sharon kept herself curled in a tight ball, waiting for the monsters to return, but their voices and splashes were replaced by the steady buzz of cicadas.

Slowly, and keeping low in the water, she crept toward the left of the tree trunk, her fingernails clawing rough bark. She craned her neck around the side and saw nothing but still black water, trees, and moonlight. She stood, water droplets falling from the hem of her tank top and elbows.

She took a step forward, and then another, that primal function of survival motoring her forward. Her thoughts wandered to her father's truck. It was still parked in the drive, but the keys were inside the house. With the bodies.

A sudden wave of sobs curved her body forward, and she buried her face in her dirty palms. All of their eyes would still be open, their bodies lifeless on the living room floor.

She thought of wading through the swamp and finding another house or road, but she didn't know the area, and she remembered her father's boss talking about gators and snakes. The truck was safer and faster.

Her legs chafed from the wet jeans, and the mud and blood began to harden over her chest and face. It tightened her skin, and the dark shades highlighted the whites of her eyes. She weaved through the path from which she came until she saw the open field that led back to the house.

Sharon paused at the clearing's edge. She gazed across the waist-high grass and reeds that stood straight and still like the house on the other side. She saw no movement, just the darkened windows of the house and the truck parked out front.

Looking at the structure now, she couldn't see anything else but death. But inside, amongst the dead, were the keys to her freedom.

Sharon crouched low, using the tall grass and reeds for cover. After the first few steps on her toes she broke into a sprint, and the rush of air stung the bite marks on her arms. She aimed for the front door, and she leapt up the porch steps, then skidded to a stop.

The door was open, the path ahead dark. Heat and a foul stench radiated from that dark plane. She whimpered and twisted the ends of her fingertips like a nervous child.

Bushes rustled to her left, and it provided the needed grit to cross the threshold of darkness, the shadows swallowing her whole as she passed through with her eyes shut.

After two full steps into the house, Sharon kept her head down and slowly opened her eyes. She stared at the floor until the tips of her mud-covered toes appeared in the darkness. She remained frozen in the foyer like a teenager caught coming home late from a curfew. She knew her parents were there on the floor. She didn't want to look at them but knew stepping on them would be worse. Finally, she gathered the courage to lift her head.

Her father lay on his back, his left leg straight, his right bent at a ninety-degree angle. His arms were stretched out from his body, and for a moment he reminded her of Jesus on the cross, his sacrifice meant to keep her alive. His face was turned toward her, his mouth slightly agape, his eyes open. Blood from the gunshot wound to his chest had pooled in a dark patch on the floor next to him.

Her mother lay on her stomach, her arms bunched under her breasts, one leg tucked under her chest while the other stuck straight out from the bottom of her dress. Her face was turned away, and Sharon stared at the tight black curls of hair on the back of her mother's head.

Quickly, Sharon skirted around the bodies and raced down the hall to her parents' bedroom. On the way, she passed the dining room where moonlight shone through the pair of skylights in the ceiling. But she didn't look up to the second-floor balcony where her and her brother's rooms had been. For all she knew, that thing was still up there.

She searched for the truck keys in the dark, not daring to turn on the lights and attract those men again. Her hands opened drawers, flung clothes, scoured the night stands, but the keys remained elusive.

She clenched her fists in frustration, and desperation made them shake. She retreated to the wall, unsure where her father could have put them. She knew they weren't in the truck. They couldn't be because her father had just gotten back from work when—

Sharon covered her mouth to muffle the frightened gasp. The keys weren't in her parents' room because her father never made it out of the living room. The keys were still in her father's pockets. Her *dead* father's pockets.

Sharon walked to the living room like an inmate on death

row, her steps slow and hesitant. Her mother watched her enter, and Sharon caught a brief glimpse of the bloody hole where her mother's jaw used to be. The entire bottom half of her face had been blown away, leaving behind stringy bits of muscles that hung from her cheeks and the roof of her mouth.

Her eyes remained transfixed on her mother's face while she maintained a slow walk forward until she stepped in something warm. She quickly recoiled her foot from the pool of blood next to her father's body. She turned away and scrunched her face, fixated on the warm liquid smeared beneath her toes.

Sharon slowly wiped her feet on the floor, refusing to look down at the red streaks staining the hardwood, and then turned back to her father's corpse. Her knees popped as she bent down, her arm outstretched and rigid.

She paused at the opening to his pants pocket, knowing that she'd have to feel her father's body. It felt wrong, but she forced herself to do it. She didn't want to die. Not here, and not now. She shut her eyes as she reached through the hole. She winced at the soft give of muscle and fat, but found nothing but lint. She quickly removed her hand, then reached across her father's waist to the other pocket, the heat of the body warming the skin of her arm.

As she moved closer to the second pocket, a curious force pulled her eyes toward her father's head where she saw a few specks of blood amongst the black stubble of his tan face. She remembered how rough it felt as a child when he kissed her goodnight, but also how comforting it was. An impulse to experience that comfort again diverted the direction of her hand. Her lower lip quivered as her fingers grazed the stubble. After the first prick against her fingertip she retracted her hand, clutching it tightly with the other, and she cried.

Snot dribbled from her nose and she quickly wiped it away. The sudden and overwhelming sense of escape flooded through her and Sharon quickly shoved her hand into the second pocket and in one quick pull, she removed the keys and jumped back from her father's body. She retreated towards the door, the keys clutched in both hands against her chest. "I'm sorry."

Sharon sprinted out the front door and hurried down the four steps of the porch, missing the last one. She landed awkwardly on her left foot and twisted her ankle. She skidded on her hands and knees in the gravel drive, fresh cuts in her palms, and then reached back for her ankle, baring her teeth with a hiss.

"There she is!"

Sharon jerked her head toward the pair of men aiming their rifles at her from the brush, and she scrambled to get her legs under her. The tiny rocks in the gravel cut into the tender flesh under her bare feet as the men hastened their pursuit. She moaned between sobs, hyperventilating as she fumbled through the ring of keys.

Her ankle throbbed painfully by the time she reached the truck and she tugged at the handle, heaving open the heavy steel door. A gunshot thundered and connected with the side of the truck. Sharon jumped from the violent blast, then climbed inside cab.

Sharon shoved the key into the ignition and jammed her foot down on the clutch as she turned the key. The engine sputtered and another gunshot sounded, this one shattering the driver side window next to her head. She screamed and ducked, lying low on the truck bench as she continued to crank the engine and hold the clutch.

The engine choked then sputtered to life, and Sharon sprung up and shifted into first gear, but as she did, the door flung open and meaty hands grabbed her arm and groped her waist.

"No!" Sharon flailed against the man that pulled her from the truck cabin and flung her helplessly to the ground. Her elbow smacked onto the gravel and a sharp crack of pain sent a thousand tiny needles up her forearm, numbing her fingers.

"Trust us, sweetheart," the man said, catching his breath. "It's better this way." He smiled, and the moonlight reflected off a silver capped tooth.

"Sure you don't want to have any fun with her first, Billy?" A thick beard covered the second man's face, a pair of hungry eyes running down the curve of her body.

"No time," Billy answered, then aimed the rifle at Sharon's head. "This place isn't safe."

Sharon held up her hands in defense, crying. "Please, don't. Just let me go." But the cries for mercy didn't budge the rifle barrel from her head, and some childish instinct curled herself into a ball as she lay on the ground. Thick, heaving sobs shook her body, and she tasted salt and blood on her lips. She shut her eyes and pictured her parents on the floor in the living room. And then she saw her brother in the arms of that creature. They shouldn't have come here. They should have never moved.

"Don't worry, sweetheart," Billy said. "It's all over now."

And with the pull of the trigger and a bullet to the brain, it was. At least for her family.

PRESENT DAY

*T*he metro rocked back and forth, the wheels clicking in the familiar rhythmic tha-dump, tha-dump, tha-dump every few seconds. A few conversations flitted through the stale air and over the noise of the screeching metal cars, but mostly everyone kept to themselves. Anyone who didn't have a phone in their hand had their eyes closed, waiting for the train to slow and the automated voice to stir them awake through the crackling speakers.

Owen Cooley didn't have a phone in his hand. He couldn't afford one. Nor could he sleep despite the dark circles under his eyes. He rubbed his knobby hands together, the tie around his neck loose with the top button of his shirt undone, the elbow patches of his jacket resting on his thighs. He stared at the black grooves on the metro floor and the piece of gum the man standing in front of him had almost stepped in for the past twenty minutes. Twice the heel of his Nike nearly landed in the pink glob, but he stayed clear, and at the next stop the man walked off, never knowing how close he came to catastrophe.

The train doors closed, the speakers beeped, and the train jolted forward, waking the large black woman who had dozed off across from him. But while the man in the white Nikes escaped doom, nothing had changed for Owen after a day of endless interviews and zero job offers. And if he had to choose between not having a job or gum on his shoe, he'd gladly take the latter.

By the time the train pulled up to his stop, the sun was setting. A nurse stood to exit, and Owen held out his arm to stop her from smashing her toe into the ABC Double-Bubble. She flashed him a pretty smile and softly touched his arm as she stepped ahead of him. It was the first good thing that had happened all day

Unlike his interaction with the nurse, there were no smiles at the end of his interviews. He either had too much experience, not the right kind, or not enough in general. He'd worked as a welder and machinist for seventeen years. And at only a few years shy of forty, he found himself jobless with a mortgage and family to feed at home.

Owen kept his hands in his pockets, a warm breeze flicking his tie lazily to the left on his walk down the side-walk. He kept his head down, his eyes scanning for any more gum mines lurking on the concrete. He rotated his shoulders uncomfortably and took his jacket off. His undershirt was soaked with sweat. Partly because of the summer heat, but mostly from nerves.

Sit up straight, make eye contact, nice dry and firm grip, but don't hold too long, and don't break off too early. It's all about the shake. At least that's what the employee down at the job center had told him. What the desk jockey hadn't told him was that the jobs he was being interviewed for all required degrees, or computer knowledge, of which he had neither.

Not to mention he was always the oldest applicant in the

room. And in most cases, he was older than the hiring manager. Compared to the spry youths that surrounded him in those hip offices, sitting in chairs that looked nothing like chairs, he was an old man. But he didn't feel old. He still felt useful. There just wasn't anyone that wanted the skills he had.

So, for the past six months since he'd been laid off at the shipyard, Owen Cooley had gone down to the job center every Monday to speak with the 'career planner' to look for jobs that paid more than minimum wage, which was what he was currently making at the McDonalds that only gave him twenty-five hours a week. The burgers and fries were a nice perk though. Not that he was supposed to take them home, but he knew they'd just throw them out at the end of the day anyway. A rich man might call that stealing. A man in his position would call it feeding his family.

A few cars rattled down the street, one of them giving him a honk, and Owen raised his hand in a friendly wave as he watched John Clarence's old Ford roll toward home. He'd been in the same boat as Owen when the shipyard closed, but he had managerial experience and ended up getting a job for some construction company as an office pusher. It paid just as well as the shipyard did, but at their son's baseball game last Saturday, he said he didn't like the environment. Too stuffy. Say the wrong thing and you're outta there.

But Owen only nodded, his mind wandering to the third notice he received in the mail that morning for being late on the water bill. It shut off the next day, and it was another three before he and Claire managed to scrape up enough cash to get it turned back on. Three fucking days.

Owen stopped and looked up from his shoes. His home was just two houses down, but he didn't know how much longer it was going to stay that way. Their savings was gone, and what had gnawed at him the most on the train ride back home wasn't the fact that the interviews hadn't gone well, or that last week his kids couldn't shower for three days. What bothered him the most was that it was his fault. A man was supposed to provide, and he'd failed. And now he'd have to walk into that house, look his wife in the eye, and tell her that at the end of the month, they'd have to move out. And go where? He had no idea.

Owen passed the mailbox out front and almost didn't open it, but knew it was better for him to check the mail, that was if Claire hadn't gotten to it first. She'd been doing that more lately. It was because he started to hide the bills and late notices from her. He did it so she wouldn't worry, but that didn't lessen the hellfire unleashed upon him when she found out.

And it was foolish for him to think he could keep that stuff from her anyway. She knew how much money they had down to the penny. But no matter how low that account got, Claire never wavered, didn't even flinch. She was tougher than him in that way, and he loved her for it.

The mailbox didn't give him anything to help lift his spirits. He shuffled through the envelopes stamped with labels in red lettering that spelled out "final notice," "past due," and "foreclosure." He paused on the last one. Those eleven capitalized red letters had been haunting him since the shipyard closed. And now the monster had finally sunk its teeth into him for good.

Owen stuffed the mail in the pocket inside his jacket and walked up the front porch steps. The laughter drifting through the open windows helped lift the weight of the day off his back and brought the only real smile he had all day as he walked inside.

"Daddy!" Chloe lifted her arms in the air triumphantly, dropped the crayon in her hand, and sprinted toward him.

Owen crouched and scooped her off the floor. He planted

a kiss on her cheek and walked her back over to the table. "Hey, bug. What are you working on?"

Chloe sighed, the tone behind it decades beyond the five year old that spoke. "I just can't get the princess' hair right. It turns out too much like spaghetti."

Owen laughed, and Chloe giggled as he tickled her sides playfully, then set her back down and kissed the top of her head. "I'm sure you'll get it. Where's your mom?"

"In the kitchen!" Claire answered, and then stepped through the cutout in the narrow hallway that was split down the middle of the house that separated the kitchen, bathroom, and bedrooms from the dining and living rooms. She clasped her hands together and arched her eyebrows with a hopeful expression. He walked to her, kissed her lips, and shook his head.

It was hard watching the hope disappear from her face. But she didn't let it keep her down for long. "Well, dinner is almost ready. Matt's out back with Grandpa. Why don't you go and get him?"

Owen arched his left eyebrow. "You left them alone?"

Claire squeezed his hand, keeping her voice low. "He was having a good day today. And it made Matt happy to throw the ball around with his granddad." She kissed his cheek and then called Chloe into the kitchen to help set the table as Owen walked down the hallway toward the back door. Before he even stepped outside, he heard the hard smack of ball in glove.

"Easy there, Ripkin!" Roger shook his hand exaggeratedly, and Matt laughed. "You're gonna bruise an old man."

"I didn't throw it that hard, Grandpa." Matt turned to the door and his face lit up. "Hey, Dad!"

"Hey, buddy. Dinner's almost ready, so why don't you come in and wash up."

"All right." Matt peeled his glove off and tucked it under his arm. He walked with his shoulders slouched.

Owen ruffled his son's hair on his way inside. "And help your sister set the table."

"Okay."

Roger tossed the ball into his glove, then closed the mitt and held it with both hands, lingering in the yard. Owen watched him closely. The doctors said the early stages were some of the hardest, and there wasn't any way to know how fast it would progress.

"You all right, Roger?"

He nodded. "Fine." He looked up but didn't smile. "How was work?"

"No work today," Owen answered.

Roger shook his head, frowning. "Right. I knew that." He hurried back inside the house, brushing Owen with his shoulder on his way past.

After the dinner table was set, Claire brought out the spaghetti and green beans, dumping conservative-sized portions on everyone's plate. The food needed to last.

Talk at the dinner table centered around the excitement for the end of school and the start of summer, and Chloe's urgent plea for more crayons in order to expand her exploration of the color spectrum. Her own words.

"We'll see what we can do, Picasso," Claire said, then looked down to Matt, who'd kept himself reserved through most of dinner, picking at his noodles with his fork. "You okay, Matt?"

Owen looked up from the last green bean on his plate and watched his son nod with a half-smile. Owen didn't buy it. "You sure?"

"Yeah," Matt answered, more confident. "I'm fine."

Both Chloe and Roger asked for seconds, and Owen declined another plate, though he knew he could have eaten one. Once the dishes were done and homework was finished (after being double-checked by Mom), it was showers and off to bed.

Roger descended into the basement without a goodnight to anyone, one of the smaller behavioral changes that Owen had noticed in the old man. When things worsened, Owen wasn't sure what they were going to do, especially if he was still unemployed. But all those worries disappeared the moment he stepped into Chloe's room. It was more gallery than bedroom, the walls adorned with the artwork that she deemed acceptable for people to view. "Night, bug."

"Night, Dad."

Owen kissed her forehead and then shut off the light on his way out and closed the door. He walked next door to Matt's room and saw his son in bed, sitting up and picking at the fringes of his glove. Owen entered and pulled the desk chair next to the bed and sat. "You want to tell me what's bothering you? And don't tell me it's nothing. I know you better than that."

Matt looked up, his eyes red and misty. "I know about the house."

His son's words hit like a one-two combo to the gut. "That's not something you have to worry about." Owen moved from the chair to the bed and lifted his son's chin, a few tears breaking from the cluster of water in his eyes. "We're going to be fine." He tapped the glove in Matt's hands. "Plus, you've got summer ball soon. That curve of yours is really coming along."

Matt wiped his eyes and sniffled. "I don't think I should do it."

"Why not? You love it."

"It's expensive. And I don't want to be the reason we're homeless."

"We're not going to be homeless. I promise. Okay?"

Matt nodded and then wrapped his arms around his dad's neck. The boy was always worrying about things beyond his ten years. It was a trait he shared with his sister, though her worries were more artistic in nature.

"All right," Owen said, kissing the top of Matt's head. "Lights out." Owen helped Matt under the sheets as the boy tucked his glove into his chest. "I love you."

"Love you too, Dad."

As Owen shut the door to his son's room, he lingered in the hallway a moment. Not once in his own childhood did he worry about whether he would be homeless. He'd be damned if he was going to let his own son do it.

After he had time to mentally prepare himself for the last conversation of the night, Owen entered his bedroom. Claire was sitting cross-legged on the bedsheets, his jacket at the foot of the bed, the bills spread out in front of her.

"We can't get an extension from the bank?" Claire asked, reading through the foreclosure notice. "We've been with them for almost fifteen years, and up until the shipyard closed, we never missed a payment."

Owen leaned back and lay down, resting his head on the pillow, staring at the ceiling, which was void of any chewing gum. "They won't budge. If we can't pay by the thirtieth, they'll kick us out."

Claire collected the rest of the bills and then tossed them on her nightstand. "Well, I think it's bullshit." She rolled over to him and rested her head on his chest. It bounced gently up and down in time with his heartbeat. "How was it out there today?"

Owen groaned. "Bad. You should see some of the looks I get when I walk into those interviews. You'd think I was marked with the plague." Owen ran his fingers through Claire's thick, wavy black hair. It was familiar. It was home. "Matt knows about the house."

"Of course he does," Claire said. "He is half me, you know."

"Thank god for that," Owen said, kissing her head.

Claire propped herself up on her elbows and looked at him. "Hey. You need to quit that. You never give yourself enough credit. Just because you're not a twenty-two year old with a degree in computer science doesn't mean you're not smart." She grabbed hold of his hands and kissed them. "You are very good at what you do, Owen. It was why the shipyard stayed in business for as long as it did in the first place. It's not your fault there isn't anyone hiring right now."

"You'd think I'd be able to find some welding work, or construction, or—"

"Something will come up," Claire said. "And until then, we'll get by. I managed to get a few more hours tutoring next week, so that'll help." She kissed him. "We'll get through this."

Owen nodded and forced a smile. "I know." But as he switched off the light and they lay in bed, he wasn't able to convince himself it was true. If he didn't get a job by next week, they were going to be evicted. He couldn't let that happen.

* * *

GARY SAT BEHIND HIS DESK, computer monitor off to the side, and typed mechanically onto his keyboard. His tie was crooked, and his nose was large enough to give his eyes an obstacle in any direction he looked. "Okay, Mr. Cooley, let's see what we have today."

Owen sat in the same suit, shirt, and tie as the day before. His manager at McDonalds had cancelled his shift for the day, and with the eminent doom of foreclosure, he couldn't just sit at home and twiddle his thumbs. "I need something full time. Anything full time. And anything immediate."

Gary flicked his eyes toward Owen, then back at the screen, then back at Owen. He took his hands off the keyboard and set them down on his desk with a thump. "Mr. Cooley, you have been coming here at least once a week for the past six months. And I can tell you every job in the system available from memory, but that won't change the fact that no one is hiring for your skillset. It might be time to start looking outside of Baltimore."

"My family grew up here," Owen said. "My kids go to school here. My son's little league team—"

"I'm just saying," Gary said, lifting his hands passively, "if you're desperate, and you really want to find something full time, and in your field, maybe it's time to broaden your horizons. It couldn't hurt to look, right?"

"No," Owen answered. "I guess not."

Uprooting his family had crossed Owen's mind before, he just didn't entertain it for very long. Plus, the doctors had told him and Claire to keep things familiar for Roger, and the old man had lived in Baltimore his entire life.

"All right, so let's see what we have out there." Gary returned his fingers to the keyboard, a sudden pep in his typing. "Nothing here in the Northeast that was close to your previous salary, so let's head down south." He poked a few more keys and then scrolled again. "Oh, here's something."

Owen leaned forward in his chair. "Is it full time?"

"It is," Gary answered. "It's a supervisor position at an auto parts factory, but it says that they're willing to look at applicants with no supervisory experience."

"Where is it?"

"Louisiana."

Owen frowned. When he considered moving his family, transferring them to the south felt too extreme. And Louisiana was the *deep* south.

"Health benefits, 401k, and the salary is fifteen thousand

more a year than what you were making at the shipyard," Gary said.

"Fifteen?" Owen's jaw went slack.

"The position is looking to be filled immediately, and it says here that the company will provide housing and pay for any relocation efforts." Gary smiled. "What do you say? A position like this isn't going to stay open for very long."

"Y-yeah," Owen said eagerly. "Let's do it."

* * *

CLAIRE STOOD in front of the small fan in the kitchen, letting the whirling blades cool the sweat collecting on her face. The whole house was hot. And it was only going to get worse the deeper they went into summer. But maybe by then Owen would have found something and they could afford to turn the A/C back on. With the fan just basically blowing hot air in her face, she thought about taking a trip down to the store to browse the aisles and cool off.

She stepped from the fan, and the beads of sweat returned. Traffic noise and the occasional backfire of an exhaust pipe drifted through the open windows. At least that's where she hoped those loud pops were coming from.

The neighborhood had changed over the fifteen years they'd taken residence. The ups and downs of the economy had shifted people around. When the kids played outside, she made sure it was in the backyard, which was fenced. It wasn't as much space as the front yard, and Matt groaned over the new rule, but she wouldn't budge.

"Hey, Dad?" Claire asked, calling down to the basement. No answer. "Roger?"

"What?"

"Are you getting hungry for lunch?"

"I'm fine."

Claire lingered in the basement doorway, leaning against the frame and drumming her fingers against the wood. Her father was down there somewhere, wandering in the dark, doing his best to find the light switch. He could still find it more times than not, but that wasn't going to last forever.

The house phone rang, and she walked back to the kitchen and plucked it off the hook. "Hello?" Claire smiled. "Hi, Mrs. Channing. Yes, I'm good, how about yourself?" She paced around the hot linoleum floor in her bare feet. "I got your message this morning, and I called you back earlier just to see—" She paused and her shoulders slumped. "Are you sure? I felt like Freddy still needed some help with those equations. If my rate is too high, I'd be willing to—" She nodded and then rubbed her forehead. "No, I understand. Well, I appreciate the time, and if anything changes, or if you know of any other parents who need a good math tutor, I hope you'll recommend me. Okay, thank you, Mrs. Channing."

The call clicked dead in Claire's ear and the arm holding up the cordless phone fell limp to her side. For six months, she'd held onto the hope that tomorrow would be better. For six months, she did everything she could to stretch their savings. And amid the constant leftovers, power and water outages, bills and late notices, she never would have expected the crushing blow to come from the mother of a fourteen-year-old boy who was struggling in his Algebra I class.

A car horn blared out front, and Claire spun around, phone still clutched in her hand. The horn blasts came in quick, short bursts, with shouting echoing intermittently between the honking. Claire stepped out of the kitchen and into the hallway where she saw the front door open. She jogged to the porch, and it was there she saw her father standing in the middle of the road, looking around, the

20

driver of a rusted, faded yellow Oldsmobile hanging out the window and screaming.

"Stop!" Claire sprinted down the porch steps, her bare feet smacking against the pavement of the walkway that cut through their unkempt front yard. She waved her hands, phone still clutched in her right, as the driver stepped out. His face reddened as he continued to berate her father. "No, please, he has Alzheimer's!"

"What the fuck is your problem, old timer?" The Oldsmobile driver was short and wore matching grey shirt and sweatpants, neither able to contain the gut that split the space between them. His hair was thinning at the top and he panted heavy breaths. "Are you fucking stupid?"

But even with the driver screaming in his face, Roger kept glancing around the neighborhood, unsure of his surroundings.

"Did you hear me?" The driver shoved Roger hard, and the old man stumbled back a few steps.

"Hey!" Claire slid between the two and raised the phone in her hand to strike. "You don't touch him, asshole."

The short, fat driver scoffed, then looked Claire up and down. "And what are you going to do about it, bitch—"

The man's eyes widened in terror as Owen appeared out of nowhere and grabbed the driver by the throat and slammed him backward onto the hood. Claire jolted backward from the sudden motion as Owen thrust a finger in the fat man's face, keeping him pinned down.

"Get in your car, and get the hell out of my neighborhood," Owen said.

The driver squirmed and wiggled on the hot hood, impotently shoving his short, chubby arms into Owen's chest, his face wiggling in fear. "I-I got it, just lemme go, c'mon, man. He was standing in the middle of the road!"

Owen lifted the driver off the hood, then forcefully

walked him to the open car door, flung him inside, and then slammed the door shut. "I see you driving down this road again and you won't drive out."

Claire took hold of her father's hand, which he thankfully didn't resist, and pulled him from the road. "Are you all right, Dad?"

The Oldsmobile sped forward, swerving down the road as the driver shouted frustrated obscenities out his window. Owen walked over and grabbed hold of Claire's arm. "What happened?"

"I was on the phone, and I didn't see him go outside," Claire answered.

Roger's cheeks reddened and he let go of Claire's hand as he stepped away. "I-I just wanted some fresh air. That's all." He became lucid once more and cast his gaze to his feet in embarrassment. "I'm fine." He turned and walked briskly back into the house.

Owen ran his hand through his short crop of brown hair and exhaled, the adrenaline burning off in the light tremor of his thumb and forefinger, and when he burst into a manic chuckle Claire thought her husband had lost his mind.

"What is it?" Claire asked.

Owen flapped his arms at his sides, that wild grin still plastered on his face. "I got a job."

Claire tilted her head to the side. She pinched her eyebrows together questioningly. "Is this a joke? Are you joking right now, because if you are, this is a very bad tim—"
He pressed his lips into hers and squeezed her tight, lifting her off the pavement and into the air. When he set her back down, the news finally sank in. "Oh my god." She covered her mouth with both hands, tears filling her eyes. "That's incredible. I just—" She laughed, jumped up and down, and then flung her arms around Owen's neck and squeezed tight. "I'm so proud of you." She kissed his cheek and then lowered

herself down, unsure of what to ask next. "So what are you doing now? Who hired you?"

And that's when the excitement from Owen's face faded. "It's a factory job, a supervisor position actually. It's a great opportunity, but it comes with some changes."

Claire placed one hand on each of Owen's cheeks and looked her husband in the eye. "You did what you needed to do for our family. We'll change with you. Whatever it takes."

Owen smiled and then kissed her once more. They walked back inside, hand in hand, and for the first time since Owen came home with his pink slip, Claire felt good. Really good. Whatever happened, wherever they ended up going together, they would make it work.

*E*leven hundred miles and two days of driving finally ended as Owen turned the U-Haul truck off the highway and passed the welcome sign that read: "Ocoee, Louisiana. Stop in, have some grub, and stay awhile!" and underneath the sign was the population which sat at fifteen thousand ninety-two, soon to be fifteen thousand ninety-seven.

The cabin of the U-Haul was only large enough for two to ride, and while most of the trip he rode alone, Matt had joined him for the last leg of the journey. Apparently Chloe and Grandpa were talkers, and his son needed some 'quiet' time. Owen understood that.

"Do they play baseball in Louisiana?" Matt asked, his glove in his lap, an Orioles cap on his head.

"Sure they do," Owen answered.

"But they don't have any professional teams here," Matt said. "Does that mean we can't go see any more games?"

"Houston's not far," Owen said. "I'm sure we could make a few trips over there this summer." And with his new salary, they might even be able to squeeze in an actual vacation, though he wasn't sure how far he wanted to push his new employer. Taking time off after only working at the place for a few months felt arrogant.

"I don't like the Astros," Matt said, glancing down at his glove.

"Hey." Owen gave his son a shove. "I know the move is hard. But this place will be good for us. And who knows? Maybe the Orioles will play in Houston for an away game. That'd be cool, right?"

Matt nodded and then lifted his head, showing the start of a smile. "Yeah."

The highway aimed straight for the heart of Ocoee's downtown, and a small cluster of buildings rose on the horizon. Swamp land stretched out on either side of the road, and Owen checked his side mirror where he saw a sliver of the van that Claire was driving with Grandpa and Chloe. They'd leased it last week after the company offered to make the first few months' payment until Owen and his family was settled.

Trees sprouted up alongside the shops, long strands of Spanish moss dangling from the branches. Large pillow-top clouds drifted lazily past the sun in patches, darkening the town and the first few shops on the left.

With only fifteen thousand residents, Owen knew it would be a bit of a culture shock for the family, seeing as how Baltimore was bursting at the seams with over half a million. But small-town life had its benefits. Less pollution, lower crime rate, a better sense of community.

In his head, their future in Ocoee was filled with the stereotypical Southern hospitality that he'd seen in television shows and movies, his northeastern accent slowly morphing to a Southern twang after a few years in the country. It would take time, but they'd learn to love it here.

"Dad, look!" Matt pointed out his window excitedly. "What is that?"

Owen followed his son's finger to the sight of a woman standing out front of a shop called "Queen's." The woman had long, thick dreads that flowed over her shoulders and down her back. She wore earth-colored tones, and the one-piece jumpsuit sagged in unshapely areas around her body. White paint framed her face in thin lines, which made it hard to guess her age, but she looked older. She leaned against a tall staff, slightly warped near the top, that reached past her head. The storefront behind her had tinted black windows, blocking the views from outside. But a few tables covered with some merchandise were set on the sidewalk, though Owen couldn't tell what they were.

Owen locked eyes with the woman as they passed, and he shivered from a sudden draft of cold air. "I thought we left all the crazies in Baltimore.".

"I thought she looked cool!" Matt smiled brightly.

"Well, maybe we can go and check out her store this weekend?" Owen asked. "How does that sound?"

"Awesome." Matt slipped his glove on and pounded his fist into the mitt excitedly.

The row of shops on Main Street ended and Owen took the next left. He followed the GPS on his new cell phone until he lost reception, then tossed it in the cup holder. He reached for the paper where he'd written the directions down as suggested by his new boss. Reception was spotty on the town's outskirts.

The trees thickened on both sides of the back roads and Owen understood where their new street name received its origin. He slowed as he approached Cypress Lane, then turned onto the gravel road that led to their home. Tree branches stretched up and over the road, intertwining with one another, forming a shady roof that blocked the sun. The house came into view up ahead, and Matt leaned forward, placing his hands on the dash, his mouth ajar, and let out a low "woooah."

Sunlight broke through the clouds and hit the house in thick streams that gleamed off the windows of the two-story home with a wrap-around front porch and second-floor balcony. Inside was six bedrooms and four baths, a massive living room, dining room, den, and kitchen. It was nearly three times the square footage of their house in Baltimore, and that was just the inside. They hadn't seen any pictures of the surrounding property, which was sprawling.

"Is all of that ours?" Matt said, the house growing larger.

"It sure is, buddy," Owen answered, his own tone awe stricken.

Most of the property looked to be swamp, and Owen wondered about the potential flooding hazards. But with the company paying for the house, the move, the van, and so much more, he wasn't about to complain. You didn't bite the hand that fed you, clothed you, and helped pull you from the brink of homelessness.

A truck was already parked in front of the house, and a man stepped out the front door, smiling and giving a friendly wave. Owen parked the U-Haul off to the side of the large patch of dirt that acted as a driveway, and Claire pulled up next to him in the van. He stepped out and gave Chuck a wave in return. "I hope you weren't waiting long."

"Got here just a few minutes before you did." Chuck Toussaint offered a handsome smile and a firm handshake as Owen walked up to greet him. "How was the trip?"

"Long," Owen answered.

Claire snuck up behind him with Chloe on her hip. "You must be Mr. Toussaint."

"Please, call me Chuck." Chuck's southern drawl was followed by a southern charm as he took Claire's hand and kissed it. "It looks like our town just got a little more attractive."

Claire snorted and waved her hand as Chuck released it. Owen arched an eyebrow as she blushed. She slapped his arm. "Oh, stop it. He's just being nice."

Chuck turned his sights on Chloe. "And who is this southern princess?"

Chloe's reaction fell short of Claire's blushing, and Owen couldn't help but feel proud when his daughter looked Chuck straight in the eye and said, "I'm from Baltimore."

"Chloe, be nice," Claire said.

Chuck laughed. "Oh, it's all right. The South needs more strong ladies like you, Miss Chloe." He stepped toward the house. "C'mon, I'll show you inside."

Owen looked back to Roger as Claire set Chloe down and she raced Matt to the front door. He wasn't sure if his father-in-law was having one of his moments, or if the old man just didn't like the move. It could be both. "You coming, Roger?"

The old man shook his head. "You go on. I'll be there in a minute."

Claire tugged at Owen's hand and whispered. "He's taken the move pretty hard, and he's nervous about the new environment. He'll be fine by himself out here for a little bit."

Owen nodded and placed his arm around Claire's waist and the pair walked up to their new house.

"Welcome home," Chuck said, his arms open and another wide grin plastered on his face. And what a home it was.

The entrance opened in to a small foyer that led into a massive, open living room. A chandelier dangled from the thirty-foot vaulted ceiling, and a wall opposite the front door cut the house in half. The living room had three doorways: one directly to the left after entering which led to the kitchen, and one on either side of the brick wall that led to the back of the house. Some older furniture was covered in white sheets, and the kids sprinted around excitedly.

"I know it looks a little dusty, but I have a cleaning service coming next week to give the whole place a good scrubbing," Chuck said. "And don't feel the need to keep any of this furniture. If you don't want it, just let me know and I'll have someone come and pick it up. Just do me a favor and don't throw it away. I could sell it for good money."

"This is incredible," Claire said.

And it was. But Owen underestimated the age of the house. He'd been so excited to accept the job offer earlier in the week that he would have taken a shack if it meant he got a paycheck again. "When was this place built?"

"Early eighteen hundreds," Chuck answered. "But the house's innards are good. All the wiring and plumbing was redone a few years back, but if you find anything that doesn't work, I will replace it free of charge."

Owen glanced at some of the cracks high on the walls near the ceiling. The wooden floors underneath his feet groaned as he shifted his weight. A musty scent familiar with older homes graced his nostrils, and he'd started to sweat. He'd read that Louisiana summers were a different kind of hot than the ones he was used to in Baltimore. It was a humid heat. The sweat ring forming around his shirt was a taste of what was to come.

"We appreciate that, Mr. Toussaint," Claire said, giving Owen a shove with her elbow. "Don't we."

"Yes," Owen said, quickly. "We really do."

"Do you guys need any help moving in?" Chuck asked.

"No," Owen answered. "You've done enough. We can take it from here."

"All right then," Chuck said. "I'll let y'all get to it. Owen, why don't you walk me out. I just want a quick word."

"Sure."

The pair stepped outside where the temperature felt like it had risen ten degrees. Owen pulled at his shirt collar, trying to fan himself.

Chuck laughed. "I'd like to say you'll get used to the heat, but I know how you northerners have thick blood."

"It's something we pride ourselves on," Owen said, smiling politely.

Chuck scanned the property and pointed toward the right side of the house where a cluster of trees began after a clearing of tall grass ended. "Now, the property itself is quite large. Over seven acres, and the house is bullseye center of it. I do have to warn you that there is a small cemetery on the property, so if the kiddies go exploring, I do ask that they be respectful."

"Oh, I didn't know that," Owen said, sounding surprised. "In fact, there wasn't a whole lot mentioned about the house. You're sure everything inside is in working order?"

Chuck laughed. "I usually choose to omit certain details when selling something, but like I said, if anything doesn't look up to code, you just let me know and I'll take care of it." He stuck out his hand, smiling. "I'm excited to have you on board, Owen. You're just the man I've been looking for."

"I appreciate the opportunity," Owen said, and then watched Chuck get in his truck and drive off. As he did, Roger poked his head from the back of the U-Haul, hands in his pockets, and walked toward Owen. "Hey, how are you feeling?"

Roger stopped when he reached Owen, and he looked at the house, squinting from the sunlight. His hair was almost all gone and liver spots dotted his scalp. His skin was wrinkled and his jowls hung loose on his face.

"Seventy-three years I lived in Baltimore," Roger said, his eyes still locked on the new house. "It was where I grew up, married, raised a family, and then watched my only daughter do the same. It was my home." He gently messaged his hands, some of the fingers curved from arthritis. "I know the Alzheimer's will take all those memories from me. The worst part right now is still having the sound mind to realize that. But I want you to promise me something." He looked at Owen, his eyes red and misty, his voice quivering. "You don't let the last memories that my grandchildren have of me be an old man that didn't know them. Understand?"

Owen nodded. "I do."

Roger kneaded Owen's shoulder with his fingers. "I don't say it enough, but you've been a good husband and father." His lip quivered again, and his voice cracked. "And a good son."

Quickly, Roger clapped Owen on the back and then walked toward the house, his head down as he wiped his eyes with his shirt sleeves. Owen couldn't imagine the pain and struggle for Roger that was just around the corner. But he promised himself that he would honor the old man's request. No matter what.

* * *

AFTER BEDROOMS WERE CEREMONIOUSLY PICKED by Matt and Chloe, everyone pitched in and carried their belongings off the U-Haul. Claire and Owen handled the larger items - couches, beds, chairs, tables - while the kids brought in what boxes they could, with Roger supervising.

Once everything was unpacked and everyone was sweaty and exhausted, Owen ordered a pizza from the closest Domino's, which was thirty minutes away. After some haggling with the kid who took his order, he managed to convince them to deliver to their house for a premium fee.

And so with paper plates, napkins, two extra-large supreme pizzas with extra bacon, and a two-liter bottle of root beer to wash it all down, his family sat at the large dining room table underneath enormous skylights and ate. And for the first time in six months, Owen sighed with relief. His family was laughing, smiling, and not worried about what tomorrow would bring. The new job wasn't just a paycheck, it was safety.

If you ever wanted to know what fear and desperation looked like, Owen would tell you to go down to the local unemployment center and look in the eyes of the men and women waiting in line to speak with a clerk. Beyond the bouncing legs, fidgeting fingers, and long exhales riddled with anxiety, you'll find the worst combination of fear, anger, and hate swirling around their souls. Anger for failing, fear for failing again, and a hate for everything that put them in their situation.

It had been less than a week since Owen's interview and simultaneous hire over the phone at Gary's desk, but he'd never forget those faces or that feeling of helplessness. He was thankful to be done with it.

Chloe belched, the deep burp rattling at an octave lower than any five-year-old girl should be able to do. She covered her mouth, shocked by her own body, and Matt and Roger burst out laughing.

"Chloe Grace Cooley," Claire said, a smile in her tone. "Excuse you, young lady."

"I think it was the root beer," Chloe said, giggling.

Owen reached across the table and grabbed her cup. "I'm cutting you off."

"Daaaaad," Chloe said, whining.

"No, Dad's right," Claire said. "Time to get ready for bed. Wash that pizza off your face, and your father and I will be up in a little bit to tuck you in."

Chloe and Matt slid from their chairs and sprinted from the dining room and toward the staircase which led to the second-floor balcony and their rooms, their feet thumping against the old steps as their pizza- and soda-fueled legs carried them up the stairs.

Claire went to reach for their plates, but Roger got up quickly. "I'll take care of that."

"Dad, you don't have to," Claire said.

Roger waved her off with an 'eh.' "And I'll get the kids to bed. Why don't you two turn in?"

"You sure?" Claire asked.

"Positive," Roger answered, kissing the top of her head as he passed.

"Thanks, Dad."

They retired to the bedroom and Claire flopped on the bed, the sheets piled messily on top of the bare mattress. "If there is a harder test of patience than driving eleven hundred miles with two kids and a geriatric over the course of two days, I don't want to take it."

Owen lay down next to her and kissed her cheek. "Thank you."

"For what?" Claire asked.

"Your dad and the kids aren't the only ones who left their home."

"I'll miss it, but everything I need is still right here." She rolled closer to him, her lips less than an inch from his. "So what do you want to do now that we don't have any bedtime responsibilities?"

Owen smiled, kissed her, and turned off the lights.

* * *

IT'D BEEN ALMOST two months since they'd made love, the longest drought in their marriage. They hadn't even gone that long after Matt and Chloe were born. But with the financial pressures and the stress and exhaustion that came with it, neither of them found themselves in the mood.

The ceiling fan twirled, shaking lightly in a rhythmic cadence. Owen lay naked and exposed, tiny beads of sweat over his body, while Claire had pulled one sheet up and over herself. She lay curled up in a ball. They'd spooned for a little bit after, but it became too hot to be sustainable. Owen wasn't sure he'd be able to fall asleep in the heat, but with six months of sleepless nights behind him, fatigue won out over sweating.

And as the Cooley family slept, light creaks echoed in the house. Any rational person would have said it was just the old bones sagging from the weight of standing up for the past two hundred years.

But there was something else in the house. Something ancient. It was dark. It was evil. And it was hungry.

"AHHHHHHH!"

Owen jolted upright in bed, his tired eyes flitting around the room while his heart hammered against his chest. Claire woke in the same fright and Owen stumbled from bed, reaching for his shorts as he sprinted from the room. The screams came from upstairs. It was Matt.

Owen's feet slipped on the steps up to the second floor, and he tripped over his own feet twice, giving Claire time to catch up. He ducked into Chloe's room first on the way and saw his daughter sitting upright in bed with the covers pulled up to her chin, her sleepy eyes wide in the dark. "Are you all right?" He didn't wait for an answer as his feet thumped heavily against the floorboards toward Matt's room.

Without breaking stride, Owen shouldered open Matt's door and saw his son flailing on the bed, arms and legs bouncing off the mattress, his throat raw from screaming.

"Matt!" Owen rushed to his son's bedside and took hold

of his shoulders, trying to keep him still. The boy's eyes were shut, and when Owen wrapped his hand around Matt's arms, he felt something slick against his fingers. He examined his palm, but it was too dark to see.

The bedroom light flicked on and Owen spun around to see Claire standing in the doorway in her robe, Chloe in her arms and their daughter's face buried in her shoulder. "What's wrong?"

"I don't know." Owen turned back to Matt, who'd calmed down and opened his eyes, the flailing done as he sucked in deep breaths. Owen pressed his hand onto Matt's forehead, and his son's skin was ice cold. He brushed the sweaty bangs off and as he did, he smeared blood onto his son's skin. Owen looked down to Matt's arm and saw the bite marks. "What the hell?"

Matt continued his hyperventilating breaths as Owen gently took hold of his son's arm. Three sets of bite marks, two on his forearm and one on his bicep.

"What is that?" Claire asked, now hovering closer. "Is he bleeding?"

Owen turned around. "Put Chloe back to bed." He didn't want his daughter to see this. He turned back to his son. "Matt, what happened?"

"Someone—" Matt drew in a breath. "Was in here—" He exhaled. "I felt it."

Owen's stomach twisted into knots. He stood, looking around the room. He ripped open the closet to find it empty. He looked under the bed, nothing. He tugged at the window, locked. He turned back to his son, who was now examining his own wounds, his eyes as round as the full moon outside. Owen lifted his son's chin and felt that his skin had thawed a little. "You're sure someone was in here?"

Matt nodded, then started to cry, and Owen kissed the top of his head and gently squeezed his neck. "It's all right.

It's okay, son." He glanced back down at the bite marks, and as the adrenaline of the moment subsided, his mind slowly shifted gears. The commotion had woken everyone in the house. But not everyone was accounted for.

Owen left the bedroom, heading back down the balcony toward the stairs. "Roger!" His wife looked at him from Chloe's bedroom on his way past, but he didn't stop. "Roger!" Once he reached the bottom of the staircase, he walked back toward the den that they'd set up as Roger's room in the right back corner of the house. When he opened the door, he found it empty.

Claire stepped out of Chloe's room on the second floor and walked to the banister as Owen passed through the dining room to the front of the house. "Where are you going?"

"Stay with the kids." The answer came out steelier than intended, but there was a rage boiling in him. The doctors had told them that the disease could cause Roger to become violent, to have what they referred to as "episodes," but they didn't mention anything like this.

Owen flung open the front door and was blasted with the thick, humid night air. He swatted away the tiny gnats buzzing around his head, tickling his cheek and neck. The U-Haul truck and van were still parked outside, and he scanned the driveway, looking for any shadowed figures in the night. "Roger!"

His voice echoed over the property, and Owen stepped out onto the gravel drive, tiny rocks poking his bare feet as he made his way to the side of the house, his head on a swivel.

He looked past the tall reeds of the clearing and saw those thick cypress trees and the hanging strands of Spanish moss on the field's edge. It was there that he saw his father-in-law. "Roger!"

Owen jogged toward the old man, then broke into a sprint, his shins brushing against the long, thin strands of grass and reeds. His bare feet squished in the mud and the farther he ran from the house, the wetter the ground became. Water splashed up onto his shorts and bare stomach, and it slowed his pace. When he reached the old man he yanked Roger's arm backward, harder than he intended.

"What the hell are you doing?" Owen asked.

Roger looked at Owen then down to his arm and tried to pull himself free. "Let me go." He used his free arm to try and pry Owen's grip off him, and he tugged more violently. "Stop! Let me go!"

"Roger, calm down." Owen eventually muscled the old man still and looked into the pair of eyes that no longer recognized him. "What are you doing out here?"

Owen felt Roger's muscles relax, and the panic subsided as he blinked. "I-I saw something." He frowned, looking away. "I think." He shut his eyes, and Owen released him. The old man held his head between his hands. "I can't—" He grunted in frustration. "I can't remember."

"Were you in Matt's room?" Owen asked, but his father-in-law kept his hands pressed against the sides of his head, mumbling to himself. "Roger!"

The old man looked up at Owen, squinting. "Who?"

Owen took hold of Roger's hand, gentler than the forceful stop from earlier, and pulled him back toward the house. "C'mon. Let's get you inside."

Roger hesitated a moment, unsure if he should follow, and then turned back to look in the direction he had been walking. "I saw... something."

Owen gave a more forceful tug, and Roger mumbled to himself on the way back. A memory surfaced in the sea of muddled confusion that was his mind. It was about his late wife, Rebecca, and how they were supposed to go and pick someone up from the airport. He didn't want to be late, and he kept telling Rebecca that she looked fine.

Owen escorted Roger back to his room and into bed. The old man lay down, but he didn't sleep, just kept talking to himself. Just before Owen left, Roger called out. "Matt. Is he okay?" His voice was weak and frightened.

Unsure of which Roger he was speaking to, the old man's words from earlier that day whispered in Owen's ear. *Don't let them see me when it starts to get bad.*

"Good night, Roger." Owen returned to the dining room, then trudged back up the stairs to the second floor.

Claire was in Chloe's doorway, frowning. "Is he okay?"

Owen kept silent until his hands were around her waist, the feel of her soft robe underneath his fingertips calming. He wanted to tell her, but didn't. "How's Chloe?"

Claire pulled away from him and crossed her arms. It wasn't the answer she was looking for. "She's fine. Already fast asleep again."

"Good." Owen walked back toward Matt's room and Claire followed closely behind.

"Owen, what did my dad say?"

"We need to get Matt's arms looked at," Owen said, entering his son's room, who was still wide awake and picking at the wounds on his skin. "Don't touch that." Owen shooed his son's fingers from the bite marks and looked at his wife. "Did you unpack the emergency kit?"

Claire lingered, waiting for the question about her father to be answered, but when Owen didn't budge, she dropped her arms at her sides. "Yeah, I'll bring it up." She left and Owen took a closer look at the bite marks.

They weren't deep, just enough pressure to break the skin. The bleeding had stopped, but when Owen pressed close to the wounds, Matt winced. "It hurts?"

"Yeah," Matt answered, his eyes locked on the marks. "It feels achy."

Owen wanted to ask his son more about what he saw, but wasn't sure if he would get the truth. Matt knew his grandpa was sick, so he might try and protect him.

"You don't know who was in your room?" Owen asked.

"No."

"Matt." He waited for his son to look him in the eyes and then took hold of his boy's hand. "It's important you tell me everything that happened." Matt gulped, and Owen paused a moment before he spoke again. "Do you know who was in your room?"

"I was sleeping, and then my arm started hurting, then I felt cold. Really cold. Like that time I fell through the lake when I was skating."

Owen remembered. He was just as scared then as he was right now. "Anything else?"

"No." Matt's face scrunched in preparation for tears. "I'm sorry, Dad."

Owen wrapped his son in a hug, holding on tight. "There's nothing to be sorry about." Matt cried into his chest, and Claire returned with the medical box. They cleaned Matt's wounds, wrapped them, and then tucked him back into bed.

Both stayed in his room until he fell back asleep, and on his way out, Owen took one last look at his boy before closing the door.

In the hallway, Claire crossed her arms in defiance and kept her voice at a whisper. "Well? What did my dad say?"

"He didn't remember," Owen answered.

Claire paused, biting her lower lip and rubbing the sleeves of her robe as she hugged herself. "Do you think he did it?"

Owen drew in a breath, trying to find a way to tell her,

but his omission of an answer told her more than she wanted to know.

Claire's eyes watered, and she shook her head. "I just didn't think he'd ever do something like that. I know the doctors said he might become aggressive, but this?" She arched her eyebrows in an expression of pained disbelief.

"Look, until we can figure something out, I don't want him alone with the kids. I'll start looking at places to take care of him tomorrow. Chuck might know of something."

Claire hugged herself tighter, now unable to control the sobbing. "I just thought we'd have more time."

Owen wrapped his arms around her and pulled her close. "I know." But if the past months had taught him anything, it was that time cared nothing of feelings or circumstances. Time didn't discriminate or have prejudice, it simply marched forward, ignoring the pleas of anyone asking for it to slow down or speed up. It was a constant, steady force that never wavered. And for Roger Templeton, time was slowly devouring his mind.

*M*achinery buzzed around the factory floor as conveyer belts carried the auto parts down the assembly line. Employees operated the large mechanical arms that stamped the brake pads, and then packaged and stacked them into crates to be shipped.

Watching the process, Owen half-listened to the HR rep. It was all just standard paperwork, going over worker's rights and all that. He'd been through it before. It was interesting to find that the factory wasn't unionized. He'd never seen that before. But with the pay, benefits, and working conditions so good, he guessed that there wasn't need for one here.

"Mr. Cooley?" Jonathan leaned forward, his hands clasped tightly together over the stack of papers that required Owen's signature. "Did you hear me?"

"No," Owen answered. "Sorry. Long night." He'd chosen to wait to tell his new employer about his father-in-law's condition until after he'd signed on the dotted line.

"By signing this, you acknowledge that the company isn't liable for any injuries that you or your family sustain while staying on company property." Jonathan pushed the form forward, the pen resting on top.

"Right," Owen said, picking up the pen and placing his signature on the form. He dated it, then handed it back to the HR rep, who then checked his watch and shuffled the papers together.

"Well, it's almost lunchtime," he said. "Let's head downstairs and I'll show you where your locker will be."

Owen followed the rep through the factory floor, catching a slew of different greetings. Most of them were smiles and friendly, twangy hellos, but there were a few glares, some more menacing than others.

Once Owen had his locker squared away, the lunch whistle sounded, and Owen realized just how much he missed that sound. The room quickly flooded with workers, clustering together in small groups, heading either for their lockers or the breakroom.

"Did you bring anything to eat today, or do you need to step out for lunch?" Jonathan asked.

"I didn't bring anything," Owen answered.

"We'll take care of 'em."

Owen turned to the sight of three sweaty figures dressed in matching blue uniforms. The man who spoke stuck out his hand and flashed a corn-yellow smile.

"Marty Wiggins," he said, squeezing Owen's hand unusually hard. "You must be the new line supervisor. I was wondering who they picked to leap over me."

"No need for prickly words, Marty," Jonathan said. "Be nice."

"Yeah, yeah, yeah," Marty waved it off and once Jonathan was gone, Marty leaned close to Owen, whispering. "I'd be careful with that one. Likes taking it up the exit only hole, if you catch my drift."

"Ah," Owen said, nodding, uncomfortable from both Marty's comments and his smell. "Gotcha."

Marty turned back to the two men still standing behind him. "Let me introduce you to the crew! This here is Jake Martin and Grandpa."

"That's not my goddamn name," Grandpa said, the wrinkles on his face further accentuated by his grimace.

Marty slapped the old timer on the shoulder. "If you didn't want the title, you shouldn't have let me marry your daughter."

Grandpa shrugged Marty's hand off him. "I never said you could. You just did it." He crossed his thin arms over his girthy stomach and turned his pair of glassy eyes away. Owen wondered if the old man was going blind, and then wondered if that was better or worse than losing your mind.

Jake Martin stuck his hand out, breaking the awkward silence and giving a friendly smile. His handshake was firm and lacked Marty's over-compensating strength. "Good to meet you." Out of the three of them, Jake was the most put together. Clean shaven, combed hair, and while his uniform was dirty, it wasn't tattered and ragged like Grandpa's and Marty's.

"We're heading down to Crawl Daddy's bar for food and a pitcher if you want to come," Marty said. "Or are we not allowed to drink on the job anymore, boss?"

"I don't think you were allowed to do it before I got here," Owen answered, Marty slowly fraying his nerves. Still, he didn't want to get off on the wrong foot. Managing people who wanted to slice you open was a lot harder than those who didn't. "But I'll tell you what, after work, the first round is on me."

Marty gave a compromising shrug. "Take what you get, I s'pose."

Everyone rode in Jake's truck, Owen taking a back seat

with Grandpa, who kept his arms crossed and his cocked toward the window on the ride to Main Street. The trip took less than five minutes, but with Marty yapping away in the front seat, it felt much longer.

"So where ya from, Owen?"

"Baltimore."

"We got a goddamn Yankee working us now," Marty said, slapping his hat on his knee. "Now I know how General Lee felt after Grant won the war."

"What'd ya do in Baltimore, Owen?" Jake asked.

"I worked at a shipyard," Owen answered. "Welding mostly. But I'm a machinist by trade. I started out in assembly at a GM factory when I was younger."

"A Jack of all trades, huh?" Marty asked. "Maybe I should have learned more so *I* coulda got yer job."

"Knock it off, Marty, will ya?" Jake asked.

"Ah, hell, I'm just poking fun." Marty turned around in his seat, sweat mixed in with the jet-black stubble along his face. "You can take some poking, can't you?"

"Sure," Owen answered. "Just not in the exit only hole."

Marty bust out laughing and slapped his hat down on his knee a few times, and Jake smiled. Even Grandpa chuckled, though he didn't break from his staring contest with the view outside.

Marty was more amiable at lunch, now that he was certain Owen didn't 'take it in the exit only hole,' though he still did most of the talking. Jake got in a word when he could, and Grandpa kept his focus on his basket of fried catfish and sweet tea.

And to Owen's relief, the food was actually good. He wasn't sure how he'd adjust to Creole cuisine. Thankfully he didn't mind seafood. He foresaw a lot of that in his diet moving forward.

With full bellies and slightly more tired eyes, they paid

the tab, but only after a good ribbing from Marty about how the new 'boss' should pick up the check. When they stepped back outside from the frigid A/C, the Louisiana heat clocked Owen in the face and he let out a low woof noise from the dense, humid air.

"You'll get used to it," Jake said, noticing the flushed look on Owen's face. "I had a cousin grew up in Ohio, and he moved down here about ten years ago. Now, it gets below seventy degrees and he starts complaining it's too cold."

"Hopefully it won't take me ten years to get to that point," Owen said.

"Hey, we got some time before we get back," Jake said. "Wanna show Owen a little bit of Main Street?"

"Ain't nothing to see," Grandpa said. "Just some shitty bricks and cracked concrete."

"Now, Grandpa," Marty said. "Don't go belittling our beloved downtown like that." Marty leaned over to Owen. "It's the finest shitty bricks and concrete this side of the Mississippi."

To be fair, Grandpa's description wasn't that far off. A handful of businesses lined the road: barber, grocery shop, gas station, insurance company, realtor, hardware store, a doctor's office. It was standard small-town America as far as Owen was concerned. Not much different from some of the neighborhoods in Baltimore. It was like its own self-sustaining entity.

"Not a lot of activity today," Owen said, noting the lack of pedestrians on the sidewalk.

"Most of the town works at the factory," Jake said.

"The big boss's family has kept most everyone employed since the thirties," Marty said.

"And the bastard won't ever let you forget it," Grandpa said, spitting on the ground, his arms crossed and that permanent scowl etched on his face.

"Ah, Grandpa's just sore cuz he's worked there longer than anybody and still has the same damn job," Marty said. "Not the big boss's fault that you never tried to climb that ladder."

"Ain't no fucking ladder," Grandpa said, his mouth downturned in a petulant frown. "Just a bunch of pussies playing dress up in those suits. I ain't no fucking doll."

Owen watched the old man carefully. There was a sharp edge to his words. He aimed to cut, but what for, Owen didn't know.

With his eyes on the old man, Owen missed the table to his left and his leg knocked the corner hard, spilling some of the table's contents to the pavement. He reached out his arms in a knee-jerk reaction to catch whatever it was that was falling but failed.

"Oh, shit, someone's gonna have some bad juju now!" Marty exclaimed, hysterical laughter shrieking from his mouth as he jumped up and down like a child.

Owen bent down to pick up the merchandise, unsure of what his hands were touching. They looked like jewelry but were made out of rope, bones, feathers, and rocks. He picked up tiny packets with different-colored dust in them, and small glass tubes with a variety of different-colored liquids inside corked at the top. Two of the glass tubes broke and stained dark patches of grey over the concrete that quickly evaporated in the heat.

Owen stood and put what he could salvage back on the table as a woman stepped out of the shop. He recognized her long dreads and baggy clothes from the day before. She stared at him now the same way she did when he drove past. Her face didn't have the white paint like before, but the familiar shiver crawled up his back.

"Careful, Owen," Marty said, taking an over-exaggerated step back. "Miss Voodoo will cast a spell on you!" His accent thickened in satire and he waved his arms and squatted down, making some primitive noises with his mouth, then laughed while Owen gaped at the old woman, getting a better sense of her age now that he was up close. She was older, her face weathered and wrinkled, but what captured his attention most were her eyes. They were a light hazel, and tiny specks of yellow flickered like gold in the sunlight. Owen wasn't sure if he'd seen a pair of eyes that beautiful before in his entire life.

"It has seen you." The voodoo woman's words crawled from her mouth in a deep, slow drawl, hitting Owen like an unexpected wave at the beach. She clutched her staff, which Owen now saw had a large rock tied to the top of it with thin leather straps.

Owen gestured to the broken items. "I can pay for what broke, I—"

"Cana-linga-too-mara-hee-so." She stepped forward and pounded her staff into the pavement. "Cana-linga-too-mara-hee-so. Cana-linga-too-mara-hee-so." She repeated the words and motions in a rhythmic cadence as her eyes widened and locked on Owen.

Owen heard Marty's laugher and felt a tug on his sleeve, but there was something hypnotizing about the way she spoke. He couldn't peel his eyes away from her.

"C'mon, Owen," Jake said, pulling Owen's arm down the sidewalk. "Let's go!"

Owen stumbled after them, his head turned back to the woman slowly following to the edge of her store and tables of trinkets, repeating the same words over and over until her voice disappeared from the distance.

"You all right?" Jake asked once they were at a safe distance.

"I'm fine," Owen answered, shaking his head like he had a dizzy spell. "Who was that?"

"Our local crazy woman," Marty answered. "You didn't have one in Baltimore?"

Jake's eyes widened and he shook his head. "Her name is Madame Crepaux. That's her shop. It's got all kinds of weird voodoo stuff in it. I wouldn't go near that place, man. I'm not a religious man, but I don't need to push my spiritual luck."

"Yeah," Owen said. "I can understand that." He tossed one last glance to the woman's shop and saw that she'd disappeared. They circled back to the truck at Crawl Daddy's and drove back to the factory to finish out the day.

But the ride back felt different for a couple reasons. One, Owen was cold, like he just stepped out of a freezer even though he'd been sweating like a pig just minutes before. His skin was almost icy, like how Matt's felt last night.

And the second was the old man. While Grandpa ignored Owen on the way to lunch, the old man didn't take his eyes off Owen the whole ride back to the factory. And just before they all clocked back into work, Owen watched the old man snarl at Marty over something he'd said, this time wide enough to reveal a silver-capped tooth. The same silver-capped tooth that a young girl saw under the Louisiana moonlight twenty-five years ago.

* * *

CLAIRE UNPACKED the rest of the dishes, loaded them in the washer, and turned it on. It'd been a while since she'd had that luxury. And it felt good. But despite the house, the financial stability, the knowledge that she'd be able to buy groceries next week and not have to stretch one meal into four, Claire couldn't stop biting her nails.

It was a habit she picked up as a little girl. Her mother scolded her every time she caught her doing it, but the habit wouldn't break. What Owen had said last night rang in her ears all morning. She'd barely slept a wink because of it, and she'd avoided her father all morning. She glanced out the front kitchen window and saw Matt playing catch with Chloe. When he moved his arms, the sunlight brightened the white of his bandages against his lightly tanned skin.

She just couldn't believe that her father would do something like that, failing mind or not. But she had to remind herself what the doctors had said. Alzheimer's could unveil some frightening tendencies, and if that should happen, they should start considering their options. The only problem was that all the options were shit.

"Gah." Claire winced and looked down at her ring finger. She'd gnawed off a hangnail and was bleeding. She reached for the sink knob, and the pipes groaned. The faucet rattled, and instead of water a black sludge spewed from the pipe, which smelled of sewage.

Claire covered her nose and quickly shut off the sink, letting the black water funnel down the drain. She backed out of the kitchen, still sucking on her finger, making a mental note to tell Owen about the pipes. She hoped that water didn't funnel through the dishwasher.

In the doorway between the kitchen and the dining room, Claire heard the faint murmur of her dad's television in the den. She'd set it up just like the basement in Baltimore in hopes of giving him some familiarity. But she wasn't sure if that mattered now.

She paced the dining room, working up the nerve to go and speak to him, and in one swift turn marched down the right rear hallway, the television growing louder.

Roger sat in his favorite chair, unaware of his daughter's presence. Perhaps even unaware he had a daughter. She knocked on the door frame as she entered. "Dad, I need to talk to you." When he didn't respond, her heart cracked, and she took another step inside. "Roger?"

He looked up at her, squinting the way he did when he wasn't himself. "Yes?"

She hesitated. If he wasn't lucid, then maybe now wasn't the best time. She raised her nails to her mouth but stopped herself and knelt at the side of her dad's chair. She looked up at him like she did when she was a little girl. "Do you know who I am?" Her voice was small and quiet, fearful almost.

Roger smiled. "Of course, Claire-Bear." He cupped her cheek, his large hand calloused but warm.

Claire leaned into it and then took hold of his hand in both of hers. "Do you remember last night?"

The smile faded. "A little."

"Something happened to Matt, and—"

"Oh my god." Roger leaned forward, his voice suddenly frightened. "Did I—"

"He's fine, Dad." She gave his hand a reassuring pat. "But there were some marks on his arm. Bite marks." She felt him shudder. "Do you remember anything like that?"

Roger's eyes searched the floor as if the answers were written there in front of him. He squeezed her hands. Even at seventy-three, and with Alzheimer's, he was still strong. Still resilient. "No." He looked at her. "Did I do it?"

"We're not sure," Claire answered.

Roger wiped his mouth, the wheels of his mind slowly turning, some of them completely broken now, and then he dropped his hand and moved close. "Was there blood in my teeth?"

Claire recoiled. "What? No. I-I mean, I don't think so." She thought about it last night. She didn't really see her dad after it happened. But Owen never mentioned seeing anything like that, and she let herself feel hopeful.

"Well," Roger said. "I would have had blood on me if I did, right?"

Claire reassuringly squeezed his hand back. "Yeah. I guess

you would have." She stood and kissed his forehead. When she pulled back, his face looked confused again.

"Do I know you?"

She smiled sadly, knowing that they'd have so many more interactions like this over the next few months. Just before she spoke to answer, Chloe screamed.

Claire spun on her heel and sprinted out of her father's room, Chloe's high-pitched wail guiding Claire toward the front door and then out into the gravel drive. "Chloe! Matt!" The afternoon sun was bright, and she stumbled blindly. "Chloe!"

"Mom!"

Black spots from the sudden brightness clouded her vision, but she pivoted right toward the sound of her daughter's voice. Shin-high grass brushed her knees as she weaved around trees and rocks. She blinked quickly, ridding herself of the blinding spots, and found Chloe next to a tree.

Bright red blotches sat high on Chloe's cheeks that were wet from crying. As she rounded the tree, she saw Matt on the ground, unconscious, a snake slithering away from his body.

"Get back, Chloe!" Claire's voice was angered, and frightened, and the tone only triggered another wail of sobs from her daughter. She knelt by her son's body, his eyes closed. "Matt, can you hear me? Matt!" She gently shook him, then checked for a pulse. He was sweating profusely, but his skin was cold to the touch. She noticed the pair of punctured holes in his forearm next to one of the bandages. She checked his breathing and felt the light puff of air from his nose. She picked her son off the ground, struggling with his weight. "Chloe, get to the U-Haul, now!"

Her daughter did as she was told, and she stumbled toward the moving truck, running ahead of Claire, who kept

Matt close to her chest, her legs sinking into the soft Louisiana mud, slowing her sprint toward the U-Haul.

With the muscles in her arms burning from Matt's weight and mud speckled over her legs, she heaved Matt into the U-Haul's passenger seat, and then helped Chloe inside after. "Put your seatbelt on and then put one on your brother."

Claire skirted around the truck's hood to the driver side door and climbed inside. The keys were still stuck in the ignition, Owen's way of testing true Southern hospitality. She cranked the U-Haul to life, then floored the accelerator and swerved down the gravel road.

Matt shivered in his seat, and Claire removed one white-knuckled hand from the wheel and placed it on her son's arm. His skin was ice-cold but he was moving, and that meant he was alive. Crying, Chloe laid her head down on Matt's shoulder.

A few low hanging branches smacked the top of the U-Haul and a truck driving in the opposite direction honked at her speed, but she ignored them. The National Guard couldn't slow her down.

Traffic thickened the closer they moved to town and the tires screeched as Claire maneuvered between the cars, their blaring horns growing angrier. Main Street appeared, and she leaned forward until her chest pressed against the steering wheel, her eyes scanning the row of buildings for Dr. Talbert's office. She was scheduled to visit today at three for the bite marks on Matt's arm.

Signs for the hardware store, grocery, and gas station flew by, but she jerked the wheel sharply to the left of the road when she spied the letters MD in her peripheral.

With the engine still running, but the U-Haul in park, Claire grabbed hold of Matt and pulled him across the seats. His limbs dragged behind him as he lay limp, and Claire cradled him in her arms. "Chloe, come on!" Her daughter followed, her short legs struggling to keep up with her mother, who shouldered open the doctor's office door. "I need help!"

Heads snapped in her direction, looking away from their phones, magazines, computers, and waiting room television playing a rerun of Friends. An elderly woman behind the reception desk rose from her chair as Claire adjusted Matt's weight in her arms.

"What happened?" she asked.

"Snake bite," Claire answered, her voice cutting in and out. "I don't know what kind it was."

A man stepped out from behind the wall separating the waiting room and the examination rooms, and Claire noticed *Dr. Talbert* inscribed on his coat. "Let's get him in the back."

Claire followed the doctor to the closest available room and laid Matthew on the table.

Dr. Talbert opened Matt's eyes and flashed a light in them, pressing his fingers against the side of Matt's neck. "Rachel, bring in the cardiac monitor." Dr. Talbert removed his stethoscope and checked the boy's breathing as Rachel wheeled in a machine and lifted Matt's shirt. She placed small suction cups over his chest and stomach. "Let's get an IV hooked up as well."

"What about anti-venom?" Claire asked. "Don't you have something like that?"

"Without knowing what kind of snake bit him, we don't know what anti-venom to use," Dr. Talbert answered. "But the fluids will help keep his organs functional until it passes."

"How long with that take?"

"I'm not sure."

Matt convulsed on the table, and foam bubbled from the corners of his mouth. The nurse and doctor stabilized his head and placed a wooden bit in his mouth to keep him from biting his tongue off.

"Oh my god," Claire said, covering her mouth.

"Mommy."

Claire spun around and saw Chloe in the doorway, her eyes locked on Matt. She went to reach for her, but one of the nurses in the hallway pulled her away from the traumatic scene.

"Keep his arms steady!" Dr. Talbert said, but even with the nurse, they could barely keep all of Matt's one hundred pounds on the table, the convulsions worsening.

Claire jumped in to help and watched the foam bubbling at the corners of Matt's mouth turn red. His eyes popped open and he screamed, spewing blood in speckled bits like a volcano. He arched his back, his legs and arms pinned by the three of them, and he squirmed.

The green lines of the cardiac monitor spiked up and down in jagged peaks, beeping wildly. Matt's body offered one final spasm and then he collapsed on his back, his body limp. The green line plummeted and the fast-paced beeps were replaced with a single monotone beep as Matt flat lined.

"No!" Claire howled like a wounded animal, helplessly clawing at her son's legs as the doctor pumped Matt's chest, his small body convulsing with each heavy-handed compression. The nurse pulled at Claire's arms, but she resisted, taking hold of Matt's left foot that tilted lifelessly to the side. Her knees buckled as the steady beep of the EKG filled the examination room.

A tightness took hold of Claire's chest, and she clutched it as the nurse holding her by the arms tried to pull her up. Another wave of sobs scrunched her face and creased her lips into a painful, solid line that lay as flat as the cardiac monitor for her son's heart.

Dr. Talbert stepped back from the table, his shoulders sagging with his arms limp at his sides. He turned to Claire and said something. But those words weren't right. They couldn't be. Matt was ten. He was healthy. He loved baseball and being a big brother. He was a good kid. He was her son. Her first born.

"God, no!" Claire's face reddened and she grew more hysterical.

"Ma'am, please," the nurse said, trying to pull Claire back. "It's best if you don't stay. Please."

Claire smacked the hands that reached for her or Matt. "Don't you touch him!" She hovered over his body protectively, holding his face, his skin still ice cold. She pulled him to her chest and slowly rocked him.

Tears dripped from Claire's face, raining over her child like an afternoon shower. She shook her head, feral moans escaping her lips. She stroked his hair, pushing the bangs from his forehead, and then gently leaned down and kissed his cheek. When she removed her lips, she laid her head on his chest.

A faint beep echoed through the room. Claire lifted her head and looked back to the monitor, the green line still flat. She looked at the nurse and doctor, both of whom were staring at the screen as well. "Did you hear that?"

Claire turned back to Matt, fanning the flames of hope. "C'mon, Matty. Come back. Please, come back." She shut her eyes, praying. She wasn't sure who was listening, or what was listening, but as she whispered promises to a being she wasn't even sure existed, another beep sounded. And then Matt opened his eyes.

3

*W*hen Chuck delivered the news to Owen about his son, he sprinted to his van and sped toward Main Street. The ambulance's flashing lights revealed the doctor's office, where he also spotted their U-Haul parked at a slanted angle, half on the street and half off, blocking three other cars from leaving. Owen parked in front of it, blocking another two cars himself.

Claire and a team of paramedics were in the examination room, hovering over Matt, when Owen entered. They checked Matt's blood pressure and lungs, placing their stethoscope over a skin that looked a sickly pale grey.

Owen saw the red stains at the corners of his son's mouth and didn't even notice Claire groping his arm until she started speaking.

"Owen, he came back." Tears lingered in her eyes as she sniffled. "He was gone, but he came back."

Owen shook his head, trying to make sense of his wife's hysteria. "Came back from what?"

"Your son flat lined, Mr. Cooley." An elderly man in a white coat spoke up, and Owen saw the name Dr. Talbert inscribed on the upper right breast of the coat. "He was dead for almost a full minute."

Owen slowly reached for his son's hand. It was ice cold. "I-I don't understand." He turned back to Claire. "What happened?"

"It was a miracle," Claire answered, hugging Owen with the same wondered surprise in her voice. "Our boy came back."

"Mr. and Mrs. Cooley?" The paramedic on Matt's right side removed the Velcro blood pressure strap from Matt's arm. "We'd like to take your son over to Southern General and run a few tests to make sure he's all right. It's just a precaution."

"Okay. Sure," Owen said.

"We'll give you guys a minute, and then we'll load your son into the ambulance."

"Thank you," Claire said.

With the medics, nurses, and doctor gone, Owen gently placed his calloused palm against Matt's cheek. "How are you feeling, bud?"

Matt's eyes were half-closed, and his lips barely moved when he spoke. "I'm okay." The words were cracked and dry like a desert earth. "Is Chloe all right? I saw the snake coming, but I didn't know if she got away in time."

Another wave of tears flooded Claire's eyes, and Owen smiled proudly. "She's okay. But you need to rest. Try to sleep, all right?"

Matt nodded, and Claire kept hold of his hand while Owen beckoned the medics to return. They loaded him onto the stretcher, Claire hovering over their boy protectively.

"I'm going to ride with him," Claire said, then looked to the paramedics. "That's okay, right?"

"Yeah, but we only have room for one more, so we can only take you."

"It's fine," Owen said, touching Claire's arm. "I'll follow with Chloe in the van."

Claire gasped. "Oh my god. I forgot about Dad. He's still at home. I didn't even tell him we left. I just got in the van and—"

"Claire," Owen said. "It's fine. I'll go home and check on him. Do you have your phone?"

She nodded.

"Call me if anything changes," Owen said, giving Claire a reassuring kiss. "I'll see you guys in a little bit." Owen retrieved Chloe from the nurses in front while Claire accompanied the paramedics into the ambulance that loaded Matt inside, then quickly sped away.

Chloe didn't say much, just wrapped her arms around Owen's neck and buried her face into his shoulder. Her little body was hot, and she quickly formed a Chloe-sized sweat stain on his shirt in the sixty seconds it took to walk her out to the van. He strapped her in the seat and gave her a kiss. "You all right, bug?"

She shook her head.

"I know it was scary, but everyone is safe now." Owen gently stroked her fine light-brown hair. "The doctors are going to make your brother better, and then we're all going home together."

"But what about Grandpa?" Chloe asked, her voice small with her head tilted down.

Owen raised his left eyebrow but kept his tone kind. "What do you mean?"

"Matt said that he might have to go away," Chloe said, her chin buried in her chest as she picked at the hem of her shirt with a large rainbow over the front. It was one of her favorites. "He said that Grandpa was sick." She looked up at him, those curious eyes searching her father's face for reassurance. "Can the doctors make him better?"

"They're going to try." Owen kissed her cheek and then climbed behind the wheel. He started the van and headed back to the house, hoping Roger hadn't gotten himself into too much trouble while he'd been alone.

* * *

ROGER'S SHIRT had soaked through with sweat. He turned in a half circle, his feet sinking in the mud as he stepped in the swampy reeds. As he turned, he saw a house. It wasn't the house he'd lived in in Baltimore, and the thick trees with long strands of moss weren't the branches he'd climbed in the city park as a boy. He shut his eyes and tried to remember.

Why did he come outside? Where was he? Why didn't any of this look familiar? He opened his eyes and looked down at the pair of hands now foreign to him. The gold band he'd worn since his vows was nothing more than a constricting piece of jewelry that he could no longer remove because of his swollen arthritis. When had his hands gotten so old? He clenched those unrecognizable hands into fists and grunted in frustration, his head growing fuzzy.

He stumbled through the hallways of his mind, groping at the darkness, his fingers searching for a light switch that would show him the way, but found nothing. And that's when he heard it.

A rattle. It echoed down those dark corridors and gave the illusion of an omnipresence. It clanged in a rhythmic dance. The noise was familiar, but he couldn't remember where he'd heard it before.

Roger turned back to the house. He lived there. Yes, he remembered now. Louisiana. That's where he was. He glanced down at his legs, which were covered in mud all the way up to his knees, a few hardened specks on his shorts. The rattle sounded again.

Had he followed that noise out here? No. It was coming from the house. He needed to go back inside. Claire would be home soon. At least he thought she would. Where had she gone? The store?

Slowly, Roger lifted one foot in front of the other, the commands from his brain slower than they should have been. His body felt broken, like his muscles were thick with hardening concrete. It hurt to move.

Roger smacked his feet against the steps up the front porch and knocked the mud off, then halfway through the motion, he stopped and stared down at his shoes in confusion. He grunted and then tracked mud into the house.

Inside, he shied away from looking at anything for too long. It worried him that he didn't recognize where he was. It felt wrong. All of this felt wrong.

A whisper tickled the back of his mind. Roger stopped. He scratched the back of his head. The voice wasn't his own. He leaned against the wall for support as he started to feel dizzy again. He was sick. Now he remembered. But what was he sick with? He didn't feel like he had a cold.

Another rattle. It was louder than the one he heard outside, closer. It preceded another whisper, and then the rattling fell into a rhythm with the whispers. Someone was speaking, but he couldn't understand what was being said. Was it because he was sick? Claire would speak to him sometimes, and he didn't recognize her words. He didn't recognize because... of the disease.

He was sick with something bad, but what was it? Cancer? Liver disease? Some vital organ failure? A clouded memory of his doctor visit floated by, and he tried to read the doctor's lips, but nothing looked familiar. He chased after it for a while, trying to remember, trying to figure out why he couldn't remember, and then—

Roger stopped in the hall, the sudden recall of his illness slamming into his chest like a pillowcase filled with bricks. A hopeless dread took hold, and he started to hyperventilate. He'd requested the tests and had gone by himself. It was like his mind and body took one step further away from each other every day. It wouldn't be long until they couldn't hold onto one another anymore. But such was life. The older you grew, the more you had to say goodbye to.

At first it was the strength of his youth. Then his tenacity. Then his career. Then his sweet Rachel. And now the last pillar of resolve that he clung to, his mind, was crumbling away.

Another rattle, more whispers.

Roger remembered that the doctor told him he would still have moments of lucidity. And when those moments presented themselves, the doctor recommended to focus on a single memory, a very important one. A focal point to rally behind. He closed his eyes and swiped at the cobwebs of his mind, frantically opening doors to find it, and just when he was about to give up, he saw it. Claire's birth.

His first and only child. He pulled the memory over him like a warm blanket. Never in his life had he felt more purposeful than that moment. For the first time, he understood what the word 'unconditionally' meant.

Another rattle, and more whispers penetrated his thoughts. But these noises weren't from his illness. He'd heard these noises before. Last night, he saw something. He chased something.

The old bones of the house creaked and groaned as Roger followed the noise down the left hallway from the living room, then past the dining room.

Thunka-dunka-dunka. Thunka-dunka-dunka.

The rhythm of the rattle quickened and the whispers grew louder in Roger's head. The chanting, the rattling, all of it seemed to work in coordination with his heart that pounded faster and faster. He wasn't sure which was leading which, but when he arrived at the last door on the rear left of the house, the noises stopped.

Roger wiped the sweat trickling toward his eyes. He reached for the old brass door knob, and despite the heat, the metal was cold. He opened it, and the hinges creaked loudly until the door came to a rest. Roger lingered in the doorway, glancing around the room and saw—

Nothing. No furniture, no decorations on the walls, no closet. Only a dirty window that clouded the afternoon sunlight.

Roger tracked more mud into the room as he stepped inside, his footprints following him to the center of the room. He squinted into the corners and glanced up at the ceiling. Those noises were coming from inside here. He was sure of it. At least he thought he was.

Roger looked down at his feet, and his mind grew heavy and clouded. He struggled to keep hold of the clarity that brought him here, but it was like fighting a riptide pulling him out to sea. The current was too strong. He turned around to leave but the door slammed shut.

Water flooded through the crack at the door's bottom, and Roger splashed his feet in the stream, tugging at the brass knob, the door sealed shut. The water darkened to black and quickly rose to his ankles, then his shins. He twisted and yanked at the knob, but no matter how hard he pulled, the door wouldn't budge.

Roger turned toward the window, the water up to his waist now and emitting a stagnant stench, like sewer water. He waded toward the window, his movements slow, hoping he could open it to escape. But just before he reached it, the door burst open and a wave of black water crashed against his back, dunking him into the black. He clawed toward the surface and gulped air as he broke through, his hands scraping the ceiling.

Roger turned back toward the door, which disappeared as the water level rose. He paddled toward it, every breath through his mouth, his head tilted upward avoiding the taste of death that surrounded him.

Something brushed against Roger's leg under the water and he jerked his foot away in a panicked escape. When he got close to the door, he took one last breath and plunged into the black abyss. Even with his eyes open, he couldn't see underwater. He patted the wall with his hands, feeling for the door, and discovered that it had shut again. His fingers grazed the brass knob and he gave it a tug, but it remained locked.

The water neutralized any power as he kicked and punched the door, unsure of how it even closed. His lungs ached for breath and he swam back to the surface and gasped for air. He coughed up some of the black water, his head dipping below the waterline twice as he struggled to stay afloat.

A cramp bit his left leg, and his arthritic fingers clawed at the walls to keep himself from drowning. And then, with his head tilted up toward the ceiling, thinking he was taking his last breaths, the water leveled off.

Less than three inches of space separated the water's surface from the room's ceiling. And as Roger bobbed up and down, clinging to life, he noticed that the water's surface never rippled, not even from his own movements. His breaths echoed like he was in a cave and then suddenly stopped.

All sound was sucked from the room. Roger's left arm numbed, and a fleeting fear of a heart attack struck his mind.

But the numbness spread to the rest of his limbs, the water growing cold. He took breaths, feeling the motion of air filling his lungs, but still couldn't hear them. However, the smell remained, and it grew more pungent.

Water bubbled on the other side of the room, but the surface didn't ripple. The small, rounded mounds of black burst then blended back seamlessly with the water's surface. And then, just as inexplicably as the water appeared, it began to recede.

Roger bobbed up and down more freely, and his muscles shook with relief when his toes felt the floor. He collapsed against the wall for support, catching his breath, and the water leveled off to the height of his chest. He looked over to the door, which was still closed, and then reached for the knob. Still locked.

"Help!" Roger weakly pounded on the door. "Please! Someone! Help!" No answer, and when Roger turned toward the window, something penetrated the surface on the other side of the room. It was a skull.

Black water rolled from the empty eye sockets, giving the illusion that the skull was crying as it rose from the dark water. Roger tilted his head to the side and saw the skull was attached to a staff.

The skull was thrust forward in a quick jerk, then pulled back, and it triggered the rattling noise. The sound he heard was bones, smacking together in a violent orchestra. He remained glued to the wall behind him, and he shivered uncontrollably, still unable to hear his own panicked breaths, the only noise in the room that rattling skull.

More water bubbled to Roger's left and he squinted into the black water, seeing something white rising from the depths. It grew larger as it neared the surface and when it broke the black water's plane, Roger jerked away.

Human bones floated like buoys, bobbing up and down

until they came to a motionless rest like the water itself. More water bubbled, and as Roger retreated to the corner of the room in horror, more bones floated to the surface. Ribs, femurs, shoulders, skulls, they all thickened the water like vegetables in a stew.

Roger smacked the bones away whenever they floated close, and then the water bubbled again near the staff and something else emerged from the darkness. Black, matted hair appeared first, blending into the water from which it came. The flesh attached to the hair was scaly, like a snake's skin, and shimmered the color of grey ash. A formidable brow hovered over eyes as big as lemons, but black as a starless night sky. The creature stopped once its eyes rose above the water's surface, and it stared at Roger, unblinking.

The creature gave the staff a shake, and Roger felt his own bones rattle. He clawed back toward the door, pulling the brass knob harder and harder, bending the very wood of the door, but nothing budged. Bones rattled again, and Roger looked behind him. The creature glided through the water, slowly, continuing its rhythmic dance of the staff and skull. *Thunka-dunka-dunka. Thunka-dunka-dunka.*

Roger felt the vibrations in his throat as he screamed but heard only the rattle from the creature's staff. He spun around, his back glued to the wall as the creature drew closer.

The rattling quickened. *Thunkadunkadunka, thunkadunkadunka, thunkadunkadunka.* The creature never blinked, didn't twitch, just shook its staff and when it was less than an arm's reach away, it pushed its head farther out of the water, exposing a mouth full of dagger like teeth, jutting out in awkward and painful directions. And that's when Roger finally heard his own scream.

4

*B*y the time Owen shifted into park and turned off the engine outside the house, Chloe was fast asleep. Her head was tilted to the side, her mouth was open, and a little pile of drool had formed on her shoulder. "Like mother, like daughter."

Owen lifted her out of the seat and placed her tiny furnace of a body over his shoulder as she remained asleep. He shut the van door and turned to the house. He stopped at the sight of the muddy tracks that led up to the front porch steps and open front door.

Owen shifted Chloe in his arms and scanned the property as he walked toward the door. He didn't see Roger in the trees or the field.

"Roger?" Owen's voice echoed in the massive living room, but only the old floors groaned in response to his footsteps. He followed the mud tracks through the living room and into the dining room, and that's when he started to hear it.

A low mumble, like chanting. There was a rhythm to it, and it echoed through the walls down the hallway. Owen followed it past his own bedroom on the first floor and back toward the closed door of the spare bedroom where the tracks ended.

Owen glanced at Chloe still asleep on his shoulder and knocked, unsure what Roger was doing on the other side. "Roger? You all right?"

More mumbles answered, and Owen jiggled the door knob. Locked. He returned to the dining room and pulled out one of the chairs. "I'm gonna set you down, okay sweetheart?" Owen gently placed her in the chair, and she grumbled something as she folded her hands on the table and laid her head down.

Owen returned to the room and pressed his ear against the door and heard more mumbling. He pounded on the old wood with his palm. "Roger, you need to open up right now!" Nothing.

Owen rammed his shoulder into the door, and the old wood buckled but didn't break. He backed up, giving himself a running start, then rushed the door again. Wood splintered off from the frame and the door flung open. Owen stumbled three steps before stopping and saw Roger on his back, his eyes staring at the ceiling, soaking wet.

Owen knelt by the old man's side and gently took his hand. "Roger, can you hear me?" He cupped his father-in-law's cheek, but the old timer didn't react, only repeating his rhythmic nonsense. And his skin was ice to the touch.

Owen leaned closer to Roger's mouth, trying to understand what was being said, but it might as well have been a foreign language.

Chulung-Oola-Awaola-May.   Chulung-Oola-Awaola-May. Chulung-Oola-Awaola-May.

"Daddy?" Chloe poked her head around the door frame, rubbing her eyes sleepily.

Owen left Roger to his nonsense and scooped Chloe off the floor and jogged down the hallway with her in his arms, then dropped her on the couch in the living room. "Sweetheart, I need you to stay right here and don't move, okay?"

Chloe's eyes widened, and she nodded as Owen ran out to the van and grabbed his phone. He dialed 911 and returned to the room where Roger was still on his back, mumbling the same words over and over.

The operator picked up. "911, what's your emergency?"

"Hi, I need an ambulance for my father-in-law. He's an Alzheimer's patient, and I think he might have hurt himself."

Owen nodded along and answered the operator's questions as the woman assured Owen that help would get there soon. He pressed two fingers into the side of the old man's neck and checked his pulse. It was racing. Owen pinched Roger's wet sleeve and then touched the floors of the room and noticed that they were wet too. The whole damn room was wet.

* * *

MATT FADED in and out of consciousness on the ride over to the hospital, but Claire never let go of his hand. The paramedics didn't say much, only answering her repeated concerns of whether her son was okay, to which they always replied 'yes.'

The ambulance slowed to a stop outside the ER entrance of Southern General, which had been a thirty-minute drive. It was twice as long as a trip would have taken from their house in Baltimore to the nearest hospital. She didn't know why that popped into her head, but it did.

Claire thanked the medics for their help, repeatedly, and she and Matt were transferred into the care of a team of nurses and a doctor who looked one step from retiring and two from the grave.

"We'll draw some blood and keep him here for a few

hours for observation," Doctor Medley said, his upper back permanently curved forward from a hump formed by either old age or fatigue. "Then we'll release him to go home. Food here isn't great, so if you need to step out and grab yourself or your son something to eat, you won't find anyone objecting. Security will give you an eyeful, along with Nurse Hatcher, but I assure you both are harmless as long as you're not trying to steal anything." He scribbled something down on his clipboard. "I'll be on call, so if you have any questions, just ask one of my nurses and they'll page me."

"I did have one question," Claire said. "Since the bite, he's been very cold, almost clammy to the touch. Is that normal?"

Doctor Medley didn't look up from his clipboard as he waved his hand, dismissing the notion. "He's still in shock. I imagine you don't run into many venomous snakes in Baltimore." He looked up, smiling, but Claire didn't return the gesture. "He'll be fine, Mrs. Cooley. He just needs rest. Keeping him here is just a precautionary measure. Nothing more." He patted her arm with his old, liver-spotted hand the way the elderly did to those younger than them when they felt it necessary to evoke their superiority, and then left to check on his other patients.

Claire pulled up a chair and resumed her position at Matt's bedside, holding his hand and gently running her fingers through his hair. She engulfed his small hand in his, trying to warm him, but despite her touch, his fingers remained icy.

"Mom?"

Claire smiled. "Hey, baby. How are you feeling?"

Matt offered a fatigued groan, his lips barely moving. "I'm thirsty."

"Okay," Claire answered, kissing his forehead. "I'll get you some water. Do you need anything else? More blankets?" His forehead was colder than his hand.

"No," Matt answered. "Just water."

"I'll be right back." Claire stopped at the doorway and turned back to her son. She lingered, watching him sleep. She'd never been so happy to see him sleep.

A nurse passed and Claire reached for the woman's elbow, who looked up from her phone at Claire's touch.

"Is there a water fountain here somewhere?" Claire asked.

"Down the hall and to the left around the corner. There'll be cups in a dispenser right next to it."

"Thanks." Claire looked back to Matt, his eyes still closed, then weaved down the hall around the traffic of nurses and doctors. She pulled a cup from the dispenser and tilted it to the side, tapping her foot as it filled. When it reached the top, she quickly turned back down to the hallway, careful not to spill the water on her hurried return.

"Here you go, baby," Claire said, lifting the cup to his lips and helping him sit up to drink. He sipped at first, then gulped the water vigorously. He drank until it was gone, and then coughed a little as Claire gently laid his head back down onto the pillow. "Do you want some more?"

"No," Matt said weakly. "Thanks, Mom."

"You're welcome." Claire crumpled the paper cup and tossed it in the waste bucket, then returned to her sentry chair, watching over her son, her hand over his while he slept.

In the quiet of their room, Claire retraced everything that had happened since they arrived in town. She did her best not to obsess, but after what she'd just seen, it was hard not to. The rational side of her brain reassured her that this was simply a combination of unfortunate events. But the other side, the maternal side, whispered different thoughts.

Claire had never been a religious woman. Neither was her family. The only time she'd set foot in a church was when Owen and her were married, and that was only because that's what both of them thought that's what the occasion called for.

But everything that happened so far felt like... signs. Bad omens warning her to leave. And the more she thought about it, the more she worried.

Claire rubbed her forehead in exasperated fatigue. She took a breath and convinced herself that she was simply overwhelmed and lacked sleep, which was true. The move, the new house, new environment, all of it was catching up with her.

She kissed Matt's hand again and then placed it under the blankets in hopes of warming it up. But after two more sets of blankets and twenty minutes later, his skin was still ice cold. She flagged down one of the nurses to check his temperature.

"Ninety-eight point five degrees," the nurse said, shrugging her shoulders. "He's fine, Mrs. Cooley."

Claire stared at the bright green numbers of the digital display. She shook her head. "How is that even possible?" She turned to the nurse. "Why does he feel so cold?"

"It's probably a side effect of the snake venom," the nurse answered reassuringly, then gestured to the monitors keeping track of his vitals. "Heart rate, blood pressure, all of that is fine. He just needs rest."

The nurse left, but the repeated squawking of 'he just needs rest' didn't offer much comfort. Claire sat in her chair, staring at her son under all of those blankets, trying to convince herself that Matt really was fine, that she just needed to trust the doctors and what they were telling her. But that second voice wouldn't shut up.

Claire stood and then walked back into the hallway to grab a drink of water for herself. When she reached for the paper cup dispenser, a commotion at the ER entrance stole her attention.

Another team of medics wheeled a man in on a stretcher, their bodies blocking the patient from view. She turned back toward the water fountain and filled her cup.

"Claire!"

She jumped at the sound of her name, then turned and saw Owen carrying Chloe down the hallway. She dropped the cup in her hand and it splashed to the floor, forming a puddle around her feet. A million thoughts raced through her mind. Chloe was hurt, her dad was hurt, her dad was missing, her—

"Where's Matt?" Owen asked, handing Chloe off to Claire, who wrapped her tightly in a hug.

"Down the hall," Claire asked, then examined Chloe. "Are you all right, baby?"

"Grandpa's sick." Chloe buried her face into Claire's shoulder after the comment and Claire looked to Owen.

"What happened?"

"He locked himself in one of the rooms on the first floor. He was whispering to himself, talking nonsense. The paramedics checked his vitals and said they were fine, but he's not responsive. I think he's having an episode."

Claire shut her eyes and then stepped backward into the puddle of water she'd made after dropping the cup, then handed Chloe back to Owen. "I want to see him."

"The doctors are looking at him now, but Claire." Owen took their daughter and then blocked her path. "We need to talk about what we're going to do with him."

"What do you mean what do we do with him?" An unintended wickedness laced her tone, and she immediately regretted it when she saw the pain on Owen's face. "I'm sorry. I just—" She drew in a breath and regained her composure.

"It's okay, but listen, I spoke to Chuck, and he told me

there are some good places in New Orleans," Owen said. "He's willing to help us pay for it until we're all set up."

"You don't think that's strange?" Claire asked.

"What?"

"How accommodating he's been? It's like he'll do anything to get us to stay."

Owen laughed in exasperation. "And you think that's a bad thing? Jesus, Claire, we were about to lose our house."

"Shh!" Claire glanced down to Chloe and shook her head. "Let's not talk about it now." She bent down to pick up the paper cup she'd dropped, then tossed it in the trash. "I need to see him."

Owen gestured down the hall. "They said they were taking him to examination room three. Where's Matt?"

"Room one seventeen. He's sleeping, so don't wake him up." Claire started to walk away, but stopped, turned around, and kissed Owen on the lips. "I'm sorry."

"Yeah," Owen said, letting out a sigh. "Me too."

They separated, their hands breaking apart at the last second, and Claire hurried toward her father's room, which she found with the door open and the paramedics already gone. She clasped her hands together and held them tight to her chest as she watched a nurse remove one of the blood pressure wraps from his arm.

She saw his lips moving, but couldn't hear his words. She had never seen her father look so old as he did right there. The nurse began to undress him, then noticed Claire in the doorway.

"Can I help you, ma'am?"

Claire wiped her eyes. "He's my father. Can you give us a minute?"

The nurse offered a sympathetic nod. "Don't be too long. Those clothes are damp, and I want to get him out of them before he catches something." She left, and Claire slowly approached her father's bedside.

Roger's words remained softer than a whisper and he lay as still as water, staring up at the ceiling with his arms and legs strapped down to the bed.

"Dad?" Claire asked, slowly reaching for the bar that ran along the side of the cot. "Are you there?"

Roger didn't break his concentrated gaze on the ceiling tiles, nor did his lips stop moving. Claire gently took hold of his hand, but then recoiled her arm when his skin was icy cold. She stepped backward, her instincts screaming at her now, ordering her to get out of that house.

But she stopped and forced herself back to her father's side and picked up his hand, her mouth downturned in grief. She sniffled. "I thought we'd have more time, Daddy." She kissed his fingers and then set them down.

Why was it whenever things started to come together, they immediately fell apart? The job and the move were supposed to be a blessing, but now they felt more like a curse. Her son almost died, and her father's disease had progressed faster than the doctors predicted. She felt the walls crumbling down, and she wasn't sure how much more she could take before the whole damn house came with it.

---

5

*T*he van headlights illuminated the front of the house, and Owen slowed as they approached, then parked, killing the engine and the lights. He paused a moment, his eyes transfixed on the house in the moonlight, and Claire reached over and touched his arm.

"Are you all right?" she asked.

Owen nodded quickly. "Fine." He turned toward the back seat where both Chloe and Matt were asleep.

The doctors found nothing wrong with Matt after their slew of tests, and they said they'd have the blood work back in a few days. But while Matt could come home, Roger was still mumbling in that catatonic stare of his, lying stiff as a board on his cot.

Claire carried Chloe inside while Owen handled Matt. "We should probably just let them rest. We'll get them upstairs and if they wake up, we'll fix them something to eat."

"All right."

They put both kids to bed, tucked them in, and then lingered in the hallway, watching both doors and leaving them open. Owen followed Claire downstairs and they collapsed on the couch in the living room. Claire rested her head on Owen's chest and sighed.

"You know I'm thankful for you getting this job," Claire said, her words hesitant but deliberate. "But I'm wondering if we made the wrong move."

"I know it's been hard," Owen said, taking her hand in his own. He rubbed her skin, which felt unusually soft against his own. He shifted on the couch so he could look her in the eye. "We just have to stay the course. If we're smart, we'll be out of debt in three years. And after that, the job market could be different and we could look into moving somewhere else, maybe back to Baltimore. Things will get better."

Claire nodded and then rested her head back onto his chest. He wasn't sure if his words were more for her or himself, but either way, they seemed to help.

"Oh," Claire said, tapping him on the chest and lifting her head. "I forgot to tell you that there was something wrong with the plumbing this morning. It happened before Matt's accident."

"The plumbing?" Owen asked, recalling the sopping wet floor he found Roger lying on.

"Yeah, in the kitchen," Claire answered. "Black water was spitting from the faucet. You might want to tell Chuck about it so he can have someone come take a look."

Owen stroked Claire's hair, nodding to himself, trying not to sound alarmed. "Yeah. I'll tell him." His stomach growled.

"Hungry?"

"Getting there," Owen answered.

Claire pushed herself off of him and crossed her legs Indian-style on the couch. "I didn't even get to eat lunch today. There isn't much in the fridge, and the last thing I want to do is cook."

"Pizza?" Owen asked.

"Sounds good to me," Claire answered.

"All right, you order it and I'll pick it up."

Claire kissed him on the cheek and rolled off the couch to grab her phone from her purse. Claire's voice drifted from the kitchen, and while she ordered, he got up and went back to the room where he'd found Roger lying unconscious, wanting answers to the questions circling his mind.

The door was still ajar from his violent entrance, and he stepped over some of the wooden shards from the broken door frame. He knelt, pressing his hand against the floorboards that were bone dry. He shook his head in disbelief, then squat-walked around the whole room, checking different spots, but everything was dry. Even after all day in this heat, it was impossible for it to dry out that quickly. Wasn't it?

"Hey," Claire said, standing in the doorway. "What are you doing?"

Owen spun around, quickly standing and wiping his palm onto his jeans. "Just wanted to double check Roger didn't bring anything in here with him during his episode." Claire glanced around the room, hugging herself. He walked toward her. "He's going to come back from this. Remember that the doctor told us that the beginning stages of the disease could be managed with the right mix of medications and therapy."

"It's not just my dad," Claire said, glancing to the room and inching closer to Owen. "Do you feel like there's something wrong with the house?"

"It's old, Claire," Owen answered. "We'll get the plumbing fixed and—"

"I'm not just talking about the plumbing," Claire said. "I mean something else. Something more... I don't know." She lowered her head and massaged her temples. "I feel like I sound like a crazy person."

"You sound like a hungry person." Owen kissed the top of

her head and walked them back into the dining room. "When's the pizza going to be ready?"

"Twenty minutes," Claire answered.

"I'll leave now. It'll take me thirty minutes to get there anyway." Owen noticed that Claire wouldn't stop looking back at the room. He gently pulled her face toward his. "There isn't anything for you to be worried about, all right? The house is old. We live in the swamp. Bad plumbing and snake bites were inevitable."

"Right," Claire said.

Owen grabbed the van keys and walked outside. But before he started the engine, he sat there in the quiet dark for a moment, looking around the property. Night had turned the trees and moss and swamp into something more sinister. And the longer his eyes lingered on the darkness, the more tricks they played on him.

The rustle of leaves and branches was supernatural. The swoosh of water was some demon lurking underneath the surface. The darkness itself became a creature hunting him in the night. Owen shut his eyes and pushed the thoughts from his mind.

His son had been bitten by a snake. The pipes were old and corroded in the house. His father-in-law had Alzheimer's. Those things weren't the work of some demon, it was only the reality of life.

* * *

AFTER OWEN RETURNED with the pizza, Claire ate a few slices, then walked back upstairs to check on the kids. Chloe was sound asleep, her mouth open and drool pouring onto her pillow. Claire shook her head, hoping that whoever she married found it as endearing as Owen found her drool.

Matt was asleep too, and Claire hovered over him in bed.

Hesitantly, she placed her palm onto his forehead, afraid that she'd feel the same icy touch as she did in the hospital. But as her palm contacted his skin, relief washed away the worry. He felt normal, and Claire immediately felt silly for letting her imagination run wild. She kissed Matt's cheek, and then left him to rest.

Owen entered the dining room from the kitchen as she stepped off the last step of the staircase. "Everyone all right up there?"

"Yeah," Claire answered, smiling for the first time all day. "Sound asleep." She wrapped her arms around his neck and they kissed.

When she pulled back, Owen smiled, his eyes still closed. "I think they put something in your pizza."

"Maybe," Claire said. "Let's go find out."

She pulled him to their bedroom, the pair disrobing along the way like they did when they were first married, and relieved some stress. Once finished, sweating and exhausted in bed, they kissed goodnight and passed out on top of the sheets.

It was just past three o'clock in the morning when Claire awoke on her stomach, sweating and thirsty. She wrestled uncomfortably with her pillow then rolled onto her back. She looked at Owen, finding him sound asleep.

Naked, she grabbed the silk robe off the back of the door and wrapped it around herself before she headed toward the kitchen for a glass of water. On the way, she passed through the dining room and then glanced up at the kid's rooms.

Chloe's door was still wide open, but Claire slowed when she noticed that Matt's door was closed. She paused, staring up at it, trying to remember if she'd closed it before going downstairs. She frowned, looking at the floor. No, she was sure she left it open.

The thought made Claire's heart skip a beat as she

ascended the staircase. She peeked into Chloe's room to check on her and saw that her daughter was still in the same position she left her. She walked softly over the noisy floorboards to Matt's room, not realizing that her hands were clenched tight into fists. A noise filtered through the cracks of Matt's door, and she froze in her track so she could hear.

Whispers, nearly soundless, echoed inside. There was a familiar rhythm and cadence to them, and Claire swore she had heard them before. Softly, and quietly, Claire reached for the door knob. "Matt?"

Her silhouette spilled into the darkened room. Her son's bed was empty. She followed the whispers to the rear left corner of the room. Matt was crouched down, his back turned to her.

"Sweetie, are you all right?" Claire asked, stepping inside.

Matt's words grew louder, and the closer she moved, the better she heard.

"*Tonga-Keira-Awalla-Liseta. Tonga-Keira-Awalla-Liseta. Tonga-Keira-Awalla-Liseta.*"

The words pounded in Claire's ears and heart as she drew closer to her son. "Matthew, get off the floor and back into bed." Her voice had a panicked anger to it, but her son didn't move. She stepped toward him hesitantly, afraid. "Matt, you need to—"

Matt spun around and belted out a piercing scream. His eyes were all black, void of the colorful blue that he was given upon his birth. A snake slithered from beneath his legs, its mouth open and fangs exposed.

Claire screamed and fell backward. Her feet and hands smacked against the floorboards on her retreat. The snake slithered toward her and Claire caught a brief glance at her son, staring down at the snake with those pitch-black eyes and repeating the same mantra louder and faster.

The high-pitched hiss of the snake followed her to the

door, snapping twice for her feet that narrowly missed. Claire shrieked as she backpedaled out of the room and smacked into the banisters of the second-floor balcony.

Matt's bedroom door slammed shut on its own, sealing her son and the snake inside. Black water, the same as from the faucet, flooded out of Matt's room through the bottom door crack. Claire jumped from the floor as the putrid water rushed against her feet.

"Matt!" Claire pounded on the door with both fists, then jiggled the handle, which remained locked. The water rushed through the side cracks of the door frame now, soaking Claire's robe.

"Mommy?" Chloe stood in her doorway, her eyes wide and her blanket pressed close to her chin.

"Stay in your room!" Claire pointed back toward her daughter's bed, and then spun around and gripped the banister, her actions so quick and forceful that she almost thrust herself over the side. "Owen!"

Chloe screamed, and Claire spun back around, her mouth gaping in shock and horror. Hundreds of tiny black spiders crawled out from the top of the door, moving in wave-like layers up to the ceiling, an endless army of disgusting creatures.

Water gushed from the cracks faster now as Claire's fists pounded on the door. Half of the spiders then shifted their path from the ceiling to Claire, and she frantically smashed them, their black bodies plastered flat against the door or falling to the floor in a lifeless heap.

She smacked at the ones crawling over her arms, their tiny legs tickling her skin, a few trying to get underneath her robe. The water on her feet grew ice cold and the door buckled like it was ready to burst. "Matt!"

Hands suddenly yanked her backward, and she watched Owen look at the spiders that had disappeared into the ceiling and the water still seeping through the cracks. "Stay back!"

Claire stepped aside as Owen smacked the door with his heel, the contact eliciting a loud crack as the door and wall rattled from her husband's forceful hit.

The rush of water slowed to a trickle and the flow of spiders ended as Owen struck the door repeatedly. A crack in the wood crawled up the door frame on one of the kicks, and the next fractured off an entire piece as the door flung open.

Owen rushed in first, feet splashing against the puddles on the floor, Claire close behind. Matt was sprawled out on the hardwood, his eyes wide open, staring at the ceiling and mumbling to himself, the same words that he was whispering when she first walked in.

"Matt!" Claire patted her son's body, but the boy remained unresponsive, his eyes cast upward as she looked for the snake. She didn't see it anywhere.

"What happened?" Owen asked.

"I-I don't know," Claire answered, her voice hoarse from screaming. "Matt's door was closed and when I opened it, he was in here with a snake."

"Check his arms, make sure he wasn't bitten again."

"He wasn't," Claire said. "He was... controlling it."

And underneath the dismissive wave Owen gave her, Claire saw a glint of fear in her husband's face. Fear because he believed her.

he night sky outside Matt's bedroom window morphed into a muddled grey just before sunrise. It was that moment right before the day began, when everything was still and quiet. And like his son, who had finally stopped his mumbling and fallen asleep a few hours ago, Owen remained still as water in the chair he brought in from the dining room downstairs.

Dark grooves imprinted under Owen's eyes, and he sat slouched in the chair, one hand on his chin, the other resting lazily on the chair's armrest. He'd sat there all night, eyes red and dry from staring at his son, trying to make sense of what was happening and why it was happening to them.

Hadn't they gone through enough? Wasn't all of the shit they trudged through the past six months enough to grant them some semblance of peace?

Owen rubbed his face and leaned forward, his muscles and bones creaking from the restless few hours he managed to catch before he awoke to his wife screaming bloody murder.

A hand gently grazed Owen's shoulder, and he reached up

and rubbed Claire's fingers. Everything she said had been bouncing around in his mind since he busted down that door. It was absurd. Unreal. And yet, here he found himself, beginning to believe that there was something wrong with this house. Something wrong with his son.

"You need to take him back to the doctors today," Owen said, still rubbing Claire's hand while his eyes remained fixated on Matt. "There must have been something they gave him that he was having a reaction to, or something from the snake bite that—"

"Owen, stop." Claire emerged from behind him and crouched by his knees, her eyes wide and bright in the darkness. The way she looked reminded Owen of when they first started dating. She was the most beautiful thing he'd ever come across, but it went beyond the flesh and traveled behind those pair of dark brown eyes. There was certainty in them. And that certainty, that decisiveness was what pulled Owen into her. Those same attributes now scared him to death. "You saw what I saw."

Owen drifted his eyes to Matthew. "I don't know what I saw."

"This is more than just snake bites and my dad's Alzheimer's," Claire said. "You saw the water, the spiders, and then they just disappeared?" She shook her head, her hands digging into his legs. "The water spilled over the banister and into the living area, which should have soaked the furniture downstairs, but everything's dry. We need to get out of this house."

"And go where?" Owen asked, exasperated. "Back to Baltimore? Back to almost being homeless? I'm not putting our family through that again."

"You want us to stay?"

Owen took Claire's hands in a firm grasp. "I want us to not have to worry about where our next meal is going to come from. I want us to have a life that doesn't revolve around clipping coupons and buying everything on sale." He let go of her hands and stepped back, afraid of the words that had been boiling over in the back of his mind. Words that if spoken, he couldn't take back.

Claire's father was a good man. Owen knew that. But after Claire's mother passed, the man gave up. He moved in with them and while he was collecting money on Social Security, he became another mouth to feed, another person to rack up the utilities bill, more weight for Owen to carry, which was fine until he lost the job at the factory. And then when Roger was diagnosed with Alzheimer's, those medical bills started piling up and drained their savings faster than he could replenish it.

"Owen, it's not safe for our son to be here," Claire said, her voice on the edge of crying again.

"And it's not safe for him to be homeless," Owen replied, his answer harsher than he intended. "Or hungry."

Claire squeezed his forearm tighter. "Just talk to your boss and see if he can get us into another place. Or we can look into something else we can buy. I know that's not something we wanted to do because we were trying to get out of debt faster, but we have to try *something*."

Owen pulled his arm back. "They paid for our move, they paid for the house, they paid for all of Matt's medical bills, and on top of that, they're paying me fifteen thousand more a year than I made at the shipyard." Owen flapped his arms at his sides. "And now you want me to go to my boss and ask him for us to move?"

"I understand everything that they've done, and believe me, I'm grateful," Claire said. "But I'm not going to let my family stay here one more night."

""There isn't anywhere else to go!" Owen hissed through

his teeth, his volume a harsh whisper. "This is it! This *has* to work."

Claire's eyes watered, and she shook her head. "You're putting our family at risk."

Frustration muddled Owen's senses, and the fatigue of the past few days eroded the will to hold his tongue. "And keeping your dad around wasn't?"

Claire immediately clammed up, and her body offered a light tremor of rage. The moment he saw her reaction, Owen slumped his shoulders in regret.

"Claire, I'm—"

"My father did not hurt Matt," Claire said. She closed the gap between them, her eyes red, that certainty and decisiveness burning right through him. "And I will not keep my children here another night. Do you understand me? We are leaving, Owen. With or without you."

Owen watched her exit, and he leaned back against the window. The muddled grey of morning was suddenly diffused by sunrise, and the first rays of light broke over the horizon. But despite the new day and the beautiful morning outside, Owen felt anything but hopeful or happy.

The drive to the factory was restless, and Owen regretted not saying goodbye to Claire before he left. It irked him when they weren't on good terms, but it was going to take some time before she forgave him about the comment regarding her father.

The bulk of the factory was arriving when Owen parked the van and stepped out. He spotted Marty Wiggins and Jake Martin getting out of their truck, Marty talking loud enough for everyone to hear him in Baltimore.

"All I'm saying is that if Drew Brees can win one more Super Bowl, then I think he should be in the conversation for greatest quarterback of all time." Marty shrugged in an over-dramatic fashion, his eyes bulging from his sockets like his own words were on par with Ernest Hemingway and he didn't understand why everyone wasn't praising his voice. "He's done more than everyone else, and with less."

"You think he's better than Archie Manning though?" Jake asked. "I mean the guy is—"

"Hey, can you tell me where Chuck's office is?" Owen asked as both men turned toward him, Marty spilling some of his coffee on his hand from the quick jerk.

"Goddammit, Yankee-Doodle numnuts," Marty said, shaking off the hot liquid. "Made me burn my damn hand."

"Hey, Owen," Jake said, his voice soft. "I heard about your boy. He all right?"

"He's getting better," Owen answered. "My wife is taking him back to the hospital today for a check-up."

"Say," Marty said, taking a sip from his coffee. "You want to get in on this Saints debate? You could be a neutral party."

"I really don't have—" And that's when Owen spotted Chuck across the lot, heading toward one of the factory entrances. Without another word, he sprinted toward his boss, waving his arms.

"Owen," Chuck said, lines of concern forming over his face. "How's your boy doing?"

"The doctors said he should be fine in a couple of days, but I need to talk to you about something."

Chuck gestured toward his office door. "I'll put some coffee on."

The office was simply decorated and designed. A metal desk and matching filing cabinet took center stage, and the walls were covered with different pictures of the factory's history. One picture in particular hung prominently on the wall behind Chuck's desk.

"First day we opened," Chuck said, pointing to the black and white photo as he smiled. He tapped on a man in a plain white shirt and dark slacks that held a cigar. "That's my great

-grandfather. Hell of a businessman, and could outwork anyone he hired." Chuck took a seat and gestured for Owen to do the same. "He always joked that was the only way to stay the boss."

"Mr. Toussaint, I can't tell you how much I appreciate what you've done for me and my family. This job was a godsend for us."

"Well, we're happy to have you on board," Chuck said, smiling as the whistle blew and the factory's machines began to hum.

The commotion caught Owen's attention, and he looked out the window to the floor as everyone started to fall into work. Everyone but him. "Mr. Toussaint, what I'm about to ask you is more than I should, but I'm doing it for the same reason I took the job here in the first place. It's for my family."

"Is everything all right?" Chuck asked.

Owen chose his words carefully. "It's the house. I don't think it's going to work out."

Chuck sat there for a moment, the concern slowly fading, and he leaned back in his chair, folding his hands over his stomach. "And what's the problem?"

"I think it's just too much space for us, honestly," Owen answered, lying through his teeth. He wasn't about to tell the man his wife thought the place was possessed or that his son was speaking with snakes. And just sitting there thinking about it, he felt silly even bringing it up. But that's what happened when you stepped out of the strange and back into reality.

"I see," Chuck said. "So, I give you a job, then move you down here, and your first complaint to me is that the house you're living in for free is too big?" Chuck laughed.

"I know," Owen said, closing his eyes and taking a breath. The sleepless night preventing his mind from piecing together his thoughts. "And, again, I'm very grateful. But the move has been tough on everyone. And with what's happened with my father-in-law, and my son, I just think that my family is funneling a lot of that frustration into the house."

And so Owen waited, his heart pounding wildly in his chest. It was the first time he'd felt anything but a welcoming presence from his boss, and this hardened version was someone he'd like to avoid in the future.

"There aren't any other houses available right now," Chuck said. "I'll check with the real estate office this afternoon and see what we can move you into later." He opened the bottom left drawer of his desk and flopped a few pieces of paper on top. "I'll have a contractor come by tomorrow to look at the house, make sure there hasn't been any damage since you've moved in." He scribbled something down on the papers, then looked up. "It's the best I can do for now."

"That'd be great, Mr. Toussaint, thank you so much." Owen retreated toward the door, dying to escape the room. "But just so you know, for the contractor, I think there's something wrong with the pipes."

"Pipes?" Chuck asked, frowning.

"Yeah," Owen answered. "There have been a few plumbing issues since we've moved in. Leaking pipes, bad water. That sort of thing."

"I'll let the contractor know." Chuck returned to the papers on his desk, and as Owen reached the door to leave, he stopped him. "And Owen."

"Yes, sir?"

"I suggest you do your job well. The last foreman I had on the line was too chummy with his subordinates. I don't want you giving off the impression that these people are your friends. Everyone is expendable here. And if you wish to make yourself valuable, I suggest that you get to work.

Unless you want to find your family on the streets after you find yourself fired."

Owen nodded, his tone flat, defeated. "Yes, sir." A headache appeared in the center of his forehead, and he wanted nothing more than to disappear into his work, and then go home to find that his family was fine, and that the past few days had been nothing more than a fluke. But as his headache worsened, so did his doubts.

* * *

THE HOSPITAL WAS BUSY. Staff and patients roamed the halls, and there was a constant echo of doctors being paged over the PA system.

Sounds of sickness, fear, and grief escaped the rooms down the halls. News delivered by doctors and nurses, some of it good, some bad, all of it having consequences. A woman's shriek caused Claire to shudder.

Chloe squirmed in Claire's arm as the doctor checked Matt, whose cheeks were still pallid and cold to the touch. She bit her lip anxiously, passing Chloe to her left arm. "Everything all right?"

The doctor removed the stethoscope from his ears and turned around. Thankfully it wasn't the same old man from yesterday. "Lungs are clear, blood pressure is normal, and he doesn't have a temperature."

"But you felt his forehead?" Claire asked, even though she watched the doctor do it. "Why is it so cold?"

"I feel fine, Mom," Matt said, his voice meek.

"Could be a sensitivity to cool air," the doctor said, though his tone suggested he might as well have been guessing. "Medically speaking, your son is perfectly healthy. I'm sure he'll be back to normal in a couple of days."

But Claire didn't think that Matt would be okay in a

couple of days, or weeks or months. A storm cloud hovered in the distance. It flashed lightening and rumbled thunder. That storm was getting closer and it would only get worse.

Claire took a moment, trying to figure out how to explain to the doctor what she'd seen without sounding like a lunatic. And she wanted to be careful of what she said in front of Matt. He hadn't remembered anything from last night. The only thing he recalled was waking up this morning with her watching over him, asking why she was crying.

"What is it, Mrs. Cooley?" The doctor placed a gentle hand on her arm, and Chloe finally stopped squirming, resting her head on Claire's shoulder.

Claire set Chloe down. "Matt, take your sister into the waiting room. I'll be out there to meet you in a minute, okay?"

"Okay," Matt said, climbing down from the patient table. "C'mon, Chloe."

Claire trailed both her children to the doorway, her eyes on them until the reached the waiting room down the hall. She bit her lower lip, twisting the hem of her blouse, and then turned back to the doctor. "There have been other things happening with Matt. Things that I know will sound crazy the moment I say them out loud."

The doctor nodded and smiled politely while Claire paced the room, her head tilted toward the floor as she turned from the wall and passed the doctor. "He's talking to himself and it's like…" The words were there, but she was suddenly frightened to speak them aloud. "It's like he hasn't been himself. He's started keeping strange animals as pets. Snakes, and… spiders." She tossed the doctor a quick glance to see his reaction and saw that he was still listening politely. "And his eyes have been dilated." Images of Matt's dark eyes flashed in her memory. "It's just been some very strange behavior."

Claire stopped her pacing and looked back to the doctor, whose mouth had slightly parted, a creaky moan escaping the physician's lips before he spoke. "The pets could be a way of him coping with what happened. Trying to conquer his own fears, so to speak."

Claire nodded, looking for any reasonable explanation to grasp hold of. "Yeah, that makes sense. He's always been a brave kid, never too scared of anything."

"And the dilated pupils could be a side effect from the venom still working its way through his body," the doctor said. "As could be his skin's sensitivity to cold." He grabbed hold of Claire's hands comfortingly, and offered a warm smile. "I'm sure the move has been difficult for him. Plus, he's on the edge of puberty, so those behavioral changes will become more and more prominent." He patted her hand and laughed. "Best get used to that."

But despite the reassurances and the doctor's friendly smile, Claire didn't believe him. Her mind had groped for a reasonable explanation of her son's behavior and after everything that happened in that house, the doctor's answers didn't satisfy her like she'd hoped.

"It's more than hormones." Claire removed her hands from the doctor's grip, and that warm smile cooled.

"Mrs. Cooley, I understand that you and your family have been through a bit of a shock, but jumping to conclusions without any facts is dangerous. Just go home and have Matthew rest, and make sure you do the same." He placed his hand on her back and guided her out of the room, pushing rather forcefully. "You look like you could use some sleep yourself."

Claire stepped forward, separating herself from the doctor's hand. His arrogance and dismissal only prodded the anger that Owen had stoked in her that morning. She quickly left, grabbing Matt and Chloe by the hand, and walked toward the exit.

Chloe struggled to keep up with her mother's pace, and Claire eventually bent down to pick her up.

"Mom, is everything okay?" Matt asked, looking up at her.

"It's fine, sweetheart." Claire pulled him close. "We just need to make one more stop before we go home." If a doctor couldn't give her answers, then she'd speak to someone who could.

A nurse played on her phone at the sign-in station, and after finishing a text she looked up. "Can I help you?"

"I need Roger Templeton's room number?" Claire asked. "I'm his daughter."

The nurse pointed to the hallway on the left. "Fourth door down."

"Thank you." It wasn't a coincidence that her father and Matt were sharing the same strange behavior. It was connected somehow, and she might be able to pry it out of her father's weathered mind.

Claire stopped at the doorway to her father's room, leaving both Claire and Matt in chairs in the hallway. She didn't want them to see him if he was still incoherent, and she didn't want to scare Matt by having him listen in if she did learn something. Despite the brave showing, she knew her son was nervous.

Roger lay asleep in his bed, no longer mumbling and whispering to himself, his chest slowly rising and falling with each breath as he lay strapped to the bed. Even though she'd seen him just yesterday, he looked to have aged a few years.

She was glad her mother wasn't alive to see him like this. If there was one blessing in her death, it was that. Claire's mom was a sweet woman, but she lacked the mind and grit that Claire inherited from her father. But she was a wonderful mom, always armed with the right words at just the right time.

Claire wished she could channel her mother's voice at that moment. She had no idea of what to say. *Hey, Dad, sorry for sending you off to a home, but you're too dangerous to be kept around your grandchildren anymore.* Or, *so you're sick now and we don't want to take care of you anymore so we're sending you away. We'll try to visit when we can!*

The words churned her stomach sour just thinking them. The man in front of her had driven her to all of those softball games as a kid. The same father who would call in to the school and tell them that she was sick, and then take her to the Orioles game.

"Daddy?" Claire gave him a gentle shake, and Roger turned his head toward her, blinking awake. "How are you feeling?" She waited to find out if this was her father or the stranger that Alzheimer's had created.

"Claire?" Roger spoke her name like a child, unsure if what he was seeing was real.

Claire gripped his hand and squeezed, smiling. "It's me."

A single tear rolled from the corner of his right eye and trailed straight down to his pillow. He produced a sad smile and the pressure of his hand gave what strength he had left. "I can't remember why I'm here."

"You had an episode," Claire said, pulling a chair behind her to sit, and she inched closer to the bed. "Owen came home and found you passed out on the floor. Dad, do you remember what happened?"

Roger squinted hard, then wiggled underneath the straps. He looked at them quickly, then up to her. "Did I hurt someone? Is that why—"

"No," Claire answered, placing her hand on his chest to calm him. "They just didn't want you wandering around the hospital when you woke up. But before, when I spoke to you yesterday, you said you thought you heard someone the night Matt was hurt. You said you were chasing something outside. Do you remember what it was?"

Roger sighed. "I don't know." He shut his eyes, shaking his head. "There was a noise."

Claire's heartbeat quickened. "What kind of noise?"

"Like a rattling," Roger answered, his eyes still closed. "I heard it again, when I was alone at the house. I followed it to a room, and then…" He trailed off, opening his eyes. "There was water. Pitch black water."

"Were there animals in there with you?" Claire asked.

Roger shook his head. "Not an animal. Something else. And it was cold. The kind that seeps into your bones. Worse than any winter up north."

"What was it, Dad?" Claire gripped his arm tighter. "What did you see?"

Roger's eyes widened. His mouth opened, and he moved his lips soundlessly, like a car trying to start but unable to catch. "Th-th-the eyes." He spoke in horrified whispers now and gazed ahead of him into the empty space, like he could see the creature right in front of him. "It was death staring at me. *Everything was dead.*"

Claire shook her head, trying to understand. All she could see was Matt with those same black eyes, and the water, the spiders, and the snake. "Dad, you need to—"

Roger took hold of her arm, his massive hand engulfing it easily, his grip incredibly strong as he pulled her close. "Don't go back in that house, Claire. Something is there. Something b-b-b-AAAAAHHHHH!" His mouth opened wide as he screamed. He thrashed in the bed, the straps struggling to keep him still.

The machines hooked up to her father beeped in the same wild ferocity of his body, and a team of nurses and orderlies flooded into the room as Claire stepped back with her hand over her mouth. One of the nurses grabbed a needle filled with a clear liquid and gave it a quick spurt, the fluid squirting out of the top. Her father roared in defiance as she stuck the needle into his arm and emptied the solution.

Roger's thrashing calmed along with the machine's commotion, and Claire fought the tears wanting to break free. She removed herself from the room, and regrouped in the hall. She drew in deep breaths, her eyes closed. *What now?*

If she went back to Owen and told him that her delusion father told her they needed to leave that house they'd only argue again. She needed proof of what her father said. And that's exactly what she was going to get.

7

The whistle blew and the loud clanking of the factory ended as workers stepped away from their stations and headed toward their lockers, ready to go home for the day. Owen fell in line behind everyone, his shirt collar soaked with a ring of sweat as he removed his hard hat and glasses. It felt good to get back into a routine like that, and for at least a few hours, he felt like his life was back to normal.

But after Owen tossed his uniform into the locker, he caught his boss staring at him from his office window. Chuck's eyes followed Owen all the way out the door, and even outside, Owen felt them linger on his back. He shivered and got into the van.

With the workday over, the troublesome thoughts of home returned. His last words to Claire had been gnawing at him all day. He didn't want to go home without some sort of peace offering, so instead of turning right onto Main Street and heading toward the house, he took a left and found a parking spot in front of the small realty office, the sign in the window still flipped to open.

Owen checked his appearance in his rearview mirror, hoping that he didn't look too derelict for someone to think he couldn't afford a house, though his creditors might have a few things to say about the matter, and stepped out of the van.

A bell on the front door jingled as Owen entered. He scraped his boots on the welcome mat before stepping onto the old hardwood. "Hello?" The small space was empty with the exception of a desk jimmied up alongside the front door and the dozens of pictures hanging on the walls, all of them showing people in front of houses, smiling as the realtor handed them keys.

"Hi there!" A middle-aged gentleman stepped from a small doorway in the back, wiping his hands with a cloth. He was clean shaven, and his pearl-white teeth contrasted against his unnaturally tan skin. "What can I help you with?" He tossed the cloth on his desk and adjusted the belt around the waist of his plaid tweed suit. It was a thick jacket for such a hot climate.

"I was hoping you could tell me the properties you have in the area?"

"Of course!" He grabbed hold of Owen's hand and gave it three hearty pumps. "Nate Covers. If you want a house, I've got the dream home for you." He spoke the words like a cheesy local commercial and then gestured to one of the chairs.

"I just need to know what you have for immediate occupancy," Owen said, taking a seat.

Nate smiled, and thrust his index finger in Owen's direction. "Right down to business. I like your style." He clicked the mouse of his computer, then started typing. "So do you already live in the area?"

"Yes," Owen answered. "Just moved here actually."

"Where from?"

"Baltimore."

"Long way from home." Nate laughed loud and quickly. "I see the wedding ring. Have kids?"

"Two."

"All right, let's see." Nate kept his eyes on the computer screen, which was turned away from Owen, and he typed a few more keystrokes and then leaned back in his chair, portions of the faux-leather armrests cracked, exposing the yellow-foam stuffing inside. "I've got a few three and four bedrooms on the market right now. What kind of budget are you looking at?"

"I haven't really gone to the bank to check that stuff out yet," Owen answered, rubbing his hands nervously. But he probably knew the answer they would give him: small. "I told my wife I'd start looking. She's not really in love with our current house."

"Where are you at now?"

"Fourteen Cypress Lane."

Nate ended the light rock in his chair, and that unnatural tan color drained from his cheeks. "So you work for Chuck Toussaint then." He drummed his fingers on his stomach.

"Yeah," Owen said.

Nate forced another wide, cheesy smile. "He's a great guy. Normally pays for his employees' housing. Did you not have the same arrangement with him?"

"No, I did, but—" Owen cut himself off, suddenly embarrassed and wanting to leave. "You know what, maybe I should just talk to him about it some more." Owen stood and Nate mirrored him. "I'm sorry for bothering you."

"Not a problem, and, hey, if anything changes, just drop by and I'll see what I can find for you."

The bell at the top of the door chimed as Owen left, and

he fished the van's keys out of his pockets, feeling uneasy about his interaction with Nate Covers. Had he crossed some sort of line going behind his boss's back like that?

He turned toward the driver side door and abruptly stopped. Across the street he saw the sign for Queen's, and standing outside her own shop of bizarre trinkets and bobbles stood the dread-haired woman, staff in hand, those pair of hazel and yellow glinted eyes fixated on him.

Owen fisted the keys in his hand and marched over to her. "What do you want?" he shouted from the middle of the street, but even as he got closer, the woman didn't move. "Is it you?" He stepped onto the sidewalk, the heat of the day and his anger flushing his cheeks a bright red. "Are you the one who's been sneaking around my house? Huh?"

Even with Owen only inches from her face, the woman didn't move. Owen caught a whiff of her musty clothes, sweat and body odor all mixed together. She shifted her weight on her feet, and some of the bone necklaces clinked lightly against one another like a morbid wind chime.

"You stay away from my family," Owen said. "And you stay the hell away from me." He snarled and thrust a finger in her face, then spun around to head back to his van.

"Your son doesn't belong to you anymore." The woman's voice was slow, her accent not as muddled as some of Owen's coworkers.

He turned around. "What the hell did you say to me?" He marched back in three quick strides, then smacked some of the items off the table out front in a violent blow. "You speak of my son again, and I will come back here with the police. So back. Off." He gritted his teeth, but while he trembled in anger, she remained still.

Owen stomped back to his van, got behind the wheel, and peeled out of the parking spot.

* * *

CLAIRE SAT cross-legged on the couch, laptop open between her knees, and sifted through everything that she could find about snake bites and which types were native to Louisiana. From what she researched, the most common venomous snake in the area was the Cottonmouth. And judging from its description, a black colored or dark-brown with black blotches on its underside, she thought that might have been the snake she saw slithering away from Matt after he was bit.

Aside from hallucinations, nausea, and vomiting, there wasn't anything else to explain her son's behavior. And the more and more she read, she realized that whatever was happening to her son went beyond the snake bite. There was something else.

Claire opened another tab on the browser, and she typed in the name of their town and waited for the search fields to populate when the front door opened and she heard Owen's voice.

"Claire?"

She snapped the laptop shut and set it aside on the couch. "Hey." The pair lingered in silence for a moment. She was still angry with him, but after a day of being able to digest his words, she understood where they were coming from.

"How's Matt?" Owen asked.

"The doctor said everything was fine," Claire answered, waiting for the I-told-you-so that never came, which she was glad to escape. She'd never felt uncomfortable with him, but with what she wanted to say, the feeling was inevitable.

"About this morning—"

"I'm sorry," Claire said, cutting him off. "I know, you thought you'd be the one apologizing."

"What I said about your dad, it was wrong." Owen walked

over and joined her on the couch. "It's just everything that's happened... I think I've let it get to me more than it should."

"We both have." Claire leaned her head against his chest. It was still damp with sweat, and he smelled the same way he did coming home from the shipyard in Baltimore. The familiarity was comforting. "But I'm not wrong about what's happening. Something is off, Owen. I still want to leave. I haven't changed my mind about that."

Owen sighed. "I spoke to Chuck. He said he'll find us a place, but he doesn't have anything open right now." Claire started to speak, and Owen lifted her hands. "It's just one more night, Claire. Just one more. Okay?"

Claire drew in a deep breath. "All right. But we leave tomorrow."

"Right." Owen kissed her forehead. "How was your dad?"

"Not good," Claire answered. "He was himself for a little bit, and then... well, he wasn't."

"Putting him in a home is the best way for him to get the help that he needs," Owen said, doing his best to sound reassuring. "They'll be better equipped for stuff like that, and I promise that we'll go and visit him at least once a week. Plus there's phone calls, and video—"

"I don't want to put him in a home," Claire said. "I've thought about it a lot, and it's not what my mom would have wanted." She straightened her back. "It's not what I want."

Owen stood silent for what felt like an eternity before he sat down on the couch's armrest and nodded slowly. "And you're comfortable leaving your dad around the kids?" He looked her in the eye. "He's only going to get worse."

"I know, and yes, I am." Claire stood firm, hoping that Owen couldn't see her trembling. "I still don't believe that he bit Matt. He wouldn't have done that. I know him."

"We'll talk more about it later." Owen turned toward their bedroom. "I'm going to take a shower."

Claire crossed her arms then glanced up to the second floor where Chloe had spread out a series of blank white papers and spilled all of her crayons on the floor. Matt was sound asleep, but Claire made sure to keep his door propped wide open. He'd passed out the moment they got home from the hospital. She'd never seen him so tired, but she figured it was good he was sleeping.

The laptop was still on the couch, the power light glowing and blinking slowly. She sat down next to the computer, looking but not touching, wondering what she would find on her Google search of the town. Just as she was about to open the tabs, Chloe called for her upstairs. Claire left the computer on the couch, making a mental note to check those results later.

* * *

AFTER OWEN SHOWERED he tried rousing Matt from bed, but he wouldn't budge, settling for a glass of water instead of dinner and fell right back into his semi-coma. Chloe joined them for dinner briefly, and then returned upstairs to continue her drawings.

Owen cleared the dinner table while Claire helped Chloe get ready for bed. When he walked back to their bedroom he saw Claire sitting on the edge of their bed, picking at her nails nervously.

"Hey," Claire said, her voice so small and fragile it was like her teeth were made of porcelain and if she spoke too loud they would shatter.

"Hey." Owen sat down next to her, then grabbed her hand. They hadn't spoken over dinner, and he'd been avoiding bringing up the subject of her father. But he couldn't stop thinking about the promise he'd made to Roger. "I know you love your dad. I love him too. And what you said about your mom not wanting to put him in a home if she was still alive, I think you're right. She wouldn't have."

Claire's expression softened.

"But you have to understand that things have changed," Owen said. "Your dad would never hurt the kids, but he's also not in his right mind. We can't think of him like he was anymore. We can't—"

Claire sniffled, wiping a tear from her eye. "I'm sorry." She squeezed his hand, a desperation in her touch that he'd never felt before. "With the move, and everything happening with Matt, it just feels like I'm losing my family." She looked up at him, her eyes red and watering, the tiny red veins of her eyes irritated from the tears. "I don't have a dad anymore."

Owen rested his chin on her head as she leaned into him and sobbed. He held her tight. "But you're not going to lose your family. I won't let that happen. I promise."

Claire took deep breaths, exhaling slowly, doing her best to regain control of her emotions. She shook her head and wiped her eyes. "You can't promise that."

"I can," Owen said, looking at her. "And I will." He never wanted to see his wife break like this again. "We'll keep your dad here. We'll do what we have to do. But he will eventually need to be sent somewhere for care. I don't want the kids to have their last memories of their grandfather being what he'll become. And he wouldn't want that either."

Claire kissed him, and then wiped her eyes. "I'm gonna take a shower before bed."

"Okay," Owen said.

When she was finished, Claire stepped out of the shower like a wet zombie and collapsed into bed with the towel still around her body. Owen helped her out of it, then pulled the thin sheet over her, kissed her cheek, and then turned off the light.

Owen lay in bed with his eyes closed, but his mind wouldn't turn off. He found himself trying to rationalize everything that happened. He kept brushing it off as coincidence, but there was something about last night, the way Claire had looked, the spiders, the water, even that Voodoo woman, it was all connected.

Just the thought of her caused Owen to shiver with anxiety. And it wasn't just her, it was that whole goddamn store. And while he never believed in religion, there was something satanic about the place. Something evil.

Owen tilted his head on his pillow toward Claire. His family was the only great thing he'd done in his life. Growing up, he had dreams, like all little kids did, but there was always something that kept him from ever trying to peek over the edge. It wasn't fear of failure, just an understanding of who he was at a very early age. He wanted a wife, to own a house, raise kids, work hard to provide for his family, and come home at the end of the day sweaty and satisfied. But now it all felt like it was slipping away.

A heavy thump sounded upstairs, and Owen jolted upright out of bed.

"What was that?" Claire asked, wakening with a violent jerk.

Owen swung his legs off the side of the bed, his eyes watching the ceiling, listening. He kept still, his muscles tense, and another heavy thump echoed upstairs, this one accompanied by a rattling noise.

"Oh my god." Claire jumped out of bed, the towel she fell asleep in falling to the floor as she rushed around the end of the mattress before Owen snatched her arm to stop her from leaving. "That's the same—"

"Just stay here," Owen said, reaching for the Louisville slugger he kept behind the nightstand. He left Claire to dress and stepped into the hallway, the heavy thumps and rattling growing louder upstairs as he sprinted toward the kids' rooms.

He dashed through the dining room and looked up to the second balcony. Oddly shaped shadows formed on the walls in the darkness, but Owen felt his heart skip a beat when he saw one move into Matt's room.

"Hey!" Owen sprinted to the staircase, his body in such a hurry that he cracked the side of the dining table with the bat as it dragged behind him. He leapt up the stairs, but the moment his foot hit the first step of the staircase, the ground trembled.

Owen's foot slipped against the wood, and gravity body-slammed him awkwardly on the steps. The staircase shuffled him side to side, the whole damn house shaking like they were in an earthquake. "Matt!"

The rumbling worsened as Owen ditched the bat and was forced to crawl up the stairs on his hands and knees. The noise blared like a freight train speeding through the house, and Owen's bones rattled more violently the closer he reached the second story.

But as Owen climbed, there was another noise among the freight train, an undertone that he'd heard before. It was a whisper, a chanting, and he could have sworn he heard the woman's voice from that voodoo shop.

The trembling ground thrust Owen into the wall, then the bannister, his legs twisting beneath him on his serpentine sprint to his son's room. The door was shut, and the vibrations of the house were so intense that Owen's vision blurred. "Matt!"

The whispering undertones grew louder, and they were accompanied by a rhythmic rattling that grew as violent as the tremors.

Owen stretched his arm and reached for the knob, pulling

himself toward the door and shouldering it open in one motion. The moment he stepped inside, the trembling stopped.

Owen stumbled a few steps, his legs wobbling on steady ground, and found Matt's bed empty, the sheets messily strewn about the mattress. Owen's heart plummeted toward his stomach and he frantically searched the room. "Matt! MATT!"

"Owen!" Claire screamed from downstairs, her voice cracking.

"He's gone!" Owen pressed his hands into the side of his head, the panic overwhelming him as he spun in circles in the dark.

Moonlight filtered through the dirty bedroom window, and Owen passed his eyes over it so quickly that he nearly missed the figure in the tall grass. He rushed to the window, his hands plastered against the dirty glass like a mad man trapped in an asylum.

Amidst the tall grass he saw something carrying his son toward the swamp. "Matt!" Owen smacked the glass and then sprinted out of the room and back toward the spiral staircase, passing Claire on her way up.

She grabbed at his arm, but he was too quick for her to stop. "What happened?"

"Someone took him!" Owen jumped the last three steps of the staircase, landing hard on the balls of his feet, breaking into a sprint toward the front of the house. The heavy thump of his feet echoed loudly through the house and ended when he slammed into the wall of humid Louisiana swamp air outside.

Owen cut a hard left that sank his feet into dirt and mud, causing him to trip. "Matt!" The tall grass in the clearing tickled at his legs and waist. He pumped his arms and legs hard, ignoring the tingle in his bare feet and the growing numbness of his body.

The clearing ended and Owen smacked aside the hanging Spanish moss as dirt morphed into mud that splashed up his legs with every step, sucking his feet into the depths of Louisiana swamp.

The overhanging branches of trees blocked the stars and moonlight and while the air had been hot and muggy when he first stepped outside, Owen felt a crisp chill run up his back.

"Come out here!" Owen screamed at the top of his lungs, stumbling through the mud like a drunkard. Rage coursed through his veins, laced with the fear of losing his son and the unknown of the darkness he saw take him. "Matt!"

The rattling noise sounded to his left, and Owen snapped his head in that direction. He lifted his foot, and the mud gave off a low suction noise as he stepped forward. The darkness thickened, and water started to bubble up from the mud the farther he walked. "You can't hide out here forever!"

Gnats and flies buzzed around his head, and despite the growing chill, sweat oozed from Owen's skin. The water level rose to his shins as he followed the rattling and then a quick, heavy swoosh sounded to his left. He jumped from the noise and watched the ripples wrinkle the still water. "Matt?"

Dark patches of grass and debris floated lazily over the black water, and the cypress trees grew more frequent the deeper he waded. He couldn't stop shivering, and when the water reached his knees, that's when he saw it.

It wasn't human, though it had legs and arms and stood upright. Thick cords of matted black hair sprouted from the top of its head and traveled down its back. Its head was large, its torso short but muscular. Its entire body was covered in a scaly grey flesh that glistened and shimmered under the moonlight. It held Matt in its arms, six-inch black claws stretched out from three stubby fingers on each hand.

"Let him go," Owen said, doing his best to keep his voice steady.

The creature didn't answer. It just stared at Owen, holding Matt, half its body below the waterline. Then, slowly, it opened its mouth, wide. A throaty croak escaped ending in a long, drawn-out hiss. The sharp teeth were pointed toward Owen and the creature hunched forward while it held his son.

Water rippled to Owen's left and right, and he saw something gliding through the water just below the surface. He turned back to the creature, and it slowly lowered into the water, taking Matt with it.

"NO!" Owen lunged forward, erupting the still, rancid swamp water. Quick, thrashing movements to his right stole Owen's attention, and those croaking hisses grew louder. It wasn't until the gator was less than a foot away that Owen realized where the sound was coming from.

He jerked to a stop, backtracking as the pair of gators blocked his path toward his son. He splashed the water, trying to push the gators back, but they wouldn't budge. "Matt!" The creature was submerged to the chest now, sinking lower. His son's head was nearly underwater, his eyes closed as he lay unconscious against the creature's body.

The gator to the left lunged and snapped, and Owen fell backward, his arms and legs flailing wildly on his retreat as the creature finally disappeared beneath the water's surface.

"NO!" The scream rivaled the gator's fierce hiss as both animals pressed forward, pushing Owen from the water. The pair followed him all the way up the mud, Owen's backside sliding in the thick muck as he kicked his legs. The gators slithered on their bellies over the dark mud, water dripping from their jaws as they exposed the hundreds of short, jagged teeth that still had bits of flesh on them from their last meal. Owen got to his feet, backpedaling, and the gators ended their pursuit. Mud and water dripped from Owen's body as his mouth hung slack.

This wasn't real. This was a bad dream and he'd wake any minute. "Matt!" His voice echoed off the water and bounced through the swamp until it disappeared into the darkness like that creature.

Headlights caught his attention toward the road. They turned down the long driveway to the house, and Owen immediately sprinted toward the truck, waving his arms in panicked frenzy, his legs cramping. "Hey! Help!"

The truck's headlights bounced up and down over the encroaching cypress roots that curved over the dirt path to the house. It slowed to a stop, and the lights and engine remained on as Owen drew closer, the adrenaline that fueled him nearly gone. "My son! Something took my son!"

A pair of shadowed figures said nothing as they stepped out of the truck, and Owen slowed. The truck looked familiar, but before Owen made the connection, a gunshot thundered from one of the silhouettes.

Owen ducked, and sprinted to the back of the house. Three more gunshots fired, each making Owen flinch. His heavy legs and arms suddenly grew light in his flight, and he didn't stop until the house was between him and the shooters.

Gasping for breath Owen hunched over, resting his hands on his knees. The gunmen shouted at one another, their voices carrying in the night, and then Owen heard the front door groaning as they stepped inside. His eyes widened. *Claire. Chloe.*

Quickly, he snuck through the back door, gently closing it

behind him while the men up front stomped loudly through the front living room.

"We know you're here!" The voice echoed down the hallways but was slightly muffled from the walls. "You're just going to make it harder on yourselves!"

Owen paused just before the hallway in the back led into the dining room. He knew that voice. It was Jake Martin from work. That was his truck parked out front.

"C'mon out, Owen! Let's get this over with."

Owen quietly crept around the edge of the stairwell, his eyes falling to the baseball bat that had fallen from his hand when the house started shaking. Halfway on his approach, the floorboards creaked and gave away his position.

He snatched the bat and sprinted toward the back just as a gunshot fired across the dining room and put a hole in the wall three inches from Owen's head. He ducked into the den where Roger's room had been located and crouched low by the door.

Slow, deliberate footsteps moved closer. Owen had a white-knuckled grip around the slugger's handle and he shivered, each breath rattling from the tiny convulsions from his body. The footsteps ended after a final groan from the floorboards and Owen forced himself still, holding his breath.

A bullet blasted through the wall to Owen's left, followed by three more shots that nipped at his ankles. Jake rounded the corner of the doorway and when he entered, Owen spun around, leading with the bat in his hands, connecting with the rifle.

The weapon clanged to the floor and as Owen lifted the bat to strike, Jake charged, leveling both men to the ground. The harsh contact into the hardwood knocked the wind out of Owen, and elbows and knees struck the floor in harsh smacks as the pair grappled with one another.

Jake's meaty fingers curled around Owen's throat, then tightened like a vice. Spit dribbled from Jake's foaming mouth, his eyes wild and dark like the creature he saw out in the woods. Owen's face reddened and he bucked his hips trying to push Jake off, but the man wouldn't budge. Slowly, Owen lifted his right leg, wedging it between the two of them, and pushed into Jake's gut.

Jake held on for a few seconds, but Owen managed enough leverage to fling him off, and Jake was lifted backwards onto his ass. Owen gasped for air and he rolled toward the rifle, Jake making a move at the same time.

Both men collided, their shoulders cracking into one another as two sets of hands fought over the weapon, Owen grabbing hold of the stock with Jake on the barrel.

Owen yanked it toward him, and Jake came with it, using the momentum to drive Owen back against the wall. Pictures crashed to the floor as Jake kept Owen pinned. Both men's faces flushed red, their expressions pained and angry as they locked like a pair of horned rams.

Owen jammed his knee into Jake's stomach and the man's grip loosened. He then yanked the weapon hard left, spinning in a half circle as he stole the gun. Jake lunged, but Owen had a half second on him, and that was all he needed as he butt-stroked Jake's forehead.

Jake collapsed to the floor like a limp noodle, a gash cut across his forehead that leaked blood over his face and the floor. Owen held the gun loosely in his right hand, staggering to the left and right as he caught his breath, gently rubbing the red marks on his neck.

Chloe screamed, and Owen jerked his head toward the sound. He jumped over Jake's unconscious body, rifle raised as he followed the noise toward the master bedroom, and that was where he saw Marty's father-in-law, the old man that Owen only knew as "Grandpa," with a knife to his wife's throat and Chloe unconscious in the corner.

"Let her go!" Spittle flew from Owen's mouth as he aimed the rifle at the old man's face. His eyes looked grey and dull in the moonlight, but the steel shimmered brightly under Claire's chin. "I will shoot you."

"No, you won't," Grandpa said, his expression stoic as he shifted Claire's body in front of him as a human shield. "I doubt you've ever even pulled a trigger before."

Owen's cheek was pressed up against the rifle's stock as the small tick marks of the rifle's sight offered a narrow window to the old man's head. "The cops are on their way." Owen took a dry swallow. "They'll be here any minute."

"Bullshit," the old man said. "Nobody's coming. It's just you, and—"

Claire thrashed backward, thrusting both her and the old man onto the bed. Owen rushed to her side as she elbowed the old man's ribs and the knife nicked her throat. Claire whimpered, placing her hand over the fresh wound, but scurried away.

Owen aimed the barrel only a few inches from the old man's chest as he lay helpless on the bed. He had his finger over the trigger, but the old man didn't flinch.

"You don't have it in you, boy." The old man lifted his head off the bed, his grey eyes locked onto Owen. "You don't have the look."

The weapon trembled in Owen's hand. His grip tightened, but the old man was right. He couldn't pull the trigger. Owen loosened his grip but kept the rifle aimed at the old man as he took the knife away. He backed toward Claire. "Are you all right?"

Claire removed her hand from the wound, blood smeared over her fingers. She hissed in pain. "I think so." She walked around the bed toward Chloe and picked her up off the ground. "They knocked her out with some rag."

"Chloroform," the old man said. "She'll be fine in a few hours."

"Who sent you?" Owen asked, aiming the rifle at the old man's head. "Who took my son?"

The old man shook his head. "Boy, you have no idea the shit you've just stepped in."

"Owen, we need to call the police," Claire said, clutching Chloe closely.

Owen gestured the end of the rifle barrel up. "Move." The old man complied and Owen walked him out into the dining room and had him sit down at the table, He handed Claire the knife and then retreated back to where he'd left Jake, keeping the barrel of the rifle on the old man until he was no longer in sight.

Owen stepped into the den and the gun barrel dropped to the floor. Jake was gone. Owen spun toward the back door and stepped outside, scanning the yard, and then looked toward the tree line where the swamp water began. He saw nothing.

He returned to the dining room and the old man was still in the chair, Claire holding the knife and Chloe. When Owen walked back in alone, the old man smiled.

"Why?" Owen asked. "Why are you doing this to us? Where is my son!" Claire flinched from the sudden burst of anger, and Owen rammed the rifle's barrel into the old man's left cheek, cocking his head at a harsh angle.

The old man grimaced. "Your boy's gone, Yankee."

"Please," Claire said, pleading. "You have children, don't you?"

The old man gave Claire a side-eye. "You're not getting him back, lady. Accept it."

"No," Owen said, shoving the end of the weapon into the

old man's head. "You tell me where my son is or I blow your brains out and toss you out in the middle of the swamp." He gritted his teeth and felt a wild hate take control of him that he'd never felt before.

The old man stared at Owen for a minute, and then the left corner of his mouth twitched upward. "There's the look." He smiled, revealing that silver capped tooth of his. "There's the killer."

*a*ll but one of the factory's lights had been shut off. Chuck Toussaint's office was still illuminated, and he sat in his chair, sipping a glass of bourbon as he gazed out onto the still quiet of the factory floor. He hated it when it was like that. He loved the noise and commotion of production. If he could keep the factory open twenty-four hours a day, he would. What he saw now was just wasted money.

He set the glass down and checked his watch. It was a Rolex. His father had given it to him when he took over the business.

"Time is money, Chuckie. And like money, you can never have enough time."

His father's words lingered in Chuck's head for a long time, rattling around in some of the blank spaces of his mind. It should be done by now, but neither Jake nor Billy had called. They were off schedule. And if there was one thing he hated more than losing money, it was being off schedule.

A hurried knock banged at his door, and Chuck snapped his head toward the commotion. It was too late for someone to be calling at this hour unexpected. He opened the bottom desk drawer and removed a .38 revolver and cocked the hammer back. "Who's there?"

"It's Nate! I need to talk to you!"

Chuck grunted in annoyance and gently lowered the hammer and then pocketed the weapon. He flung open the door and a very haggard, very panicked real estate agent rushed inside.

"I tried calling you, but it keeps going to voicemail," Nate said, pacing the office floor in quick circles.

"What?" Chuck hurried back toward his desk and picked up his phone. No service. "Shit. You'd think by now we'd get some goddamn towers in this fucking town."

"You didn't tell me you filled the Cypress house," Nate said blatantly. "Your new tenant paid me a visit today."

"It doesn't matter," Chuck said, taking a seat and reaching for his bourbon. "It should be done by now."

Nate flattened his palms on Chuck's desk and hunched over. "You need to tell me when you do that. I almost started talking too much. And you know I have a problem with that."

"Relax," Chuck said sternly. "Have a drink. Bourbon's behind you."

Nate had always had a heavy hand, something that Chuck used to his advantage. "I don't need this kind of stress, Chuck, I really don't." He poured himself a glance, gulped down a mouthful, then exhaled. "Thank God we only have to do this once."

"Yeah," Chuck said, his voice muffled in his glass as he took another sip. "Thank God."

* * *

THE LATE HOUR had turned Main Street into a ghost town. Crawl Daddy's Bar shoved out its last few drunks and flipped the closed sign, then shut off the lights. The pair of Louisiana bachelors put their arms around one another, swaying back and forth down the sidewalk.

"I don't care what they say, Tommy." The man hiccupped and then burped, leaning into his friend. "You could have played pro-ball if you had gone to college. Go 'Dawgs!"

Tommy slowed on their way down the sidewalk. "Woah, woah, Kenny, hold up." He tapped his friend on the chest. "I-I don't wanna walk in front of that store. Bitch inside might get us."

Kenny, with all of his eight beers, four shots, and two plates of nachos under his belt, scrunched up his face skeptically. "You mean old crazy Crepaux? You really believe all that horseshit?" Kenny removed his arm and stumbled right up to the door, the closed sign exposed in the window, and pressed his greasy face up against the glass. "Hey! You in there, voodoo woman?" He laughed drunkenly and then turned back to Tommy, who started to chuckle himself. "I bet she ain't even—"

A bright flash lit up the windows, and both Kenny and Tommy yelped as they shut their eyes and lifted their arms to block out the blinding light. Kenny fell backward and landed on his ass, scraping up his back and shoulders, while Tommy hunched over with his elbows on his knees.

The light disappeared, and it took them both a minute before Main Street slowly filed back into their vision.

"Tommy!" Kenny said, reaching out his hands and groping air. "Tommy, whe—" Kenny screamed and jumped when a hand touched his arm.

"C'mon, man, let's get the hell out of here!" Tommy pulled Kenny toward his truck down the street, leaving whatever shit that woman was up to behind those closed doors.

Inside the shop, that voodoo woman, Madame Crepaux, stood over a wide, shallow bowl that took up the entirety of the card table she'd set it on. She sat alone, eyes closed with those white paint marks over her face, chanting over and over to herself.

A mixture of corked tubes and emptied baggies lay discarded on the table. The woman chanted the same phrase over and over, her eyes shut tight and her muscles tensed. "Chulung-Oola-Awaola-May. Chulung-Oola-Awaola-May. Chulung-Oola-Awaola-May. Chulung-Oola-Awaola-May."

The words grew faster and she rocked back and forth. The water in the bowl was black like the night sky void of stars. It was still at first, but as she spoke the words faster, the water rippled from the center and outward toward the edges.

The woman lifted her arms and head toward the ceiling and opened her eyes, her throat bobbing up and down along with the chanting that had grown as loud as screams. The water in the bowl bubbled but as she reached the crescendo of the chant, the water fell flat as glass.

The chanting ended. Her arms and head lingered upward, her eyes open, and there she stayed until she heard the familiar rattle of bones cracking against one another. She looked down and in the water, she saw the creature. It snarled and hissed, those long, jagged teeth and black eyes fixated on her.

Slowly, she lowered her arms and clutched the sides of the bowl as a smile spread across her lips. She'd been waiting for this moment for a long time. The reckoning was near. The righting of all those wrongs so many years ago was at hand. Now all she needed was the father.

9

It felt like a dream at first. A dream of darkness. But when ten-year-old Matt Cooley opened his eyes, the world was just as black as the nightmare that woke him. At least he thought he was awake. He shivered. It was cold here, and it felt like someone had plunged him into snow wearing nothing but his underwear.

A weightlessness had overtaken his body and he floated through the blackness. Was he in space? One of his science teachers had told him it was cold and dark in space. But there were no stars here, and a numbness stole the use of his legs and arms. He shut his eyes, trying to force himself to stand, but couldn't. And then he heard a whisper carried from an echo far away. He thought he knew the voice, but it was so quiet he couldn't be sure.

Where was he? Why couldn't he move? Why couldn't he see? The last thing he remembered was... was... What? The move from Baltimore? The snake bite? No, there was something else, something he—

A rattling echoed in the darkness. The noise was harsh and sharp like a bunch of baseballs cracking against a dozen wooden bats. The sound vibrated his bones, and it repeated itself, over and over, bringing a throbbing ache to his body.

Matt shut his eyes hard, wishing he could cover his ears to block the noise, but his arms remained numb and useless. And suddenly he had the sensation of falling, a force tugging at the pit of his stomach, the same one he felt when he got on that roller coaster with his dad two years ago at Six Flags. The sensation stayed like that for a long time, then slowed and eventually stopped. And then, just as mysteriously as this darkness appeared and covered him like a blanket of ice, it was lifted.

He blinked a few times, his vision blurred. The ceiling he stared at was different than the one in his bedroom. He rolled to his side, but stopped when he reached the edge of the concrete slab he'd awoken upon.

Startled, he pushed himself back to the center. Concrete walls enclosed him, a narrow hallway offering the only exit. Dirtied and broken stained glass windows lined the top of the walls just below the ceiling, but only a grey haze could be seen beyond them.

Carefully, he swung his legs over the side, every scrape of his feet and breath into his lungs echoing like he was underwater. He pressed his palms on the edges of the slab, the tiny grains of concrete digging into his skin.

He examined his body and found himself still dressed in the faded Orioles shirt and shorts that he'd fallen asleep in on his bed. He looked to his bare feet, then wiggled his toes in confirmation that he was still alive.

The cold worsened, and Matt shivered as he gently slid from the concrete slab, hugging himself for both warmth and a sense of security. He walked through the narrow hallway and then whimpered at the sight outside.

Rows of graves lined the confines of a short, rusted, and tilting iron fence. The headstones crumbled from years of neglect, the names and dates engraved in the stone no longer legible. He turned behind him to look at the structure he'd walked out of and saw that it was a mausoleum, towering high above the other tombs.

A fog crawled over the ground, and the air gripped icy fingers around Matt's neck. The world around him was a hazy spectrum of greys and blacks, void of any color. He lifted his head toward the sky, and his jaw went slack. Where there should have been a night sky, there was nothing but a grey canvas. No stars, no moon. It was like the sky was blanketed with permanent overcast storm clouds.

He shivered again and tiptoed between the graves. The ground was cold like the air, and his weight gave way to the soft clumps of muddy swamp.

A sharp pain cut through from the back of his head, and Matt winced, reaching for the pain's origin. His fingers grazed something sharp, and he quickly retracted his hand. A prick of blood oozed from the tip of his finger, and then a tickle ran across the top of his head.

Matt stomped his legs in quick hopping motions, his hands scouring his hair in search of the critter roaming his scalp. Another sharp prick hit his finger, followed by a crunch under his palm as he pressed down hard. He peeled his hand off his head and examined a squashed spider the size of a quarter.

Matt scraped the guts off onto the bark of a tree, then thoroughly patted the rest of his head, relieved after finding nothing else. He then weaved around the tombs, taking a closer look at the swamp that surrounded him.

The trees were dead. Leafless branches reached up toward the dying sky, their bark various shades of grey and black like the rest of the environment.

"Mom! Dad!" His voice echoed, and it sounded as if he were screaming from underwater. His lungs ached, and he leaned up against a tree to catch his breath. He hunched over, placing his hand on his knee. He'd never felt so tired before.

A hiss sounded from above and Matt jerked his head up as a snake slithered down one of the tree branches, its tongue flicking the air, catching Matt's scent.

Matt jerked backward, but only got a few steps before another snake slithered from the left of him, leaving a serpentine trail through the mud. More followed. Three, then five, soon dozens were chasing after him with their exposed fangs and forked tongues.

Matt sprinted away, casting himself deeper into the swamp. The mud beneath him swallowed his feet and slowed his pace. The hissing faded, but sharp knives stabbed at his sides and lungs from the exertion. He slowed, fatigued, and glanced back into the darkness, finding nothing but fog and trees.

He collapsed to his knees in the mud and clutched his chest. Liquid gargled in his lungs, and when he coughed, a spray of black crud blew over his hand. He examined it in horror and quickly wiped it off on his shorts.

Matt stood, and pressed forward. Mud eventually gave way to water, and he waded through the ankle-deep swamp slowly, unable to see beneath the surface of the pitch-black darkness. But the closer he looked down at the water, the more he realized that there was something different about it.

Despite his movements, the water remained still. No ripples. No splashes. But it still felt like water.

He passed more clusters of dead cypress trees, their thick trunks a collection of tubes reaching deep into the earth. He coughed, a phlegmy tickle in his throat. He used his bandaged arm to cover his mouth, and when he lowered it, more black specks flicked over the white gauze. He started to panic.

Was he dead? Had he gone to hell? He'd heard Tommy

McDoyle talking about that one day, saying how if you were bad you were sent to hell and you would burn. Except it wasn't hot here. But, maybe you froze to death in hell. It's not like Tommy had ever been.

Matt wandered aimlessly, shivering, unsure of where to go except forward. Slowly, the water receded, and the ground solidified under his feet.

Ahead, between the trees, he saw a clearing of dirt, and on the other side of the clearing was a house. The same one he'd been living in for the past few days. It looked darker, more ominous, but if his family was here, then that's where they'd be.

Matt broke into a sprint, his feet slinging mud. His lungs still burned, and he wheezed on his mad dash over the dirt field, which felt soft yet brittle against his feet, like ash.

"Mom! Dad!" Matt's voice echoed as he veered toward the front porch, tracking muddy footprints inside as he skidded to a stop on the groaning hardwood floors. "Mom? Dad?"

Matt walked to the kitchen's entrance but quickly veered away when he saw a snake slither out of the sink faucet. He ran down the hallway, past the dining room, and toward his parents' room on the first floor. He found it empty, the sheets on the bed torn and strewn about messily. The pictures on the dresser were broken in their frames, distorting the happy smiles and cheerful moments.

Staring at those pictures, he felt that he might shatter like that glass. Just break, unable to be whole again. Maybe he was like that already.

A drop of something wet landed on top of his head, and with the fear of the spider from earlier still fresh in his mind, he clawed at it, smearing the warm liquid on his fingers and hair. Matt removed his hand and rolled his fingertips together, feeling the slick grime of the substance. He sniffed at it wearily, then quickly pulled away, grimacing from the stench. The scent was akin to an alley dumpster on a hot summer day after having baked in the sun for a week without rain.

Matt turned toward the door, and another drop of the black, tar-like substance plopped directly in front of his feet, freezing him in place. He looked up to the ceiling and saw more black droplets hanging above, wiggling in their struggle to break free.

Matt sprinted into the hallway to avoid the rain, and when he entered the dining room, two gators appeared from the back hallway, jaws exposed and growling in a throaty hiss, their bodies decrepit. Their scaly backs had decayed to bone and their clawed feet oozed bloody prints over the floor.

He spun around to head back toward the front of the house, but found the hallway to his escape blocked with snakes.

More drops of black goo fell as Matt retreated toward the kitchen table, quickly scurrying off the floor as the snakes and gators circled him. He cried, the black substance raining harder now, plopping over his body in heavy thumps, darkening his beloved Orioles shirt, their stink filling his senses.

The snakes covered every inch of the floor, bringing it to life in writhing movements. Thousands of spiders crawled along the walls. The house had come alive with creatures, and Matt knew they would eat him, digging their fangs into his flesh to tear him apart. And then suddenly, the hissing stopped, and the snakes near the hallway parted to form an opening, cramming themselves against the walls.

A pair of stumpy, clawed feet appeared, and Matt fell backwards onto the table when the creature came into full view. It stood six feet tall, and its long, muscled arms led down to a three-fingered hand, each of them armed with six-inch claws that were black as night. Its head was wide, and when it opened its jaws, its lipless mouth exposed an array of jagged, three-inch serrated teeth. They clustered clumsily in the creature's mouth, but when it closed its jaw, they fit together like pieces in a jigsaw puzzle.

Its torso was short, but thick like a barrel. A scaly grey skin covered thick muscles, and matted black hair sprouted from the top of its domed head and down its back. One of the long claws attached to a three-fingered hand twitched, and it stood there, unblinking, teeth exposed, staring at Matt.

Cold seeped into Matt's bones and froze his heart, and he suddenly choked for air. He clawed at his neck and flattened on his back. More drops of blackness rained over him and his eyes bulged in panic. His lungs tightened to the point of bursting.

The creature hovered over Matt, and pressed the tip of one of its razor-sharp claws into Matt's shirt collar, then ran it down the length of his chest and belly, tearing the fabric and exposing Matt's pale and tender flesh. Matt couldn't move, but he felt a light prick from the tip of the claw on his skin as the creature applied pressure.

Matt opened his mouth to scream but emitted no sound. The creature cut a line from the top of his chest to his belly button, just deep enough to draw blood, and Matt's brain lit up like fire from the pain.

After the first line, the creature then placed the same claw just below Matt's left nipple. It drew another line, drawing blood like before, and intersecting the vertical line. The pain reached a crescendo and his body went limp. He tilted his head to the side and saw the snakes, gators, and spiders scurrying across the floor.

Matt turned his head lazily back to the creature, catching a glimpse at his chest and stomach and the black cross now carved into his flesh. Blood poured between his ribcage, collecting in tiny pools on the table.

The creature tilted its head back and opened its mouth wide, giving a primal roar that scattered the rest of the animals from the house and elicited a tremor of fear from Matt's body. It wasn't like anything he'd heard before in this world. It was like the creature was calling out to someone, or something.

Silence lingered after the creature's roar, and Matt's limbs remained useless. He'd forgotten that he couldn't breathe, this state of suspension growing more normal the longer he was kept in it.

And then, like an echo in the far distance, he heard a voice. It was familiar, and it seemed to answer the creature's call. But the sounds were human. Someone was calling Matt's name. Someone he knew. His grandfather.

$\mathcal{M}$ ain Street in Ocoee, Louisiana was quiet. Not even a tumbleweed blew through at this time of night. A few of the street lamps flickered, most of them burned out and never replaced. The town folk preferred the view of the stars and moon over the harsh fluorescents of city lighting. Not that Ocoee qualified as a city. But nobody argued about the view.

Closed signs and darkened windows lined the businesses along Main Street, but beyond the one-story buildings was the auto factory where most of the town worked. It was owned by the Toussaint family, had been for nearly five generations. And the man in charge was Charles Toussaint VII, the firstborn male son and only child of Charles Toussaint VI.

The Toussaint family had been intertwined with the fate of this town for its entire existence. In the early 1800s, the first Toussaints arrived and cleared farmland to harvest crops. They hunted and traded, they fished and bartered, and from their humble beginnings, they grew into a name recognizable by every man, woman, and child in the great state of Louisiana.

The current heir to the Toussaint throne knew his family's history very well, better than anyone else, save for one. And while the Toussaints were beloved by the townspeople, who saved them from the crippling Great Depression in the thirties after Chuck's great-grandfather turned their canning factory into an assembly factory for military vehicles for the efforts during the Second World War, they were also responsible for some of the township's more unsavory history.

Actions were taken, secrets were buried, and the Toussaints endured on. But while the rest of the town had forgotten what had happened over the years, a few held onto the truth of the past. And none more so than Madame Crepaux.

A patch of broken streetlights cast one particular building into a darker shadow. Above the storefront on the ledge of the roof stood the old worn letters of the shop: Queen's.

There were always whispers about that store and its proprietor, Madame Crepaux. Say her name aloud amongst the townspeople and they'd harshly tell you to shut your trap. "A devil worshiper she is!" "A no-good woman, that's for sure." "A phony. Just a dirty trickster."

People had whispered about her ever since she could remember. She didn't care what the town said, because the townspeople had forgotten what had happened. But she didn't. The circles of those she trusted had passed down ancient knowledge to her, and she practiced and practiced until she grew into her own kind of legend. And finally the time had come. All of the pieces were in place.

The curse had started with fathers and sons, and that's how it would end, or so she had seen. The future was fragmented, cloudy, like looking through a keyhole.

Inside her shop were items that most people would find repulsive. Animal skeletons, jewelry made from bones, feathers, and furs. Shelves of potions lined the walls, ranging in color from dark blues, blacks, and purples, to light yellows, greens, and blues, packaged in different-sized glass tubes, some in odd, twisting shapes. The walls were painted a dark, earthy brown, and the wooden floorboards were splintered and worn from decades of customers, mostly tourists, browsing her goods.

A cash register sat on top of a large glass case that contained more potions, more herbs, more tokens. Despite her knowledge and devotion to her religion, if she wanted to stay in this town, she still needed to pay rent. So the knick-knacks and novelties helped get her along as people passed through on their way to New Orleans or Texas.

But behind the door to the left of the register was another room, one that remained closed during business hours, but was open now. A faint glow shimmered from inside, and there Madame Crepaux watched Matt Cooley be taken by the creature. Her eyes watered, and she quickly wiped them before tears could fall. It was hard watching such innocence be harmed, but what was necessary was rarely easy. And if all went according to plan, the boy would be returned home.

The glow from the large shallow basin slowly faded, and she struck a match and lit a candle. The flame flickered and revealed Madame Crepaux in her baggy, earthy-toned clothes that concealed the harsh realities that time bestowed upon the body. Her long dreads remained thick and black at the ends, but had started to thin and grey at the top. Her joints groaned, and she didn't move as quickly as she used to, but her mind was sharper than it had ever been. And while well-worn lines were imprinted on her face, revealing the travels and stories of a lifetime, the pair of hazel eyes glowed with flickering specks of yellow. They were bright, intelligent, and the only part of her that was still beautiful.

Behind her was a table with old books and scrolls, their covers and letters faded and worn after almost two centuries of study. They had been passed down from priestess to priestess, from bokor to bokor, and then finally to her.

Much of the world was blind to the practice of Voodoo. Gris-gris, charms, and potions were viewed as nothing more than sideshow attractions. People did not understand the power that it gave, the good it could do… or the bad.

Voodoo was a religion that took from all forms of worships. It possessed symbols from Christianity and from the African tribes of her ancestors. Rituals were passed down by song to connect with the deities and the spirits of this world and the next. These songs also opened gates between worlds, and she had craved to open one gate in particular for as long as she could remember. But she needed something. A powerful amulet that she could not retrieve herself, created by a bokor who had sold out for the material goods of this world.

Madame Crepaux hovered her finger over one of the books, searching for the first lines of the words to the enchantment, smiling when she found it. She needed to move the other pieces together quickly. The longer the boy remained with the creature, the stronger it would become, and the harder it would be to open the doorway to its domain.

The father would come to her, that she was sure of. But the grandfather would need help. He had already been marked by the creature, and he was the chosen conduit to connect this world and the next.

She closed her eyes and lifted her arms, a low throaty hum escaping her lips. "Khan-Mah-EEE-Nochtway." She stomped her foot, feeling the vibrations of the rhythm run through her. "Khan-Mah-EEE-Nochtway." Another stomp, then a quick clap of her hands.

Madame Crepaux turned back to her shallow bowl, the light glowing once more, repeating the chant as she quickened her rhythm. Roger Templeton stirred as she reached within the depths of the old man's broken mind.

"KHAN-MAH-EEE-NOCHTWAY!" The light in the bowl flashed bright and Madame Crepaux opened her eyes as she felt Roger Templeton awake in his hospital bed. She felt his panic, his confusion, and then his fear as she showed him what had become of his grandson.

They were only quick flashes, glimpses of what happened, but that was all that was needed. Madame held the connection as long as she could, but the man's disease made it difficult, and after a few minutes, she dropped her hands to her sides and her knees buckled as she crumpled to the floor.

She gasped for breath, sweat trickling down her sides under her robes. She gathered her strength, focusing on her regaining control of her breathing. When she sat up, her knees popped and she clutched the table for support.

The years had stolen much of her strength, and she longed for the power she felt in her youth. But time cared nothing of the yearnings of the past.

The glow in the bowl faded, and only the candle flickered light. She looked back to her books, to all that she had studied. She clutched the bone necklace around her neck, drawing strength from her own gris-gris. She would need it for what was to come. They all would.

* * *

OWEN SAT on the edge of Matt's bed, staring out the single dirty window of his son's room. Red and blue lights passed in sweeping shades over the darkness outside. The cops had arrived twenty minutes ago, and Owen had come upstairs in a trance-like walk. It all felt like a dream, and he thought that if he walked up here, he'd find his son safe and sound in his bed. But Owen found only an empty room.

The sheriff asked questions downstairs that Owen didn't know how to answer. Every time he moved his lips, he stopped at the absurdity of his own words. His son was taken not by the men who'd come to kill him and his family, which he still had no idea why, but by some... thing.

Owen shut his eyes and massaged them with the palms of his hands, trying to rid himself of the image of his son in the arms of that creature, sinking into the depths of the swamp. He turned his gaze from the windows and cast them over the walls.

A large Orioles poster was plastered at the head of Matt's bed. A bat stood in the corner. Dirty cleats and a bucket of baseballs sat beneath the window in front of him. A shelf to the right displayed one of his son's most treasured possessions, a ball signed by every player of the 2012 Orioles team.

Matt's glove rested beneath his pillow, and Owen reached for it. He flipped it over, the straps of the glove dangling from the thick, flat fingers. The leather was well worn and oiled properly. His mother had shown him how to do it. He got his love of baseball from her.

Voices drifted upstairs, and Owen could hear Claire as she spoke with the officers. It was muffled, and faint, but she was still there, still talking.

The tips of Owen's fingers whitened as he squeezed the glove harder. How did this happen? The move down here was supposed to solve everything, it was supposed to be a fresh start, an escape from the woes of Baltimore. But the job, the house, it was all too good to be true.

Desperation had a way of blinding you to rational thought. When faced with the prospect of your family being tossed into the streets with no food, no water, no roof over your head, you started to see things differently. And so when he was offered the job down here in Louisiana, he had moved his family without hesitation. He did it to save them. He did it to be the hero.

And now his son was gone. His family nearly dead. And he had no idea what to do next.

"Owen?"

He turned and saw Claire standing in the doorway. She was still wearing her robe, though she'd added a shirt and shorts beneath it.

"Hey," Owen answered, still holding his son's glove.

Claire entered the room softly, not even the floorboards groaning from her steps. She joined him on the bed's edge and placed her hand over his. "They want us to come down to the station. Fill out some paperwork and make a statement."

Owen nodded, rubbing the inside of the glove. "Do you remember his first game? He was four, wasn't he?"

A smile waned over her face, and she nodded. "Five." She gestured to the glove. "We got that for him at the stadium."

"We bought him his own seat, but he just sat on my leg the whole game."

"Owen, we need to go and speak with the officers," Claire said, her voice kind, but the patience thinning.

"The jersey we got him was like a dress." Owen's voice cracked and he felt tears gather in his eyes. "That was a good day." Owen glanced out the window to the edge of where the swamp began. Where that creature had disappeared with his son.

"Owen—"

"I lost him, Claire," Owen said, his voice trembling as a tear fell to the glove, darkening the leather. "And I don't know how to get him back." He turned to her, the same desperation in his voice when he came home with that pink slip from the shipyard six months ago. "I don't know what to do."

Claire pulled him close, struggling with his size and weight, his body engulfing hers in the darkness. He sobbed into her shoulder and she whispered into his ear. "None of this is your fault. We're going to find him. We'll get him back."

Owen held onto her words, climbing them like a ladder from the depths of despair. His head broke the surface and he took his first breath of strength. That's what she was for him, that perpetual engine that pushed him forward.

"The sheriff's downstairs?" Owen asked, wiping his eyes.

"Yeah," Claire answered.

Owen gently set the glove back on the bed before taking Claire's hand, and they walked down the stairs together.

Dozens of officers scoured the dining room while others searched the rest of the house, tagging random items for evidence, combing the place for anything that would help them in their investigation. But how would it bring his son back from the clutches of that monster? He had no idea.

"I want a clean sweep of the whole property!" The sheriff bellowed his orders from the front porch over to the line of deputies walking through the tall grass from the house to the trees on the edge of the swamp.

Dogs barked in the back of squad cars as their handlers prepped them with a few items of Matt's clothing. Owen thought about giving them the glove but wasn't sure if the hounds could smell past all of that oil.

Sheriff Bellingham turned when Claire tapped him on the shoulder, his belly surprisingly flat for a man of his age and size. He was eye level with Owen in regards to his height, but his shoulders were a little broader, and the senior authority figure kept his fists pressed into his hips, giving himself a superhero-like stance.

"Ma'am," Bellingham's tone softened. "You folks ready to head to the station?"

"How long will this take?" Owen asked, remembering Chloe still upstairs in her room.

"Not long, Mr. Cooley." The sheriff's voice offered a thick but articulate twang, his lips bristling the bushy grey mustache that sprouted from his upper lip. "I just want to make sure we cross all our t's and dot all our I's. It makes it easier in the long run."

Owen gestured to the line of deputies, who had now reached the edge of the swamp. "That's all you brought?"

"I've coordinated with some of the sheriffs in the other parishes," Bellingham said. "They're sending men over so we can put together a search party."

"And you think that'll be enough?" Owen asked, an unintentional hardness to his voice.

"If the man who took your son—"

"It wasn't a man." Owen stiffened.

"I know what it might have looked like, but—"

"No," Owen said. "You don't."

"Some of these guys like to wear masks," Bellingham said. "It's a psychological game they play. About ten years ago, I had this fellow taking kids dressed up like a woman. And let me tell you, he didn't look like no woman. Taller than me, and just as wide. He shaved three times a day to keep the stubble off. Wore wigs, dresses, makeup. It's easy to get caught up in it all when something like this happens."

"He's telling the truth, Sheriff," Claire said. "The things that have happened in this house, they've... defied normal."

The sheriff gave them each a look up and down, then clucked his tongue and raised his eyebrows. "Well, the sooner we get your statement down, the sooner we can start pressing charges against the people responsible."

Owen searched the squad cars out front and finally

spotted the one carrying the old man. He had his hands cuffed behind his back, and he was staring straight at Owen. The wrinkly, white bearded face snarled and revealed a single, silver-capped tooth. The second man who attacked his family, Jake Martin, had disappeared into the swamp when Owen rescued Claire and their daughter. Both men worked at the factory where Owen had just started his new job.

A deputy stepped out of the house, holding up a cell phone. "Sheriff? This kept going off in the bedroom. It's got eleven missed calls."

"That's mine," Claire said, frowning. The deputy handed it over to her and she scrolled through the missed calls, then looked at Owen, her cheeks as white as the robe she wore. "It's the hospital."

Claire turned her back to them as she returned the call, her head down. Owen couldn't see it, but she was biting her nails, chewing the ends nervously while she waited for someone to answer.

Like Claire, Owen already knew what the call was about. Owen's father-in-law was diagnosed with early onset Alzheimer's four months ago. But after the move from Baltimore, his condition worsened, so they admitted him to the nearest hospital. At least Owen had made himself believe it was the disease. However, after what he saw last night, he wasn't so sure.

Claire lowered the phone then spun back around, stuttering a bit before she found her rhythm. "They said my dad won't stop screaming, that he keeps asking for me. They want me to come down to the hospital and talk to him, but I don't—" She shut her eyes, inhaled a deep breath, and then exhaled slowly. The breath rattled with an anxiety that made her lower lip tremble. White knuckles clutched the phone, and she shook her head.

"I'll handle the police report," Owen said. He turned to the sheriff. "You can get her statement after?"

"Sure," Bellingham said. "We'd be able to get the ball rolling as long as we have one of you on record. But we'd still eventually want to get your wife's version of the events."

Owen took his wife's hand, feeling the sweat on her skin. "Go. I'll see you right after."

"I'll take Chloe with me," Claire said, tossing a glance to the old man with his silver-capped tooth in the back of the squad car. "I don't want her being around the station with those people."

"I'll have one of my deputies drive you over to the hospital," Bellingham said, then turned out to the field, pressed his fingers to his lips, and let out a loud whistle that turned every officer's head. "John!" He followed the name with a big, sweeping motion of his arm, and one of the deputies broke from the pack and jogged over.

The young man's face dripped with sweat and he panted steadily upon his arrival. "Sheriff?"

"I need you to escort Mrs. Cooley and her daughter to the hospital," Bellingham answered, then turned to Claire. "You think you could answer a few of Deputy Hurt's questions on the way there?"

"Sure," Claire answered.

"Mr. Cooley?" Bellingham asked.

"Hm?" Owen snapped his head away from the staring contest with the old man.

"Do you want to ride with one of my deputies to the station downtown, or will you be taking your own vehicle?"

"I'll drive," Owen answered.

"All right then, we should get going."

The sheriff and Deputy Hurt started the walk to their cruisers, and Claire leaned into Owen as he wrapped his arms around her. "I'll call you when I'm done at the hospital."

Owen kissed the top of her head. "I'm sure he's fine. And you're right. We will find him."

"I know," Claire said, and she walked back into the house to grab Chloe.

On his way to the van, Owen tossed one more glance toward the squad car with the old man, but he'd turned away.

Owen didn't know why the old man and Jake had attacked him, but he was willing to bet it had something to do with that thing that took his son. He climbed into the van and just before he started the engine, he glanced at the house through the windshield.

The police lights bathed the old wood blue and red, but the windows remained dark. Unnatural shadows engulfed the structure greedily, and Owen felt a chill run through him, his mind kept circling the one question that he couldn't answer. Why his family?

The bourbon inside the crystal bottle at the wet bar in Chuck Toussaint's office was gone. Most of it disappeared into Nate Covers's stomach, but a fair amount was currently working its way through Chuck's liver. He'd stayed awake as long as he could, but the liquor's foggy haze eventually won out and he'd fallen asleep on his desk, his empty crystal glass near his limp and outwardly stretched hand.

Papers were strewn about his desk, a few new contracts that needed his approval before shipments could be sent out to his distributors. A large window exposed the guts of the factory that Chuck owned. He inherited it from his father, and his father inherited from his father, and his from his father, and so on all the way back to the factory's conception at the turn of the twentieth century.

And so Charles Toussaint VII's fate was sealed generations ago as he was to inherit the family business that had been the staple of Ocoee, Louisiana's community and economy.

But the business wasn't the only thing Chuck inherited.

Underneath the wealth and status that his family held, there was a secret that had been forgotten since his ancestors first settled in this godforsaken piece of swamp land. It haunted his dreams. Especially tonight.

Chuck spasmed in his drunken slumber, groaning as he shifted to a more comfortable position on the desk. He figured that thing would visit him tonight, and he'd put off sleep as long as he could to avoid it. But the liquor and fatigue had finally caught up.

He'd seen it once in person. When he was eight, his father took him to that house on Cypress Lane. His father hadn't said anything on the ride over. His mother had cried when they left, and that alone frightened him.

The anxiety only worsened when they turned down the gravel road and Chuck saw that house in the distance. Clouds drifted over the moon and shifted the shadows, bringing the darkness to life.

A freezing terror struck at Chuck's heart, and he looked to his father in that moment, whose gaze was straight ahead as he slowed the truck and parked.

"You said we weren't supposed to come here," Chuck said, his eyes wider than a full moon. "You said it was dangerous." Tears rolled down his cheeks despite his best efforts to control them. He hated crying in front of his father because he knew how much his father detested weakness. But the fear ran wild, and he couldn't contain the sniveling whimpers that followed.

"You need to see something," his father said, still staring at the house while the seat underneath them vibrated from the truck's engine. "Something that you'll have to face as a man. Like I did." His father was colder and more distant than usual. "Get out of the truck."

"W-why?" Chuck asked.

His father turned to him and his expression hardened

into steel. The same steel that the machines were made of at the factory, the same steel of the factory itself. It was immovable, unswayable. "Now!"

Chuck jumped at his father's bark and quickly unbuckled his seat belt and pulled the door handle. The door groaned as it opened, and he slid off the bench seat and his knees buckled when he hit the bumpy gravel. He looked up to his father, the tears still streaming down his face. His dad gestured to the field and then pointed to the swamp beyond it.

"Head to the cemetery. You stay there until I come and get you. Understand?"

Chuck slowly turned and looked to the trees and swamp across the swaying tall grass and reeds. He shook his head. "I-I don't w-wanna go."

His father's expression remained hardened and unyielding. "Do as I say, boy."

Chuck didn't bother controlling the sobs now as he turned away from the truck and placed one wobbling foot down in front of the other and stepped into the field. He thought his father would leave him here to rot, and he kept wondering what he had done to deserve it. He turned back only twice, and each time he saw that his father's truck was still in the drive.

The tall grass tickled the exposed skin of his arms, neck, and the back of his legs. And each time he jerked and recoiled from the grass's touch, his imagination and the darkness got the better of him. The tall grass finally ended, and the large cypress trees sprung up from the thick mud that sucked his shoes down with each step.

Chuck dodged the hanging moss that swayed in the breeze, reaching for his shoulders like monster's fingers. The squish of the mud grew wetter the farther he ventured into the swamp, and through the trees he saw the pieces of concrete that comprised the cemetery. He veered along the edge of the muck and water toward the raised tombs, his new shoes now completely ruined with grime up to his knees.

The hot stink of the swamp filled his lungs, and by the time he reached the graves, the muscles in his legs had turned to jelly and his shirt was soaked with sweat. He remembered his father telling him that this was his family's cemetery. And that one day, like the rest of the Toussaints, he would be buried here with them. He just hoped it wasn't tonight.

Death terrified him. The idea that he would no longer exist, no longer feel, or think or see or hear, it was too overwhelming. How could things just stop? How could he just end and not even realize it? He expressed those fears and questions to his best friend Aaron Jessup. And Aaron told him that you never die if you know Jesus. He'd get to go to heaven and see his whole family up there and he'll never get scared, or tired, or hurt ever again.

Chuck didn't know who Jesus was, but that night at the dinner table he'd told his father what Aaron had said, and his father pounded his heavy fist against the thick oak and rattled the plates and silverware.

"The only things in life that matter are what you can see, feel, hear, and taste. If you can't hold it, then it's not worth your time. If the Jessups want to spew that shit to their kid, then fine, but I won't have you become a weak-minded fool like their boy. You hear me?"

Chuck nodded and never brought it up again. But he sometimes still thought of what Aaron had said, and it made him feel better. He'd like to see his grandmother again. Beside his mom, she was the only other family member that he liked. Every visit to his grandparents' house was like an escape, as long as he didn't have to be around his grandfather very long. The old man was meaner than his father and looked scarier because of the saggy skin and wrinkles. Mammie had wrinkles, but she didn't have his grandfather's scowl.

Chuck found his Mammie's grave among the dead and pressed his back against the firm concrete of her tomb as he sat down. If there was a safer place to wait, then he couldn't think of one.

Cicadas and insects buzzed in the night air, and every once in a while, the water would swoosh from a gator or snake. Chuck kept himself tucked into a tight ball, hugging his knees tight against his chest. The longer he lingered there in the dark, the less frightening it became, and soon he grew sleepy. He released his knees from his chest and lay down along the side of his Mammie's tomb.

Eventually, Chuck dozed off, and he wasn't sure how long he'd been asleep, but he awoke to a low growl and high-pitched hiss echoing from the depths of the swamp. He pushed himself up on his elbows and wiped the sleep from his eyes. He shivered from an unearthly chill in the air, unheard of at this time of summer. Even in the nighttime.

The cold worsened as Chuck sat upright, the growl and hiss growing louder and coming from different directions. Chuck backed himself into the tomb as a rattle knocked the air. It was slow at first, but then grew into a steady rhythm, vibrating the air with each clackity-clack.

Chuck retreated from the graveyard, the cold seeping into his bones now and chilling every breath. His heart hammered in his chest, and he tripped over his own mud-crusted shoes and smacked into the muck face first.

The rattling grew louder and Chuck panicked, rolling in the thick mud that refused to let him go. The more he struggled, the quicker he sank. He crawled on all fours, his arms and legs burning as the rattling grew louder.

Another low growl and hiss echoed to his right, then another to his left, and Chuck burst into tears again. He couldn't even see what was out there, and he knew that his father had said to wait until he came and got him, but he didn't want to die. He didn't want to be cast into darkness forever. He wanted to hear his mother's voice again. He wanted to see his friends. He wanted to feel the warmth of the sun on his face.

The rattling stopped and Chuck's ears popped as the air was sucked from his lungs. Panic took hold and he flailed more violently in the mud. And when he finally flipped to his back he saw the creature standing over him in the darkness.

Black good dripped from the wide mouth full of jagged teeth. Scaly grey skin covered its body, and long claws extended from its hands. But out of all the menacing features, it was the creature's eyes that frightened him most. It was like they were staring into his soul, sucking the very life from him every second their gazes were locked together.

Suddenly, it lunged forward, arms stretched out and claws extended and gleaming under the moonlight. The roar that bellowed from its core rattled Chuck's bones and froze him as he turned away and shut his eyes, waiting for the monster to eat him and then fall into the nothing that was death. He'd be buried in this cemetery, maybe next to his mammie, and there he would rot away into nothing.

Chuck shivered, waiting for the vicious kiss of the creature's teeth. But after a while, nothing happened.

"You saw it."

Chuck snapped his head toward his father's voice and saw him standing motionless and cloaked in shadows. "I don't— I'm not—" He felt the tears coming again, and he turned his mud-splattered face away from his father so he couldn't see.

But his father knelt and pulled Chuck's gaze upon him.

The hardened expression he'd seen at the truck had softened, but it was a far cry from anything that could be considered kind.

"What you saw tonight wanted to kill you," his father said. "But it won't. Because it can't."

"Wh-Wh-Why?" Chuck asked, the will to fight back the tears growing stronger.

His father extended his hand and pulled his son from the muck with ease. He then steadied his boy and gripped him firmly by the shoulders. "You'll find out when you're older. But I wanted you to see it, like your grandfather showed me. Because it's important to know what you're facing. What our family will always face. But as long as you do what I tell you, it will never be able to hurt you. Understand?"

He didn't, but he nodded anyways. And then his father walked him back to the truck, forced him to wipe the mud off himself before he climbed back into the cab, and they drove home.

Chuck's phone buzzed, vibrating the desk in steady, rhythmic motions. Slowly, it pulled him from his drunken nightmares, and he raised his head in annoyance at the phone.

He snatched at it angrily, ending the loud drumming against the desk that split his throbbing head. Without looking at the number, he answered, thinking it was Billy or Jake finally calling to let him know that it was done.

"About time you called," Chuck said, his throat raspy and croaked. He smacked his lips dryly. His breath tasted like shit.

"I didn't realize we scheduled a call this late, Mr. Toussaint," Bellingham said.

It took a few seconds for the sheriff's voice to register in Chuck's mind, but when it did, a shot of adrenaline flooded through him like a freight train. "Sheriff, I apologize. I thought you were someone else." Chuck's stomach twisted in knots at the sheriff's silence.

"I picked up one of your employees tonight," Bellingham said.

The knots in Chuck's stomach worsened and he doubled over on his desk in pain, a rumbling in his gut. "Who?" But Chuck knew. He just hoped the pair hadn't rolled over on him yet.

"Billy Rouche," Sheriff Bellingham answered. "Apparently Jake Martin was with him as well. They attacked another one of your employees; Owen Cooley. They broke into his house on Cypress Lane. Mr. Cooley managed to subdue Billy, but Jake ran off into the swamp. I have my deputies looking for him, but I wanted to give you a courtesy call seeing as how everyone involved works for you and that the incident happened on one of your housing properties."

"Thank you, Sheriff," Chuck said, trying to hide the shaking in his voice, his back arched with his forearms flat against the desk. "I appreciate that."

The sheriff paused again and the rumbling in Chuck's stomach worsened. "Can I ask where you've been this evening, Mr. Toussaint?"

"I was working late," Chuck answered. "At the office. Nate Covers is here with me. He came over for a drink and we accidently finished a bottle of bourbon." Chuck laughed, but the sheriff didn't reciprocate. He cleared his throat and shut his eyes to stop the room from spinning. "I'll have the company lawyer come by the station first thing in the morning. We'll get all of this sorted out."

"I hope we do," Bellingham said. "Good night, Mr. Toussaint."

"Night, Sheriff." Chuck hung up and then immediately rushed to the trashcan at the edge of his desk. Half a bottle of bourbon along with his catfish lunch emptied from his stomach. The taste of vomit that lingered on his tongue wasn't much worse than the taste he woke up with, but it definitely wasn't better.

"Shitshitshitshit!" Chuck wiped his mouth with the back of his hand and then looked up to see Nate passed out in his chair, the half-drunk cup of bourbon still sitting on his lap and dangerously close to spilling over his trousers. "Nate!"

Nate tilted his head from left to right, then adjusted his ass on the seat. The bourbon spilled in a large dark patch against his grey jeans, making it look like he'd pissed himself.

Chuck stumbled over and violently shook him by the shoulders. "Nate!"

Nate finally stirred, impotently batting away at Chuck's arms. "Whatduyawant?" He briefly opened his eyes, then readjusted in his chair, trying to go back to sleep.

"Get up!" Chuck yanked Nate from the chair, and he rolled to the floor with a smack.

Nate groaned and floundered like a turtle stuck on his back. "What?" He squinted up at Chuck, who grabbed hold of him by the collar.

"Listen to me. The sheriff arrested Billy, and Jake's gone missing." Another low rumble sounded in Chuck's stomach, but the anger helped keep the vomit down. Though he wouldn't have minded puking all over Nate if it would wake the bastard up. "Do you hear me? The Cooleys are still alive!"

Somewhere in the fried circuits of his liquor-soaked brain, Nate slowly made the connection, and a mixture of surprise and fear spread over his face as Chuck let go of his collar. "Shit!" He rolled to his side and stood, wobbling to the desk for support. "Does the sheriff know?"

"I just told you the sheriff is the one that called me!" Chuck grunted in frustration. "I don't know how much he knows."

Nate glanced down at his pants and then frowned in disgust. "Christ, did I piss myself?"

Chuck lunged forward and Nate recoiled. "The sheriff is going to ask you where you were tonight, and you'll tell him you got plastered with me in my office. You and me were here all night. Got it?"

"Y-yeah," Nate answered. "All night. Got it." When Chuck backed off Nate's body loosened again, and he nearly collapsed to the floor like a wet noodle, but he kept hold of the desk to keep him upright. "What are you going to do?"

Chuck shook his head. He'd done exactly what his own father had done. He'd even enlisted Billy, who'd done the dirty work before. There was no playbook for this mess. And suddenly, as if he were having one of his nightmares, Chuck saw the creature lurking in the back of his mind. Snarling, growling, waiting for the moment to strike. Those black eyes waiting to drag him into oblivion. And while his father said there wasn't any heaven, he never said anything about there not being a hell. And if he didn't end up in jail, that's exactly where that creature would take him if he didn't fix this soon.

* * *

CLAIRE NODDED, only half listening to the deputy's questions on the ride to the hospital. She kept thinking about her father, about Matt, about Owen, about what came next. "Chloe, sweetheart, sit still." Her daughter squirmed in her lap, and the deputy looked over.

"Mrs. Cooley, did you hear me?" Deputy Hurt asked.

"I'm sorry," Claire answered, Chloe burying her face into her chest.

"What was Matt wearing the last time you saw him?"

Claire sighed, exasperated, trying to think. "Um, he had a baseball shirt on. The Orioles. And gym shorts." She focused her dark brown eyes on the empty road. Morning was beginning to break, and the night sky lightened to grey.

During the six months where Owen was unemployed in Baltimore, that first part of the morning where the sunshine broke through the windows had been her favorite part of the day. There was something hopeful about a new beginning. Things could change. The page was blank, and you could write whatever you wanted.

"Mrs. Cooley?" Deputy Hurt asked.

"Hmm?"

"Have your children interacted with anyone in town? Or has anyone stopped by the house?"

"Um, no. We haven't seen anyone except the staff at the doctor's office and hospital." But now, staring up at the grey mud of a morning sky, that feeling of hope eluded her. She didn't know what to write on today's blank page, because she wanted to rip apart the whole book. "Have things like this happened before?" Claire looked over at him. "Have there been kidnappings in Ocoee?"

"Not during my tenure with the department."

Which couldn't have been for very long, Claire thought. The boy looked like he graduated high school last week, and the press of his uniform still had the creases from being taken out of the bag.

"How long have you been with the sheriff's department, Deputy Hurt?" Claire asked as Chloe shifted again in her lap.

"Seven weeks." Deputy Hurt's neck and cheeks flushed red, and he wiggled uncomfortably in his seat. "I may not know all of Ocoee's crime history, but I do know the SOP for a missing child, and I can tell you that Sheriff Bellingham won't skip on the details." He cleared his throat, trying to regain his nerve. "The sheriff runs a good department."

Claire hoped he did. She'd gotten a good feeling from the sheriff when he showed up. He wasn't oozing with personality and charm, but he was competent. She gently stroked Chloe's hair and her daughter started to calm down. "Any chance we can get there faster than this?"

Deputy Hurt straightened in his seat and stiffened his arms against the wheel, a hint of a smile on his face. "Yes, ma'am." The engine revved, and Deputy Hurt flicked on the lights and siren.

The rest of the trip was in silence, and when they arrived at the hospital, Deputy Hurt pulled right up to the ER doors and parked in one of the emergency lanes. He quickly ran around the car to her door like a valet hoping for a good tip and helped her and Chloe out of the cruiser.

The ER doors swooshed open and Claire caught a glimpse of the lobby. It was vacant, the patients inside waiting in misery with packs of ice over their injuries or wrapped up in bloodied gauze.

Claire passed them quickly as she found the nurses' desk, the deputy by her side commanding an attention that she wouldn't have gotten without him. "I'm Claire Cooley, I was told my father was asking for me?"

The nurse, dark circles stamped under her eyes and a nearly empty coffee cup next to her elbow, sluggishly got out of her seat and walked around the counter. "He woke up a few hours ago, screaming nonsense." The nurse led them past a few open rooms, the hospital quiet save for the few beeping machines she heard and the random paging of doctors and nurses over the PA system. "The doctors tried sedating him, but nothing has worked. It's quite... odd."

They turned a corner down the hallway, and Claire's heart skipped a beat when she heard the faint cry echoing through the tiled halls. The screams grew louder, and when they reached the end of another hallway and turned right, Claire saw that some of the other patients were out of their beds and peeking down the hall to the source of the noise.

"Matt! Get out of there! MAAAATT!!"

Chloe squeezed Claire tight, and she stopped, Deputy Hurt stopping with her while the nurse continued her walk toward Roger's room.

"Will you take her back to the lobby?" Claire asked.

"MAAAAATTTTT!!!"

Deputy Hurt's Adam's apple bobbed up and down as he nodded, extending his arms as Claire transferred Chloe over.

"I'll be right back." Claire kissed Chloe on the cheek and then jogged to catch up to the nurse. Her father's screams sounded unnatural. It was primal and fearful.

Claire slowly stepped into the room and saw her father struggling against the straps on the bed that kept him in place. The room was dark, and a pair of orderlies stood off to the side, watching him.

"I'll let the doctor know you're here," the nurse said.

It wasn't until the nurse was gone that Claire responded with a thank you. Her mind was elsewhere, back when she was a little girl and she sat on her father's lap. That felt so long ago.

"Dad," Claire said, walking up to the bedside. "Dad, you need to calm down."

Roger shook his head back and forth, his eyes wide open in a frenzied panic, the veins and muscles along his throat and neck throbbing and tight. "We have to get him out of there! MAAAATT!!"

A mixture of hope and confusion arose within Claire and she gripped her father by the shoulders. "Do you know where he is?"

Roger stopped his thrashing and his grey eyes locked onto her. "I saw what took him. I saw its eyes. Its eyes, Claire!"

Claire looked back to the orderlies still in the room, both

of them glaring at her like bouncers at a nightclub. "How long has he been screaming like this?"

"Hours," one of the orderlies said.

Claire turned back to Roger and saw that he had shut his eyelids. His eyeballs throbbed underneath the thin pieces of skin. "It's… cold. Very cold. And dead. Nothing's alive in that place."

"What place, Dad?" Claire didn't know how her father was seeing these things but the more her father spoke, the more she believed him. This wasn't his Alzheimer's.

"Your house," Roger answered, popping open his eyes. "You can't stay there, Claire. You have to get everyone out."

"No," Claire said, shaking her head. "Dad, Matt's not at the house. He was taken." Tears filled her eyes, and she realized that the tips of her fingers had whitened from the pressure she applied to her father's shoulder. "You said you saw him. Who took him, Dad? Who took Matthew?"

Roger sank deeper into his pillow, his voice growing toward a whisper. "I can hear him, Claire. He's scared. He wants to come home. But I can't—" His lip quivered. "I'm sorry, sweetheart. I'm sorry."

Claire lowered her forehead on Roger's arm and cried. It was all madness. Everything. Her father's disease. The house. Matt's abduction. None of it was meant for her or her family. This was some altered reality, not her life.

"I can feel that creature," Roger said softly. "It wants something."

Claire lifted her head, her eyes red and watering, a string of snot hanging from her lip. She wiped it away. "What does it want?"

"Something it can't get by itself." Roger shivered as he spoke, staring up at the ceiling. "It knows where it is, but it is forbidden to touch it."

Claire tucked her lower lip into her mouth and gently

stroked the thin wisps of hair on her father's head. "Dad, I don't know what you're talking about."

Roger turned to Claire, his expression dripping with desperation. "We have to go to her, Claire. She can help us. You have to take me to her!"

Claire clutched her father's hand. "Who?"

"Queen's."

Owen's gaze kept drifting back toward the cells. He could almost see the old man behind the bars, but the harsh angle blocked everything from view except for his hands. The same pair of hands that had held a knife to his wife's throat and smothered his daughter with a rag of chloroform.

"Mr. Cooley?" Bellingham asked.

"What?" Owen answered, turning back toward the sheriff.

Bellingham sighed in exasperation and then leaned forward over his desk, the man's hairy forearms thumping heavily over the report he was filling out. "Mr. Cooley, I understand the stress of the situation. But the faster you can help me understand what happened at your house, the quicker my people can get to work." He lifted his arms and flipped back a page on the report. "You said there was someone else there besides Billy and Jake?"

"Yeah." Owen fidgeted in the chair, his nerves fried from the long night, and the past three days, trying to figure out a way to explain what he'd seen for the tenth time.

"What did it look like?" Bellingham asked.

Owen rubbed his eyes, trying to ebb his growing frustration. "It was tall. About my height. It had grey, scaly skin, a big head with black eyes, and sharp teeth. And claws." Owen separated his hands and measured six inches. "They were this long, and black, like its eyes."

"I see." Bellingham paused, then looked down to his notes. "And have you had any problems with either Jake or Billy at work?"

Owen exhaled. "The only other co-worker I really interacted with was Marty Wiggins." He dropped his hand on his thigh with a slap. "Look, I've been here less than a week. You really think that's enough time for someone to develop a grudge like this?"

"Mr. Cooley, I'm just—"

"No!" Owen slammed his palm on the sheriff's desk. "I know what I saw. It wasn't a person, or an animal, or some guy in a fucking costume." Owen rose from the chair, leaning over the desk and inching closer to Bellingham's face. "Something snuck into my house, took my son, and then disappeared beneath the swamp. So put *that* in your goddamn report!"

Owen shoved the chair aside and it cracked against the floor as he stormed out of the sheriff's office. The receptionist jerked her head toward him on his way past, and when he reached for the handle of the front door to leave, it swung open, the first few rays of morning blinding him as a pair of shadowed figures stepped inside. He blinked rapidly, trying to rid himself of the sunspots that blinded him. When his vision cleared, Owen saw Mr. Toussaint and a man he didn't know.

"Owen," Mr. Toussaint said. "How are you holding up?"

Owen grabbed Chuck by the shoulders, harder than he intended. "Mr. Toussaint, something is going on at the house."

Mr. Toussaint recoiled a bit and then gestured to the stranger next to him. "Harold, you can go and speak with the sheriff in the back." He gently removed Owen's hands from his arms. "The sheriff filled me in. I can't imagine what you're going through."

Owen watched Harold walk past, his eyes following him until him until he disappeared into the sheriff's office. "Who is that?"

"Company lawyer," Chuck answered.

"You're protecting that guy?" Owen took a step back, his voice sharp.

"I'm protecting the company," Mr. Toussaint answered. "And if you need any legal help, I'd be glad to—"

"I don't need legal help. I need my son!" Owen pointed back toward the cells where the old man was locked up. "He knows something." He leaned close, catching a whiff of the faint scent of booze on Mr. Toussaint's shoulder that made him wrinkle his nose.

"Owen, it's best to let the law handle this. I don't want you to make anything worse." Mr. Toussaint reached for Owen's arm, but Owen knocked it away before it touched him.

"We don't need any more help from you." Owen shouldered Mr. Toussaint on his way past and stormed outside.

The harsh wall of damp heat smacked Owen's face and he violently kicked his van's tire, his foot jerking back harshly from the recoil of the rubber. He leaned against the door that was already hot from the morning sun, his head aching.

Every second that passed was one more that blurred the memories of last night. Had he seen something? Was it all in his head? From the outside looking in, he would have thought he was crazy too.

But there was more than just the creature that took his son. The house itself felt like it was alive. And Claire had seen things too. Owen shut his eyes, clinging to that knowledge. He just needed proof, a connection to the unexplainable. He turned, his eyes finding the narrow stretch of real estate outside of Queen's. He grimaced and clenched his fists.

Leaving his van at the sheriff's station, Owen marched across the street to the voodoo woman's store. The heat and hurried paced brought a gleaming sheen of sweat over his upper lip.

The windows to Queen's were darkened, and the contents normally strewn on the sidewalk had been pulled inside. It was still early, and the sign hanging on the door was flipped to close. Owen pressed his face against the glass, warm from the sun. "Hey!" He pounded on the door.

After receiving no answer, Owen stepped back. He reached for the handle and gave it a pull; a bell jingled as it opened. Owen lingered in the doorway, his eyes adjusting to the darkness inside. Slowly, he entered.

The door swung shut behind him, cutting off the sunlight that illuminated his entrance. It was quiet, and the musty scent of old wood filled the air. Owen maneuvered past the shelves and tables lined with odd and mysterious items: strange elixirs with names he couldn't pronounce, drawings of creatures he'd never seen, and jewelry made of bones, twigs, and rocks. There was an alternative beauty to the store, and he walked toward the glass case where a cash register sat on top, his eyes locked onto the painted skulls that rested inside.

"You have seen it."

Owen spun to his right and saw the old woman squinting at him. Thick cords of black hair cascaded down her back and over her shoulders. The earthy-brown colored dress she wore hung loosely on her body, and she supported herself with a tall staff that was warped like a crooked and deformed spine, a rock resting at the very top like a crown.

When she shifted her weight, a necklace of bones swayed. It was that same rattling of bones he remembered hearing when Matt was taken. His face twisted into a snarl. "What did you do?"

Madame Crepaux remained silent for a moment, then gave a gentle shake of her head. "Nothing."

"Nothing?" Owen's face was cast in shadows and those hot coals of rage burned in the pit of his stomach, stoking the flames of anger. "Then I guess it doesn't matter if I get the sheriff and have him take a look around." Owen spun around and headed for the door before he acted on the impulses racing through his head.

Owen's fingers grazed the door handle and he managed to pull it open an inch before it slammed shut, the bell at the top jingling violently. Owen turned back to the old woman who stood there in the same stoic manner, her weathered hands still gripping the staff.

"The police cannot help your son," Madame Crepaux said, the little flecks of yellow in her eyes glowing in the dark. "But you can."

Owen laughed, the chuckle soft at first, light-hearted and hysterical, and then faded with the shake of his head. "Lady, I don't know you." He stepped toward her, a drunken swagger to his movements. "My son is gone." His eyes teared up, and he gestured back toward the door. "And I think you're lying to cover up for yourself." He clenched his fists, but even as he drew closer to the old woman, she remained still. "You tell me where he is, and you tell me now." Owen came to a stop only inches from her face as his cheeks grew hot. "Because if you don't there is no amount of law and order that will stop me from hurting you."

The ground rattled beneath Owen's feet, vibrations running up through his legs. A jolt of panic rushed through him when he couldn't lift his feet. Madame Crepaux stepped backwards, her legs motionless behind the cover of her frumpy clothes, giving the illusion that she was floating. Or maybe it wasn't an illusion.

"You must see now, Owen Cooley," Madame Crepaux said. "You must understand what you will face, what your son is facing now." She pounded the end of her staff against the floor, and the rock at the staff's crown illuminated.

Owen lifted his hands to shield himself from the bright light, his feet still glued to the floor which shook more violently now. A crack split between his feet, the fault line cutting the floor in quick, jagged movements. His eyes widened in terror and he looked back up to the woman still staring at him, those yellow eyes brighter than the stone at the top of her staff.

"Keep your eyes open." Madame Crepaux lifted the staff and then pounded the floor again, which widened the crack into a dark crevasse between Owen's legs.

Owen screamed as he fell, flipping over and over, his stomach swirling from the sensation of free fall. His scream suddenly cut out and he jerked to a stop harshly. His feet gently touched solid ground and his knees buckled slightly as the weightlessness disappeared, though the darkness remained.

A soft glow appeared like a cloud in the distance, and Owen stopped dead in his tracks. He squinted, unsure of what it was. It took shape slowly, growing larger.

It looked like the swamp outside his house, but was filtered through a grey haze. Owen squinted, trying to understand what he was seeing, and that was when he saw his son. "Matt!" Owen's voice echoed throughout the darkness. He sprinted toward his boy, who lay motionless on the ground. "Matt!" But no matter how fast he ran, his son remained far off in the distance, trapped in that cloudy glow.

And then, just before Owen was about to scream again,

that creature appeared, stepping from the darkness of the swamp.

"No!" Owen's legs churned faster, his body a blur in the darkness. The creature bent down, its claws outstretched in preparation for an attack. Tears blurred Owen's vision, his heart pounding frantically in his chest, shaking his whole body.

The glow faded, and Owen stretched out his arms. "Matt! MATT!" A force tugged at his stomach and he was sucked from the darkness.

Another flash of light, and Owen felt the grain of wood beneath his palms. He blinked rapidly, his body covered in sweat. A black, weathered hand was thrust into the plane of his vision, and he looked up to the stoic expression on Madame Crepaux's face, the bright glow of her eyes gone. He grabbed hold of her hand, her strength surprising as she helped him to his feet.

"What was that?" Owen asked.

"A glimpse into a world that you must enter to save your son," Madame Crepaux answered. "And it must be done quickly. Come." She turned, and Owen followed.

The room was small. In its center was a table with a large, shallow basin resting on it with water as black as the eyes of the creature.

"The creature that took your boy is Bacalou. And it is a cursed thing. Born from the great spirits Damballah, god of snakes and protector of trees and water, and Baron Samedie, the god of death. It controls the dead and the nature of this world." She circled the basin as she spoke, the tip of her finger running along the edge, then stopped when she reached the opposite side of the table, raising her eyes to him.

Unlike the coldness Owen felt when he saw the monster, a warm sensation bubbled in his chest. It was as if he had known her for a long time, and as she closed the distance between them, he caught the scent of her breath as she spoke. It was hot, but sweet.

"Fathers will risk much for their children. Especially their sons," Madame Crepaux said. "What are you willing to risk, Owen Cooley?"

Owen stiffened, but his voice cracked. "Whatever it takes."

Madame Crepaux's lips curled in a smile, and she patted Owen's left cheek. She turned to a shelf lined with different-colored elixirs next to the skull of a small gator then returned to the shallow bowl filled with black water.

"How did this even happen?" Owen asked. "Why my son?"

Madame Crepaux began mixing the ingredients together. "Over a century ago, the house where your family now lives belonged to a powerful Voodoo Queen. She was a healer. Stories of her abilities spread throughout the swamp lands, and her name became a whisper of hope. Samba."

She closed her eyes and a single tear rolled down her face. "A father heard of the Queen's powers and brought his dying son to her to save his life. But the boy was too far gone, and in the Queen's attempt to save him, the boy died." The floor groaned as she stepped toward Owen. "The father's grief drove him mad, and he blamed Queen Samba for his son's death. He turned the town against her and raided her home, sentencing her to death by fire." A half-smile curved up the side of the woman's face. "But the Queen used the father's rage and grief against him, setting a curse on his family that would last until the last roots of his family tree were dead. She conjured Bacalou to kill every firstborn male of the Toussaint family that was taken by the creature. The Queen's curse stole son after son from the man's family until one of the man's descendants bribed a bokor to try and end the curse. But the Queen's gris-gris was too powerful to be broken without the destruction of the family's bloodline, so the bokor channeled the curse into an amulet, keeping the creature tied to the Queen's former house and grounds. But the creature still required a firstborn son's soul to be sacrificed every twenty-five years to keep it contained. That is the reason you were brought here, Owen Cooley. Your son was taken so the heir of Charles Toussaint could live."

Owen stumbled backward, his head spinning, his stomach churning at the fate he'd sentenced his own son. *He* made the decision to take the job. *He* moved his family in that house. *He* refused to believe that there was anything wrong until it was too late. And now it could cost him his son's life. Chuck may have laid the trap, but Owen took the bait. "How do I stop it?"

"There is an amulet that keeps Bacalou chained to the house and its grounds. It protects the heir of the Toussaints. And it is the key to unlock the door into the creature's world." Madame Crepaux guided Owen to the table where the basin sat. "I have tried to retrieve the amulet myself, but the Bokor who forged it ensured that no other follower of Voodoo could set foot on that land." She pressed her finger into his chest. "I have waited a long time for you, Owen Cooley. Bon Dieu guided your family here so you could end this evil and restore the balance of the spirits. It is time for wrongs to be righted."

The house. Mr. Toussaint. The move. All of it swirled in Owen's mind, the connections slowly coming together. He looked to Madame Crepaux, a sense of clarity washing over him. "Chuck sent Billy and Jake to kill us so there wouldn't be any questions after my son was taken. He was just going to… erase us."

Madame Crepaux nodded gravely. "It was what his father taught him, and his father before him. He will do whatever he can to keep himself alive. He is dangerous, and he has influence in this town. He will use all of it to keep your son in the creature's possession and then silence you and your family."

The lawyer, Owen thought. Chuck came to the sheriff's station to make sure the old man didn't talk. He grabbed hold of Madame Crepaux, her arms bone thin under the bulky robes. "My family. I have to get them someplace safe."

"Your wife will call you soon." Madame Crepaux gripped the sides of the basin and stared into the blackness. "She will bring your father-in-law, and your daughter." She lifted her head. "They will be safe here."

"My father-in-law?" Owen asked.

"He was in contact with the creature and now shares a connection with the beast," Madame Crepaux answered. "Once you bring me the amulet I will need that connection to help open the portal to the creature's world."

Owen glanced down into the bowl that the woman was so intently focused on. He wasn't sure what she saw, but only his reflection stared back at him. "How is all of this even possible?"

"In Voodoo, the primordial god Bon Dieu works through the spirits and souls of this earth to test us." Madame Crepaux lifted her eyes to the ceiling with an expression of uncertainty. "Even the most studied and powerful bokors and priestesses cannot fully understand Bon Dieu's purpose. But I have learned that Bon Dieu values life and balance. And that is what we must restore." She turned toward Owen. "But we must hurry."

Madame Crepaux touched the center of the black water in the basin, which sent a ripple to the edges of the bowl. "The creature is draining your son's soul as we speak. And if we cannot retrieve him by midnight tonight he will be lost forever."

Owen started to speak, but stopped when his phone

buzzed in his pocket. He retrieved it and gave Madame Crepaux a quick look of disbelief as he saw Claire's number.

"Claire." Owen closed his eyes as she started to tell him everything that happened. "I know. I-I know, listen. Discharge your father from the hospital and then bring him and Chloe to the voodoo shop on Main Street. It's called Queen's." He opened his eyes and looked at Madame Crepaux. "I know how to get Matthew back."

---

*B*illy saw a sliver of Chuck as he entered the sheriff's office, but it was only a quick glance. The view between the bars of the cell were narrow, and after the door closed, he retreated to the back of his cell, snarling, exposing that silver-capped tooth.

The tooth had been chipped during a fight in high school. Lenny Calhoun called him a pussy and that he came from a whole family of pussies. And without a word, Billy rammed his fist into Lenny's face and knocked him to the ground flat. But with Lenny on his ass, Billy didn't stop.

A rage, deep within Billy's heart, bubbled to the surface. It was a rage born from the dirt floor shack he lived in with his parents. Rage from the stares he received in the hallways at school with his dirty shirt and pants that were hand-me-downs from his older brother, his feet flopping in shoes that were too big with holes in the toes. Rage from the frustration in his studies, and the fact that no matter how much time he put into his homework, he couldn't muster anything higher than a C-. And with every punch he landed on Lenny's face, Billy's smile widened.

"Knock it off, Billy!" Sam Leland had tried to pull him off, and Billy had jabbed him in the ribs. That had made Sam's older brother shove Billy from behind and sent him sprawling onto the concrete where he chipped that front tooth.

It hurt worse than a bee sting, and he cursed and groaned as he rolled to his side, Lenny's motionless body right beside him. "Fuck, Johnny! What'd you do that for?" The tooth's exposed nerve sent a spasm of pain for every breath that passed over it. It was like someone stuck a knife in his mouth.

Lenny Calhoun had to go to the hospital, but he kept his mouth shut about who beat the piss out of him. And that was how Billy learned how fear worked. You hurt someone bad enough, and they'll do whatever you want. Fear was the tool he could use to get himself out of the piss-poor, dirt-floored, tin roof shack that he had been born into. And he did.

Billy Rouche graduated high school by the skin of his teeth and the very next day, he walked himself down to the auto parts factory dressed in the nicest clothes he could find in his daddy's drawers, and burst right into Charles Toussaint's office, interrupting a meeting. He'd told Mr. Toussaint that he'd do any job he'd give him and he'd do it better than anyone as long as there was the promise of a bigger paycheck down the road.

That boldness and determined spirit earned Billy a job, and Mr. Toussaint took an immediate liking to him. And so he worked his way out of that shithole shack and moved into one of the factory-owned housing units. It had power and tiled flooring with carpet in the bedroom. To Billy Rouche, it was a palace.

And so Billy worked for the Toussaints doing whatever the boss asked him to do, knowing that his reward would come Friday when he picked up his paycheck. He developed a rapport with Mr. Toussaint, and in those early years as a young man, he began to look at Mr. Toussaint as a father figure. The man was everything Billy wanted to be: rich and powerful. And he'd do anything to get there.

So when Billy's adopted father pulled him aside at the end of his shift twenty-five years ago and opened a crystal bottle and poured him a glass of the finest bourbon he'd ever tasted, he didn't hesitate for the job that Mr. Toussaint had in store for him.

All he had to do was kill some family that just moved into town. Husband, wife, and daughter. And in return, Billy would get a new house, higher salary, and a trip to New Orleans for a few weeks where he'd be set up with cash, liquor, and women.

And so he did it. He killed all three of those people at that house on Cypress Lane and then partied his ass off for three weeks in New Orleans. He screwed women he'd never even dreamed of and thought himself a king.

It was like that for a while, until Mr. Toussaint retired and his pissant son took over the factory. And if it weren't for everything that Mr. Toussaint had done for him, Billy probably would have quit after that first year. But Mr. Toussaint came to him one night after announcing his retirement and asked Billy for one last job.

Mr. Toussaint had brought over that same bourbon they'd shared so many years before, and to Billy it tasted just as good as he remembered. "My son will come to you one day in the future and ask you to do the same thing I did. Will you stay on and do that for me, Billy?"

"Sure, Mr. Toussaint," Billy answered, and then Mr. Toussaint smiled and they finished that bourbon together, talking about women and gambling and liquor until both were too drunk to even remember why they were drinking in the first place.

Last night, he'd tried to keep his promise to Mr. Toussaint. But the result wasn't the same, and he'd spent the past several hours in that cell feeling like he did when he walked the halls of his high school: a failure.

The sound of the sheriff's door opening and mumbled conversations drifted through the cell bars and pulled him from his memories. A few minutes later, the sheriff appeared. The old man put his fists on his hips and glared at Billy like a rabid dog.

"Problem, Sheriff?" Billy asked.

"You've got friends with deep pockets." Bellingham gripped the bars with those old hands. Hands that Billy knew hurt from years of work, just like his did. "Who told you to go to the Cypress house, Billy?"

Billy scratched at his chin which lay under a thick tuft of white beard. "Did I make bail?"

"You did."

Billy flicked a piece of dirt under his fingernail to the floor. "The law says that if I make bail, I get to leave." He smiled a little when he saw the sheriff's grimace. It was nice when the law worked for you instead of against you. And it didn't hurt that it also pissed Bellingham off.

Bellingham removed a set of keys from his pocket, and the lock in the old jail cell clanged loudly as he turned the key. The hinges groaned as the door to freedom opened, and Billy's knees popped as he pushed himself off the cot. A petulant smile creased his lips after he walked past the sheriff and toward the station's exit.

"Don't leave town, Billy," Bellingham said.

Billy flipped the sheriff the bird and then squinted into the sunshine on his way out. The sunlight hurt his eyes and it wasn't until he heard the horn honk to his left that he saw the black sedan. It was one of Chuck's cars. The passenger side door opened, and Billy made his way over. Once inside, he shut the door. "Took you long enough to—"

Chuck gripped Billy's collar and pulled him across the seat. A drop of spittle landed onto Chuck's chin as he wrung Billy's shirt. "What the hell happened last night? You were supposed to finish them off. And now they're going to the police?" Chuck shoved Billy away. "This wasn't supposed to happen!"

"Owen got the drop on Jake," Billy said, smoothing out the front of his shirt.

"And where the hell is he?" Chuck asked, his tone irritated.

"I don't know," Billy answered, adding his own note of frustration. "He's probably hiding out in one of his uncle's shacks in the swamp."

Chuck massaged his temples and then rubbed his eyes. "I want this swept up before it gets anymore out of hand."

"And how would you like me to do that?"

"This didn't happen before!" Chuck screamed. "My father said I could trust you when this day came! If I'd known that you'd fuck it up, I'd have hired someone else to do it."

Billy sat in the seat, thinking back to the time when he knocked Lenny Calhoun to the ground and how he'd like to do that to the pissant sitting next to him. But the memory of Mr. Toussaint kept his hands from curling into fists and giving Chuckie Toussaint a few silver teeth of his own. "We just need to find Jake."

Chuck stewed in his anger, but after being unable to figure out a solution for his own problem, he went along. "You said he's at his uncle's?"

"That's where I'd start looking."

"Fine. Tell me where."

Billy gave the directions through the back roads, a smile on his face at the thought of Chuck's expensive shoes and nice slacks being ruined after a trek through the Louisiana swamp.

* * *

AS OWEN HELD CHLOE, Claire and Roger listened to Madame Crepaux speak. The longer the old woman spoke, the paler Claire's cheeks became. Nausea spread from the pit of her stomach and outward to her arms, legs, and head. Everything ached and when the woman had finished her piece, Claire turned toward Owen, tears in her eyes.

"You believe her?" Claire asked.

"Yeah," Owen answered.

It was Owen's steady tone that convinced her more than the word itself. Claire nodded and then looked at her father, who she wasn't even sure understood everything that the woman had said. "Dad, are you all right?"

Roger nodded, then turned to Madame Crepaux. "What do I have to do?"

"Come with me." Madame Crepaux took Roger's arm and led him to another room in the back. "We must make your mind stronger."

Roger followed hesitantly as Claire let the news sink in. She walked over to Owen, who was gently rubbing Chloe's back after falling asleep in her father's arms. "If Chuck knew about this, then we have to tell the police."

"We tell them the truth and they'll ask us for proof," Owen replied. "They're not going to believe us, and they're sure as hell not going to believe that woman."

"So he just gets away with it?" Claire asked.

"You heard what she said," Owen answered. "We have until midnight tonight to get Matt back. We worry about that first, then we'll deal with Chuck." He stood and handed Chloe back to Claire, the girl still fast asleep even after the exchange. "I want you and Chloe to stay here with your dad. Don't leave, not even if it's to go to the police. I'm not convinced that the sheriff isn't on Chuck's payroll."

"So we just trust her then?" Claire asked, looking back at the room where the woman had disappeared with her father, her mind noting that she at least left the door open.

"She doesn't have any reason to lie to us," Owen answered.

But Claire wasn't sure if she believed him. She noticed the expression of disdain on the woman's face every time she spoke about Chuck's family and what they did to that Voodoo Queen. Not that Claire was fond of Chuck herself, but there was something to be said about vendettas.

She remembered when she was seven and told her best friend Betty Davidson that she liked Tommy Hursh, and made her promise to keep it a secret. Betty said she would, but the next day on the playground, Claire watched Betty kiss Tommy on the cheek and the pair "dated" for about a week before they called it off.

Seven-year-old Claire was pissed, and she not only broke off her friendship with Betty, but kept hold of that rage all through second grade, just waiting for a chance to get back at her, and eventually an opportunity presented itself.

Samantha Wurley spilled the beans to Claire one day at lunch that Betty was afraid of spiders. So that night after dinner, with the hot coals of revenge stoked in her belly, she walked to the oak tree in her backyard where she'd seen spiders crawling around, armed with a piece of plastic Tupperware she stole from the kitchen, to try and catch one.

Unbeknownst to seven-year-old Claire, the spiders that she had so rightly avoided on that oak tree were Brown Recluse spiders. And when she reached out to grab one, it bit her hand, and she sprinted back to the house crying, her revenge on Betty Davidson the farthest thing from her mind.

Vomiting, fever, and aches followed for the next several hours, and she missed almost a week of school. After she'd felt better, her father asked her what she had been doing and she broke down crying. She came clean and told him what she'd planned to do. After she was done, her father remained quiet for a moment and then wiped the tears from her eyes.

"People hurt other people, Claire," her father said, his calloused hands on her cheek. "But you can't let the actions of others define who you are."

"What do you mean?" Claire asked.

"You only acted this way because of what Betty did, right?"

"Yeah," Claire answered sheepishly.

"You changed your behavior based off how someone else treated you, and look what happened." He leaned in close enough to where she could smell his aftershave, that oily, wood scent on his cheeks. "That's not who you are."

Claire lowered her eyes, and all the rage and revenge that had accumulated inside of her transformed into shame and guilt.

"Hate will eat you up inside until there's nothing left in you but fear. And when you reach that point, there isn't any turning back. Be strong, Claire. Keep hold of hope even when it's dark."

And for the past thirty years, that's exactly what Claire did. She just needed to do it a little while longer. She turned to Owen and kissed his lips. "Be careful."

"I will."

Claire's stomach twisted into knots as the door closed behind Owen. But she clung to the hope that they'd get Matthew back, and she stayed strong for the family here with her now. She set Chloe down in a chair and walked back to the room where the woman had taken her father. She saw him lying flat on a table. Madame Crepaux hovered over him, her hands floating over his chest. A low, throaty hum escaped her lips, and she slowed her hands to match the rhythm of her voice, then gently laid them on Roger's chest.

"This won't hurt him, will it?" Claire asked.

"No," Madame Crepaux answered.

Claire stepped to her father's side and gently took hold of his hand. "Do you know what he's sick with?"

Madame Crepaux raised a finger and then tapped the side of her skull. "His mind wanders in darkness, searching for a light he cannot find. The deeper he walks, the more lost he becomes."

"What is all of this?" Claire asked, examining some of the elixirs, herbs, and odd jewelry in the room.

"A collection of my knowledge." Madame Crepaux raised the bowl to her nose and sniffed. She brought the bowl to Roger's lips and helped raise his head to drink.

Claire jolted forward, stretching out her hand in protest. "What is that?"

"Gris-gris," the woman answered. "This will help light the path of his mind."

"It's okay, Claire," Roger said. "I can do it." He looked at her like he did on that day thirty years ago in her room when she'd told him about the spider. It was the strongest she'd seen him in a long time.

Claire removed her hand and her father sipped the purple water from the bowl, some of it spilling down the corners of his mouth, until it was gone.

"Not the tastiest concoction," Roger said, grimacing.

"Your mind will feel lighter, but your body will grow heavy," Madame Crepaux said, reaching for her staff with the skull on it. She walked around to the head of the table and placed one hand over Roger's eyes while the other gripped her staff. She tilted her face toward the ceiling and inhaled deeply. "Calla-Wem-Oola-Shan-Deelo." She ended the chant with a heavy thump of her staff. "Calla-Wem-Oola-Shan-Deelo." Another hard smack between staff and floor rattled the room. "Calla-Wem-Oola-Shan-Deelo."

Claire jerked from the loud thump of the next hit, and she noticed that her father's muscles relaxed, his mouth growing slack.

"CALLA-WEM-OOLA-SHAN-DEELO!"   Madame Crepaux slammed her staff against the floor and the entire room darkened, a rush of cold sweeping over Claire's body like a frigid winter wind.

The cold and sheer panic of the moment made her heart pound like a jackhammer in her chest. Claire turned around to look at Chloe, who was still sound asleep in her chair.

"It's dark," Roger said.

Claire whipped her head back around and saw her father still as pond water, his glowing eyes staring up at the ceiling.

"You are between worlds now," Madame Crepaux said, gently running her fingertip over his forehead in the shape of a cross.

"Everything looks dead," Roger said, a tinge of horror in his voice. "It's colorless."

Claire squeezed her father's hand that had turned cold as ice as his eyes wandered over the ceiling.

"There are trees, and a cemetery." Roger swallowed, his Adam's apple bobbing up and down. "The house. I can see it from the swamp across the clearing."

"The creature's world is replicated out of the prison from which he cannot leave," Crepaux said.

"W-wait." His voice grew soft, but excited. "I think I see something. Matt. Matt!" He called out like her son was there in the room with them. "He turned. I think he heard me. Matt!"

"Grandpa?" The weak voice echoed through the room, and Claire quickly covered her gasp.

"Yeah," Roger answered happily. "It's me. Are you all right?"

"I feel tired," Matt answered, his voice muffled and distant.

"Matt?" Claire asked, her voice thick with grief. "Can you hear me?"

"Only your father can speak with him," the woman said.

Claire clawed at her dad's arm. "Tell him that I miss him and love him and that we're going to get him out of that place soon." Tears rolled down her cheeks as her dad relayed the message.

"Mom's there?" Matt asked.

"I'm here, baby," Claire answered aloud. She shut her eyes, whispering to herself. "I'm always with you."

"Roger," Madame Crepaux said. "Ask your grandson the color of the sky."

Roger cleared his throat and repeated the message, and they waited, Claire wiping her eyes.

"It was grey, but it's closer to black now," Matt replied. "Like night, but darker."

Claire looked to Madame Crepaux for an understanding of what that meant, but the old woman's face hardened as she returned to her herbs and potions. "Is that bad? Good?"

"Our window is closing faster than I expected." Madame Crepaux dumped one of the potions into the bowl and then sprinkled green bits of herbs over it.

"AHHH!" Matt's scream pierced the air of the room.

"Matt? Matt!" Claire shook her father. "Dad, what is it?"

"I-I don't know," Roger answered. "I can't see anything anymore." The glow from his eyes began to fade. "Matt!"

"Mom! Help!" Matt's voice was breathless and panicked.

"I'm here, baby!" Claire searched the darkness of the room as if she could find him.

Matt sobbed loudly. "It's coming for me again… it's going to… to— AHHH—"

The darkness of the room faded and the lights returned as the glow from Roger's eyes disappeared. He blinked rapidly as the familiar dark brown replaced the glowing light. He looked to Claire when he was done, and she lunged for him, wrapping her arms around his neck like she did when she was a little girl. "Daddy."

"It's all right, Claire," Roger said, patting her on the back. "He's going to be fine. He's strong. Just like you."

Claire shut her eyes hard, squeezing him tighter.

"Mommy?"

Claire turned around and saw Chloe standing in the doorway, sleepily rubbing her left eye. She walked over and scooped Chloe off the ground and kissed her cheek. "It's okay, baby. Everything's fine."

"Is Matt here?"

Claire kissed the side of Chloe's head again. "No, baby."

Madame Crepaux handed Roger another elixir. "Drink this, it will help keep your strength up."

"Why couldn't he hear me?" Claire asked, tears lingering in her eyes.

Madame Crepaux leaned against the cabinet of potions and mixtures. "He is in Bacalou's world. And Bacalou controls what he sees, what he hears." The flecks of yellow in her eyes offered a light glow as she set her eyes on Claire. "And as Bacalou grows stronger, he will have more control over his world and ours."

Owen, Claire thought. "And what does that mean for my family?"

Madame Crepaux's face darkened. "More pain."

*C*huck grimaced as he lifted his Italian shoes out of the Louisiana mud, the black color hidden underneath all those clumps of grey. A mosquito buzzed around his neck, and he slapped his reddening skin that baked under the hot summer sun.

Billy was up ahead, periodically glancing back at Chuck with a smirk on his face. Laugh it up, Chuck thought. He knew the old geezer had never taken to Chuck like he had with his father, and the feeling was mutual.

"How much farther is this fucking place?" Chuck asked, his suit pants shin deep in the stagnant swamp water.

"Not sure," Billy hollered back.

"No shit, old man," Chuck said, muttering under his breath, losing his balance as another section of mud swallowed him up.

The only positive Chuck had pulled from the long trek out into the middle of Bum-Fuck-Egypt was the time to think about his next moves. And so far every solution had its complications.

Only three other people knew about his intentions with the Cooley family at the house on Cypress Lane. The first was his real estate agent, Nate, who he knew would keep his mouth shut out of fear of jail time.

The second was Billy, but despite Billy's disdain for him, Chuck didn't think the old timer would rat. The old man was too stubborn and too proud. He'd think he'd be dishonoring the memory of Chuck's father.

The third was Jake, and out of the three, he presented the most trouble. He was younger, less loyal, and money hungry. It'd been why Chuck had picked him to help with the job in the first place. He liked people who could be bought. It made things easier. But even money had its limits.

"Got something," Billy said, stopping near a tree up ahead.

Chuck caught up and followed Billy's finger toward a sliver of a cabin on a raised platform above the water. It wasn't any bigger than a shack, but Chuck saw its advantages. The occupant had a three-hundred sixty-degree view of anyone coming their way.

Chuck wiped his brow, the sweat coming off him in buckets. "You think he's there?"

"Maybe," Billy answered. "But we better be careful. After what happened, he's bound to be trigger happy."

Chuck felt the weight of his own revolver tucked in the back of his waistband. It was a last resort, but one that he hadn't ruled out.

"Jake! It's Billy and Chuck! Don't shoot!"

Chuck grew fidgety and Billy kept his hands in the air as they pushed through the stagnant swamp water. Billy shouted again, but the shack remained quiet. Chuck squinted through the tree branches to try and find any movement.

"You alone?" Jake asked, his voice echoing.

"Yeah," Billy answered. "Just the two of us."

"I've got a bead on you, so you better not be lyin'," Jake said.

Chuck eventually saw the barrel of Jake's rifle sticking out of the corner of one of the windows. It followed them to the stepladder on the east side of the shack, and then finally retreated when he couldn't keep a line of sight from the window's harsh angle.

Water and mud fell from their shoes on the way up the ladder, and when Chuck stepped through the shadowed entrance, it took a minute for his eyes to adjust to his surroundings.

The inside of the shack was bare bones: A cot sat in the corner, which was probably the source of the mildew scent that graced Chuck's nostrils, a table, one chair, and an old iron stove with a top for cooking. No source of fresh water that he could see, and no food to cook. And Jake looked more ragged for it.

"How the hell'd you get here?" Jake asked, the rifle lowered but still clutched in his hands against his stomach.

"You blabbered about this place last month at the poker game," Billy said, panting. "You got water?"

"No." Jake turned to Chuck and grimaced. "You said this was supposed to be an easy job."

"It was," Chuck answered. "They didn't know you were coming. What the hell happened?"

"You said they'd be scared, that they wouldn't put up a fight!" Jake rotated his shoulders, sulking. "So what the hell do we do now?"

"Cops are looking for you," Billy answered.

"No shit," Jake replied. "You think I'd come out here for a vacation?"

"My lawyer was able to get Billy out on bail," Chuck said. "You turn yourself in and I can get you the same deal."

"Like hell I'll turn myself in!" Jake stiffened, and Chuck's eyes immediately fell to the rifle.

"It's our word against theirs," Chuck said. "You do exactly as the lawyer tells you to do and you get out of this with minimal jail time."

"Jail time?" Jake paced the floor, rifle still in hand, shaking his head. His muscles tensed. "No way. Not this Cajun."

Heat and fatigue drained Chuck's remaining patience. He lunged forward, teeth bared. "Listen to me, you redneck prick! You don't get a deal until you turn yourself in, and the only way you're going to get out of this alive is if you do what I tell you. Got it?"

Jake's knuckles whitened over the stock of his rifle and his cheeks burned a fire red. "You think you're still calling the shots, boss man?" Quick as a snake bite, Jake raised the rifle, and Chuck found himself staring down the dark barrel less than a foot from the tip of his nose.

"Easy, Jake," Billy said, the floorboards groaning as he took a step toward both of them. "We need him to get out of this. He's got the money to make all of this go away, don't you?"

"Yeah," Chuck answered, his voice wavering, his thoughts already wrapped around the revolver tucked in his waistband. "I got the money."

Jake puffed quick, short breaths from his nostrils, and when the floorboards groaned again from Billy's direction, Jake aimed the rifle at the old man. "Don't move!"

With the rifle aimed away from him, Chuck reached for the gun, but the first tug made it catch on his belt. By then Jake saw Chuck's movements and shifted his aim. With his hand still behind his back, Chuck sprinted into Jake, knocking both men to the floor with a loud crack from some of the wood planks that fractured beneath their weight.

The pair grappled, the rifle wedged between them, and

Chuck felt hands groping his shoulders, pulling him back. He flung his elbow backward, connecting with a thick hunk of muscle, and he heard Billy gasp for breath and the hands released him.

Jake thrust his knee up, catching Chuck in the gut, and then bucked Chuck off him. Chuck rolled to the side, and Jake scrambled to his feet to try and fire the weapon, but the long rifle barrel made it awkward to handle in the tight space.

Chuck finally freed the revolver from his waistband, and Jake's eyes bulged from their sockets as Chuck drew down on him. He squeezed the trigger, the harsh recoil from the gun reverberating up his arm and the high-pitched whine of gunfire ringing in his ears.

Chuck blinked away the gun smoke and saw the first bullet missed wide left. He squeezed the trigger again, and the second bullet connected with Jake's gut, where it spread a bloom of red over his grimy wifebeater that dripped down the front of his pants. The third and fourth shots smacked his chest and dropped him to the floor.

High on adrenaline, Chuck didn't even feel the heavy impact of Billy ramming into his shoulder, knocking them over. Billy pinned Chuck down, keeping the hand with the revolver pressed against the floor as he reached for Jake's rifle.

"GAAHHRR!" Chuck flopped his body on the floor, trying to buck Billy off him, and his right knee grazed Billy's ribs with enough impact to knock some of the wind out of the old man. Billy rallied and lunged again, this time landing a fist under Chuck's chin.

The blow chattered Chuck's teeth together, and a hot burst of warmth flooded over his tongue as he tasted the metallic flavor of his own blood, and the pair twisted like snakes over the floor.

Billy cocked his free left arm back and rammed it awkwardly into Chuck's head and stomach. Chuck twisted away, the dull ache from the blow lingering at the points of impact. Eventually, Chuck rolled to his stomach, and Billy's weight disappeared.

Chuck turned and saw Billy's backside as he scrambled toward the rifle next to Jake's body. Billy snatched the rifle on the run and then jumped through the window. Chuck aimed for Billy's back, but exhaustion from the scuffle stole his accuracy. The bullets splintered the wood around the window, missing Billy on his escape.

A harsh plunk of water broke through the deafening whine from the gunshots, and Chuck scrambled to his feet, rushing over to the window and looking over the side where he saw nothing except the remnant ripples of the splash.

With his body aching, he turned away from the window, clutching his ribs where Billy had struck him. Jake's lifeless eyes stared upward. The hot scent of blood, guts, and fresh bowel movement emptied from Jake's body combined with the thick, humid heat of the cabin churned Chuck's stomach and he hunched over, spewing up the food he'd shoveled down just a few hours ago.

Chuck wiped his mouth along his sleeve and watched the vomit mix into Jake's blood. The sight triggered another gag, but he managed to keep the rest of his breakfast down. His throat and chest burned from the vomit, and he stomped away from the body, bursting outside to the fresh air and away from the scent of death.

A gunshot thundered, and a geyser of splinters shot up through the decrepit floorboards. In a motion that was more instinct than practical, Chuck covered his head and sprinted back inside the shack, the bullets following him in periodic fashion.

Billy was underneath, screaming as he fired round after

round through the shack's floor. Chuck cowered in a corner as bullets exploded through the rotten wood.

"Fuck you, Chuck! Fuck you!" The shouts were spit intermittently between gunshots, and Chuck covered his ears, trying to block out both noises. "You prissy little mamma's boy!"

Chuck flinched at another gunshot, and then silence. He opened his eyes, shivering, but didn't move from the corner until he heard the hurried swoosh of legs in water below.

Chuck sprinted onto the wraparound porch, squinting between the thick clusters of trees. The swoosh of legs faded, and Chuck circled the tiny catwalk porch and spotted a shoulder and arm between two tree trunks. He raised his revolver and fired, the bullet ricocheting off bark.

Billy spun around at the sound of the gunshot, and for a brief moment the pair locked eyes and Chuck saw that silver-capped tooth revealed behind a snarl.

Chuck squeezed the trigger again, screaming as the gunshots veered aimlessly into trees, then lowered the .38 in frustration, breathing heavily, wiping the collection of snot from his upper lip. Billy was gone.

Chuck leaned back into the wall and collapsed on the floor. It was all slipping away. Billy would go to the police and tell them everything.

In the growing afternoon heat, Chuck inhaled the stink of the swamp, and he suddenly grew hot with a hate that permeated through his bones. He hated this town, this state, the whole goddamn swamp. His eyes watered like a toddler in a tantrum.

All of it was stupid. It wasn't his fault that his family was cursed. It wasn't his fault that Billy and Jake were too incompetent to get their jobs done. It wasn't his fault Jake had run out here in the middle of nowhere and shoved him to the ground. He wasn't dead set on killing, but Jake forced his hand. What choice did he have?

Chuck glanced at Jake's body. The blood had stopped pouring from the gunshot wounds, and a few bugs began to circle the corpse. He opened the revolver's chamber. One bullet left. Chuck slapped the wood and cursed. He'd have to make the last bullet count.

15

The van's brakes squealed as Owen stopped in front of the house and then killed the engine. A humid wave of heat blasted his body when he stepped outside and walked toward the front door. The windows were darkened, and police tape guarded the entrance in a yellow shaped X. Even in the daylight, the house looked ominous.

Inside, the police had left their boot-prints all over the floor of the living room. A few items were tagged, but it was mostly left the way they found it. Owen lingered in the living room, half-expecting to find the home infested with snakes and spiders upon his arrival, the walls oozing blood and the floor covered in a thick layer of Louisiana muck. But the normalcy provided its own horror. It was like nothing had happened.

Owen reached into his pocket and removed the picture Madame Crepaux had given him of the amulet. The drawing was old and faded, but it was a clear enough picture. The amulet was a simple green stone wrapped with thin strips of deer leather in a spider web pattern. But while he knew what the amulet looked like, neither he nor Madame Crepaux knew where in the house it resided, so Owen started with the living room first.

Couch cushions were thrown from the sofa, chairs over-turned, and books flung from shelves, their pages scanned quickly. After the room was torn apart and messy, he entered the kitchen.

Pots and pans clanged against the floor, and Owen left a wake of opened cupboards and drawers as he traversed the long counters, working his way to the dining room. There he opened more drawers, checked closets and the china cabinets along the walls, finding nothing but cobwebs.

Next came his bedroom, then Roger's room, then the downstairs bathroom where he found a cluster of dead roaches piled beneath the sink, their paper-thin exoskeletons nearly disintegrated from the gust of wind when Owen opened the cabinet door.

Sweating now, he hurried up the stairs and searched Chloe's room. He went through her things more gently, knowing he'd catch hell if he left her drawings and art supplies scattered in a mess on the floor. The five-year-old was more organized than he was. Still, he found nothing.

Owen stepped from his daughter's room, and then looked to Matt's room down the hall. He approached slowly, treating it like sacred ground. He paused at the door, and as he looked inside, he felt that ache from the missing piece of him that was carved out after Matt's abduction.

With his heart pounding like a hammer against his chest, Owen sifted through his son's belongings. The gloves, the bats, the baseballs, the dresser, closet, under the bed, night-stand, desk, the bin in the corner, and after turning every-thing upside down, he found nothing.

Owen sat on the edge of the bed and reached for one of

the shirts on the floor. He held it delicately between his fingers as he slowly rocked back and forth, his veins coursing with anxiety. He pressed Matt's shirt against his cheek, trying to figure out where else to look. But every room had been checked. And if it wasn't here then... *The property.*

The shirt slipped from Owen's fingertips as he slowly walked to the window. Madame Crepaux had said the creature was contained to the property, not just the house. And he remembered Chuck telling him about a cemetery in the swamp.

Owen pivoted toward the door and when he stepped out onto the second-floor balcony overlooking the dining room, he heard a rattle. *Thunka-clunka-thunka.* He froze, the noise so faint he thought he'd imagined it. And then it rattled again. *Thunka-clunka-thunka.*

Owen turned in a half circle, the old bones of the house groaning in distress, searching for the noise's origin. A black spot landed on his left arm and tickled his skin. Owen smacked it, and it fell to the floor. It was a spider.

Another landed on his right arm, and then his shoulder. Soon they fell like raindrops clustering before a downpour. He sprinted toward the stairs, frantically smacking at the dozens of tiny pricks from their teeth that sunk into his skin like the tip of a bobby pin.

Once down the stairs, Owen sprinted out the back door and into the open field, eyes shut and batting at the spiders he felt still crawling over him. But when he opened his eyes in the sunlight, they were gone.

Owen spun in a circle, panting, checking every inch of him to make sure they were gone, then looked back to the house. Standing there, he could have sworn he heard the echo of a laughter in the distance. It was inhuman, malicious.

Owen stepped toward the swamp and then stopped,

craning his neck back toward the house. Quickly, he jogged back inside and toward the front living room closet. He stepped over the landmines he'd left behind from his search and found what he was looking for among the shovels, picks, lawn equipment, screwdrivers, and wrenches: a ten-pound sledgehammer that sat on its head with the handle propped at an angle in the corner.

Owen curled his fingers around the smooth wooden handle and felt the fear shake loose. Between the creature, the house, and everything he'd experienced with Madame Crepaux, Owen felt like he was grasping in the dark at things he couldn't understand. The weight of the hammer in his hands was like taking hold of sanity in an insane world.

On a shelf at eye level, a small black box caught his attention. He knew what was inside. It was Roger's 9mm Glock. The old man had bought it over a year ago, before he was diagnosed with Alzheimer's.

Owen had fired it once before, and only once. He was about as proficient with the weapon as he was in speaking Spanish: zero. Regardless, he reached for the box and shoved the loaded magazine into the pistol. It clicked into place and he tucked it in his waistband, trying to remember everything that Roger had told him about the weapon. He wasn't sure if it would even hurt that creature, Bacalou, but it made him feel better having it.

Still batting at his arms occasionally, Owen lugged the hammer through the swamp, the hot sun beating down on his neck. Shade from the cypress trees offered a slight reprieve from the rising afternoon temperatures, and the ground softened the deeper he traveled into the swamp.

A sudden chill grazed the back of Owen's neck and he snapped his head around, expecting to find the creature, but saw only his muddy footprints. The deeper he walked the higher the black water rose, eventually stopping at Owen's ankles.

He swatted the insects that buzzed annoyingly at his face and neck, and that was when he saw it between a pair of thick cypress trunks. A slightly raised mound of land among the mud and water, the first three headstones of the grave-yard in view. As he drew closer, dozens more appeared, creating a small lake of concrete in the middle of the swamp.

The tombs rested above the ground, the soil too watery for a proper burial. In the center of the graveyard was a large mausoleum that stood twelve feet high with stained glass windows at the top of its walls just below the roof.

The structure itself was simple, boxlike, but the name Toussaint was sculpted meticulously over the gate's rusted iron, and its raised platform gave the deceased an esteemed place of rest among the dead. Thick cypress branches from multiple trees intertwined above the tomb, its entrance dark-ened and cast under a perpetual shadow. Owen was certain there was something alive in there. Maybe the creature he saw, maybe something worse.

Owen paused, his eyes darting around the swamp when they weren't locked on that dark entrance. Some of the older concrete tombs had sunken into the soft mud, the ground slowly giving way to the weight of the dead through the years. The tombs were of different casts and molds. Surrounded by stone, he wondered how many sons the crea-ture had taken.

Every grave was a member of the Toussaint family, all of them part of the same evil that had taken Matt. And the sight of the graves, the knowledge of what this family had done, bubbled a rage to the surface of Owen's consciousness. It was an anger derived from Matt's abduction, from the pink slip he was given by the shipyard in Baltimore, from the following six months where his family struggled to survive as he searched for work.

Owen lifted the hammer, charging for the nearest tomb, and swung all his weight behind it as the heavy chunk of iron smashed the headstone to pieces, flinging dust and bits of rock over the ground. He worked his way through the graveyard, waking the dead from their tombs and exposing them to a world that was no longer theirs.

Sweat poured from Owen's face, soaking his shirt that clung to his body like a starved animal. The more he destroyed, the angrier he grew. Hate flooded through his veins as he smashed tomb after tomb, checking the remains of the dead inside in search of the amulet.

Paper-thin skin clung to the skeletons like Owen's sweat-soaked shirt. A blast of heat and the scent of the embalming process radiated from every coffin, some of the bottoms rotted and leaking water. A litany of dead rats and other creatures lay alongside the corpses.

Tombs crumbled under the weight of Owen's sledgehammer, and the wake of disturbed dead widened behind him until all that was left was the mausoleum. Panting, he sprinted toward its gates.

"GaaaaAHHH!" The throaty groan reached a crescendo along with the hammer's highest arc and then crashed violently against the chain and lock. The face of the hammer ricocheted off the head of the lock and hit the ground with a heavy thud. Owen smacked the hammer against it repeatedly, and the rusted chain finally gave way.

Owen's hands were raw and red as he passed through the gates, the hammer's head dragging behind him, scraping against the concrete floor.

Inside, the air grew silent and still. The temperature dropped drastically and his footsteps echoed. The old stained glass windows beneath the ceiling filtered dirty light inside, giving it the aura that even on the brightest days, the mausoleum would always remain dark.

A raised tomb, much like the ones outside, rested atop a concrete pedestal, covered with a thick slab of stone that sealed the dead inside, and hopefully, the amulet.

A plaque rested at the tomb's foot with an inscription. The name read Charles Toussaint V, born 1928, died 1988. Another phrase was written in what looked like Latin underneath. *Mors Mihi Lucrum*.

Owen ran his fingertips over the inscription, unsure of its meaning, but then tightened his grip on the handle of his sledgehammer. His muscles burned as he lifted it and brought it down forcefully onto the tomb's stone cover. The contact rattled his bones, but his grip remained steady. He lifted it again, swinging with the momentum from the weight of the hammer, his eyes locked onto the same spot from before and made contact.

Another rattling crack ran through his arms and shoulders, but this time the concrete splintered. Owen swung again, bringing the tomb's roof crumbling down over the coffin.

Owen cleared the debris and then tugged at the coffin's handle. With the casket finally out from beneath the stone, Owen hesitated to open it.

A sudden and incomprehensible fear took hold of him. He imagined his son in the coffin, his eyes sunken in and his clothes tattered and torn like the corpses in the graves outside. Owen closed his eyes and in the same motion lifted the casket. He suddenly pulled in heavy breaths, unaware that he'd held his breath, his body aching for oxygen. He opened his eyes and looked down, a wave of relief flooding through him.

An old man with his eyes closed and his arms folded over his chest slept undisturbed on the white plush cushions inside. A chain hung over his neck, its end clutched underneath Charles Toussaint V's dead hands.

Owen slowly reached for the corpse's fingers, grimacing in disgust before he even made contact. He shuddered when his fingertips pressed against the wrinkled skin, the body cold and brittle.

The bones were stiff, and the joints cracked painfully as Owen peeled the fingers of the left hand first that revealed the right hand clutched around the end of the necklace. The last crack of joints released the dead man's grip and Owen stared down in confusion. The corpse clutched nothing but air, the pendulum at the end of the necklace no longer attached to the chain.

"No," Owen said, moving the man's arms and checking down by his sides, feeling his pronounced ribs and hip bones, the body incredibly light from its decomposition. But after searching every inch inside, he found nothing.

Owen retreated deeper into the mausoleum, sulking. The sunlight from the stained-glass windows faded, and he leaned against the cool concrete wall, the hammer on the ground to his right. A wind gusted through the mausoleum's entrance, cold like a northeastern winter that bit at his bones. And with it was a stench of death.

Thunder clapped overhead and a spittle of rain thudded against the roof. From the entrance, he saw the rain thicken and then lightening flashed.

The downpour worsened, and Owen stared at the sheets of rain that moved in waves from the harsh wind that brought an occasional burst of icy water into the mausoleum. But outside in the storm Owen saw something. It was hunched over, struggling against the wind and rain.

Owen moved closer to the entrance to get a better look. A frosty mist spritzed his face as neared the entrance. Lightning flashed again and Owen's eyes widened in terror at the empty eye sockets of the skull stumbling toward him.

The animated corpse snarled and rushed toward the mausoleum in a half sprint, half limp. Owen reached for the gate, slamming it shut as the corpse collided into the barricade, its bony fingers curled around the iron bars and its permanently exposed teeth snapping viciously.

More corpses emerged from the rain, collecting at the rusted gate, reaching their mangled and decayed arms between the bars. Owen retreated deeper into the mausoleum, his eyes fixated on the terror outside when a sharp vise clamped down on his shoulder.

Owen gasped and spun around to find Charles Toussaint V reaching for his neck with those cold, frail hands. In a knee-jerk reaction, Owen reached for the pistol still in his waistband and fired into the dead man's stomach.

The gunshot thundered worse than the storm, leaving Owen's ears ringing. Charles stumbled a few steps before regaining his balance, and then quickly lunged forward once more. The clothes hung loosely off the decaying body and the trousers sagged at the waist, held up only by a pair of suspenders that clung to the thin shoulders.

Owen fired again, the bullet impotent against the walking dead. He dropped the pistol and reached for the sledgehammer. He white-knuckled the sledgehammer's handle and backpedaled in a circle around the coffin, avoiding the animalistic lunges of the dead as dying moans echoed between the claps of thunder outside.

With enough space between them, Owen swung the hammer upwards in a high rising arc, the flat head of the ten-pound chunk of metal connecting flush underneath the zombie's chin with a resounding pop as the head was separated from the top of the spinal cord. But even with the head gone, Charles's body still walked aimlessly, its arms outstretched, clawing for Owen's flesh.

Owen looked to the gate still clustered with the dead and then sprinted toward it as fast and as hard as he could. He snatched the pistol off the floor on his sprint, then lowered his shoulder and shut his eyes as a sheet of icy rain and wind blasted him when he connected with the gate.

The clustered bodies of the dead added resistance to the door, and Owen's acceleration slowed to a strenuous push as the corpses clawed at his face and arms. The sharp ends of exposed finger bones drew blood along his right cheek and the left side of his neck.

Owen twisted left and right at the waist, flinging the dead off him, swinging the hammer wildly and clumsily. The cold stung the fresh wounds, and Owen squinted to avoid the stinging pelts of rain in his eyes.

The horde of the dead all turned toward him, their reanimated bodies awkward and cumbersome. A streak of lightning split the clouds above, and the harsh roll of thunder quickly followed. Owen turned from the horde and sprinted toward the swamp, but stopped after only a few steps.

A black mass moved toward him on the ground, like rising swamp water, and Owen shook his head in confusion. Dozens of tiny fangs were exposed and he realized that the moving blackness were snakes slithering over the mud, snapping at his legs that churned in a panicked retreat.

Caught between snakes and the dead, Owen abandoned the hammer and sprinted left into an open patch of swamp. Branches and long strands of hanging moss whipped wild and violent from the storm. After a while he glanced behind him, but the snakes and the dead were lost in the rain.

The storm worsened, and the harsh sting of the icy raindrops slowed Owen to a walk as he stumbled blindly through the swamp. He turned right, thinking that was where the edge of the clearing was, and after what felt like an eternity he was rewarded with the sight of the house across the clearing.

Wind flattened the tall grass and moved it back and forth like ocean waves in a violent squall. Owen clutched his arms, no longer able to feel the skin underneath his fingertips. His teeth chattered together and his blood flow slowed to an icy glaze. His eyelids fluttered and consciousness grew elusive. Another flash of lightning lit up the swamp and a figure caught his eye, standing in the distance.

At first Owen thought it was one of the corpses, but lightning flashed again and it revealed Bacalou. Its exposed teeth stretched wide across its mouth and those pair of black eyes stared through Owen's soul.

Owen trembled, clenching his fists together, stumbling forward with his eyes locked onto the creature's lifeless stare. "Where is my son?" His voice was weak against the violent rage of the storm.

The wide mouth and exposed teeth gave the impression that the creature was smiling, and it opened its jaws and released a throaty series of croaks, as if it was mocking him with laughter, and then it slowly dissolved into darkness.

"No!" Owen stumbled forward, trying to force his body to move quicker, but the cold had transformed him into one of those corpses, and his brain struggled to command his body. "Give him back!" Owen broke into a sprint, his body hunched forward, everything numb and frozen. His foot caught a root and he smacked into the thick mud with a splat. When he lifted his face, the creature was gone.

Mud fell from his chin and cheeks, and the rain subsided, morphing to a drizzle until the water shut off completely. Clouds parted overhead, and the sun returned along with a blast of humid heat that Owen welcomed with relief. He lay there in the mud for a while, letting his body thaw, and then finally pushed himself off the ground.

Owen turned back to the house, and the world returned to normal. As he climbed back behind the wheel of the van a thought broke through the fatigue and stress of his mind. If the amulet wasn't here, then that meant someone had already taken it. And he knew exactly who would have wanted to take it.

$\mathcal{S}$ heriff Bellingham sat behind his desk, chin resting in his hand, and blinked at the statements he'd been staring at all morning given by Billy Rouche and Owen Cooley. He'd been staring at that report for the past hour and still couldn't force himself to believe that what Mr. Cooley had said was real. He was a father who had just gone through something incredibly traumatic. The man had obviously made something up in his head for him to cope.

Bellingham remembered a case from his days as a deputy where a young man had come back from the war in the Middle East. He was diagnosed with PTSD, but unfortunately didn't seek out the proper care that he needed in order to help him cope with everything he'd seen in the battle. Instead, the man self-medicated with booze and drugs, and one night he stumbled down Main Street with a 9mm Smith and Wesson shooting at random cars and buildings

There was an hour of negotiation between authorities and the gunman as they cornered him down a side street. And after that hour, Bellingham watched the man put the gun to his temple and in a knee-jerk reaction Bellingham fired his weapon, winging the suspect in the arm that dropped him to the pavement. Paramedics rushed him to the hospital where they managed to save the man's life.

Bellingham was publicly torn a new asshole for his actions by the sheriff at the time. But behind closed doors, Bellingham remembered how the sheriff had thanked him for what he did. If he hadn't taken that shot, then the man would have died.

"Sheriff?"

Bellingham drifted out of the memory and saw his assistant in the doorway to his office. "Yeah?"

"Sheriff Barker over in Vermilion Parish wants to know if you need them for the search party tomorrow, and if you do, how many?"

"Yes, and whatever he can spare," Bellingham answered.

"Gotcha."

Veronica disappeared and Bellingham reclined in his seat, folding his hands behind his head, one on top of the other. The search for Jake Martin had turned up nothing. The dogs couldn't catch a scent, and the trees grew so thick in those back waters that they couldn't fit boats. They'd have to go in by foot, and even with the number of men that Bellingham was borrowing from across the state, he wasn't sure if they'd be able to find him.

Like a lot of the people in town, Jake came from a family that had been here for a long time. Bellingham knew that Jake had an uncle with some swamp houses out in the middle of god knows where from back in the twenties when they used to smuggle moonshine during Prohibition. Now they were used to drink and gamble, howling like animals under the hot summer moon.

There was a lot of that in Ocoee, more than he liked to admit as the head of law and order in his parish. The swamp would always be full of rats. He just tried to make it so they

JAMES HUNT

didn't scurry into town. But he had a feeling there might be one or two that had set up shop right under his nose.

It was no secret that Bellingham's predecessor was chummy with the Toussaints. Chuck's father came into the station often and was a contributor to the previous sheriff's re-election campaigns. And then when Bellingham ran, Chuck Toussaint wasn't shy about filling the campaign coffers, a sly smile spread over his face as he did so, giving a wink as if there was an unspoken agreement between them.

But Chuck Toussaint could cough up as much money as his pockets were willing to part with and it didn't change Bellingham's policy: everyone was equal on the scales of justice, and no amount of money could tip them one way or the next. It was a policy Bellingham shared with Chuck after his election, and the sheriff could have sworn he saw smoke spewing from Chuck's ears.

Bellingham's gut rumbled with unease at the way Chuck had answered his call earlier that morning. And while no names were dropped, Bellingham suspected that Chuck thought it was either Billy or Jake calling him back. That knowledge, combined with the fact that everyone involved worked with Chuck, made for an unsavory connection.

"Veronica!" Bellingham drummed his fingers over the statements on his desk as Veronica poked her head inside. "I need any reports on file for Toussaint owned property. More specifically at the house on Cypress Lane."

"It's in the computer, Sheriff," Veronica said, gesturing to the unused laptop on top of the bookcase behind Bellingham.

"Just the same, I'd like the paper copies."

Veronica rolled her eyes, unaware that he saw it, and returned a few minutes later with a single vanilla-colored folder. It drifted lazily to the top of his desk as she dropped it and stood in front of his desk, hands on her hips, head cocked to the side. "You know the department paid good money for that laptop. It's more efficient."

"It can be hacked," Bellingham said, staring at the one sheet of paper inside the folder.

"That's why we put a security system on it," Veronica replied, leaning forward, her large hooped earrings swaying from her lobes. "You just don't want to learn something new, because it scares you."

Bellingham frowned, but it was in reaction to the document in his hands. "This is it? This thing is twenty-five years old."

"You asked what we had on file," Veronica said, turning back toward the door, then stopping and looking at the sheriff with a smirk on her face. "You want more, then you know where to find it." She narrowed her eyes. "On the hacker machine."

Bellingham grimaced as she left, and then turned around to stare at the laptop underneath some of the case files he worked on last week. Reluctantly, he pulled the machine from its perch and rested it squarely on his desk. He opened it, then pressed the power button. A blurred image appeared on the screen and he reached for his glasses. He frowned at the two boxes labeled username and password.

"Veronica!" Bellingham shouted. "What's—"

"First initial, then last name. Password's your birthday."

Bellingham grunted and entered the information. He found the police database and searched the files for any more information on the property on Cypress Lane. The only consistency he found was that the property remained unoccupied. It wasn't until earlier in the week that an application for residency was filed by the Cooley family, and Bellingham had to go back another twenty-five years to find another family that resided there when Chuck's father ran the factory in town.

The previous residents to the house was Donald Kieffer, his wife, and two children. He scrolled the old pages and compared it with his notes on the Cooley family and found a few similarities. Both families had two kids; one boy and one girl. Both worked for the Toussaint family. And there was a notification that the Kieffer's left the house less than a week after they moved in, citing structural problems with the home as their reason for vacating. But when he went to look for a forwarding address, Bellingham found nothing.

"Veronica!"

The light patter of feet ended when Veronica poked her head around the corner, her eyebrow arched and staring at the phone on Bellingham's desk. "You do know that device right there has the ability to connect us without the need for yelling across the station."

"Get Judge Harlow on the line for me," Bellingham said, his concentration on the pair of reports in front of him. "I need to subpoena the factory for some records, and I also need you to find me a family that moved out of the Cypress Lane house twenty-five years ago."

Veronica shifted her body into the doorframe, her face scrunched together. "You want to subpoena the factory? Is something wrong?"

Bellingham looked up from the computer. "Two of their employees kidnapped the child of another employee and then tried to kill the rest of the family. So yes, Veronica, something is wrong. Now, go on!" He shooed her away and she scurried back to her desk

That uncomfortable feeling returned in Bellingham's gut as he stared at the report that was signed off by the sheriff at the time. A sheriff that was awfully chummy with the Toussaint family.

* * *

A GREEN LAYER of mossy film covered the top of the black swamp water, and Chuck waded through it carefully. Red, bloodshot lines filled the white space of his eyeballs as he glanced between trees and hanging moss, just waiting for Billy to jump out from behind one of them.

The old man knew the swamps well, and while Chuck may have had the advantage of a younger body, the old man tipped the scale with experience.

A mosquito buzzed by and landed on the back of Chuck's neck. With a quick strike, he slapped the bug and wiped his hands off on a dangling piece of moss. The revolver was still gripped in his left hand, his thoughts circling the one remaining bullet.

Even as a boy, Chuck always knew when he was in trouble. It was like a sixth sense. And his elevated pulse combined with the hairs standing up on the back of his neck were all the symptoms he needed to experience to know the shit storm coming his way.

More than once, Chuck glanced behind him at the thought of Jake's corpse rising from the dead and seeking vengeance. But each time he checked, there was nothing but swamp and trees and that hot sun burning a hole from the blue sky above.

Sweat trickled down every inch of Chuck's sunburnt skin. He'd shed his dress shirt on impulse a few miles back and now with the sun beating down on him, he cursed himself for not keeping it to cover his head and shoulders which had turned a bright pink.

And with the dress shirt gone, Chuck exposed a thin strap of a necklace. It traveled beneath the front of his undershirt, a light bulge from the jewelry at the necklace's end. Chuck had pawed at it nervously during his walk, unaware he was even touching it.

Water swooshed somewhere to his left, and Chuck spun

in the same direction, leading with the pistol. His heartrate skyrocketed, and he trembled. "Come on out, Billy!" No answer. No movement. "Jake pulled the gun on me! It was all self-defense."

Chuck circled in the water, mosquitoes buzzing around his eyes as if he were already dead. "I know we've had our differences, but I'm willing to let it go. We need each other right now, Billy. I know you respected my father. If you don't want to do this for me, then do it for him."

Chuck slowly scanned the swamp, waiting for the old man to show himself. He'd hoped that the comment about his father would lure him out. There was a layer of mushy sentimentalism beneath that calloused exterior. He turned right in a half-circle, then a quarter turn back to his left. A steady swell of panic rose in his stomach at the swamp's silence. "Shit."

Lost in the uncertainty of his own future, Chuck didn't hear Billy's ghost-like footsteps as he glided through the water, nor did he see the twisted, murderous expression plastered on the old man's face as he thrust all of his weight into Chuck's back, dunking both of them into the hot swamp water.

The black water rushed up Chuck's nose as Billy kept him pinned beneath the surface. Chuck immediately brought his hands to his neck to try and peel Billy's grip from his throat, and in the process, he dropped the revolver and it nestled in the mud.

Chuck violently twisted left, then right, trying to buck Billy off of him. His lungs tightened, desperate for air, and a primal surge of survival flooded his muscles. He leapt from the water, thrusting Billy off him, and gasped for breath.

Chuck coughed up a belly full of swamp water, but the reprieve was short-lived as Billy charged Chuck again. He led with his fist and connected with the right side of Chuck's face. A bright flash of pain lit up at the point of contact, followed quickly by a lingering throbbing.

Billy landed another heavy punch to Chuck's left side that forced him backward into a tree trunk and the pair locked horns. Water splashed and rippled violently as they pushed back and forth, their hands gripped on each other's arms and shoulders.

The longer the two held on, the more Chuck gained an advantage. Beneath his grip, Chuck felt the old man start to waver. Billy's beard dampened with water and sweat, the sunlight reflecting off the tiny droplets caught amongst the thick white hairs.

Chuck drove forward, pushing Billy back into a tree, and then quickly punched the old man's gut that all but ended the vise grip around Chuck's shoulders. Chuck followed up with a hard right to the old man's cheek, and the contact elicited a crack that hurt him as much as it did Billy.

"Fuck!" Chuck retreated a few steps, shaking his right hand that throbbed like his head and ribs. The old man had propped himself against a tree, wheezing breaths. Chuck remembered the gun and immediately started patting the mud with his feet for the revolver.

"You know your daddy never liked you," Billy said. "Said you were nothing more than a wasted jizz stain."

Chuck's cheeks flushed red. "Yeah, well, he told me that you were nothing but a trained dog. Housebroken, but still too dangerous to be unchained in the front yard. He never saw you as a son, no matter how much you wanted that to be true."

Billy lifted his head. "So we were both disappointments then." Billy added a sorrowful chuckle. "A pair of bastards with our father's names."

"I had to kill Jake." Chuck blurted the words out involuntarily. "He was out of his mind. He would have killed me if I hadn't."

"Yeah," Billy said, slowly straightening himself out. "He probably would have."

The pair stood there, sweating, aching, tired, hungry, and thirsty. It was a stalemate that neither wanted. Chuck filtered through the options that were left to him and what to do next. On his next step back, his heart skipped when his foot touched metal.

"So what now, Chuckie?" Billy asked, those cloudy grey eyes locked onto him. "I want to kill you, and you want to kill me, but neither of us are in a position to pull a trigger."

Chuck prodded it further, outlining it with tip of his shoe, the object taking shape.

"The sheriff won't find Jake's body out here." Billy gestured to the surrounding swamp. "Not unless one of us tells him. But it won't do either of us any good to talk to the cops now, so you're going to get me the best attorneys money can buy and keep me out of jail. In exchange, I'll keep my mouth shut."

"And what happens if my attorneys and my money can't keep you out of jail?" Chuck burrowed the tip of his foot into the soft sediment below the .38.

Billy took an aggressive step, the snarl revealing that silver-capped tooth, which was the only piece of that old man that didn't look worn and rusted. Though Chuck was sure some of the shine had disappeared over the years.

"So what's it gonna be, Chuckie?" Billy asked.

Chuck's foot was now entirely underneath the revolver. "Fuck you, Billy."

Billy exploded forward, and Chuck lifted his foot with the gun, reaching down with his hand in the same instance. His fingers slipped around the muddied and slick weapon and he clumsily raised the barrel as Billy cut the distance between them in half. He aimed, pressed his finger against the curve of the trigger, and squeezed.

A harsh bang ejected from the barrel, and the recoil jerked Chuck's arm back and the pistol wavered wildly in his hand. Billy's body collided into Chuck with a meaty thud, but then fell limp into the water face first.

Chuck stumbled backward, the gun gripped awkwardly in his hand. Billy's body bobbed up and down in the water, his arms and legs splayed out as he floated lazily.

The same eerie feeling when Chuck expected Jake's dead body to come stumbling after him occurred again as he kept the revolver trained on Billy's lifeless body. He wasn't sure how long he stood there, watching the back of Billy's head wander aimlessly in the three feet of water, but his eyes had grown incredibly dry from staring, and they ached from the sun's reflection on the water.

With a shaking hand, he pinched the bridge of his nose together and scrunched his face, feeling the tightness of his skin and the burn on his cheeks. He shook his head. "If you had just fucking listened in the first place. If you had just done your job, I wouldn't have—" But he stopped himself, knowing that the corpse couldn't respond.

The stagnant heat of the swamp hit Chuck from below and above. The knee-high water he waded through boiled his legs, and the sun above blistered and reddened the back of his neck. He turned around in a dazed glare. Jake's body and the shack that Chuck had left him in was long behind him.

He shielded his eyes with the cover of his hand as he looked to the sky. It was getting later in the afternoon, though he couldn't be sure exactly what time it was. He licked his lower lip and felt the chapped rawness of his skin, along with the salt of his own sweat.

"Bullshit," Chuck said, whispering to himself. "Fucking bullshit." He leaned against a tree trunk and closed his eyes.

Like a child reaching for its comforting blanket, Chuck tugged at the necklace then fisted the piece of jewelry at its end. "You can't get me, fucker. No, way. Not with this. *Not with this.*" He opened his fist and revealed a green stone wrapped in thin cords, the pattern a spider's web.

But even with his safety net, Chuck still felt the thumping of his heart against his chest. It beat firmly, and the dehydration only added more strain.

Two of his loose ends were dead, and like Billy had said, the likelihood of the sheriff finding them out here before they were gator food was zero. All that was left to deal with now was the Cooley family.

17

---

*O*wen was still shivering by the time he reached Queen's, his clothes wet and clinging to his body. For once he was glad for the hot Louisiana sun as he hobbled toward the front door.

A little bell jingled upon his entrance and he saw Chloe sitting at the front counter, standing on a chair and hunched over a paper with a cluster of crayons, pens, and pencils. She didn't bother looking up to see who had come inside, too involved with her work.

"Chloe, where's your mother?" The store looked empty and the tinted windows up front kept the inside of the shop in a perpetual state of darkness.

"With Grandpa," Chloe answered, her concentration still on the drawing spread out over the desk.

"Hey."

Owen turned and saw Claire stepping from the darkness of the room on his left. Her eyes were bloodshot and the tip of her nose was red, both of which only happened when she'd been crying. "You all right?"

Claire's eyes watered, and she pulled in her lower lip as she shook her head. "I heard him, Owen. I heard Matt."

He pulled her close and she cried into his chest, the fact that he was soaked to the bone not even registering in her current state of mind. A small thump hit the back of his legs, and Owen turned his head around to see Chloe hugging his knees. He smiled and bent to pick Chloe off the floor and she nestled in the crook of his arm.

"Daddy, you're all wet," Chloe said, poking at his shoulder.

"Oh my god, you are," Claire replied. She looked at him, confused. "And cold. God, your skin is like ice." And then her eyes widened with fear and she clutched his arm tighter. "You saw it?"

"I did," Owen answered. "But I couldn't find the amulet."

Footsteps and the third echoing thump of Madame Crepaux's staff smacked against the floor as she emerged from the same dark room as Claire, an expression of fear carved along the wrinkles of her face. "It has to be there."

Owen stepped away from his girls and walked to the woman. "It was, but it's not anymore."

Madame Crepaux's face slowly twisted from fear to anger, and she pushed past Owen, limping toward the room on the other side of the shop, a string of curses streaming from her lips as she disappeared.

Owen followed and found her pulling book after book from the shelves and stacking them half-hazard on a table in the middle of the room. The covers were old and worn, the spines warped and dusty. Owen picked at the corner of one of the books and lifted it an inch before the old woman slammed another book down on top of it, then returned to her shelves.

"It's Chuck," Owen said. "He's the one who has to have it."

"That's wrong, it's all wrong." Madame Crepaux started

flipping pages, quickly scanning the old pieces of parchment, shaking her head.

Owen caught a glimpse of some of it, words and phrases that weren't written in English along with shapes and drawings that looked abstract. He grabbed her wrist and forced her to stop. "What is it? What are you doing?"

Madame Crepaux yanked her hand back with a surprising strength. "It was part of the bokor's magic that the amulet must remain on the property!" She stewed in anger. "That mongrel peasant lied to me."

"What difference does it make that the amulet isn't on the property?" Owen asked. "All that matters is that we find it, right?"

Madame Crepaux circled around the table between them on her path to him. "If that amulet is not there to hold the creature back, then its power will grow!" She pointed a long finger into his chest. "And that power could mean your son's soul is slipping away even faster than expected."

"Then find Chuck," Owen said. "I know he has the amulet. There's no one else that could."

Madame Crepaux looked to her books, then to the shelves with the remaining potions and herbs. A brief moment of hope filled her eyes, but her shoulders slumped and the light dimmed. She shook her head. "The amulet protects him from me as well as the monster. Until it's destroyed, he will elude me."

Owen's pocket buzzed, and he jolted, forgetting he even had the cellphone on him. The number wasn't recognized on his phone, but the area code was local. "Hello?"

Silence lingered on the other end of the phone, and then Chuck finally spoke. "I know what you think, Owen. But you need to know that there's more to it than—"

"You brought me here so my son could die," Owen said.

Another pause. "Let me make things right. Let me—"

"I want the amulet. Bring it to me and I'll consider not going to the police."

"Yes. Yes, of course. It's just... I need some time."

"No time," Owen said, baring his teeth. "Now."

"Then you'll have to come to me," Chuck said. "But just you. No cops."

While Owen didn't buy Chuck's act for a second, he understood. The man was out to protect himself. But Chuck held all the cards. Even if Owen went to the police, they wouldn't be able to do anything in the time needed to get Matt back before midnight. He had to play by Chuck's rules. "Fine."

"Get a pen and paper," Chuck said.

Owen complied, scribbling an address on a notepad next to the register. The moment after Chuck was done telling him the location, the call ended. Owen didn't realize he was shaking until he felt Claire's hand on his shoulder, and with her touch came a soothing focus of what needed to be done. He cupped her face, staring into the eyes he loved so much, the eyes that had saved him so many times from himself.

"Listen, if I don't come back, then you go to the Sheriff," Owen said. "You tell him everything."

"Do what you have to," Claire said, her eyes watering but her voice strong and clear. "And know that whatever you do, and however you do it, it's not wrong." She placed her hands over his. "It's *not* wrong."

Owen kissed her and saw that Chloe was watching. He walked over and kissed her cheek as well, and before he left, he noticed the picture that she'd been working on. It was of their family, and they were at their house in Baltimore.

"I miss home," Chloe said, looking at her father.

Owen kissed her again and asked if he could keep the picture, and she nodded that he could. He folded it gently and carefully into his pocket and then left with Claire's words echoing in his mind.

Owen had been mad before. He'd thought about punching people, and he'd whispered wishes of evil onto people that hurt him. But never had he felt such calmness when he experienced those emotions like he did right now. The reality of murder felt too real. He remembered what Billy had said after they'd broken into their house the night Matt was taken.

"You don't have the look of a killer, boy."

At the time, Billy was right. But not anymore.

* * *

SHERIFF BELLINGHAM REACHED for the coffee mug to his left without looking, his fingers grasping at nothing but air until it grazed the white handle and he lifted the rim to his pursed lips. The coffee was bitter and cold.

Bellingham wiped the dryness from his eyes and flipped through the old reports that Veronica had brought him from the factory. He'd managed to pull the HR records on Billy Rouche and discovered that the old man had a grievance filed against him twenty-five years ago. The name at the top of the grievance was redacted to protect the other employee's identity. He put in a request to the HR department to find him the name of the individual who filed it, but he already had a pretty good idea the employee was Donald Kieffer. Still, he needed to be sure.

He'd tasked Veronica with staying on top of the clerk over at the factory, and while he was waiting on that information, he'd spent the past hour searching for Donald Kieffer's current whereabouts, which had proven difficult.

With no information in regards to Mr. Kieffer's social security numbers or driver's license, Bellingham had done a search for Donald Kieffer in his database and discovered over five hundred around the country. He managed to whittle that number down to twenty-three after cross-referencing middle initials.

So far twenty-two of those twenty-three Donald Kieffers had never lived in Ocoee, Louisiana. And while Bellingham waited for the confirmation of number twenty-three, he remained hopeful that the last Donald Kieffer was the same man who worked at the Toussaint factory twenty-five years ago.

He reached for the statements made by Mr. and Mrs. Cooley, along with what the deputy had written down from what he'd seen of Mrs. Cooley's father at the hospital. The nonsense he was spewing seemed to match the descriptions of what Mr. Cooley had seen. And unless the pair coordinated their stories together before the police arrived, a very unlikely theory seeing as how Mrs. Cooley's father was strapped down to a hospital bed all night without any access to a phone, that created another connection, which started to string up a loose theory.

The world was random, chaotic, and for the most part a big mess in the sheriff's eyes. But every so often there was a moment of clarity, a ray of light that shone through the dark and revealed a path. Bellingham was getting glimpses of that path now, and his muscles tensed.

The phone on his desk rang, and Bellingham cleared his throat and picked up the receiver.

"Sheriff, this is Kyle Warber over at the DMV's office in Oregon, how are you?"

"Fine, Mr. Warber."

"I found the information you wanted on Donald Kieffer. It looks like Mr. Kieffer passed away last year, but according to our records, he lived in Oregon his entire life. Never had a residence in your town."

Bellingham lingered for a moment, those connections growing stronger. He thanked Mr. Warber for the information, and then hung up. So now he had a missing boy, and a family missing from twenty-five years ago, both of whom lived in a house owned by the Toussaint family.

Bellingham reached for the coffee mug and walked over to pour himself a fresh cup. The majority of his deputies were out scouting for the Cooley boy. And with Veronica over at the factory waiting for the final word on that grievance report, he was all alone. Not that he minded it. He'd discovered that being sheriff rarely afforded him a moment of peace and quiet.

It was his wife that had made him run for the position in the first place. He would have been content to retire four years ago after thirty years in the department, but Laura said he still had some gumption left in the tank. And while he didn't want to admit it, he knew she was right. The woman could read him like a book, especially when he didn't want to turn the next page.

Truth was she'd been the driving force pushing him to be better since the moment they met. He smiled at the memory of their first date as he reached for the coffee pot. He'd picked her up at her house. His jaw nearly dropped to the floor when she opened the door to her parents' place. She was dressed in a low crop tank top, with her hair done up like Farrah Fawcett, and cut-off jean shorts. It was a hot summer night, and he was glad to see that she had dressed for the occasion.

It was a stark contrast from the uniform Bellingham had seen her wear at school, but while a physical attraction began their courtship, it was a friendship that kept it going.

Bellingham walked her out to the car, doing his best to try and not stare at her chest, and parted when they got close to hop in the driver side.

JAMES HUNT

"What are you doing?" Laura asked.

Bellingham stopped at the hood of his Trans-Am, which he'd bought a month before after a year of saving. He pointed to the driver seat. "Getting in?"

"And you're not going to open my door for me?" She raised her eyebrows in coordination with her tone and crossed her arms.

"I thought women didn't like that?" Bellingham answered, still lingering at the hood of the car. "You know, cause of feminism."

"Addler Bellingham." Laura uncrossed her arms and placed them on her hips. "I hate to be the bearer of bad news, but not opening a door for a woman or any person in general is not helping to promote feminism, just bad manners." She glanced down at her own chest, and his eyes quickly followed, but lingered there much longer than hers did. "And I did not wear this outfit for you." He lifted his eyes and blushed. "I wore it because it's hot outside, and god forbid I'd want to be in something other than the potato sacks they make us wear at school." She stepped to the car door and opened it herself. "Women do things for themselves because they *want* to do them for themselves."

Bellingham stood there, mouth open.

"Now, get in," Laura said, sliding one tan, smooth leg into the car. "I have to be back by ten."

And that's how it went for the majority of their first date, with Bellingham doing his best to not look like an even bigger ass. By the end of the night, he didn't think he succeeded.

But when he walked her back to the front door of her parents' house, she leaned in and kissed him, long, hard, and passionate, slipping in a very talented tongue that triggered a burning hot coal in his stomach and woke up his manhood.

Laura pulled back, and he stood there with an embarrassing erection that she looked down at, and then smirked. "There. You've got a peek at mine, and now I've got a peek at yours." She laughed and then stepped inside, leaving Bellingham on the front porch, trying to hide the bulge in his pants.

Nearly forty years later she was still teaching him, and in a place like Ocoee, it was well-needed preaching. He took a sip from his mug, throwing up a thank you to the man upstairs for strong women and strong coffee.

The phone in his office rang again, and Bellingham hurried back, balancing the full-to-the-brim mug carefully in his hand on his way back to his desk. "Sheriff Bellingham."

"Sheriff," Veronica said. "I finally got a name on that grievance you wanted information on."

"Who was it?"

"Donald Kieffer."

"Make a copy of that report and then bring it back to the station and add it to the Cooley file." Bellingham hung up, and took a sip from his Saints mug before setting it down and reaching for his car keys. It was time to pay Billy Rouche a visit.

18

Owen's phone navigation flitted out twice on the winding dirt paths that were a result of his journey to the address that Chuck had given him. They were even farther out from town than the house on Cypress.

The 9mm Glock sat in the passenger seat, loaded with a fifteen-round capacity magazine. Its presence made Owen both nervous and safe at the same time.

Owen slowed, spying the turn up ahead through the trees and swamp. He stopped the car just before the turn, looking farther down the path. A small house stood at the very end. The roof sagged, the windows were dirty, and the paint had long ago faded and peeled from its exterior. There was a truck parked out front, one he didn't recognize.

Shadows from the trees crawled over the car as he came to a stop ten yards from the house. He parked, grabbed the gun, and took a deep breath before stepping outside.

The gravel drive crunched beneath Owen's feet. Sweat broke out on his forehead and his heart pounded like a jackhammer. By the time he reached the shade of the short awning over the front door, he couldn't stop shaking.

The door was cracked open, and Owen aimed the pistol at the gap, then pushed it open. The contrast of darkness inside blinded him for a moment, and he panicked, but it calmed once the shapes of chairs and couches filled the living room.

Owen kept the gun pointed in front of him as he scanned the room. A few steps later he noticed a smell, hot like the weather, but fleshy. And when he turned the corner into the kitchen he saw Billy Rouche lying belly up, a bloody wound on his stomach and his clothes and body wet and soaking the floor around him.

"Drop the gun, Owen."

Owen shuddered from the pistol jammed in his back. Slowly he held up his hands, and then Chuck relieved him of the weapon.

"The police know I'm here," Owen said.

Chuck scoffed. "No, they don't." He spun Owen around and had both guns gripped in his hands, aimed at Owen. "They don't know you're here because you knew I wouldn't show if they did. And I have something you need."

"He's only ten," Owen said, his eyes watering. "He's a boy. He's scared. And he's my son."

Chuck stepped back a few paces. He was wet and dirty and sunburnt like the dead man on the floor, complete with a matching lifeless stare. "Kill or be killed, Owen."

"You mother—" Owen stepped forward, and Chuck raised the pistols a little higher, shaking his head.

"Nah, ah, ah," Chuck said. "You've still got a few things to do." With his head, he gestured to a chair. "Sit down. Call your wife."

The sunlight from the opened front door behind Chuck cast his body in shadow. Only his silhouette was visible, the gun part of the outline. Owen stiffened. "No."

Chuck stepped forward, the features of his face filling the

closer he moved. The southern charm from their first meeting had disappeared. The varnish wiped clean and exposing the dirty truth beneath all of the money and nice clothes. "Then I'll kill her after I kill you."

"You kill me and she goes to the police," Owen said.

"After what you tell her it won't matter what she tells the police," Chuck said, then he pressed the pistol against Owen's chest. "Call. Her."

Owen carefully reached for his phone, and took a seat in the chair; his eyes fixated on Chuck the whole time.

"Good boy," Chuck said. "Now, when she answers, you're going to tell her that you're very angry, and that you know Billy and Jake have your son, and that you're going to do something about it." Chuck's eyes widened. "And make sure you sell it."

Owen shifted his eyes from the phone to the dead body. "So you put a bullet in my head after I make the call and frame me for Billy's murder? Is that it?"

"And Jake's," Chuck said, his voice on the brink of madness. "Let's not forget about Jake, Owen." There was a light tremor to his arm. "Call." Chuck walked forward and cut the distance between the two of them in half. "Now."

"I've seen cowards before," Owen said, grimacing. "But I've never seen one like you."

"And you've never been backed into a corner?" Chuck asked, spitting the words back like venom. "You've never had to do things that you weren't proud of? Never had to crawl through the shit on your hands and knees to get out on the other side?" Chuck shook his head, crying now. "Oh, I think you have. I think that's why you took the job down here in the first place. I think that's why even after you started noticing things wrong with that house, you stayed. Because this was it, your one shot at redemption, and you ignored everything else for the job and the money I offered you. It was too good to be true, and you knew it. But you kept your family here anyway. You could have left days ago, but you didn't. This isn't on me." He shook his head in wild defiance. "No. Your son's blood is on *your* hands. Not mine." He shook uncontrollably now. "Not mine!"

Skipped meals. No showers. No power. Wearing the same dirty clothes to school. Owen knew the shit Chuck was talking about. The job down here at the factory was supposed to save them, not damn them to this new hell. He didn't listen to Claire when she told him there was something wrong. He'd ignored her when she said they should leave. Matt was gone because of him. And he couldn't wash that blood off, no matter how hard or how long he scrubbed.

"Well?" Chuck asked. "What's it gonna be?"

Owen looked down at the phone. He wasn't sure what he would say. A version of what Chuck had told him to be sure, but what else? Tell her that she was right? That he was sorry? No. His last words to his wife wouldn't be so selfish as to clear his own conscience. Not when they were still in danger.

He dialed Claire, his heart caught in his throat as the phone rang. A small portion of him didn't want her to pick up, and after five rings he thought she wouldn't, but then...

"Owen? What's going on? Are you all right?"

Owen closed his eyes, and he nearly broke down right then and there. But he held it. He still had one last job. "Hey, baby." He opened his eyes and saw the black emptiness of the gun barrel. He'd never been shot before and suddenly wondered if it would hurt, and then in an almost premonition type of warning, a hot pain filled his chest. "I'm sorry, Claire. I should have listened to you before. We should have left. You were right."

Claire was crying now. "Whatever you're doing, Owen, don't you dare!"

"I had to, baby," Owen answered, fighting back his own

tears now. "It's not safe for you and Chloe. I have to make it safe for you."

And so this was it. The final push. Owen briefly wondered if his life would flash before his eyes as his tongue turned to sandpaper in his mouth. "Take Chloe and your dad and leave town." He opened his eyes, Claire stuttering in his ear. "Chuck just killed Billy Rouche and he's—"

Chuck lunged forward, screaming at the top of his lungs as he cracked the weapon against Owen's cheek, knocking the phone from his hand and Owen to the floor. Trembling, Chuck picked up the phone and then ended the call as Owen rolled and moaned on the floor. "You fucking prick!" He hovered over Owen and then jammed the pistol's barrel into Owen's temple. He foamed at the corners of his mouth like a rabid dog. "You fucking shit! You—"

Red and blue lights flashed outside. Both Owen and Chuck snapped their heads towards it at the same time and the violent turn caused the necklace around Chuck's neck to pop from his wifebeater and dangle right in front of Owen's eyes.

The bright green stone sparkled in the leather spider web that held it in place. The pistol's pressure on the side of Owen's head lightened, and he punched Chuck's nose, knocking the man off him and to his side. He ripped the amulet off Chuck's neck, and then sprinted out the back door.

Owen's feet splashed in the water and he turned back only once. In the brief glimpse behind him, Owen saw Chuck stumbling out of the back door and the sheriff's car pulling up next to his van. For a moment, Chuck thought about stopping, but stopping meant explaining, and explaining took time. With the sun fading lower in the sky, it was time he didn't have.

Owen sprinted into the trees, the mud slowing his pace

and Chuck gaining on him as he disappeared deeper and deeper into the wilderness. In his last glimpse of the house, Owen saw the sheriff walk out the back, gun in hand and scanning the edge of the swamp.

Owen tightened his fist around the amulet and while the rest of his body remained hot and sweaty, the hand holding the amulet grew colder.

Splashes alerted Owen to Chuck's distance behind him and he knew it was only a matter of time before he used that pistol. The only reason Chuck hadn't fired yet was because he didn't want to give away their location to the sheriff. Chuck was still hoping to finish this quietly.

Owen's muscles burned as the distance lengthened, and a thousand tiny knives stabbed his lungs with each breath. Directionless, he wandered through the swamp, pushed only by the fact that if he stopped, Chuck would kill him, or the Sheriff would arrest him, and his son would be lost forever.

The swamp water rose to his chest and significantly slowed Owen's pace. He twisted his body left and right, his legs churning under the water like he was running on the moon.

"You can't keep this up forever, Owen." Chuck's voice carried over the water, bouncing off the trees like an echo chamber. "Whatever you think that stone can help you do is a lie."

Owen turned back, searching for Chuck amongst the trees. He kept quiet and trudged forward, doing his best to limit his own noise.

"The cops won't believe you," Chuck said, his voice swirling around like a hurricane. "You don't have any proof. You can't do this on your own."

Owen dodged a piece of moss dangling from a tree, some of its wiry tentacles brushing the side of his neck where the dead had scratched him. He looked to the stone, knowing that this was the only proof he needed.

Water rippled to his left and Owen snapped his head in the same direction, frozen terror icing his veins as he imagined Chuck there with pistol in hand, smiling as he squeezed the trigger. But there was nothing.

He glanced up to the sky, the sun growing dimmer and dimmer the farther he waded into the swamp. He had no idea where he was now, and even if he was able to evade Chuck, he had no idea of how to get back to the road.

Owen stopped, noticing the silence. Insects buzzed and another ripple of water, this time to his right, caught his attention. He spun in a circle, arms still above the water, the knuckles on his right hand white from the tight grip on the amulet.

Gunshots thundered, and bark from the tree trunk only a foot from Owen's head splintered off and fell to the water. Wide-eyed, Owen turned left and saw Chuck between the trees, Roger's 9mm Glock aimed in his outstretched arm.

Another gunshot triggered Owen into action, and he sprinted forward as fast as his legs would allow in the high water. He kept his head ducked low, his body moving at a tormenting slow pace as more bullets zipped over the still black water.

"You're a dead man!" Chuck said, screaming now as he chased Owen through the trees, his motion just as slow, but aided by the long reach of the pistol.

One more bullet ricocheted off a tree trunk to Owen's left, and a harsh burn spread across his shoulder. Owen gritted his teeth and winced, clutching the wound, but kept moving. He was hesitant to look down at it, afraid that he'd discover he'd been shot, a trail of blood leaking from him and into the water which would catch the scent of gators looking for a quick, easy meal.

But when he finally glanced down and removed his hand from his shoulder, he saw nothing more than a red line. The bullet barely nicked him.

Bullet-size splashes erupted to his left in three geyser-like sprays, and adrenaline powered him onward. One more gunshot thundered, but Owen didn't hear a ricochet as he continued his slow-motion sprint through the water, which had risen to his shoulders now. He started to swim, which propelled him faster than the tippy toe walk through the water.

Behind him, Chuck's voice echoed in the swamp. "I'll kill you! You hear me? You're a fucking dead man! I'll get to your family first! I'll get there and slit their throats, and then I'll kill you when you show up! It's all on you now! You hear me? Your family's death is on you!"

And while Chuck's voice faded the farther Owen swam, the words resonated. He looked to his fist that held the amulet. His family's fate did rest on his shoulders. And he didn't have any plans on letting them down.

19

*C*laire stood near the front windows of the shop, her arms clutched protectively around her body in a tight hug, her left foot tapping nervously as she chewed on her lower lip. She stared out to the beautiful evening sky that had transformed into an array of oranges, pinks, purples, reds, and blues. And what should have been a beautiful sight was nothing more than an impending doom for her son.

She turned away from the window, her head down as she paced back to the counter where Chloe was still working on her drawings. She was glad that her daughter had something to do, something to distract her young mind from the worry of all the strange things happening around her.

Owen should have been back by now. He'd been gone for hours. She tried going to the police station as Owen suggested if he didn't return, but when she arrived, she'd found it empty. So she returned to Queen's.

"Mary. Mary? Is dinner ready yet?" Roger's incoherent thoughts filtered from the back room. Since Madame Crepaux used him for opening the door to whatever realm the creature lived, he'd relapsed into his dementia further and longer than he'd ever done before. "No, I don't want to go to the movies tonight. Nothing good to see."

She walked back to the room where he was kept and saw him lying down on a table. Roger swayed his head back and forth, his cloudy eyes glancing up at the ceiling, his mouth moving and forming words, but his brain not making the connection of the reality that surrounded him.

She wondered what it would be like to look at his mind, to see what he saw in those moments where the circuits were crossed and confusion set in. She knew he didn't even realize it was happening and was glad for it. This wasn't Roger Templeton on the table. This was Alzheimer's. And he was a son of a bitch.

"Goddammit, Mary, I said no!" Roger slammed his fists against the table, the muscles along his arms and neck thickening from the strenuous pull. "I-I'm fine," he answered, keeping his eyes tight shut. "I'm okay. I'm not hungry, Mary."

Claire's mom had been dead for almost three years, but anytime he said her name like this, it still wrenched her heart. When Alzheimer's took control, it brought the ghost of her mother to life. And it was always haunting.

"I'm not hungry!" Alzheimer's opened his eyes, staring up to the ceiling and screaming at the top of his lungs. He looked at Claire. Those angry, violent eyes were upon her. They didn't recognize her, and she didn't recognize him. He got up from the table and Claire stepped in front of the door to keep him in the room.

"Dad, you need to calm down," Claire said, approaching slowly, her hands held up passively. "Just lay back down on the table."

Alzheimer's lunged forward, grabbing Claire by the shoulders, her father still surprisingly strong. "Who are you? Get out of my house! Mary! Mary!" His voice grew angrier, more frantic, more violent.

"Dad! You need to—"

The harsh crack of the backhand knocked Claire off balance, leaving a hot, burning mark that sat high on her cheek. She remained hunched over, one of her fingers grazing the mark, and Alzheimer's stood there, panting heavily.

"GAAHH!" Alzheimer's lunged forward, fists swinging wildly, and Claire flung herself in his path to protect him from Chloe.

Claire braced for the inevitable impact, shutting her eyes and turning her face away from the monster in her father's body. But after she tensed, there was nothing. She opened her eyes and saw Madame Crepaux standing behind her, the rock at the top of her staff glowing and Alzheimer's frozen in mid-step.

"Get him back on the table," Madame Crepaux said. "Tie him down."

Claire did as she was told, moving the shell of her father with surprising ease. Once he was tied down, the rock ended its glow, and Alzheimer's slowly returned, blinking and thrashing against the straps.

"Let me go! Let me go!" Alzheimer's howled and snarled, and Claire retreated until a hand fell on her shoulder.

"The trip into the monster's world has only tired his mind," Madame Crepaux said. "He will be better soon."

"And he has to do it again? Help open up that... door?" Claire asked, staring at her father, who blinked absentmindedly at the ceiling. "Can his mind handle that?"

Madame Crepaux stared at Claire, and then at her father. "It must. There is no other way to reach Bacalou's domain without your father as a conduit."

"Will it kill him?" Claire asked.

Madame Crepaux shook her head. "I do not know." She

handed a bowl of something that she had mixed. "Give this to him. It will help get him ready."

Claire took the bowl, and Madame Crepaux left, leaving her alone with Alzheimer's. He thrashed on the table, his eyes shut, mumbling something. "Dad?" He didn't respond. "Roger?"

Alzheimer's looked at her, then to the bowl. His tone was stern, but some of the anger had lessened. "I'm not hungry."

Claire forced the rim of the bowl to his lips and lifted his head. "It's good for you." She forced his head steady, and he grimaced as she funneled the concoction down his throat.

Alzheimer's consumed about half of it before he closed his lips and the liquid spilled over his face. He violently shook his head. "Poison! It's poison!" He thrashed and knocked the bowl from her hands and it crashed to the floor, some of the liquid spilling over Claire's clothes.

Alzheimer's screamed and howled, snarling at the woman who used to be his daughter, but had transformed into a demon trying to kill him.

The raised welt where she'd been struck burned hot, and Claire trembled. Her son was gone, her husband was missing, and the one man in her life that was still here wasn't really here at all. "Stop it! Just stop it!" She gripped her father by the shoulders and his thrashing ended, but he kept the snarl. "I know you're going to take him from me. I know what you're going to do to all of the memories of him and his family. But you give him back to me now. You hear me? You let him go for a little while longer."

Alzheimer's gave a mistrusting look, but the snarl disappeared.

Desperation was plastered over Claire's face, and she was ashamed at the hate coursing through her veins, but she needed something to help her get through this.

"Please," Claire said, tears in her eyes now. "Let me have him back."

The cloudy haze vanished, and for a moment Claire believed that her father was back. The anger disappeared and he squinted at her, the rusted wheels of his mind trying to make a connection that would have been the easiest thing in the world just a year ago.

"Do I know you?"

And just like that, the brief ray of light was snuffed out. Claire shook her head and backed away, sobbing openly now as she lifted her hand to the welt on her cheek. "No. You don't." She turned and saw Chloe crying, and she wrapped her arms around her, the past twenty-four hours flooding out of her like water from a busted dam.

* * *

THE COTTON CANDY sunset had turned pitch black, clouds covering the moon and stars, casting the earth below in darkness. Owen panted, stumbling a few steps out of the water until he collapsed against one of the trees for support. His eyes had adjusted to the darkness and in the shades of night he saw the trees, the moss, the swamp, and the tiny ripples of water among the reeds and water from the wind or whatever animals lay beneath the surface.

Owen tilted his head back, his mouth open. Despite the swim on his escape, the day had dried him out. The night concealed the sunburns on his face and neck, but when he ran his tongue over his lips, he felt the cracks and chapped skin. His muscles spasmed randomly in fatigue and defiance of movement. But if it was already nightfall, then the window to save his son was nearly closed.

Owen pushed forward, catapulting himself off from the tree trunks like a monkey swinging from branch to branch.

He paused for another breath, his muscles forcing him to stop. He glanced down at his fist and then uncurled his aching fingers.

The green stone glowed in the darkness, and Owen tried to understand how something so small, something so ordinary could possess so much power. He closed the stone back into his fist, thoughts of Matthew pushing him onward. He'd circled a few memories of his son over the past day, but all of them led back to one.

It was spring, about four years ago. Chloe was still a baby at the time, and both Owen and Claire had expressed to their eldest how proud they were of him for being such a good big brother. He fell into the role like a natural, holding her, giving her kisses on the top of her head, helping her eat once she transitioned from breastfeeding to baby food.

He and Claire wanted to do something special for him on his upcoming birthday. With the attention that Chloe required, that any new baby required, they knew that they sometimes had put Matt on the back burner. And because of the type of kid he was, so soft-spoken and well-behaved, it was easy for him to go unnoticed. Out of the two of them, Chloe had always been the squeaky wheel, and as the old saying goes, she got the grease.

When Owen was still at the shipyard in Baltimore, he worked with a guy whose son was in the PR department for the Orioles. And if there was a bigger Baltimore Orioles fan than Matt Cooley, Owen had yet to meet them. So, after handing over a week of vacation time, Owen managed to score some front row seats along the first base line right next to the Orioles dugout. Matt also got to throw out the first pitch of the game and had his baseball signed by every player in the dugout. Matt couldn't wipe the smile off his face for the whole four hours the game lasted.

And while the joy of watching his son's face light up at

the players, the game, the crowd, the food, and the atmosphere was rewarding, it wasn't until the end of the game and they had walked back to the parking lot that he finally got to the moment that had replayed in his mind like the favorite scene in a favorite movie.

"Dad?" Matt asked after Owen had clicked on his seatbelt.

"Yeah, buddy?"

Matt kept his head down, twirling the baseball in his hands, the smile faded a little bit but still creasing his lips upward. "Thank you."

Owen brushed his son's hair back behind his ear and smiled. "You deserve it, buddy. You've done such a great job this past year."

Matt looked up at him, his eyes wide but sleepy.

"So," Owen asked. "What was your favorite part of the day?"

"Right now," Matt answered.

Owen laughed, shaking his head. "Really? It wasn't the game or the fact that you got to throw out the first pitch?"

Matt was quiet for a moment, and then looked up at Owen. "You made this happen, Dad. And when I grow up, I want to be just like you so I can make my son feel the same way."

With his son's words ringing clearly in his memory, Owen shut his eyes and dropped to his knees in the middle of the swamp. His shoulders bounced, sobbing, as his mouth downturned and he drew in a snot-riddled breath, trying to regain his composure.

Most kids think their dad is Superman. Owen thought that about his own father when he was younger. But Owen knew Matt would discover how much better he was than him as he grew older. Still, hearing those words come out of his son's mouth filled him with a pride that couldn't be bought, sold, or replaced. It was priceless.

A pair of lights flashed in Owen's peripheral vision. He turned to the sight, blinked a few times, unsure if the moving illumination was real or just a mirage derived from hopeful thoughts. But then he heard an engine, and he realized the road was close.

He waved his arms, his voice cracking as he called out. "Hey!" He didn't care who it was out there on the road so long as they could take him back to Main Street. The closer he drew to the road, the clearer the headlights came into view. They were attached to an old truck, the driver in the cab hidden by darkness.

Owen broke through the edge of the swamp and stumbled up the embankment of the road, his dirty hand outstretched to flag the driver down. His fingers penetrated the cones of lights from the headlights, then collapsed onto the asphalt.

Brakes squealed as the truck slowed, casting the top half of Owen's body into view. The truck's engine rumbled as the driver shifted into park. Door hinges squeaked, and boots scraped against the asphalt.

Owen could barely find the strength to lift his head. His fingernails clawed at the bits of exposed rock on the road, which was still warm from baking in the sun all day.

"Holy mother of Christ. Owen?"

Owen lifted his head, the voice unfamiliar as the pair of boots moved closer. He felt hands on him and was then flipped over onto his back, blinking as Marty Wiggins's face came into view.

"What the hell happened to you?"

Owen moved his mouth to try and respond, but nothing escaped his lips except for a wheezing groan. It was the weight of the amulet in his hand, which had grown oddly heavy, that finally snapped him out of the dazed confusion muddling his brain.

"Town," Owen said, taking a hard, dry swallow of spit. "Take me into town." He rolled to his left, groaning as Marty's hands fell over him and provided the needed strength to lift him off the ground.

Once on two legs, Owen wobbled but Marty steadied him by taking hold of his shoulders. Marty pinched his eyebrows together, a single, greasy brown line down his chin that could be traced to the wad of dip protruding from his lower lip.

"Damn, Yankee, you look like shit." Marty steered Owen toward the truck and opened the passenger side door, then helped him up inside.

Goose bumps suddenly formed over Owen's skin from the cold A/C, and he hugged himself as he shivered. His mind swirled with fatigue, and he glanced down at his closed fist.

The driver side door shut, and the cabin rocked as Marty stepped inside. The truck's transmission grunted in defiance before spurting them forward.

Owen caught himself drifting to sleep twice, and he jerked himself from rest, sucking in deep breaths of air as he kept his eyes on the illuminated road that stretched for miles with nothing on either side but the swamp that Owen had traveled through.

"Everybody was talking about what happened to your son today at work," Marty said, hawking some brown spittle into an old Diet Coke can. "My wife's been having a fit all day trying to get a hold of her dad. I knew the old bastard was crooked, but I didn't know he was *that* crooked."

Owen frowned, Marty's words slow to sink in, but he finally remembered from his first few days on the job that Billy Rouche was Marty's father-in-law. He turned to Marty, slowly, unsure of the man's allegiance. "Did you know?"

Marty glanced over, and with the man's lower lip puffed

out from the dip, he looked like a sulking child that had been caught with his hand in the cookie jar. "Look, Yankee, I might be an asshole, but I'm not a criminal. Not on the scale of ol' Billy Rouche." He raised his eyebrows and briefly took his hands from the wheel and held them up in defense. "Why would I have picked you up if I was in cahoots with the old man? Huh? It would have made more sense to just run you over!"

And in Owen's fractured and tired mind, he conceded the Southern drawling, dip-spitting, self-proclaimed ragin' Cajun had a point. Owen's muscles relaxed and he leaned back on the seat. "Take me to Queen's."

Marty nearly swallowed the dip in his mouth, and then coughed brown spittle over his dash and windshield. "Ah, shit." He wiped his lips with the back of his hand, and then reached for a dirty rag in the center console and cleaned up the mess. "What the hell you want to go there for?"

Owen glanced down to the rock in his palm. The green glowed brighter now.

"What the hell is that?" Marty asked, his attention more on Owen now than the road, and they drifted more freely over the lanes of traffic, which were thankfully empty on both sides.

"It's how I'm getting my son back," Owen answered, then looked up to the window outside and the starless, moonless night. "But I don't have much time left."

20

*S*heriff Bellingham eyed Queen's from across the street. The windows were tinted, and the closed sign was flipped at the door. While he had always thought Madame Crepaux strange, he never considered her a danger to anyone, not the least some Yankee who just moved down from Baltimore.

The house on Cypress Lane was empty when Bellingham checked after leaving Billy Rouche's residence, so the sheriff thought Madame Crepaux's shop would be a good place to start, seeing as how this was the last place Mrs. Cooley was seen after the hospital.

Two of the sheriff's deputies were with him, and both men had taken a few steps back when the sheriff walked toward the store. He was almost halfway across the street when he realized he was alone.

He turned around and frowned, giving them the same hard stare their fathers would. Both men looked at each other, then reluctantly followed, their eyes cast sheepishly down to their feet, still keeping a safe distance as Bellingham pounded on the front door.

"Ms. Crepaux! It's Sheriff Bellingham. Open up!" He took a step back, hands on his hips. He looked back to his deputies, who had remained in the road and off the sidewalk in front of the store. "You know that you two are going in there with me."

"Sheriff, we shouldn't be bothering this woman," Deputy Hurt said. "She's," he looked down to his feet, wiggling uncomfortably like a kid in church. "Well, she's crazy!"

"Yeah, Sheriff," Deputy Lane said. "I'm not saying I believe in all of this stuff, but no reason to go and kick the hornet's nest, you know?"

"You two nancys get your asses up on this sidewalk now!" Bellingham pointed down to the concrete with his right index finger extended, revealing his swollen and knobby knuckles that had started to ache. He wished he had some type of future telling to go along with the aches. His grandmother had a knee that swelled up just before it rained, and he recalled a great aunt that had a hip that ached whenever a high tide was coming in to break the levees. The only thing that he saw in his future was an Ibuprofen.

Bellingham knocked again, then tried the handle, which was locked. He leaned closer, trying to get a look inside, but whomever the woman had gotten to tint her windows had done a damned fine job. He spun around, and both deputies jumped from the old man's speed. "You two stay put and you radio me the moment you see anyone come by."

A unanimous "yes, sir" rang through the air, and Bellingham marched back across the street, the night air still lingering with the heat of the day. He checked his watch. If he was lucky, he'd be able to pull Judge Harlow out of bed. The old hag was probably already asleep in her coffin. The judge should have retired ten years ago, but she was still useful for getting a warrant at still hop up on her bench and spell out the law better than any other clerk of the court this side of the grand ol' Mississippi.

He walked back down to his office and had Veronica try Chuck Toussaint again. The bastard hadn't picked up his phone all day, and no one at work had seen him. He didn't like how slippery the man was becoming, and he sure as hell didn't like the fact that one of his suspects was dead.

Veronica poked her head into his office. "Still can't get a hold Mr. Toussaint, Sheriff."

Bellingham slammed both fists onto the table and rattled a cluster of pens and his nameplate off the desk. His jowls flushed red and contrasted brightly against the white mop of hair on his head. "I want an APB for Owen Cooley, Jake Martin, and Chuck Toussaint, and I want all three of those men in my cells before morning!"

Veronica skittered away without a peep and Bellingham reached for the statements again, trying to find something that he was missing. In all of the investigations that he'd conducted over the years, nine times out of ten, the simplest answer was the correct one. If all the evidence pointed to the butler with the candlestick in the library, then by God that's what it was.

But the simplest answer in this scenario just didn't make any sense. All the background checks he ran on Owen Cooley revealed the past of your average red-blooded American male. One instant of drunk and disorderly conduct when he was nineteen, where he was also charged with underage drinking, a few speeding tickets, but other than that, he was clean as a whistle.

Then on the other side Bellingham had Chuck Toussaint, known greaser of elections and a profound wealth and power in town, and old Billy Rouche who had been intertwined with the Toussaints for as long as he could remember. Not to mention the family that had suddenly disappeared off the face of the earth twenty-five years ago who lived in the same house as the Cooley's.

Bellingham thumped his elbows on the table and massaged his temples. Was he actually considering believing what Owen Cooley had told him? Then what? Put out an APB for a creature with large black eyes, long claws, and a mouth full of teeth? He'd have more gators brought in than he'd know what to do with.

Bellingham reached for his truck keys and grabbed his hat. He watched Veronica shoot up out of her chair in his peripheral vision on his way out. "Keep me updated on those APBs."

"Where are you going?" Veronica asked.

"Monster hunting," Bellingham answered.

* * *

OWEN CHUGGED a half bottle of warm water that Marty pulled from the back of the truck, and while it worsened his thirst, it did provide a needed boost of clarity. The fog of fatigue was briefly lifted and he sat up a little straighter in his seat. "What time is it?"

Marty glanced at his wrist. "Quarter after eleven."

"How much farther till town?"

"Not much longer."

Owen drew in a breath, eyes closed, gathering the needed strength to keep pushing forward.

"So," Marty said, switching his glance between the road and Owen in nervous throws. "You wanna fill me in on what's going on?"

"You wouldn't believe me if I told you." Owen leaned his head against the glass, feeling the vibrations from the road as a car passed in the opposite direction. When he noticed that it was a sheriff's deputy he immediately ducked lower in his seat. His eyes trailed it in the rearview mirror until it was out of view.

The truck slowed and then rumbled as Marty pulled off the asphalt and onto the gravel on the side of the road. "You wanna tell me why you clenched up like a whore in Church when that cop passed?"

"Your father-in-law is dead," Owen answered. He blurted it out faster than he intended, but in the essence of time, he didn't have much to waste.

Marty remained stoic, blinking a few times, that lump in his lower lip nearly dissolved. Owen tensed, waiting for Marty to speak, or to reach across the seats and try and choke him out. Owen had the size and muscle on Marty, but in his tired state, he wasn't sure if he'd be able to fend the man off.

"You do it?" Marty finally asked.

"No."

"You think it was Chuck?"

"I know it was Chuck."

Marty nodded slowly and then leaned back against his door. "Shit." He rubbed his eyes, groaning, and then smacked his palm against the wheel. "Dammit! That stupid old man. I told him not to get too close to those Toussaints. Ain't nothin' but a bunch of aristocratic asshats." He wrung the wheel, the thin cords of muscle along his forearms tensing from the tight grip.

"Marty," Owen said. "I need to get to Queen's."

"We need to go to the police," Marty said. "I don't need this kind of heat, Yankee."

"After you drop me off at the shop, you can do whatever the hell you want," Owen said. "I just need to get there."

"I don't know—"

"He's ten!" Owen's voice thundered inside the cabin, and the strength in which the words escaped surprised even him.

"He's afraid, and alone, and wondering why his father hasn't come to find him." Desperation clung to those last words like morning dew to grass. His eyes watered and when Marty kept silent, Owen reached for the door handle.

"Hold your horses," Marty said, waving at Owen's hand. He shifted the truck back into drive and both men bounced in their seats as he pulled onto the road.

"Thank you," Owen said.

"Yeah, well, you're just lucky I never liked that old bastard," Marty said. "Though my wife is going to be upset. Damn, you Yankees sure do love causin' a mess for us boys down South, don't you?" Marty looked over, but there was a hint of a smile on his face.

When Main Street finally came into view, Owen jolted upright in his seat. He pointed toward Queen's, but Marty waved him off.

"I know where it is," Marty said. "Not that I'd ever go there willingly." He slowed as he approached, and as Owen's eyes adjusted to the dark patch out front of the voodoo shop, Owen saw why. "Looks like someone else had your same idea."

The pair of deputies looked toward the headlights of Marty's truck, which he had stopped conspicuously in the middle of the road. Owen ducked below the dash and smacked Marty's arm. "Drive past and park down at the end of the street. I'll circle around back."

Marty bid as he was told, giving a wave to both deputies on the way past, the cheesy smile spread across his face anything but natural. He found an open spot at the end of the street and parked, killing the engine as Owen kept low on his exit.

"So what the hell am I supposed to do now?" Marty asked as Owen was slipping away.

"Just act like you're walking up toward Crawl Daddy's and say you're going in for a beer."

"If I'm going to Crawl Daddy's, then why the hell did I park all the way down here?" Marty asked, exasperation in his voice.

"You wanted the fresh air," Owen answered, and then slipped around the back of an insurance adjuster's shop before scurrying up the backside of the strip of buildings.

He glanced down at the rock in his hand and saw that it glowed even brighter now, the green light escaping through the cracks of his fingers. Owen tucked it into his pocket to keep himself hidden in darkness, and when he arrived at the back window of Queen's, he tapped the glass, hoping everyone was still inside.

After the first round of poking, no one answered, and he tapped the glass harder. He stole quick glances of the darkness around him and saw a rat scurry out from a hole at the bottom of a trashcan. A few A/C units hummed quietly farther down the road, but he heard no footsteps or shouts from the deputies out front.

"Claire!" Owen whispered, this time knocking on the glass. "Claire, open—"

A suction noise popped and the window pulled inward. "Owen?" Claire kept her voice a whisper, and then the window pushed outward even more, and she lunged through the open space and wrapped her arms around Owen's neck, squeezing tight. "Thank god."

Owen kissed her cheek and brought her face in front of his. "Everything all right?"

"It's fine," Claire said, still keeping her voice down. "The deputies have been out front for a while. What happened?"

Owen held up his hand, then briefly revealed the amulet, the luminescent glow filling the back alleyway, before closing his fist. "Do we still have time?"

"Yes." Madame Crepaux appeared next to Claire, her yellow eyes flickering in the darkness. "But we must hurry."

Both of them stepped back and Owen pulled himself inside, his muscles quivering from the exertion, and then landed awkwardly on his feet, his ankles giving way. Claire caught him before he fell.

"Christ, Owen, you're shaking like a leaf," Claire said, helping him through the room toward the door and across the shop to the second room where Roger was being kept.

"I'm fine," Owen said, doing his best to ensure that his voice didn't quiver. A small heavy thump smacked against his leg as Madame Crepaux closed the door, then lit a candle, revealing Chloe latched to his leg. He bent down and picked her up. "Hey, bug."

"Daddy, you stink," Chloe said, wrinkling her nose, and then kissed him on the cheek. "But I'm glad you're back."

Owen smiled, kissed his daughter, and then squeezed her tight, a few tears leaking out of the corner of his eyes. He set her down and Madame Crepaux brought a candlelight to his face, her eyes wide.

"Let me see it," she said.

Owen uncurled his fist with the amulet, and Madame Crepaux released a low gasp as she gently plucked the stone from his palm, holding it close to the candlelight, her eyes reflecting the green glow.

"Powerful," she said, whispering to herself. "The bokor who forged this did his work well."

"So what now?" Owen asked.

The woman closed her hand around the amulet and then turned to Roger, bringing the stone and setting it around his neck. "He will open the portal into the creature's world. It will be small, and it will be brief, but you will have entrance."

"How does he get out?" Claire asked, holding onto Owen's arm. "How does he come back?"

Crepaux walked quickly to her table and cabinets of herbs and solutions. She emptied a handful into a bowl, which glowed with a white light, and the water moved and danced across the ceiling. "The house will be the strongest point in the creature's world, and the most human. It is there you will be able to find the door back to this world." She turned around, bowl in hand, and set it down between Roger's ankles on the table where he was still strapped down.

The front door rattled with fists, and through the closed door of the side room, they all turned their heads toward the commotion of the deputies out front. "Open up! Search warrant! Open up!"

"We haven't much time," Madame Crepaux said, and quickly grabbed hold of Owen's hand and linked it together with Roger's, who was still unconscious. "Keep hold of him, and hang on tight."

Claire picked up Chloe and took a step back as Madame Crepaux raised her hands high and tilted her face toward the ceiling. She closed her eyes and opened her mouth, a low, throaty moan escaping her lips as the pounding on the door out front grew louder.

"Search warrant!"

Madame Crepaux swayed back and forth, the throaty hum steady as the light flickered in the bowl and the amulet around Roger's neck grew brighter. "Demallah-Ooo-Nah!" She stomped her foot and clapped her hands, both noises echoing loudly in the room and dwarfing the pounding on the front door.

"Sherriff's department, open up!"

Owen looked back to Claire as he held onto Roger's hand. She kept Chloe close to her chest, and in the glow of the green and white lights, he saw that she was crying. "I will bring him back."

"Demallah-Ooo-Nah!" Another stomp and clap, the rhythm growing faster.

"I know," Claire said.

A crash of glass and the stomping of feet snapped Claire's attention to the closed door, which quickly rattled. Feet shuffled, and another fist pounded violently on the other side.

Owen squeezed Roger's hand tighter, the light inside filling up the entire room now, a clash of green and white so blinding that Owen lifted his free arm to shield his eyes.

"Demallah-Ooo-Nah!" Stomp. Clap. "Demallah-Ooo-Nah!" Stomp, clap. "Demallah-Ooo-Nah!" Stomp-Clap. "DEMALLAH-OOO-NAH!"

The ground rattled under Owen's feet and he felt a harsh tug at the center of his chest, yanking him forward, and suddenly he was falling, the world around him still blinded by light. His skin grew cold, and with his eyes still closed, he caught a whiff of death, like road kill that had been baking in the afternoon sun.

Owen stepped back from the smell, and he stumbled, his mind disoriented from the sudden stopping motion of falling. He felt the ground squish beneath his feet. He blinked a few times, the brightness fading and replaced with shades of grey.

Trees sprouted from the swamp, their trunks broken and cracked, their branches void of leaves, with scraggly-looking pieces of moss that looked as dead as the trees they hung from. The leafless branches spiraled toward a sky void of sun, moon, stars, or clouds. It was a pitch black that Owen had never seen before, looking as dead as the world beneath it.

Owen paced in a half circle, getting his bearings, and then saw the house through the trees. He took a step toward it when a voice echoed from above. It was inaudible, nothing more than a water mumble, but it was enough to cast Owen's stare toward the cemetery.

The headstones and tombs he smashed in with the sledgehammer were still whole in this place, and he found himself drawn to it. Owen jogged over and his breaths stung with each inhale. He only made a few feet before his muscles ached and he clawed at the dead bark of the trunks to stay upright.

The cemetery widened the closer Owen moved through the trees. Another watery echo sounded from the darkness above, but this time he recognized the voice. It was Roger.

"The tomb." Roger's voice rang in clearer now, and Owen understood. He picked up his pace, and each labored breath sent a series of daggers into his chest.

"Matt!" Owen's voice echoed, and he cast a quick glance at the first grave he passed, wondering if the dead would rise again and what the hell they'd look like in a place like this. He saw the barren tree branches were clouded with thick spider webs. Tiny black dots crawled along them, moving together in a synchronized wave.

A pea soup fog rolled in thick around Owen's ankles, and he sprinted toward the mausoleum centered in the grave-yard. He swung open the wrought iron gate, this one not chained like the one in his world, and a mind-numbing rush of cold air struck him as he stepped inside. The stained glass windows at the top of the walls were broken, the beautiful artwork transformed into dagger-like shards.

A large concrete slab covered the top of a coffin that rested on a pedestal. Owen placed his fingers underneath the slab and lifted, his muscles straining, and he only moved it an inch before his grip gave out.

Owen sucked in another ragged breath, and he doubled over in a fit of coughing. The hearty hacks rattled his lungs and burned his throat. He spat on the ground, and his eyes widened from the bright sight of blood on the concrete. He'd been here only a couple minutes and that was what was happening to his insides?

He forced himself to stand and then repositioned his grip, and pushed this time instead of lifting. The concrete slab scraped against the pedestal and slowly exposed the coffin inside. Owen's arms shook, and his back and shoulders burned. His lungs ached, and he coughed up another spray of blood over his chin and shirt as the slab finally crashed to the floor.

Owen reached for the coffin's lid, and ripped it open. Inside, Matt lay on his side, his skin grey and clammy, curled up in a ball. He took sharp, wheezing breaths, and when Owen rolled the boy to his back, he saw that blood had crusted around his mouth and chin and stained the front of his shirt.

"Matt!" Owen scooped his boy out of the coffin and cradled him. He felt like a block of ice, his little chest rising quickly from his fast, panting breaths. "Matt?"

Matt's eyelids fluttered open, revealing blackness where his once vibrant blue eyes had been. He opened his mouth like a fish sucking water, finding the strength to speak. "Dad?"

Owen kissed his son's forehead, his lips burning from his son's icy touch. He pulled him closer and then stepped toward the mausoleum's exit. "I'm getting you out of here. Just hang on."

Shadows covered the sky above when Owen jogged out of the tomb, his son heavy in his arms as he weaved around the graves. The world darkened, and when he looked up to the spiders in the webs, all of them scattered toward the trunks, chasing him.

His feet splashed in ankle-high water, and to the left and right of him, growling and snapping their jaws, were gators.

One of the gator's mouth was split down the middle, and another had large, gaping wounds exposed on its back and sides.

Owen pushed through the pain and fatigue and the life-sucking nature of the world around him, and focused only on getting his son to the house. More creatures emerged from the swamp on his sprint: rats, snakes, spiders, lizards, gators, all of them decrepit and dying. They chased Owen through the trees, nipping at his ankles, a few scratches slashed on his calves. But when he broke the tree line and his feet padded into the dead soil of the field before the house, the animals didn't pursue him.

Hundreds of dead creatures lined up at the edge of the field, their glassy eyes staring at Owen, their animalistic calls both of this world and some other that he had never heard. Owen hobbled up the front porch steps and shouldered open the door, stumbling inside, barely able to keep Matt in his arms.

"I'm here!" Owen screamed toward the ceiling, the inside of the house a near replica, save for the fact that everything had aged horribly inside. The wood had rotted along the walls, boards were missing in the floor, what paint there was had been stripped and torn away. The house resembled the carcasses of those animals outside.

The walls rattled and Owen pulled Matt close to his chest. He retreated back to the front door, but it slammed shut on its own, sealing him inside. Black water flooded through the bottom crack, and Owen rushed toward it, tugging at the doorknob to escape, finding it locked.

The water rushed inside faster, then started to bubble up from between the floorboards. Owen ran down the hallway and into the dining room, the water rising to his ankles, and then his shins by the time he reached the staircase and bounded up step after step, the swirling black liquid looking more like tar than water.

"Get us out!" Owen screamed, and then spit up another hacking wad of blood, some of it dribbling onto his son. The black water reached the second-story banisters and flooded onto the balcony, and it was here the water stopped.

Noise was sucked from the room, and Owen's ears popped. He rotated his jaw, the dull throb in his ears turning painful. And that's when he heard it. The rattle pounded like the tossing of bones on concrete, clanging violently against an unforgiving surface. Owen backed all the way to the wall as the water to his left bubbled. Another rattle, this one louder and faster than before.

The creature's head appeared from the bubbling water near the stairs, its back to Owen as it ascended the staircase from the black muck, which dripped from its grey, scaly hide. The razor-sharp claws shimmered, and as it turned down the balcony, it set those dark eyes on Owen and his son, its mouth spread wide with all of those teeth set haggardly in its mouth.

The floor vibrated from each of its steps, and Owen's heart hammered wildly in his chest. Hot tears burst from his eyes, and Owen lifted his head toward the ceiling. "Get us out! GET US OUT OF HERE!" He felt the burn from his throat when he screamed but barely heard his own voice.

With no answer, Owen sprinted to Matt's room and shut the door, sealing himself and his son inside. He placed Matt down in the corner of the room then tried the window, but it was locked. The door burst open, and the creature approached, its raised claws like daggers poised to strike.

One of Matt's bats rested in the corner and Owen reached for it, putting himself between the monster and his son. "You won't have him, you hear me?"

The creature opened its mouth wide, saliva dripping from those sharp fangs and a low growl escaping from its throat.

Owen sprinted toward the creature, throwing all of his weight behind the momentum, screaming at the top of his lungs, a father's rage fueling him like a freight train. The bat connected with the creature's head but shattered upon impact, a thousand splinters flying through the air.

Bacalou didn't even flinch from the blow. It hissed and growled, and then spread its claws. Owen looked at the razor-sharp tips of black and took a step back, but he was too slow. The creature rammed its claws into Owen's body, the sharp knives cutting through bone and organs as the creature lifted him off the ground, keeping him impaled. Bacalou roared, sending a hot stink of breath that blasted Owen's face.

The pain from the wounds lit up Owen's mind like a hot flash, powerful but fleeting, and in its place seeped coldness. He glanced down to the creature and saw that the water was rising, consuming his feet, then his legs and stomach, his chest.

He glanced back to where he placed Matt and saw that his boy was gone, swallowed up by the darkness. Tears, red like blood, fell from his eyes and his mouth as the black water reached his chin. And as the creature let out another throaty roar, Owen knew that he had failed. His son was dead. He was dead. And then all was black.

250

*O*wen lay lifeless on the floor of Matt's room. It was exactly where the monster had dug its claws into his chest and stomach, and he'd felt those last bits of life drain from him. His body was soaked, his clothes glued to his skin and his hair dripping wet. But the floor around him was dry. The broken boards and peeled paint that had been in that other world were gone. Moonlight drifted in through the window, the clouds parting long enough to illuminate the inside of the house on Cypress Lane.

Owen's body jerked in a jackknife-like motion, and water spewed from his mouth and onto the floor as he shifted to his side, drawing in a gasping breath. His fingers immediately went to where the creature had stabbed him, but in place of blood and guts, he felt only the holes in his shirt and tiny bumps that rose like scar tissue over his chest and stomach.

He immediately looked behind him and saw Matt lying on the floor. In a panicked scramble, he crawled to his son on all fours. His son's skin had warmed, and he checked for a pulse. As he did, Matt gargled and bucked from a cough just like his father had done and vomited up the same black water.

"That's it, get it all out," Owen said, patting his son's back.

Matt caught his breath, and when he looked up, he blinked, his eyelashes still wet, and Owen stared into those beautiful blues that he was convinced he'd never see again. "Dad?"

Owen pulled his son close, squeezing tight and clawing at his boy with a father's hunger. He kissed Matt's head, sniffling from the tears starting to come, and then cried.

Matt squeezed back, though not as hard, and Owen loosened the hold on his boy and the pair remained seated on the floor. He looked down at his hands and arms, examining them and then giving them a poke, as if he expected them to not be real. When he looked back up, Matt's eyes filled with water. "It's not a dream. I'm home?"

"Yeah," Owen answered. "You're home."

"Hello?" The voice echoed from the front of the house, and both Owen and Matt jumped from the sound. "Mr. Cooley?"

Owen helped Matt to his feet, and the pair walked out to the balcony just as Sheriff Bellingham entered through the hallway to the dining room below. The men locked eyes, both in disbelief at the sight of one another, and then Bellingham noticed Matt.

"My god," Bellingham said.

Owen walked with his son toward the staircase. "He needs to go to the hospital." Matt flinched at the word, but Owen gave him a reassuring pat. "Just as a precaution, buddy."

Bellingham watched the pair walk all the way down the steps, and when Owen reached the first floor, he saw the sheriff place his hand on the butt of his pistol. "Mr. Cooley, I'm going to need you to step away from your son."

The air grew still between them and Bellingham repeated the order, which Owen continued to ignore. "Whatever you think I did, it wasn't me."

"Mr. Cooley, I don't want to have to do this the hard way," Bellingham said, his body tensed, his knuckles white against the black of his pistol handle. "Not in front of your son."

Matt had his face buried into Owen's shoulder now, and he felt the boy trembling. With effort, Owen pulled his son off of him and set him near the base of the stairs. "Hey, Matt, look at me." The pearly whites around those blue eyes had flushed red from tears that streamed down his face. "You're safe now. Nothing's going to hurt you. Understand?"

Matt nodded and then wiped his eyes.

Owen turned back around to Bellingham, who still had his hand on the pistol. "I need to get my wife over here, so she can be with our son."

"We'll drive him—"

"No," Owen said, his tone stern. He watched Bellingham fidget nervously. "He's not going anywhere in the back of a squad car, and he's not staying with anyone but family." Owen clenched his fists and placed himself between Bellingham and his boy.

Slowly, Bellingham nodded. "All right, Mr. Cooley." He removed his hand from his pistol, his shoulders relaxing a bit. "I can make that happen."

* * *

THE BEDROOM WAS LARGE, and a ten-thousand-dollar painting hung on the wall where the bed's headboard was propped against. The painting was a knock-off Jackson Pollock. Some imitator who thought they could recreate the same textures and color schemes of the famous abstract expressionist. Chuck had thought the man had pulled it off quite well. Any art critic would have disagreed.

A pair of socks flew across the room and landed onto the bedspread that was already piled messily with clothes, money, jewelry, credit cards, and legal documents. A suitcase was open and empty on the floor, and Chuck paced around the room absentmindedly, moving toward something, and then forgetting what he was doing halfway to his destination.

He was shirtless but still wore the same pants that he had in the swamp. His bare chest was covered with specks of dirt and mud, his hair dry but sticking out in wild directions. He closed his eyes and took a few deep breaths, trying to stem the flood of panic that was consuming his movements and thoughts. He had to think straight. He had to move quickly.

Ever since Owen had taken that amulet from him, he'd felt like he had a target carved on his back, and he couldn't remove it no matter how many times he clawed at it.

Chuck reached for the Wild Turkey that was half gone and chugged a few gulps straight out of the bottle. Two lines of the dark bourbon dribbled down the sides of his mouth as he scrunched his face from the burn of the liquor.

The phone rang and Chuck jumped from the noise, dropping the bottle of bourbon where the glass smacked with a dull thud before falling to its side and staining the white carpet brown. He flung pants and shirts off the bed until he found the phone. It was Nate. "What?"

"What the hell is going on?" Nate asked, his voice quiet but still conveying a sense of panic. "The police just showed up at my place."

"Listen, just tell them you were with me all day drinking at my place. You just got home a little bit ago, and you left me passed out at my house. Got it?"

"Does this have to do with what's going on with Jake and

Billy? I thought you said you were taking care of that?" Nate asked.

Through the speaker of the phone, Chuck heard the faint knocking of the police at the door and another voice that sounded far away. "I did, but I need you to tell the police what I just said. All right?"

Another series of knocks, these ones more vicious than the ones before. "Y-yeah, yeah, all right, Chuckie, all right."

The call ended and Chuck collapsed onto the side of his bed. If the police were at Nate's, then it wouldn't be long before they were here. He dug at his eyes with his palms, a storm of a headache coming on from the day out in the swamp and the liquor he'd drained.

If Jake and the old man had just done their job, then he wouldn't even be in this situation. They only had to do it this one time, and he would have been good for another twenty-five years. One fucking time, and they fumbled it at the last second.

Chuck was so angry, in so much disbelief that he actually started to laugh. He caught his reflection in the mirror and he just completely lost it. "Well, Dad," he stopped, wiping his eyes. "Looks like your boy fucked up again. Just like you thought I would."

There was a picture of his father on his dresser. He looked like he always did. Stern. Unhappy. He couldn't recall a single memory of his father smiling. Not even when things were going right. Chuck recalled a time when he brought home his report card in grade school. He had gotten straight As. It was the first time he'd ever done it, and he was so proud that he ran from the school straight to the factory to tell his father.

On the way there, Chuck imagined that his father would hold it up and show everyone in the factory what his boy had accomplished, beaming with a pride that only a father could show. But when Chuck arrived at his father's office, the reception was less than welcome.

"What are you doing here?" his father asked, not looking up from the papers on his desk, too absorbed in his work to even acknowledge his son's presence.

"Dad," Chuck answered, holding up the yellow card that showed all of his high marks in every subject listed. "I got my report card."

His father compared different sheets of paper on his desk, then scowled, shaking his head and crossing out a series of figures. He turned toward his door away from Chuck. "Bernice! I need the projections for next quarter!"

"Dad, look." Chuck extended the report card and placed it on top of the papers his father was working on. He stepped back, a smile on his face, and waited for the praise he so desperately wanted.

But as his father examined the card, the scowl on his face only intensified. "What is this?"

"My report card," Chuck said, his tone timid. "I got straight As." He looked down to his feet, and suddenly the card was flung at his legs and knocked against his shins.

"Why the hell would you bring that to me?" His father's tone thundered loudly in the office. "You wanted to have a celebration? You wanted a new toy for this?"

"No," Chuck answered sheepishly, trying to keep the tears at bay. "I just thought you'd be proud of me."

And then his father actually laughed, the heavy vibrato of his voice slapping Chuck's face like a wet towel. "School is your job. Do you think I give my employees a bonus for doing their job? No. Excellence is expected, Charles, not celebrated." He returned to his work. "Come back when you actually have something noteworthy."

With silent tears streaming down his face, Chuck picked up his report card and quickly and quietly left the office. He cried all the way home and all night, skipping supper. And his father's words stuck with him for the rest of his life, and like the words, he continued his quest to find something noteworthy for his father to finally speak the words he'd wanted to hear his entire life. But he never did. And they never came.

"I bet you're just laughing your ass off, huh, Dad?" Chuck asked, staring at that hard face. "I bet you never felt anything, did you? No fear. No joy. You weren't anything but a black hole, weren't you?" He snarled. "Well, fuck you, Dad."

And just as the words left his mouth, an icy chill hit him, followed by the rattling of bones. Chuck shot up from the bed like the piston of an engine and then reached for the pistol lying on the pillow. With shaking arms and quivering legs, he aimed the gun in the empty space of the room, jerking left, then right, searching for the noise's source, but saw nothing except the spilled bottle of bourbon that had soaked into the carpet.

Another rattle, this one louder than before. Then another, and another, the noise falling into a rhythm. A playful laughter flitted through the air. It was a woman's laughter, mocking and wicked.

"You think that black magic can stop a bullet?" Chuck asked, maneuvering his aim around the empty room, the rattling and whispers growing louder. "Why don't you come on out and we'll give it a try!"

Another laugh, this one deeper, calculated. "I see you, son of Charles Toussaint. I can feel the fear carved into your soul. You are not safe anymore."

Chuck backed up to the wall, his arm extended straight out like a piece of steel. Sweat had broken out all over his body, the sheen of liquid reflecting off of the fluorescent lighting of the room. A groaning noise echoed at the door, and Chuck pivoted his aim toward it.

A dark shadow crept into the doorway, pausing for a moment, then spread inside. Chuck's finger twitched over the trigger, but he didn't pull it. Fear had frozen him, and it kept him there as the shadow took form into the shape of a woman. Madame Crepaux.

"You have murdered, Charles Toussaint, and you have cheated," Madame Crepaux said, her legs nothing more than black, wispy clouds, her eyes glowing yellow and hot. "Your family has sipped from the cups of others and given nothing in return. But now I will come for your cup, and I will drink until there is nothing left!" The apparition thrust her head back and laughed, a cackle so wild that it shook apart the woman herself.

Chuck screamed, then shut his eyes as he pulled the trigger. The recoil of the weapon shuddered against his body. He pulled the trigger until the magazine emptied. He opened his eyes and saw only the bullet holes in the wall on the other side of the room.

The black woman was gone, and Chuck slid to the floor, crying like he did on the way home from his father's office. But unlike the despair of never having a father's affection, the despair that filled him now was hopeless. The amulet was gone. The creature was free. And it was all because he couldn't kill Owen Cooley. But that could change.

* * *

STRANGE MACHINES BEEPED, and a mixture of fear and hope lingered in the air of the hospital. People wanting to know whether or not their loved ones would survive, doctors delivering good news, bad news… final news.

Owen wasn't sure why he was thinking about all of that now, but it could have something to do with the cuffs around his left wrist that tethered him to the hospital bed while a deputy watched him from the door and a nurse drew his blood.

"All right, Mr. Cooley," she said, carefully removing the vial of blood from the needle, and then disposing of the gloves and needle in the medical waste basket marked by that awful orange and those half-death circles. "That should be everything. We'll have the tests back in a couple days, but everything looks normal so far."

Owen nodded his appreciation and then left. He'd told the nurse, as well as the doctor, about the three scars on his chest and stomach where the creature had stabbed him, though he chose to leave that last part out. Now that Matt was back, he didn't think it necessary to continue his tale of the creature from the black lagoon.

He reached for the spots and rubbed the raised scar tissue with the tips of his fingers. It felt cold. The whole damn hospital was cold. He looked to the deputy who stood straight and alert at the door, watching him intently.

The exchange between him and his wife was short when they reached the hospital. He managed to learn that Madame Crepaux had disappeared, but there wasn't much chance for conversation after that as he was whisked away. The sheriff had questioned him, but only for a little bit. The fact that Matt wasn't missing anymore seemed to vex the old sheriff. But what vexed Bellingham gave Owen relief.

A tight, tingling feeling formed in his groin and he wiggled on the chair. He'd downed three bottles of water and two portions of applesauce since he'd arrived at the hospital, and now all that liquid was begging to be released.

"Deputy?" Owen gestured to the bathroom, and the officer walked over and removed the cuffs, escorting him all the way to the restroom's door. For a second, Owen thought the man was going to walk in with him, but he remained at the door and just kept the door open.

Owen flexed the wrist now free from the cuffs and reveled in the relief that it was gone. He peed, flushed, and then went to wash his hands. But the moment his fingers touched the water, a burning pain seared in his chest and stomach. Owen hissed in pain and clutched the sides of the sink as the deputy burst inside.

"What's wrong?"

Owen shook his head. "My chest. It… burns."

"Just hold on, I'll get the doctor." The deputy ran into the hall, shouting.

Owen looked down to his chest and then gently fingered one of the raised scars where the creature had stabbed him. He touched it, and another jolt of pain rushed through him so fast and hard that his mind dizzied and he tightened his grip on the sink.

The pain subsided a little, and Owen blinked at his reflection in the mirror when something flashed. He shook his head, eyes shut and rolling in their sockets. The burning returned a little bit, and he tasted sweat on his lips.

Owen looked at his reflection once more, examining his face, shaking off what he saw as nothing more than a response from the pain. His mind was playing tricks on him, that was all. But then as he stared into his reflection, his eyes darkened and his skin broke into cracked, fleshy scales that turned grey. His mouth widened and his teeth grew sharp and long and jagged. "NO!" He shut his eyes and turned away, hearing the creature's laugh echo in his mind.

With his eyes still closed, he sprinted for the door but slammed into the deputy's body, who quickly spun him back around against the wall and pinned his arms behind his back.

"Calm down, buddy," The deputy said.

"No!" Owen thrashed against the officer's hold, but he was too weak to break free. "I'm not that thing! I'm not!"

"What the hell are you talking about?" the deputy asked,

and the cuffs clicked into place. He spun Owen around, who caught another glimpse of his reflection before being forced back into the hallway and saw that his face had returned to normal. But as he walked down the hospital hallway, escorted by the deputy, he heard a distinct rattling. This time, the noise came from within, and he heard the low growl of Bacalou in the back of his mind. It was finally free. And it was hungry.

150 YEARS AGO

*C*louds covered the night sky and drifted lazily over the stars and the moon. Underneath the peaceful night, the Louisiana swamp sat still and quiet. Darkened waters flowed between the trees, which stretched to the horizon. But amidst the wild, man had already started to tame the land.

Lights burned from a small town of trappers and loggers. Dirt roads and log houses had replaced the reedy swamps and thick cypress trees. A group of settlers had gathered outside a house, a cloud of disdain and anger growing above them.

But away from the settlement, far on the outskirts and nestled in the swamp, was another home. It was small, and poorly built. Candlelight flickered in the windows, and smoke plumed from the chimney. A woman cried, her grief disrupting the peaceful night. Here, another cloud had started to form. Death.

A young girl lay in bed. Blood had dried at the corners of her mouth and stained the white nightgown that she'd been bedridden in for the past three days. She no longer drank, no longer ate. Her parents had tried everything. The doctor in town had told them to make her as comfortable as possible, but her father refused to watch his daughter die. So he found the woman the townspeople had whispered about. He was told that she could save those on the brink of death.

People who were fortunate enough to never need her services called her a witch, a devil worshiper. But to those that she had saved, she was known by another name. The Queen.

From the stories and descriptions of the townspeople, you would have thought her an old woman, hunched over and fragile. You probably would have pictured her with an unsightly face, marked with welts, scars, and wrinkled by the fleeting years of time.

But the woman that knelt at the foot of the young girl's bed was nothing like the rumors. A face of beauty framed a pair of luminous green eyes. The robes she wore clung to the curves of her body, and while much of her skin was covered, her exposed hands were soft as silk.

"She doesn't have much time left." Queen Samba closed her eyes and lifted her hand to the ceiling. An invisible force grew heavy against her palm. She looked to the parents, the mother clutching her husband's arm. They reeked of fear, while their daughter reeked of death. Baron Samedie was close.

"Can you save her?" the father asked, his voice shaking as the mother cried into his chest.

Queen Samba examined the girl's pale skin and the lips that had turned a light shade of blue, almost violet. She turned toward the parents. A small amulet hung from her neck. The amber centered in the leather strap glowed. "The price to save your daughter's life will come at the cost of another."

The father stepped forward. "If it's a life you need, then

take mine."

"No!" the mother cried, clawing at her husband's chest, which he gently removed. He kissed her and after he pulled away she collapsed into a chair, hunched over in grief.

The father stiffened, but fought back tears. "Do what you must."

"Very well." Queen Samba took the father's hand and guided him to his daughter's bedside. She interlaced the father's fingers with the child's, and then cupped her hands over both of theirs. She closed her eyes and lifted her head toward the sky, toward Baron Samedie, who waited for the child's soul.

"La-kalla-ooo-way." The queen spoke softly, letting her tone rumble through her bones and outward to her hands. The father shuddered while the girl remained still. She drew in a breath. "La-kalla-ooo-way." The room tremored, the very walls of the house shaking.

The piece of amber around Queen Samba's neck glowed brightly. The mother had lowered herself to her knees, her hands clutched together and her eyes shut hard, tears leaking from the corners as she recited the Lord's prayer.

Queen Samba opened her eyes and she saw Baron Samedie, his skeleton cloaked in black robes, those empty eyes fixated upon the little girl. She lifted her hand up toward him, quickly repeating the incantation. "La-kalla-ooo-way! La-kalla-ooo-way! LA-KALLA-OOO-WAY!"

The amber flashed into a blinding light, forcing the father to look away. But the Queen kept hold of his hand and his daughter's. Slowly, the father's life drained from his veins and passed through the Queen. Moments of hope, joy, fear, even his darkest secrets and desires. All of it was channeled through her and offered to Baron Samedie as a sacrifice.

As life slipped away from him, the father aged. His cheeks grew sullen. His jet-black hair faded to grey, then white. Skin sagged and wrinkled, and the taut muscles along his body slackened. Queen Samba brought the father to the brink, and then stopped, leaving only a sliver of life.

"Be gone!" Queen Samba yelled, dismissing Baron Samedie with a flick of her wrist. "You have had your fill tonight! Leave these souls in peace."

Content, Baron Samedie slowly dissolved back into his realm. The father's fingers slipped from the Queen's and he collapsed to the floor. He examined his frail and weathered hands, then looked to the Queen. "What…did you do?"

Queen Samba rose, the amber around her neck no longer glowing, and sweat glistened over her skin. "Your daughter is spared, but Baron Samedie will return for you. It could be tomorrow, or it could be years from now." She looked to the girl in bed. Color had returned to her cheeks, and her breathing had soothed.

The girl woke, and lifted her head. "Mommy? Daddy?"

Both the father and mother rushed to their daughter's side, throwing their arms around their child. Their tears of grief and pain were now of joy. The mother turned back to Queen Samba, who lingered at the door. "Thank you."

Queen Samba nodded, and then left. She collected no payment, nor did she ask for one. When people sought her powers, she helped them restore balance to their lives. That was her purpose. That was Bon Dieu's will.

For years, the Queen had devoted her time and practice to the study of Voodoo. Those years of tireless work had transformed her body and mind into a vessel for the spirits created by Bon Dieu. It was a privilege to be such a vessel, and she understood the rarity of having such influence in this world. But as powerful as she was, Queen Samba could not save every person, nor every child.

The hour trek through the swamp passed quickly, and

Queen Samba emerged from the cypress trees and dangling Spanish moss with a smile.

Across a field of tall reeds and grass that drifted lazily in the breeze were the glow of candles in the windows of the two-story house she called home. Inside was her family, the disciples that had come to learn the ways of Voodoo and treat the sick and damned with no other place to go. It was a house full of life and warmth.

But of all her family, the most precious of them was waiting for her on the porch as she walked up the front steps.

"Maman!" Isadora looked up from her book and brightened with a smile. She quickly jumped from her chair and sprinted to her mother.

Queen Samba smiled as her daughter wrapped her arms around her neck. "My sweet child!" She kissed Isadora on the cheek. "What are you doing up so late?"

Isadora lifted the book still clutched in her hand. "I was learning more about Bon Dieu, and how he created the spirits for us to communicate with." Isadora pointed to the same script that Samba had studied so many years ago. "He brought life to trees, and the water, and even us!" She smiled, those beautiful hazel eyes reflecting the candlelight glow.

Samba brushed Isadora's hair behind her ear. "You will become a great Queen one day, my darling."

Isadora jumped excitedly, waving her arms. "Will I have all of your powers? Will I be able to control the spirits?"

Samba laughed and gently lowered her daughter's hands. "Perhaps." She leaned in closer. "But only if you respect them." She opened her palm, and a tiny ball of green light danced like fire. "But you must always control it, because if you let it, it will consume you." She closed her fist and the fire was snuffed out.

"Maman!" Isadora pointed toward the dirt path that led from their house to the road, her eyes wide with fear.

Samba turned and saw torches burning on the horizon, held by the fists of angry men. She quickly ushered Isadora inside. "Wake the others, child. Hurry!"

The girl sprinted away, taking the book with her as Samba eyed the mob marching toward her. The father of the boy had corralled the townspeople at last, and now he had come to destroy her. He had promised he would.

Fear and ignorance caught like wildfire. And now Charles Toussaint had brought the fire to her house, ready to burn everything and everyone that she loved. She had held on to hope that he wouldn't be able to convince so many to join him. She was saddened to discover that she was wrong.

Queen Samba rushed inside and found her disciples awake, their eyes frantic, clawing at her robe.

"Queen! What do we do?"

"Why are they coming? What have we done?"

"The Great Bon Dieu has forgotten us!"

Queen Samba held up her hands, and all fell silent. She looked to her followers, their eyes and ears eager for comfort. "Bon Dieu will never forget us, even when we forget him." She cast a harrowing glare at Damas, who'd spoken the last words, and he cowered, but then Samba placed a finger underneath his chin and raised his eyes toward her. "He has not left you."

The young man and the others nodded, their confidence growing. Queen Samba pulled the four of them close, her green eyes providing an unearthly glow. "Move all of the sick and ill from their beds and hide in the swamp. Wait there until these men have gone. Take my scrolls, and books, and the clothes on your back. There is no time for anything else."

"What of young Isadora?" Damas asked.

Queen Samba turned to the mob out front. She knew what Charles Toussaint wanted, but she would not let him have it.

"Queen?" Damas asked, gently prodding her arm.

Samba faced her followers. "She will go with you, and you will keep her safe. I trust you, Damas. But no matter what, you do not give her up, understand? No matter what the man chooses to do to me. Do not give her up." She squeezed his arms tight. "Say it."

"I-I won't give her up," Damas answered. "No m-matter what."

Samba kissed his forehead and then jumped into action, helping move those that were still under her charge. Old, young, black, white, men, women, children, there were all walks of life that sought shelter under her roof. She helped thieves and monks up from their beds. She stirred whores and teachers, drunkards and craftsmen.

All of them fled out the back, Samba pushing them toward safety, her faithful followers leading them into the swamp. As the last few patients were helped down the stairs, Isadora lingered on the back porch, tears streaming down her face, with Damas trying to pull her away as the torch lights grew brighter out front. "Maman! Don't leave me, Maman!"

Samba rushed to her daughter's side, kissing her forehead as she cupped the little girl's cheeks. "My sweet girl, you will never be without me."

Isadora sniffled and then threw her arms around her mother's neck. "I don't want to go without you, Maman. I'm scared."

Samba squeezed her daughter tight. "You are strong, Isadora. And I promise you that we will see each other again. No matter what."

Isadora whimpered, but nodded as Damas took her hand. She stretched out her arm, her eyes locked onto her mother, crying again. "I love you, Maman!"

If a heart could break, then Samba's split in two at her daughter's words. Her lip quivered, but she steadied her voice. "I love you too!" She waited until she could no longer see them in the darkness, and by then the wolves were howling at her front door.

"Kill the witch!"

"Burn her!"

"She's nothing more than a devil worshiper!"

"Send her back to the hell she came from!"

A heavy thud hit the front door that buckled the wood. It was followed by another, then another, and finally the frame cracked and the door flung inward, slamming against the wall. A tall, broad-shouldered silhouette filled the doorway. Torches flickered behind him like the flames of hell.

Charles Toussaint entered, fists clenched at his sides, his expression of hate and disgust hardened like the steel rail of train tracks. "I told you I would come, woman." He glanced around at the house, snarling like a rabid dog. "I had to pay off a lot of people to find this place."

Queen Samba stood in the living room, the glow of the torches illuminating her face and casting long shadows behind her. "I did what I could for your boy." Her voice softened as she tried to reach past his calloused grief and anger. "Treasure the memories you had with your son. Do not soil them with such destruction now."

The wooden floorboards bent and warped with every step that Charles Toussaint took inside. "Do not tell me how to honor my son." Spit flew from his mouth, and the flickering flame from the torch triggered the shadows on his face to dance. "You killed him. You and your witchcraft." He snatched Samba by the wrist, his large weathered hand engulfing her with ease. "I've come to repay you in kind." He regarded the empty house, and he squeezed her wrist hard.

The bones in Samba's wrist groaned in pain, but she did not waver. She narrowed her eyes. "My death will bring you no joy."

Toussaint yanked her close enough to where she could smell the sweat of his body and the stink of his breath, which puffed hot on her cheek. "No. But your daughter's death will."

Queen Samba's eyes flashed bright green, and she slapped Toussaint's cheek. The vicious crack released Toussaint's hold on her wrist, and he stumbled to the side. When he turned to face her again the mark left behind on his cheek burned a bright red.

Toussaint screamed, lunging for Samba, his size and strength overpowering as he muscled her to the crowd outside. She was brought out to the roar of cheers. The mob parted as Toussaint threw her to the ground.

Samba slowly pushed herself up, the crowd circling around her. "You do not want this." She pointed to Toussaint. "You have followed this man here, but that does not make you evil. It's what comes next that will define your souls."

"The only evil here is you, witch." Toussaint grabbed her by the throat and practically lifted her off the ground. He looked to the dark swamp around him. "If you want your Queen to live, then give me the girl! If not, then you'll all watch her burn!"

Samba struggled for air, trying to peel his fingers off as Toussaint waited for a response. And Samba was glad to hear nothing but silence.

"Fine," Toussaint said, and then tossed Samba to the ground. "String her up!"

The crowd cheered, and Samba clawed at the dirt, gasping for breath. From the ground, she saw the wood and oil they'd lugged with them and the cross that she would be tied to. She shut her eyes and whispered. "Bon Dieu. Hear me. Please."

Angry hands grabbed her arms and dragged her toward the pyre. Coarse rope tightened around her wrists and ankles, her arms pinned behind her back on the cross. She lifted her head to the night sky. She knew the pain that would come. She knew she would feel everything. But her daughter would live.

"Witch, you have been found guilty in the practice of unholy rituals," Toussaint said as the wood around her feet was doused with oil. "For your crimes, you will be burned at the stake and sent back to the hell and devil that you worship."

A man cheered, and it triggered a chain reaction that rippled through the crowd. They were all drunk off the hate that Toussaint had funneled down their throats.

Samba could only keep her eyes locked to the night sky as the heavy doses of oil were then flung over her clothes. "Please, Bon Dieu," she whispered. "Take me quickly."

Toussaint grabbed one of the torches and stepped to the edge of piled wood, his cheeks a cherry red. "To hell with you, witch." He raised the torch high, and Samba closed her eyes, but just before Toussaint dropped the torch, a cry echoed from the house.

"Maman!"

Isadora stood on the porch, crying and alone. Toussaint and the crowd turned just as Damas reached for her arm, giving her a harsh yank backward.

"NO!" Samba tugged against the restraints as Toussaint tossed the torch into the dirt and reached for the pistol at his side. He aimed for Damas, his eyes white and fearful in the glowing firelight.

A gunshot shattered the night air. Damas twisted his body

violently on his collapse to the floor. Isadora screamed as the blood oozed from his chest.

Toussaint snatched Isadora off the porch, and Samba fought impotently against the ropes that bound her. "Let her go! She has done nothing!"

Toussaint manhandled Isadora and dropped her at the edge of the wooden pile. He handed the pistol to a man on his left. "Reload it."

"NO!" Samba cried.

"Maman!"

"QUIET!" Toussaint accompanied his bark with a harsh jerk that rattled Isadora like a doll. He looked to Samba, smiling, his eyes reflecting the fire of the torches. "You have always preached of the balance of life and death." He held out his hand, and his associate gave him the reloaded pistol. "A child for a child."

Samba shuddered when Toussaint pressed the end of the barrel against Isadora's head, his free hand on the back of her neck, keeping her in place. "Take my life. Torture me, but don't harm my daughter." Tears dripped from her chin and she tasted the snot from her nose. "You know the pain of losing a child. Taking mine won't ease your suffering."

Toussaint cocked the pistol's hammer.

"Maman," Isadora wept and trembled. "Save me."

Samba smiled with tears in her eyes. "It's okay, baby. Everything will be fine. Everything will—"

Smoke filled the air in a swirling puff of grey. Isadora collapsed into a small, lifeless pile at Toussaint's feet.

Samba screamed, the veins and muscles along her neck tight as her throat grew raw. She convulsed and heaved against the restraints. She shook her head, her grieving howls born from the depths of her womb where Isadora was born, a light shining in the dark. But now that light had been snuffed out, so had Queen Samba's sense of balance and peace. She lowered her head. "If Bon Dieu will not hear me, then I will call on death to listen."

Her eyes flashed a bright green, and her voice started low and deep, then grew into a fast rhythm as she called upon Baron Samedie and Demballah-Wedo for justice. "Calla-Wen-eee-ooo-la. Calla-Wen-eee-ooo-la. Calla-Wen-eee-ooo-la. CALLA-WEN-EEE-OOO-LA!"

A black darkness swirled around the house, around the crowd of angered townspeople, who suddenly gasped in horror. All but Toussaint cowered.

"Hear me, Baron Samedie! Hear me, Demballah!" Queen Samba lifted her head and locked eyes with Toussaint, her face greying and flecking with scales. "I call upon you to drain the life from the Toussaint name. For as long as a first-born son of the Toussaint family walks this earth, they will not be safe! Their souls will be taken, trapped in the underworld and cast to wander aimlessly in eternity." She convulsed, and she saw Baron Samedie smiling down on her. He was willing, but it would take a sacrifice, one that she was more than willing to give. "I offer you my soul for vengeance! Hear me, Baron Samedie! HEAR ME!"

Wind swirled all around, and the hot summer air suddenly grew cold. Charles Toussaint snatched a torch from one of the townspeople, its fire nearly gone, and tossed it over the oil-soaked wood. The tiny embers caught quickly, and fire swirled up and around Queen Samba, the glow from her green eyes suddenly blacker than the night that surrounded them.

"Your heirs will never be safe," Samba said, her voice low, growling and ominous. "I will snap every branch of your family tree!" The fire took hold of her clothes, the flames crawling up her body as the laughter turned into the same high-pitched screams of her daughter.

Through the fire, Queen Samba caught one last glimpse

of Charles Toussaint, and as her soul passed from this world and into the hands of Baron Samedie, she felt the cold touch of revenge. She was no longer Queen Samba. Until her curse ended, she would be known only as Bacalou.

PRESENT DAY

*O*wen stared at his reflection in the one-way mirror of the sheriff's interrogation room. He kept expecting his face to break out into the scaly grey flesh of that monster. But so far it had not surfaced. Owen shuddered at what it might do.

A whisper tickled his ear, and Owen shook his head in annoyance. The voice was weak, tired. Ever since he saw Bacalou's image in the mirror at the hospital he'd heard whispers. Sometimes they were coherent, other times they were nonsense.

First it was a man, then a woman, suddenly a child. He turned as fast as he could toward the noises to where he thought they were coming, but saw nothing. And with every whisper came a chill that stiffened his spine and raised the hairs on the back of his neck.

But for the moment, the whispers and Bacalou were the least of Owen's worries. With Chuck gone, and Madame Crepaux missing, Owen was the only suspect in custody for the murder of Billy Rouche and Jake Martin. According to the sheriff, Owen had motive and no alibi.

Owen conceded the motive, but he did have an alibi, it just wasn't believable. Because despite everything that happened, Bellingham still wasn't convinced that Owen's son was taken by an evil Voodoo spirit that had cursed the Toussaint family.

The door opened and two deputies stepped inside, followed by Sheriff Bellingham, who shut the door behind him. He was a tall man with broad shoulders. Thinning white hair complemented a bristly mustache.

"We've sent all the evidence we have to the lab," Deputy Hurt said as Bellingham stood against the one-way glass, arms crossed over his stomach, staring at Owen. "If the bullets found in those bodies match the ones on your gun then you'll get a one way ticket to federal prison." He leaned against the table, smirking at Owen.

"The bullets weren't from my gun," Owen said, talking to the sheriff and bypassing the deputy. "I'm telling the truth, Sheriff. I don't have any reason to lie."

"Yeah, except for going to jail," Hurt replied.

"Give us a minute, boys," Bellingham said, his eyes locked onto Owen. "And turn the cameras off."

"Sheriff, I don't think—"

Bellingham's glare shut Deputy Hurt down, and the young man nodded and escorted the other deputy out. A few seconds after the door was shut Owen saw the tiny red light on the camera in the corner turn off. Bellingham walked to the table, took the seat directly across from Owen, and folded his hands on the table.

"You're in a bad spot, Owen," Bellingham said. "The sooner you tell me the truth, the sooner we can put the whole thing behind us."

Owen chuckled in exasperation, his motions limited by the restraints on his wrists and ankles. "I don't know what else I can say, Sheriff, that I haven't already said. I told you everything. It was Chuck who was behind my son's abduction. But it was the creature that took him."

"The creature from the curse," Bellingham said. "The curse from some ancient Voodoo Queen." He arched his eyebrows. "You do understand how that sounds, right? There isn't a judge in this country that's going to believe you."

Owen shrugged. "It doesn't matter now. Matt's safe. That's all that matters." That had been the one pillar keeping his sanity from collapsing. His son was alive.

"Owen—" Bellingham cut himself off with a sigh. He drummed his fingers on the table and then leaned back in his chair. "I don't think you murdered those people. I don't. But you need to give me something other than what you've got." He stood and walked back to the door. "Because I can tell you that even if an autopsy report comes back on Billy Rouche, Jake Martin is still missing. And that's a body that can still be pinned on you." He opened the door and leaned his head out. "Hurt! You can come back."

After Bellingham disappeared Owen was escorted back to his cell. Because of the murder charge, he was isolated from the other inmates. Hurt removed the restraints and the pressure around his ankles and wrists were alleviated.

The metal bruised his skin, and Owen gently messaged the imprints left behind by the shackles. He collapsed onto his cot, its thin mattress springs squeaking as he bounced up and down twice before coming to a rest. He was still caught in a nightmare, one that he no longer believed he could wake up from.

He slouched in despair, his eyes on the tips of his shoes, when a spider crawled between them from under the cot. It crawled on top of his shoe and traveled up his pant leg until it came to rest on his knee.

Owen tilted his head to the left, and the spider moved left. He tilted his head to the right, and the spider moved right. He motioned backward, and the spider crawled back down his leg. Owen let out a hysterical chuckle, short and loud.

"This can't be real." But the longer Owen stared at the spider, the longer he shared that connection, the clearer that hum in the back his head became. The spider was speaking to him. And in that telepathic bridge, Owen was speaking to it as well.

Owen thought about the whispers, about the flash of the creature he'd seen in the mirror at the hospital. Did he now possess the creature's powers? Could he control the creatures of this world like it could? Could he raise the dead to walk again?

The dead. Those whispers.

That's what those voices were. He was listening to the dead in next world. Like his connection to the spider, he was also connected to the souls in the afterlife. If he could control the spider, talk to it, then maybe he could talk to the dead as well. And if he could find Jake Martin's soul, then he might be able to find out where his body was slain. It was a long shot, but it was Owen's only shot.

* * *

CLAIRE CHEWED the end of her left pinky nail raw. Her eyes were glued to Matt, who sat on the cot as the doctor looked him over. She hovered close by and finally lowered her pinky when she drew a prick of blood. "He's okay?"

"I feel fine, Mom," Matt said, his cheeks flushing red with embarrassment.

The doctor lowered his stethoscope and crossed his arms. "Everything checks out. We'll run some blood work to make sure everything's okay on the inside, but from what I can tell here, he's fine. Just needs to eat, drink plenty of liquids, and rest."

But despite the doctor's prognosis, Claire was hesitant to enjoy the good news. She hadn't told the doctors what really happened to her son, not that they'd believe her if she did. "So, nothing out of the ordinary?"

The doctor hesitated and then gestured to the hallway. "Can I speak with you for a moment?"

"Of course." Claire kissed Matt on the cheek before she followed the doctor out of the room, who closed the door after she stepped out.

"Mrs. Cooley, I'm aware that your son was abducted," the doctor said. "The authorities filled me in on the details."

Not all the details, Claire thought. "I just want to make sure there aren't any lingering health issues that could affect him in the future."

"I can't imagine how difficult all of this has been for you, but I think it's important for your son to start working through what happened to him." The doctor placed a sympathetic hand on her shoulder and gave a light squeeze. "But I can tell you from a medical standpoint there doesn't seem to be any findings of sexual misconduct."

"What?" Claire gasped, taking a step backward. "Is that what you think happened?"

The doctor held up his hands defensively. "I'm sorry, it's just that in the room—" He pointed toward the door, cutting himself off. "If you weren't concerned about a sexual assault, then what other health problems would you be worried about?"

"I just…" Claire slouched, arms flapping at her side, and leaned back into the wall, her head down and staring at the tile. "I just don't want to lose him again."

"Mrs. Cooley, your son is safe," the doctor said. "Matt will have quite a few mental obstacles in the future, finding a way to cope with what happened. And it'll be hard for you to relive it as well. But he is *safe*."

"I know." Claire wiped the tears away before they fell and nodded. "Thank you."

The doctor reached for the doorknob. "I'll just finish making my notes on his file and give you some time alone with your family."

Claire lingered in the hallway as the doctor stepped back into the room. She took a few deep breaths, gathering her strength, trying to heed the doctor's advice. But no matter how hard she tried, the anxiousness remained.

Matt hadn't exhibited any of the odd symptoms as before. He wasn't speaking to snakes, his skin wasn't cold, nothing wrong with his eyes. He looked normal, sounded normal, and it all added up to having her son back, safe and healthy. She just needed to start believing it.

Claire returned to the room and found the doctor done with his notes. Chloe smiled from her chair, and Claire picked her daughter up and kissed her cheek. "How are you doing, sweetheart?"

"I'm okay," Chloe answered. "I'm glad Matt's back."

"Me too."

"I'll give you a call when the bloodwork comes back from the lab, but you guys are all done if you want to head home," the doctor said, then ruffled Matt's hair. "You've been a very brave young man." He looked to Claire and extended his card. "It's the hospital number, but I'll be on call all day if you have any questions."

"Thank you, Doctor," Claire replied, taking the card from him. "For everything."

After the doctor left, Claire took hold of Matt's hand, Chloe still in her left arm, and lowered herself to his eye level. "You doing all right?"

Matt nodded sheepishly. "Fine. A little hungry maybe."

"Well, we can fix that." Claire grunted from Chloe's added weight as she stood upright, taking hold of Matt's hand, the doctor's words ringing in her ears. *Head home.*

What home? The place where that creature had tormented her son? The place where her father had lost his mind? The house where her family was nearly killed?

Just when they had something going for them, the floor was pulled from beneath their feet. And Claire was facing all of it alone. The only other person she could speak to about it had lost his mind. Since Madame Crepaux had used him to send Owen into that other world, his Alzheimer's had only worsened.

And so Claire walked down the hospital halls, slowly, with Chloe in one arm and holding Matt's hand with the other. Her husband was in jail. Her father was dying. And they didn't have a penny to their name. If it was always darkest just before dawn, then the sunrise couldn't come soon enough.

22

---

ix. That was the number of dead roaches that Chuck had counted in Nate Covers's basement. He was sure there was more hiding behind boxes and the dozens of yard signs that had Nate's face plastered all over them.

Cockroaches and Nate Covers's grinning face, those were the new realities of Chuck Toussaint's life. The police had come again this morning, a few follow-up questions for Nate about his friend, and so his "friend" had shoved him downstairs so he wouldn't be seen.

Chuck reached for the black duffel bag next to him. He unzipped the top and opened it halfway. He peeked inside at the reassuring sight of his cash and jewelry. It was everything in his safe. Close to half a million. It was more than enough to start over somewhere. He could get into Mexico easily enough. He'd spend a few weeks getting liquored up and laid and figure out his next move.

The unknown was the worst part. The creature could be anywhere now, appear at any time. That unknown had haunted Chuck since he was a child, a creature designed for no other purpose than to hunt and kill him, just like it had so many others of his family.

Every first-born male of the Toussaint name will be taken until no more remain.

And for the first time in two centuries, a first-born Toussaint male could not reproduce. He'd been to every doctor in this country and a few abroad, but all of them told him the same thing: he was sterile.

At first, it was relief that flooded through him at the news. He wouldn't spawn a child that would have to live with the fear and terror that he did as a boy. But then the fear took control. Fear for his future. If he couldn't produce a son, then the curse would stay with him, and that creature would hunt him for the rest of his life. And because of that, every twenty-five years he would need to produce a sacrifice for Bacalou in order to survive.

Chuck had done everything to convince himself that he had no other choice. It wasn't his fault his family was cursed. He hadn't burned that Voodoo Queen. He didn't want to die, so someone else had to. And that's how he'd viewed life for as long as he could remember, like numbers on a balance sheet.

The basement door creaked open at the top of the stairs, and Chuck saw Nate's shadowed figure. "Chuck," he whispered. "You all right?"

"What the hell are you whispering for? Cops are gone, aren't they?" Chuck pushed himself off the floor, grabbing the duffel bag of money as he rounded the bottom of the stairs.

"Yeah, they're gone," Nate answered.

"Good." Chuck stomped up the stairs and shouldered the door open, stepping into Nate's living room as he stretched his back. "When was the last time you cleaned down there?"

Nate quickly scurried to the living room windows, shutting the blinds, then checked the peephole at the front door.

He spun around, his face a bright red. "Do you want someone to see you? What if they come back?"

Chuck sat on the couch. "Relax. I'll leave after dark."

"Yeah," Nate replied, fidgeting as he paced the living room. "Probably for the best." Nate then caught Chuck's gaze, and his cheeks flushed red with embarrassment. "It's not that I don't want you here, it's just—"

"You don't want to go to jail," Chuck said.

"Hey, you don't have to worry about me," Nate said, that real estate charm returning now that he realized he wouldn't have to harbor a wanted criminal. He sat in the chair across from the sofa and drummed his fingers on the armrest, his cheeks puffing with air. "So... What are you gonna do?"

"The less you know, the better," Chuck answered.

Nate nodded, and then his eyes slowly drifted to the duffel bag.

"You'll get your money when I leave," Chuck said.

Nate smiled. "Right. Yeah, sure." He lowered his eyes toward the duffel bag again and then quickly pulled them away. "The cops said they're charging Owen with Jake and Billy's murders." Nate shifted in the chair. "You think that'll stick?"

"Doesn't do me any good if it doesn't," Chuck answered. With the police busy with Owen, it was less resources they could use to spend looking for him.

Nate leaned forward, his eyes wide. "So it's true then, about the curse." He shook his head in a feigned disbelief. "The way you spoke about it and after everything you've done to stop it, I mean I guess that I always believed the stories were real, but..." He narrowed his eyes, lowering his voice to a whisper. "There really is a creature after you." He collapsed back into the chair, running his hands through his hair in the process. "Goddamn. So the Voodoo Queen, the house, your great-great-great-great grandfather. The little girl?" He chuckled hysterically, rubbing his eyes until the skin around them were red. "You've got one hell of a family."

Chuck stared at the floor, focusing on a stain next to the coffee table. He wasn't sure what it was. Probably bourbon, knowing Nate. But for whatever reason, he couldn't get the idea out of his head that it was blood.

"Yeah," Chuck said, not realizing he was smiling now. "Hell of a family."

The laughter rolled out of Chuck, slow and quiet at first. His shoulders bobbed up and down, he scrunched his face tight, and a tear squeezed from the corner of his eye.

"Um, Chuck?" Nate asked.

"HAHAHAH!" Madness had finally taken hold. Chuck was nothing more than an inmate on death row, waiting for his name to be called. He'd fought so long against the inevitable, that black doom that hung over every man's head. But in the end, none of it mattered. His wealth, his power, none of it could save him now.

The laughter faded, and Chuck wiped the tear from his cheek. His eyes returned to the stain on the carpet. Though he knew it wasn't true, Chuck still saw blood. And then he felt the tears fall. Tears that his father would have beat him for showing. And if the creature got its way, then he might be joining his father in whatever hell their family was cast. All thanks to Owen Cooley.

* * *

FROM THE ROAD, the house on Cypress Lane looked abandoned and foreclosed. It had lost its glory and luster from the days when Queen Samba had lived in it. Instead of a place of refuge for the sick and dying, it had been transformed into a harbinger of death. But the Queen's legacy survived through her disciples, as did her knowledge and power.

Madame Crepaux stood at the edge of the property, staff in hand and a fresh coat of sweat from the hot summer sun. Her joints had grown stiff, her knees and feet aching despite the staff's support.

For years, Madame Crepaux had longed to set foot inside that house, to experience the history of those that she had admired. But now, with Bacalou free, she found herself hesitant to enter.

It was mostly guilt that kept her out. Guilt of the pain she had caused Owen Cooley and his family. She knew Owen's fate the moment she saw him enter town. He was a necessary sacrifice to restore the balance of life and death. Without it, Bacalou's curse would never end, and the Queen's soul would never be free.

But had she not warned Owen Cooley of the price to retrieve his son? Yes, but not the whole cost.

Madame Crepaux closed her eyes and drew in a breath. She lifted her foot and lowered it onto the gravel road. When her foot touched rock, she exhaled, her body sagging with relief. She tilted her face toward the sky, the warmth of the sun beating on her old skin like the cracked and bumpy asphalt of the road. "Thank you, Bon Dieu."

The front door groaned as Madame Crepaux opened it, the sunlight penetrating the shadows inside. Floorboards buckled underneath her feet, and the staff's thump echoed loudly as she entered. The walls, the floors, the furniture, all of it contained the history of the Queen's legend. Madame Crepaux imagined the cots that lined the rooms, Queen Samba traveling from bedside to bedside, nursing the sick back to health.

The war between life and death was as old as time itself. The gods had enlisted soldiers in that war, and Madame Crepaux had simply answered the call like so many others before her. And in this house, beneath the crusted blood of innocence lost and the curse that had taken so many, there was the woman who in her last moments had traded her soul for revenge.

Madame Crepaux lingered in the living room a moment longer, then walked out the back, keeping a path toward the Toussaint family cemetery. There was a man buried there that she wanted to see. The first root of a tree that had spawned so much death.

Deeper into the swamp, the warm black water rose to her thighs. She lifted her hand and gently ran her fingers through the dangling strands of moss. It had been a long time since she had traversed nature like this. It was quiet, serene, warm.

The cemetery appeared, and Madame Crepaux climbed the raised mound of soft mud toward the graveyard's edge. Crumbled pieces of stone littered the ground, the tomes exposed from Owen Cooley's search of the amulet. The disturbed dead slept restlessly, their bodies decaying and still in the long process of returning to the earth from which they came.

Amongst the family of murderers, she glided between the headstones, searching for *his* grave, which she found near the mausoleum at the graveyard's center.

It was one of the oldest graves in the cemetery. The dates on the headstone had nearly been wiped away by the elements of time. But the name at the top was still legible in large Roman letters. Charles Toussaint.

Inside that coffin was a man who had murdered a child in cold blood, and then burned her mother at the stake. And as a follower of the great Queen Samba and her disciples who passed down their knowledge and truth for generations, she would finally give the Queen peace.

"Your tree is nearly dead," Madame Crepaux said, glowering at the headstone. "I'll make sure it stays that way."

She could still see the faded Latin beneath the name and years of life. Mors Mihi Lucrum. "To me, death is a reward." She spoke the words gravely. She wondered why Charles Toussaint had chosen those words to be put on his family's crest after the events with the Queen. Perhaps it was regret for the burden of future generations of his family. Or maybe it was just the fear of a tired old man on his deathbed.

Grimacing, she walked east, deeper into the swamp, traversing the trees and water. The black water touched her upper lip, only her eyes and the skull from her staff gliding over the water's surface.

After the Queen had been burned and Charles Toussaint and his band of minions retreated to their town, Samba's followers had emerged from the swamp, retrieving the body of Isadora and what remained of the Queen's material self. They buried them side by side, deep within the heart of the swamp, hidden on the property where the Queen had healed so many.

For years after, the Queen's followers would pilgrimage to her grave and honor her memory. But after the bokor created the amulet that chained Bacalou to the property and barred any followers of Samba from stepping foot around the house, the pilgrimages ended.

Fifty years had passed since any disciple had seen the grave of their Queen. But her memory was still alive, still vibrant in Madame Crepaux's soul.

The stone brightened to a blinding light, and Madame Crepaux saw the raised mound of mud and the small marking of the graves. She hastened her pace, her feet sinking in the thick mud on her trek up the mound and out of the water.

The brown robes clung to her body, soaking wet and dripping. She collapsed to her knees at the foot of the graves, tears welling in her eyes as she bowed to the woman who had taught her so much.

"My Queen," Madame Crepaux's voice quivered as she spoke. "It is nearly done." She placed her weathered hand against the soft, cool mud. "Peace will find you soon." She closed her eyes and lowered her voice to a whisper. "But, please, forgive me for what I do next."

Despite all her knowledge and dedication to her studies, Madame Crepaux was not as powerful as the Queen. And while she respected the balance of life, and restoring that balance had been her sole purpose, it didn't diminish her own desire for revenge.

For decades, Madame Crepaux had been forced to sit on the sidelines, watching helplessly as the Toussaints roamed freely, untouched by the curse. It was a mockery of the Queen's sacrifice and legacy.

Madame Crepaux placed both hands over the grave, chanting. The ground rattled and then parted, revealing the coffin of Queen Samba's remains.

Buried with Queen Samba was the Queen's gris-gris that she had read about in the scrolls. Unlike the Queen's body, it did not burn, and it could not be destroyed. It held the Queen's power, and Madame Crepaux could harness it.

But stealing another's gris-gris marked one's soul with darkness, and that darkness would grow so long as the gris-gris was kept. But Madame Crepaux had come too far now. Like the Queen's final act of vengeance, she would bear the weight of this burden.

Madame Crepaux reached into the coffin and removed the amber stone from the grave. It radiated light and power, and when she clutched it in her fist, that same power flooded her veins.

The Queen's knowledge, wisdom, and strength was suddenly hers. But underneath, she felt the pain and grief of

Isadora's death. It was as real and heartbreaking for her as it was the Queen.

Madame Crepaux closed her eyes as she placed the stone around her neck. "I will help Bacalou hunt him down. And when it is done, your soul will finally be at rest."

With the Queen's amulet around her neck, her body suddenly grew lighter. Her skin tightened, the years of life rolled back, and the aches and pains of old age disappeared. She watched her weathered hands be restored to the beauty of her youth. Her eyes flickered with a brilliant gold and she laughed, raising her arms toward the sky, reveling in the Queen's power.

23

*O*wen shifted uncomfortably in his shackles, his back growing tighter the longer the trip lasted. One of the sheriff's deputies, Lacroix, rode with him in the back of the van. He held a pump action twelve-gauge and was decked out in tactical gear. Deputy Hurt drove, while Bellingham rode in the passenger seat. It was just the four of them, despite Owen's request for more firepower.

He felt the beast lurking in the back of his mind, gathering its strength, and he wasn't sure how much longer he'd be able to keep it shoved in its cage.

Owen tugged at his restraints. His movements had been constricted to breathing and blinking. But even with the added security, he wondered if it would be enough to stop the creature.

Most of the ride, Owen had preoccupied his mind with the whispers from the dead echoing in his thoughts. But the messages were short, incoherent, and random. It was like listening to a crazy person losing his voice. They had quieted some since they had gotten in the van, but every once in a while they screamed, and a flash of pain seared his brain.

Owen looked toward the sheriff through the tiny barred, square window. He saw only pieces of Bellingham's profile, and that was when he heard another whisper. His heart raced. It was louder, and this one was human. He shut his eyes, clenched his jaw, and then grunted.

"H-he's actin' funny, Sheriff," Lacroix said

Bellingham turned around. "Stop the van."

The voice grew louder, taking shape in Owen's mind. He shook his head. "No, I'm fine, it's just— Gah!" A sharp prick stabbed the center of his brain, and his body stiffened against the chains and the voice grew louder.

The swamp. Twenty miles east of Route 22. I'm here.

Owen recognized the dead man's voice. The van screeched to a stop, and both Owen and the deputy were thrust forward. Bellingham and Hurt got out of the front seats and then marched around to the back, the sunlight outside blinding in contrast to the dark of the van.

"Owen, you tell me what's going on, now!"

He turned to the sheriff, struggling to maintain control. "I know where Jake Martin is."

Bellingham lowered his weapon, and the van rocked as he climbed inside. "Where?"

"Twenty miles east of Route 22, in the swamp." Owen grunted, his mouth starting to foam. "Sheriff, it's coming." Owen's body vibrated like a taut guitar string. "You need to run. You need to— AHH!"

The two deputies backed away while Bellingham placed his hand on Owen's shoulder. "Fight it, Cooley. Whatever it is, fight it!"

"Sheriff, you need to get out of there!" Deputy Hurt screamed, gun drawn and aimed at Owen.

Owen's face reddened as Bacalou shoved Owen's consciousness aside, forcing him to watch helplessly in the corner of his mind as his own body thrashed wildly.

Bellingham backed out of the van, slamming the doors shut and covering Owen's body in darkness. But that was Bacalou's environment.

Owen's eyes blackened, his flesh greyed and scaled, and this time his teeth sharpened and lengthened in crooked rows. The hunger was insatiable, and from his view in the small corner of his own mind, he heard the sheriff on the other side of the van doors.

"Owen! Stay right where you are! Fight it!"

But he couldn't. Bacalou was in control now, and the creature had only one thing on its mind. Find the heir of Charles Toussaint.

Bacalou broke Owen's chains with one flex of its muscles. Black goo dripped from the corner of Owen's mouth, his misshapen teeth permanently exposed from the vicious snarl.

Owen's body possessed accentuated features of the creature now, complete with elongated claws at the end of his fingers. His torso had widened, and extra muscle padded his legs and arms.

Bacalou charged the van doors, causing the reinforced steel doors to buckle. It roared, its anger rising, and charged again, this time breaking through and tumbling to the ground outside. It rolled over the grass and asphalt and skidded to a stop as Bellingham and the deputies stepped backward.

"Open fire!" Bellingham squeezed the trigger and the first bullet connected with Bacalou's chest, tearing Owen's blue jumpsuit, but failed to penetrate the creature's thick hide.

Bellingham fired three more rounds before the creature lunged and the deputy by his side fired the twelve-gauge that provided enough power to knock it off course. Bacalou roared, shaking off the shotgun's heavy blow.

Bellingham and the deputies retreated from the van, each of them emptying the magazines of their weapons.

Bacalou set its sight on the nearest human, which happened to be the deputy in riot gear, and then slashed at the barrel of the shotgun, its claws swiping through the metal like paper.

Defenseless, the deputy backpedaled, and Bacalou lunged again, this time shredding the bulletproof vest and slashing the deputy's stomach and chest.

"Lacroix!" Bellingham loaded a fresh magazine into the pistol and then aimed for the creature's head.

Three heavy knocks connected with Bacalou's right temple, and three bright flashes of pain followed as the monster roared. But it provided the needed time to pull Lacroix away before Bacalou could finish its work.

All the while Owen sat in the corner of his mind and watched terror and death wreak havoc. He knew that if the creature killed a deputy or one of the officers, any chance of reuniting with his family would disappear, so Owen fought back.

But his progress was slow. Some type of invisible force kept him from retaking control. He saw Bacalou slashing wildly toward Bellingham and the deputies, its rage inflamed and fanned by its own desire for death. Owen grit his teeth. "Enough."

The creature was strong, powerful, but it hadn't reached its full potential. This was Owen's last chance, his last moment to fight for himself. "Enough!" Owen lunged from darkness, and Bacalou cried out in pain.

Light cast out darkness and Owen gasped, his cheek flush against the mud and grass on the ground. He half-heartedly clawed at the dirt and then rolled to his side, gulping air. The hot afternoon sun beat down on him. Sweat poured off him in buckets, and he lifted his trembling head to the sight of Bellingham and Deputy Hurt, their faces ghost white.

Lacroix sat on the ground, clutching the flesh wounds over his chest and stomach. "What the hell are you?"

Slowly, Owen pushed himself off the ground. "We need to move."

"You need to be locked up!" Deputy Hurt said, gun gripped tightly and keeping his distance. "Sheriff, we can't take him to the courthouse. He'd tear the whole place apart!"

Bellingham's demeanor calmed, though he still aimed his pistol at Owen. "And what are we supposed to do with him, Deputy?"

"Shoot him," Deputy Lacroix answered, his voice weak and trembling. "Kill him and get it over with."

"No," Owen said, pushing himself off the ground. He winced once he sat up, his head aching and the scars on his chest burning. "I can help you. I can take you to Jake Martin's body."

"It's a trick," Deputy Hurt said, baring his teeth.

"No trick," Owen replied, still speaking to the sheriff. If he was going to get out of this alive, if he was going to try and clear his name, then this was his only hope. "If I'm wrong, then you can put a bullet in me and leave me in the swamp. But just let me try. Please, Sheriff."

"All right, Owen," Bellingham said. "You show me where Jake Martin's body is and we'll go from there." Bellingham walked over and then extended a hand to help Owen off the ground.

The old sheriff pulled Owen up with ease, but the moment he was upright, the sheriff tightened his grip on Owen's arm and pulled him close. "You put my men in danger again and I will put a bullet in your head. Whether you're right about Jake Martin or not. Understand?"

Owen nodded. But as he was loaded into the back of the

van with new restraints placed over his wrists, he wasn't sure if a bullet to the head would be enough to stop Bacalou.

* * *

WHISPERS ECHOED through Roger's mind, fragments of a past that he couldn't remember. His mind was a blank canvas where memories were suddenly splashed with no context, and before he could understand the distorted images, they were wiped away.

Roger tried getting up, but the restraints on the bed kept him down. It was his tenth attempt, though he thought it was his first. He stared at the straps over his wrists and the long pieces of leather that crossed his chest and stomach. Who had put them there? Why couldn't he move? "Mary? Mary, come help me."

Roger frowned at his voice. It couldn't have been his. It was old and weak. He'd just turned thirty-five a few months ago. He looked down and saw the liver-spotted, weathered hand attached to his body, and he panicked.

"No," he said, his voice as quiet as those whispers in his head. "No!" He thrashed in violent spasms. "Help! Someone help!" But the more he moved, the more constricted he felt, and it didn't take long before two men dressed in white hurried into his room. "Who are you? What are you doing?"

"Just calm down, Mr. Templeton." The man who spoke had a bald head and a wide jaw. He was skinny and held down one of Roger's arms. "You're all right. You're just in the hospital. We're going to give you something to make you feel better."

Roger squinted at the man. "No, please. I just want to go home, I just—Gah!" He looked to his right and saw another man who jabbed a needle into his arm, pressing down on a syringe. "What are you doing? What is… that?" His eyelids grew heavy, and his muscles relaxed.

"Naptime, Grandpa." The orderly with the syringe had a thin, unearthly smile. Long, straight black hair dangled at his shoulders. It was wet and greasy.

The man's face grew fuzzy as Roger blinked, fighting to stay awake, but instead sank back into his pillow. "Please… Just… Go…" He tilted his head to the side and drifted off into a sleep with dreams as broken as his memories.

For Roger, sleep was a coin toss. Fifty-fifty odds for either clarity and rest or confusion and terror. Those few moments before he drifted from consciousness were always riddled with anxiety.

But hope rose in the distance, like a sunrise after a long night of cold darkness. Roger remembered his home in Baltimore, his wife, his daughter. His memories poured over him like a cleansing rain.

But amidst the warm joyful moments, he also had a front row seat of his actions when that beast Alzheimer's took control. So much anger, hate, a violence he didn't even know existed within him. He cringed as he relived them. And tonight, in the deep state of restless unconsciousness that the sedation provided, he saw a new memory shrouded in darkness.

He tried to look away, but the nightmare beckoned him closer. He was in a room, lying on a table. There were strange things around him, colored liquids in glass bottles, jewelry made of tiny bones, rocks, and leather. It was dark in the room, and he was angry, angry because he was confused, because of the disease.

Claire was there, trying to calm him, trying to get him to stay down. But it only worsened the anger. He lashed out, striking Claire on her cheek. A vicious crack sounded from the contact and Claire burst into tears as she looked at him, covering the mark on her face.

Roger's heart shattered. That wasn't him. He wouldn't do that. He tried to speak, tried to apologize, but Alzheimer's bit his tongue.

"Stop!" Roger pleaded in his sleep, a sinking feeling of hopelessness overtaking him. "Please, stop." He collapsed to his knees, crying, wanting to pull himself from this prison of hell.

But amidst the broken dreams and discarded memories, a singular voice broke through the madness. It whispered in a language that Roger could not speak, yet he understood perfectly. And as Roger wandered in darkness, groping blindly to find the voice's source, he saw it. He saw both of them.

Owen and the creature. They were together somehow, fighting for control. Because of what Madame Crepaux had done to him, Roger still shared a connection with the beast.

For Roger, his journey into the creature's mind was like being at an exhibit at an art museum, free to wander around looking at the inside, but unable to touch anything. So Roger went deeper into Bacalou's mind.

It was a cold place, dark and violent. Roger's own thoughts grew twisted, but he persevered. Bacalou wanted something. He'd wanted it for a very long time. It just needed one final push, one last surge to end its pain.

Roger searched the creature's mind for its desire with a heightened sense of urgency. He saw the faces and souls that it had taken over the years. Most were from the same family, a few were not. He opened doors into hallways that frightened him. And then Roger saw it. Felt it, actually. It stank of death and froze him. The creature wanted to kill someone. A man.

Charles Toussaint. The name was whispered softly. And at

this end, this great finality where Bacalou killed this man, Roger saw Owen's soul consumed among the calamity as collateral damage.

That thought lingered in Roger's sedated mind. It clung to him like the very disease that wanted to kill him. He couldn't let Owen be taken like that. His daughter would be devastated. He needed to do something about it.

If that thing wanted a vessel, then let it take him. He just needed to find a way to get the creature's attention.

laire kept hold of both Matt and Chloe in the back seat of the deputy's SUV. His only interaction with her were the two glances in the rearview mirror, but she was grateful for the silence.

Chloe had fallen asleep, as she did on most car rides, but Matt stayed awake. He leaned his head against her arm as he looked out the window. She had so many questions for him, but she'd kept them to herself. There wasn't any need to overwhelm the boy with more worries.

The car slowed, and Claire saw the glow of a neon sign. The dirty yellow color spelled out "Bart's Motel." And like the sign it represented, the two-story structure had lost much of its luster. Paint peeled from the walls, the iron banister along the second story flaked with rust, missing shingles dotted the roof. It was a dump, but it was the closest place to stay outside of Ocoee. And it was on the sheriff's dime.

Claire kissed the top of Chloe's head as she reached for the door. "All right, bug. Time to wake up." She groaned as Claire picked her up and brought her into the warm afternoon air. Matt followed, and the deputy walked toward the front office.

"I'll get your room keys, and then I'll help you with the bags," he said.

"Thank you." Claire adjusted Chloe in her arms and then placed her hand on top of Matt's head. "You all right, sweetheart?"

"I'm okay," Matt answered.

The answer lacked conviction, but Claire let it go.

The deputy returned holding the keys. "Let's get you settled in."

Their room sat on the second floor. It was small and simple, only the bare bones of necessities. A single nightstand sat between two twin beds, bare of any comforters, with only yellow-cream sheets that matched some of the discolored stains that made them look dirty even when they were clean.

A TV from 1995 sat on a dresser, and a sink on the back wall was attached to a small bathroom where the door scraped against the edge of the toilet when opened. There was another door on the left wall of the room that connected into the room next door, which had its own door just on the other side, but both were locked so neighbors couldn't get in unless they were invited. Claire hadn't seen a room set up like this since she went on vacation with her family as a little girl.

"It's not the best accommodations," the deputy said, "but it's the best we could do on such short notice."

"It's fine," Claire said, trying to sound grateful. "Thank you."

The deputy offered a nervous smile and handed over the keys. "I have to get back to the station, but we'll keep a squad car nearby if you need anything." The deputy swallowed and glanced at his shoes to gather his nerve. "I... also need to talk to you about your husband."

Claire nodded, her stomach tightening into knots. She turned back to Chloe and Matt. "You two stay here. I'll be back in a minute." She followed the deputy out the door and down the second-floor balcony, away from the room so the kids couldn't eavesdrop. They stopped at the stairs and Claire crossed her arms. "How bad is it?"

"The sheriff is taking Owen to the courthouse today to set bail," the deputy answered. "Because it's a murder charge, the bail will likely be set at one million. If you want to get him out, you'll have to put up ten percent."

Claire gripped the rusted rail for support. "Christ." She squeezed the iron, the muscles along her forearm wiry and thick. She took a breath and then pushed off. "Has he been assigned an attorney yet?"

"There's someone from the state office coming this afternoon," the deputy answered.

"I'd like to meet them when they arrive."

The deputy reached into his pocket and handed her a card. "It's the station number. The desk is always manned, so you can call anytime."

"Thank you."

"Good luck, Mrs. Cooley."

Claire lingered on the balcony as the deputy walked downstairs and drove away. She glanced down to the parking lot, which was empty save for two cars. She thumped the rail then trudged back to the room, trying to figure out how to explain to the kids what was happening to their father. She was sure Matt had an idea, but that didn't make it any easier.

She opened the door, catching Chloe in mid-jump on the bed, who upon the sight of her mother immediately stopped, her eyes big and preparing tears in case she was in trouble. Matt stepped out of the bathroom and washed his hands.

"Guys, I need to talk to you for a second." Claire sat on the end of the bed closest to the door. Chloe was the first to join her, and Matt took a seat in a nearby chair. "I know you probably have questions about what's going on."

"Why can't we go home?" Chloe asked. "Is it not safe there anymore?"

Claire put her arm around her daughter and gently squeezed. "We're not sure yet, but we'll know soon."

"Is Dad okay?" Matt asked.

"Your dad is fine. There's just—" She closed her eyes and drew in a breath as she rubbed her forehead. "There are some people who think your dad did something bad." She looked to Chloe, then to Matt. "But he didn't. And that's important for you two to understand. There will be a lot of people that will say otherwise, but any time you hear them say something, I want you to come to me, okay? I promise I'll tell you the truth." She watched Chloe and Matt nod in response.

"What do people think Daddy did?" Chloe asked.

"They think he hurt people." Claire watched both of their reactions carefully. Chloe pinched her eyebrows together, while Matt stared at his shoes, his cheeks oddly pale.

Chloe kicked at air a couple of times, twisting her mouth and tilting her head to the side. "If Daddy didn't do that stuff, then why are people saying he did?"

"Because of me," Matt said, his head still down.

"No," Claire replied quickly, reaching out and grabbing hold of Matt's hand. "It is not because of you."

Matt jerked his hand away. "It is. It's because I was in that place, and then he had to get me out." He slid off the chair and beelined it for the door.

"Matt, no!" Claire jumped to follow, but then looked back

to Chloe, who remained on the bed. "You stay right there, young lady, understand?" She kept her voice stern and after Chloe's quick nod, she ran after Matt, shutting the door behind her. "Matt, stop!" Her son was already at the staircase by the time she left the room, and despite her shouting, he hurried down the steps.

Claire sprinted after him, chasing him through the parking lot and behind the building until Matt stopped by the trees before the swamp. He leaned against the bark of a cypress tree and caught his breath, allowing Claire to catch up.

"Hey." Claire gripped his shoulder and knelt in front of him, still panting from the run. "This isn't your fault, Matt."

"Then whose is it?" Matt lifted his head, tears in his eyes. "If it weren't for me, then Dad wouldn't be in trouble. Right?"

"No. No, sweetheart." Claire wiped her thumb underneath his eyes, catching the tears before they fell. "None of this is your fault. Absolutely nothing. Not the move here, not what happened to you, and not your dad coming to get you." She grabbed hold of his shoulders. "And I know that if your dad was here, he would say the same thing."

Matt sniffled and then nodded.

"Say it," Claire said. "It's not your fault."

Matt's lip quivered. "It's not my fault."

Claire pulled him close and rocked him in a hug. "I love you. Your dad loves you. That's never going to change."

Matt had always been so strong for his age, taking on more than his years should have allowed. But outside that motel on the outskirts of Ocoee, he was a ten-year-old boy, sobbing his heart out to his mother, who rocked him until the tears ran dry.

* * *

THE SUN HAD SUNK low in the sky as Chuck peeked from the blinds of Nate's front living room. Despite the closed door, Nate's frantic pacing could still be heard from the bedroom. The steps had grown sporadic as Nate drained the whiskey bottle in the kitchen. He'd been at it for almost three hours now.

Chuck left his perch at the window and adjusted the strap of the duffel bag slung over his shoulder. Nate kept looking at it. Money made people stupid. And a lot of money made people violent. But Chuck still had his pistol.

Like Nate with his liquor, the pistol had become Chuck's crutch. Before this started, he could count the number of times he went to the range on one hand. And yet in the span of twenty-four hours, he'd killed two men. And if Owen Cooley hadn't gotten away, that number would have jumped to three.

"All right," Nate said, sliding out of his room and slurring his words. "We need to talk, Chuck." He pointed an unsteady finger at Chuck and shut one eye. "I don't feel comfortable with you staying here anymore." He held up his hands in a passive defense, flinging some of the whiskey out of the bottle. "I understand the pressure you're under right now, but for me, the risk has become too high." He fixed a pair of bloodshot eyes on Chuck. "I'm sorry." Then he held out his hand, expecting the payment that Chuck had promised.

At least ten feet separated the two, and Chuck let the silence linger before he answered. "No." He stepped forward, and Nate stepped back. "And if I ever find out that you spoke to the police and ratted me out, I'll come back for you, Nate."

"C-c'mon, Chuck," Nate said, retreating deeper into his own house. "You know I was just kidding around. I wouldn't do that to you. No way. I-I just thought—" His leg bumped into a coffee table, and he jumped from the contact. "I-I didn't mean it, Chuck. Swear to God."

An unexplainable urge to reach for the pistol pushed Chuck's hand to the weapon, and just before his fingers grazed the handle, the lights shut off in Nate's house.

Chuck looked around while Nate beelined it for the front door, knocking into Chuck on his frantic scurry past. Nate yanked on the doorknob, heaving his weight behind it, but the door wouldn't budge. He spun around, the bottle of whiskey still gripped in his hand. "Is it here?"

And before Chuck answered, a sudden chill filled the air. He ripped the pistol from his waistband, spinning in a circle, aiming at nothing but darkness. His heart rate skyrocketed, his pupils dilated, and his body trembled.

"Come on out!" Chuck's voice shrieked as he pivoted in jerky movements. "You've wanted to do this for a long time, so come on!" Darkness descended over the windows outside.

"I have waited a long time." Madame Crepaux's voice traveled like a cold breeze. "And now you have nothing to protect you except for the sorry piece of metal in your hands. But that cannot stop me."

The gun was yanked from Chuck's hand, and it skidded across the carpet and under the couch.

"Your ancestors murdered a great Queen," Madame Crepaux said. "Fire melted her skin from bone. It was a painful death. Torture."

Flames appeared on Chuck's hand, and he screamed. He shook his hand violently, trying to rid himself of the fire, but it danced up along his arm and over his body, then his face. Every square inch of his body brightened with pain until it became so unbearable that his scream was replaced with gasping silence.

Chuck collapsed to the carpet, rolling on the ground, batting at the flames, the pain so overwhelming that he was blinded to anything but its blaring absolution.

And then as quickly as they appeared, the flames were

gone. Chuck spasmed on the floor, flopping like a dying fish on a dock. After a moment, he rose to his hands and knees, checking his arms and legs, feeling his face. There were no burns, no scars, no disfigured flesh. The only sign of the heat was the sweat that had drenched his body. He looked to Nate, who had wet himself.

"Did you see that?" Chuck asked.

Nate remained silent. He slid to the carpet. On the floor, he hugged his knees and rocked back and forth. He shut his eyes and shook his head.

Chuck reached for the pistol beneath the couch, his eyes slowly adjusting to the darkness. He spun around, waiting for whatever tricks the old woman had for him next.

"I can burn you any time," Madame Crepaux said, her voice omnipresent. "You will live an eternity in those flames."

"A bokor set me free of this curse before," Chuck said. "I can find another one to do it again!"

"I'm too strong for that now," Madame Crepaux answered, her voice deepening. "There is no spell to stop me, no place for you to hide. No matter how far you run, Bacalou will find you!"

Knives dug into the skin on his forearm. He frantically pulled up the sleeve of his shirt and found teeth marks. Blood oozed from his flesh and dripped down his arm.

Another bite clamped down on his other forearm, then on his shoulder, then the back of his leg, calf, neck, cheek. Chuck screamed, swatting violently at the pain. He dropped to his knees and felt teeth on the back of his neck that paralyzed him. A hot breath tickled his ear, and then he heard Madame Crepaux's voice whisper softly.

"There is no escape," she said. "But I will not kill you. Your life belongs to Bacalou, and it will come for you soon. I only seek to return to you in kind the suffering you have brought onto others. I will bring you to the precipice of death."

Chuck's paralysis ended, and the darkness lifted. He checked his body again, searching for the bite marks along his arms and legs, but like the burns from the flames, there was nothing.

"It's not real," Nate said, his eyes shut, shaking his head. He started to cry. "Christ, there is no way that this is real."

Chuck remained on the floor, sweat dripping from his nose, his body clammy and cold. He trembled, his nerves frayed. While the marks were gone, the pain lingered in his mind.

The first tear that fell was mixed with sweat. And then they fell like rain, pattering against the carpet after they dripped from his chin. The finality was inevitable. He couldn't outrun the beast. He couldn't stop the beast. His life was already wasted. So what was left now?

A rage bubbled inside of him. It was that primal rage, fueled by fear and survival. It all started with the death of a son, and if he was going to die, then he would take the one thing from the man who caused all of this to happen.

*M*osquitos buzzed wildly, feasting on the backs of the deputy's necks as Owen led Bellingham and his men through the black water. They'd been wading through the trees for hours and Owen had lost track of time, but he hadn't lost the scent of Jake Martin's body.

No, a scent wasn't the right word. It was a feeling. It was a mixture of whispers, an unseen force pulling him toward the body. He wasn't sure if the whispers were from Jake Martin, the creature, or something else entirely, but he was beginning to learn that the dead were restless beings. When they wandered, they were purposeless, haunting.

Owen stole a quick glance behind him. Bellingham and the officers trailed him closely, guns drawn. The deputy in the SWAT gear had survived Bacalou's attack, the creature's claws barely breaking the skin. The Kevlar vest was a different story though.

"I thought you said you knew where to find him?" Bellingham asked.

"It's close." Owen scanned the trees, squinting, his eyes growing tired from the sun and heat.

"Sheriff, how do we know he's telling the truth?" Hurt asked, swatting at another mosquito near his neck. "He could just be buying time until he's that... thing again."

"Because he's up shit creek without a paddle," Bellingham answered, his tone short and frustrated. The deputies mumbled to themselves. "If we don't find the body in the next ten minutes, we're turning back. God help us if we get stuck out here after dark."

"God help us if I turn into that thing again," Owen replied, only loud enough for him to hear. And just when he thought that whatever force was pulling out here was sending him on a wild goose chase, he saw something between the trees.

Owen stopped, Bellingham and the deputies stopping with him. He pointed to the structure. "There. Up ahead. You see it?"

Bellingham approached, coming up on the left side of Owen's peripheral, gun slightly lowered now. "Yeah, I see it." He turned around. "Heads up! We've got contact." He looked to Owen and then gestured with the pistol. "Go on."

Owen hastened his pace, eager to bring this to an end and curious to see if he was right. The closer they moved to it, the more the structure was revealed. It stood high on stilts, the roof brushing the canopy. A ladder climbed all the way to the top, and Owen waited as Bellingham and the deputies caught up.

"Sheriff, look," Deputy Hurt said, pointing to a bullet hole in a tree.

"Tag it," Bellingham said, his eyes drifting to the top of the shack on stilts. "He's up there?"

"Yeah," Owen answered, and then lifted his wrists that were still cuffed.

"Oh no," Bellingham said. "You're staying down here. Hurt, you keep an eye on Mr. Cooley."

"Shouldn't I go up there, Sheriff?" Hurt asked.

"I've kept up with you boys this far, haven't I?" Bellingham holstered his pistol and then grabbed hold of the highest rung he could reach and lifted himself up. Water dripped from the sheriff's backside as he climbed, and both Hurt and Owen watched Bellingham until he was over the top and onto the deck.

Owen's stomach tightened in anticipation. The voices and whispers had grown louder. Jake Martin was up there, his body decayed, his soul tortured in the afterlife.

That was perhaps the oddest thing to experience. Like being sidelined in his own body when Bacalou took over, he could insert himself into the souls of the dead. It was like being inside a movie that you'd watched a million times. You knew what would happen, but you were so close to it that it was like you were experiencing it for the first time. It was an added dimension of smell and texture in addition to sight and sound.

Bellingham poked his head over the side. "He's up here. Hurt, I need some evidence bags."

Owen exhaled, collapsing against the ladder in relief, as Hurt lowered his pistol and removed the evidence bags. "The bullets will be from Chuck's gun, I know—" Owen gasped, choking for air as ice filled his lungs.

The world darkened with shadows as Bacalou lunged for control of Owen's body once more. Owen buckled at the waist and turned left. As he did, he saw the gun barrel in Lacroix's hands. A harsh sting of pain spread across his chest as Lacroix fired, and Owen was flung backward into the water.

"Hold your fire!" Bellingham thrust out his arms and quickly descended the stairs.

Shock took hold of Owen first, his senses overwhelmed.

Two seconds passed, and then his mind finally caught up with the pain signals of his brain.

With his hands still cuffed, Owen thrashed beneath the water's surface, choking on the black water as blood oozed from the gunshot wound to his chest. Distorted images of trees and sky filtered through the shallow water, and suddenly hands broke through the surface, lifting him from a watery grave.

"Christ, he's bleeding!" Hurt carried him to a nearby tree and propped him up, the water line just below the bullet wound. He applied pressure, and Owen cried out in pain. "Sheriff!"

Owen coughed and suddenly tasted blood. He lifted a shaking hand to his lips. When he pulled his fingers away, he caught the shimmer of blood under the sunlight. His eyes widened as Hurt removed his outer shirt and pressed it against Owen's chest.

"He's losing a lot of blood, Sheriff!" Hurt turned just as Bellingham splashed into the water and rushed over, kneeling on Owen's right.

"Owen? Can you hear me all right?" Bellingham grabbed hold of Owen's chin and pulled his face toward him. "Owen?"

Owen saw the sheriff. He heard the sheriff. But he couldn't find the energy to answer. His head had grown incredibly light and his cheeks had drained of color.

The deputy who'd fired the gunshot kept his gun aimed at Owen, and when Bellingham saw, he knocked the barrel away. "I think you've done enough here, Lacroix."

"He was turning into that thing again!" Lacroix said, his voice shrieking. "He would have killed us!"

"And you could have ended a murder case before it began!" Bellingham added his own shirt to the growing pile of bloody rags over Owen's wound.

"Claire." Owen's eyes were half closed, his voice a whisper. Bellingham and his deputies faded from sight. He couldn't feel the pain of the bullet anymore. Everything was cold and dark, but in the distance, he could see a shining light. It was shapeless and quiet, but he knew it was his wife.

And past her image, death called to him. Owen closed his eyes and felt the icy shroud of black fall over him. He drew in a raspy breath and adrenaline flooded his veins. He gasped for air, drawing in a rattling, painful breath.

"Owen, you still with us?" Bellingham asked.

And that's when the shadows returned, and Owen was pulled away into the corner of his mind where he was forced to watch as the creature's power strengthened. It was Bacalou that pulled him from the clutches of death, because the creature could control it. So long as Bacalou was inside of him, he could not die, not until the creature finished what it started.

Apathy glazed Owen's mind. Bacalou's power was an intoxicating drug, and with every new hit, Owen's addiction grew.

Owen watched from the darkened corner of his own mind as Bellingham and his deputies opened fire on the creature, the bullets bouncing harmlessly off its hide. He tasted their fear, oozing off them like a frightened animal.

Bacalou knocked Bellingham aside, sending the old man splashing into the water. It stomped forward, backhanding Hurt in another forceful crack that knocked the deputy unconscious in the water. And then it turned to the final deputy, the one Bacalou had nearly killed before.

"Get back!" he screamed, unloading the shotgun into Bacalou's chest, the pellets in the shell ricocheting off the creature's hide like pebbles thrown against a mountainside. He hastened his retreat, and once the shotgun was empty, he tossed it and sprinted as fast as he could through the black water, his knees bouncing high and splashing wildly.

Bacalou roared, and the water bubbled in front of the deputy's path, bringing him to an abrupt halt. Owen laughed when he heard the deputy whimper and then clapped in vicious delight when the gator appeared, its jaws exposed.

"NOOOO!" Lacroix screamed.

Bacalou turned away as the gator lunged forward and bit the deputy's leg. Owen tasted the blood and flesh, just as the animal did. The moment filled him with frightened excitement. It was animalistic, primal, and intoxicating.

Suddenly, a fresh scent lingered in the air, one that was more intoxicating than anything else. It was Charles Toussaint VII. The creature wanted him dead. Owen wanted him dead.

* * *

AFTER A FEW HOURS at the motel and two checks by the sheriff's deputies, Claire couldn't stay in the room any longer. The attorney had gotten held up in traffic in New Orleans and wouldn't be able to arrive until tomorrow. There was nothing to do, and that inaction was driving her up a wall.

When the deputies arrived for their third check, she asked them for a ride back into town. When she told them where she wanted to go, they said they'd have to radio the sheriff to make sure it was okay. And after the sheriff didn't respond, the pair sat dumbfounded on what to do next.

"Look, I just want to see if she's there," Claire said. "There is a lot that she knows that could help my husband. Please, I have to do something."

After a few minutes of deliberation, they eventually agreed to take Claire into town, and one of the deputies stayed to watch the kids. She didn't want to leave them, but taking them back to the shop didn't feel right. She said her goodbyes, and while Chloe protested, Matt kept quiet.

The closer they got to the store on Main Street, the more Claire fidgeted on the edge of her seat, chewing at her nails.

"Are you all right, Ma'am?"

Claire jumped. "I'm fine. Just… anxious to get this over with."

The deputy nodded. "It's a shame what your family has been through."

Claire smiled politely, but it vanished quickly. "Thank you." She squeezed her hands together, twisting her fingers as the first building of Main Street came into view, and then felt her stomach float as the deputy pulled into a parking spot just one building down from Queen's.

The deputy kept the engine running and then turned in his seat. "Ma'am, we weren't able to radio the sheriff about the protocols for this, but I think it might be best if I go inside with you."

"No," Claire answered, quicker than she intended, and then backpedaled after she saw the deputy's raised eyebrow. "I'm sorry, it's just… I know that you're looking to question the woman, and I might be able to convince her to come out if I go in alone." She wasn't sure if that was accurate, or even if Madame Crepaux was at the store, but she had a feeling that last part was true. "Please," Claire said. "At least let me try."

The deputy shifted uneasily, and then glanced at the storefront. He sighed. "All right." The leather groaned as he turned back to Claire. "You get five minutes."

"Thank you." Claire reached for the door handle and quickly left before he changed his mind.

The store windows were black. She tugged against the handle, finding it locked. She pressed her face against the glass, which was still hot from baking in the sun all day. A click sounded at the door and she immediately pulled her face from the window. She reached for the handle again, and this time when she pulled, the bell jingled as it opened.

Claire hurried inside, shutting the door behind her as the deputy stirred in his SUV. He got out of the car, and Claire locked the door. Slowly, she stepped deeper into the store, passing the strange trinkets and potions stacked on shelves. "Hello?"

Only silence answered, and Claire pressed forward slowly, her eyes beginning to adjust to the darkness. She walked to the back room where her father had been strapped down. Absentmindedly, she reached for the cheek where he'd hit her.

"Your father still loves you more than anything."

Claire spun around, the voice tickling the hairs on the back of her neck. She jumped at the sight of the young woman with glowing yellow eyes. "Madame Crepaux?"

Madame Crepaux smiled. "Yes."

Claire shook her head in disbelief. "How... Is that possible?"

"Voodoo transcends time itself," Madame Crepaux answered.

While the woman in front of her may be able to turn back time, Claire couldn't, and what she had left was running out. She lunged forward. "The police think Owen killed people." She took hold of Madame Crepaux's hand. "You have to help me clear his name. He didn't do what they think he did."

"I know what the police want," Madame Crepaux said, her eyes glowing a golden hue now. "But what the police do will not matter."

Claire frowned. "What are you talking about? They're taking him to the courthouse to file charges!" But her words fell on deaf ears as Madame Crepaux turned to leave. "Stop!" Claire jumped in front of her and swelled with anger. She thrust a finger in Madame Crepaux's face. "There are police outside. You help me or I let them in."

Madame Crepaux looked from Claire's finger, then to the windows out front. "The police cannot stop me." She turned to Claire. "You cannot stop me." Her eyes pulsated with a flash of gold. "Your husband knew the price of your son's return."

"Price?" Claire asked. "What price?"

Madame Crepaux sidestepped Claire, but Claire snatched hold of her arm, and Claire's hand burned from the contact.

Claire hissed at the pain, but when she checked her palm, there was no redness or marks or scars. Madame Crepaux's eyes flickered again with that golden flare, and Claire felt the cold in the room intensify.

"I understand the sacrifices that your family has made," Madame Crepaux said. "But you have your son back. Be thankful for that."

Claire circled Madame Crepaux hesitantly, again trying to block her path towards the front door. Not that Claire was sure the woman even needed to use doors anymore.

"You said my husband knew the price," Claire said. "I want to know what he paid."

Madame Crepaux regarded Claire with those glowing, golden eyes, and the darkness around her pulsated outward from her body, as if her very presence disturbed darkness.

"What happens to Owen?" Claire asked.

Madame Crepaux lifted her hands to her waist, palms facing upward. "The world is full of small parts that make a greater whole in the balance of life and death." In her right hand was a small ball of light, in the left darkness, like a black hole. "But because of Bacalou and the Toussaints, that balance is in jeopardy."

The hot, bright light was pulled apart by the black mass,

and the light dimmed, growing smaller while the darkness grew larger.

Claire's thoughts wandered to the darker corners of her mind. The places she went after Matt was taken and everything she imagined that her son was going through alone. But there was an added dimension to all those bad thoughts, a texture.

"You can feel it," Madame Crepaux said, her eyes glowing an even richer gold than before. "When Death tips the scales, it darkens everyone, everywhere." Madame Crepaux stepped closer, the dark mass still absorbing light. "I have felt the pain of people halfway across the world, simply because of the dark forces here. I have heard their cries, their pleas for mercy, but the darkness does not care of their pain, or their pleas."

Claire collapsed to her knees, her mind hazy and dizzy. "Stop." Her voice was weak, quiet. "Please." All of the bad thoughts worsened, and she looked down at her hands, which had weathered and greyed. They were the hands of an old woman, and when she brought her fingertips to her face, she felt the wrinkled skin of her cheek.

Madame Crepaux kneeled, the black mass the size of a basketball and the light smaller than a golf ball. "What you feel is what I have felt for decades. Me and so many others. You have simply had a taste, Claire. Do not risk what you have left to save your husband now."

Madame Crepaux closed both hands and the black mass vanished, along with the light, and Claire collapsed to the floor. She gasped for air like she had been holding her breath. She saw her hands return to normal, the wrinkles and spots gone.

"Please," Claire said. "What happens to Owen?"

Madame Crepaux's expression softened, and it was here that Claire received the first glimpse of the old woman she'd met before. She reached out a hand and cupped Claire's face. "Bacalou resides inside of your husband now and is controlling him as we speak. It is only a matter of time before the creature takes full control of your husband's body, completing its transformation. It will then seek out the last remaining heir of Charles Toussaint and end the curse. Once that happens, your husband will die along with the creature."

Claire's eyes watered, and she wiped her nose. "You knew that the creature would do that to him?"

Madame Crepaux paused, and then, without remorse answered, "Yes."

"Then help me save him."

"There is one way, but it would take the life of another." Madame Crepaux held Claire's hands. "Can you live with that, Claire Cooley? Can you live with the knowledge that to save your husband's life, another must die?"

Claire tightened her grip on Madame Crepaux's hands, and without any hesitation or fear of repercussions, she answered. "Yes."

*A*fter Claire Cooley left her shop, Madame Crepaux vanished in a wisp of smoke before the deputy barged in after her. She was unsure what Claire said after she left, but it didn't matter.

The sun had nearly set outside, and Madame Crepaux traveled through the air faster than light and as sightless as a breeze. The power from Queen Samba's gris-gris was immense, and she found herself latching tighter to its aura. It was intoxicating, and frightening. The deeper she entrenched herself in Queen Samba's power, the harder it would be for her to let it go.

Madame Crepaux felt the dark mark on her soul grow for every second that she possessed the Queen's gris-gris, but it wouldn't be much longer before Bacalou fulfilled its purpose.

Lights flickered inside the halls of the hospital as she passed unnoticed by the staff. She sensed the death in every room, those struggling to break free from Baron Samedie's hold. His dark cloud was everywhere, counting down until those withering lives would be his.

The Queen's gris-gris propelled her toward the rooms,

the urge to heal powerful. But Madame Crepaux refused the call. She would let Baron Samedie take what was rightfully his.

Madame Crepaux found Roger Templeton's room. He lay on the bed, asleep, his mouth open and his breathing irregular. The machines attached to his chest and arms beeped in the same offbeat rhythm. The old man's body was shutting down.

She hovered over him, examining the sagging flesh that had once been young and viral, beaten down by the years of abuse that life dealt. He was an old man losing his mind. But she also knew he was a man who loved his family. And while Roger Templeton could not control or manage the disease that ravaged his mind, Bacalou could.

Madame Crepaux gently touched Roger's forehead, and the old man woke. He groaned, blinking as she took his hand, offering him a branch of strength.

"You have been lost, Roger Templeton," Madame Crepaux said. "Let me help you find your way."

The haze slowly lifted from Roger's mind, and he took a dry swallow before he spoke. "I remember you." He squinted, and suddenly his breathing quickened. "Owen, he's—" He shut his eyes, and his voice dropped to a whisper. "The creature will kill him." He opened them and squeezed Madame Crepaux's hand back, his strength returning. "That can't happen."

Madame Crepaux's voice softened. "If you go down this path, you will lose everything. Your memories, yourself, your soul." Her eyes flickered gold, like a temptress on the rocks. "There will be no peace for you in the next world."

"Whatever it takes," Roger said eagerly.

Crepaux nodded, and the stone around her neck glowed as she placed her hand on his chest.

* * *

ONCE DARKNESS FELL, every rustle of wind or ripple of water sent a chill down Chuck's back and froze him in his tracks. He waited for the fires to return, and he kept checking the flesh on his hands. He couldn't push the memories of charred and blackened skin from his mind. He envisioned his whole body burning, reliving that pain over and over. He imagined what it would be like to burn like that forever, to never know the sweet relief of death.

Was that what happened to the souls of the people that Bacalou killed? Did they burn forever? Could they always feel those flames melting their flesh and bones? The pain never numbing, always fresh and new? Chuck started to believe they could. Everyone had to answer for their crimes in this world. He supposed that was just part of his fate.

Chuck trekked through the swampy brush alongside the highway out of town. Twice he saw a police car. But despite the wail of sirens and flashing blue lights, Chuck was surprised to find that he wasn't scared. Compared to burning in hell for eternity, the prospect of a dry bed in a cell didn't sound that bad.

He'd figured that Nate would have spoken to the cops by now, and it was only a matter of time before they radioed air support to start scanning the swamps from above. It'd be harder to find him now that it was dark though.

After a few hours of walking, the fatigue of the past two days had worn Chuck's endurance down to a nub. He needed food. He needed rest.

A small motel sat on the town's outskirts. It wasn't much farther, and he knew the owner didn't mind taking in unsavory characters. His father had used the place for all his affairs, a piece of knowledge he learned after his father passed. He wasn't sure if his mother knew. She probably did.

It was funny, the things that ran through his mind on the walk from Nate's. After such a traumatic and painful experience, he thought that he would look back and find all the fond memories of life: the time spent with this mother and grandmother, his youth before he discovered the curse, the fleeting moments of true happiness that he had with his first and second wives. But none of those memories replayed tonight.

Instead, scars were opened and fresh blood welled up from the past. He saw only the creature, and his father's scowl, and the way that his wives looked at him when he told them he was sterile. Arguments, pain, fear, hate, jealousy, they all flooded back in rogue waves.

Was it that woman causing all of this? Could she now somehow reach into his mind and drudge up all the nasty black and dead things that swirled around in his past that he wished would stay buried?

Charles Toussaint VII had come from a long line of villainous men. It was imbedded in his DNA, and no matter what mask he tried to wear to cover it up, or conceal it, somehow the bad always shone through. He could feel it in the way people looked at him. The whispers that carried through the factory and the town.

The people here didn't love his family, they needed his family. And because they were too lazy to find work elsewhere, they took the increasingly longer hours and stagnant pay in return. And with every day that passed, Chuck heard those whispers grow louder and those stares linger. Everyone wanted him dead, and he couldn't blame them. His family had stood on the backs of others for so long now they forgot what decency looked like. But none of that mattered anymore. Nothing mattered.

Chuck stared at the motel across the street as he remained tucked away in the brush off the side of the highway. He checked left and right, both lanes of traffic empty. The parking lot only had two cars in it, and the light was still on in the front office.

A quick sprint across the road, and Chuck ducked inside. The clerk at the front desk didn't look up from his television screen. Sweating, sunburnt, and stinking of the swamp, he unzipped his duffel bag and removed a stack of twenties. "I need a room."

"Eighty bucks, and I need to see your ID." The clerk sipped from a can of Miller Light, his eyes glued to the television screen.

"How much for no ID."

The clerk peeled his eyes away from the screen and looked Chuck up and down. He sipped the beer again, and then slid off his stool and leaned into the front counter. "Cops were here a while ago." He shrugged his shoulders. "Probably be coming back later too."

Chuck reached into the duffel and pulled another stack of twenties, then set both down on the counter. The two towers totaled one thousand dollars. "That enough to keep quiet?"

The clerk thumbed the cash. "Might need a little more convincing." He smiled. "You know, just to be on the safe side."

Chuck reluctantly slapped down another stack. The clerk stuffed the rest of the cash in his pockets and then reached for one of the keys in a drawer. He handed it over to Chuck. "Second floor. Room twenty-eight. Try and keep it the way you found it."

"I'm sure that won't be hard." Chuck snatched the key from the man's fingers, and then quickly scurried up to the second floor and into his room.

He tossed the duffel bag onto the mattress and the springs squeaked. Chuck went to the sink, passing a door on the inner room wall. It connected to the room next door, an old architectural element from the past.

At the sink, he splashed water on his face. It dripped from his chin and nose as he stared in the mirror. It was a face he didn't recognize, but one that he'd worn his entire life. It was his eyes that had changed the most. They were soulless.

Chuck undressed and then climbed into the shower, washing away the grime of the swamp, though the stress sill clung to him like a second skin. He air-dried, and then sat on the end of the bed, naked, and reached for the pistol he'd brought with him.

It had suddenly grown heavier on the trip here and he wondered what would happen if he killed himself before the creature got to him. Would he still burn? Would his soul still be damned? Or would the bullet not even matter? Could he not die until the creature killed him?

Chuck turned the gun barrel to face him and stared down the empty black space within. He raised it to his temple and closed his eyes as metal touched flesh, then placed his finger on the trigger. His hand didn't shake and his heart didn't pound. The only thing his brain registered was the fact that there was a warm piece of metal against his skull and that his hand had placed it there.

So what came next? Blackness? Fire? Pain? What did death really look like? What did it feel like? It was a question that couldn't be answered until the final moment; just as you took that last step over the edge and your feet were no longer on solid ground. It was that moment just before free-fall, that blip of a tenth of a second. That was where the truth was found.

Blue lights flashed outside the window, and Chuck turned his head toward the commotion, removing the pistol from his temple. He snuck to the window and saw the sheriff's cruiser downstairs. Chuck cursed the clerk at the front, thinking that he'd sold him out.

The deputies ascended the stairs, the lights on their cruiser still flashing in the parking lot, and then turned toward his room. He ducked behind the door, away from the window, as the deputies closed in. He raised the pistol, eyes locked on the door handle, ready for them to bust inside.

The officer's murmurs grew louder, and from the corner by the door, Chuck saw one of the officer's shoulders. He tensed. *A gunfight. Quick and dirty. It'd be better this way. No more waiting. No more fear. Just done.*

And then there were three knocks. But something was wrong. The noises weren't coming from his door. They were coming from—

"Mrs. Cooley, we're sorry to bother you, but we need to speak with you for a moment. Can you step outside?"

It couldn't be. It had to be a different Cooley, a different woman. There was no way that he was sitting next door to the same family that he'd tried to kill. And that meant if the mother was inside that room, then so was the son.

"What happened?" Mrs. Cooley asked.

"We finally heard back from the sheriff," one of the deputies answered. "Your husband attacked the group of officers transporting him to the courthouse and escaped."

"What? No, that's… that's not possible."

Chuck knew that if Owen was gone, then there was only one place that he'd go, and there was only one person that he'd be looking for.

"The sheriff thinks he'll try and contact you," the second deputy spoke now. "If that happens, you need to let us know."

"Did he… did he hurt anyone?"

"One of the deputies is in critical condition at the hospital."

Mrs. Cooley gasped, and the police mumbled a few more things that Chuck missed as he leaned away from the door.

If Owen Cooley was still alive, if he had escaped and grown so violent that he was willing to kill another officer, then Chuck knew the man wanted only one thing.

Revenge was a cruel beast. It twisted you into something that you weren't, forced you into positions that you'd never find yourself otherwise. And that toxic potion had seeped into Owen Cooley's veins. It pushed him beyond the limits of his reason and thought. And it brought a smile to Chuck's face.

If Owen was going to come after him, then Chuck wanted to make sure that their meeting would be memorable. And everything he needed for that to happen was next door.

*C*laire lingered on the balcony for a moment as the deputies returned to their car. She noticed that they stayed in the parking lot as she tried to wrap her head around what they'd told her.

After her interaction with Madame Crepaux, Claire knew that the cause of Owen's escape was more of the creature's doing than his own. But she didn't share that information with the police. What good would it do?

Sorry to tell you officer, but my husband has actually been possessed by the same creature that took my son and is currently hunting down one of your murder suspects to end a two-hundred-year-old curse on a family that killed an ancient Voodoo queen.

Claire steadied herself on the rail of the balcony, took a breath, and then walked back into the room. Chloe sprinted around the carpet in her bare feet, humming to herself as Matt sat in a chair and flicked through the limited number of TV channels with the remote.

Chloe knocked on the locked door that connected to the room next door. "Hello? Anybody home?"

"Chloe, stop." Claire snapped sharper than she intended,

and Chloe sheepishly stepped away from the door. "I'm sorry. It's just… just try and be quiet for a minute, okay?"

"Do you want me to turn off the TV?" Matt asked.

"No, that's fine, sweetheart."

Claire took a seat on the edge of the bed, and she twirled the wedding band around her finger. The diamond was small, but high quality. When Owen proposed, he nearly dropped it, he was shaking so much. She'd never seen him so nervous before in her life. He looked as if his whole future hinged on her answer, but she never told him that her world hinged on him asking.

She wished she could reach out to him, let him hear her voice. If she had the chance, she knew she could break through the creature's hold and reach him.

Chloe knocked on the door again, and Claire jumped from the noise. "Chloe, I said—"

A knock answered back. All three of them looked to the door. The springs of the mattress squeaked in relief as Claire stood. "Sorry!"

Another knock.

"It's my daughter," Claire said. "She won't do it again. I'm—"

Three more knocks in fast succession cut her off, and Claire's frustration went from simmer to boil. She stomped toward the door, the knocking continuous now, unlocked it, and swung it open. "Listen, if you just—"

The gun barrel poked through first. Her eyes went to the face of the man that held it. Chuck pressed his fingers to his lips as Claire gawked in stunned silence.

"Scream, and I kill everyone in this room," Chuck said, then looked down toward the kids who'd huddled together in the chair, Matt shoving his little sister behind him. Claire sidestepped to the left, slowly, blocking Chuck's line of sight to her children.

"The police are downstairs," Claire said, her voice shaking. "You try anything and—"

"They'll arrest me?" Chuck asked, now all the way in the room now. "Take me away to jail? Charge me for murder?" He cocked his head sideways. "You and I both know I have bigger things to worry about than the boys in blue downstairs." He took an aggressive step forward, and Claire shuddered. "Sit. Down."

Claire slowly complied, inching as close to her children as she could in the chair next to her, and reached out her arm to grab hold of Matt's hand.

Chuck paced the room, the gun trained on the kids now as he walked to the front door and made sure the chain lock was set. He peeked out the window and then shook his head. "Out of all the places for you to come. Out of all the places for me to hide. What are the chances?"

"It's over," Claire said. "Hurting us won't help you anymore now."

"Help me?" Chuck asked, then chuckled. "Nothing can help me, Claire. There isn't a spell, or incantation that I can speak, there isn't a lawyer that can bail me out of this, and there isn't a human being on this planet that can undo what's transpired over the past few days." He stepped closer. "But I've accepted my fate. I've come to terms with my future. Have you?"

Claire watched the pistol in Chuck's hand. It didn't waver, or flinch, it was steady as a rock, and just beneath the cool calm expression on Chuck's face, Claire could see the reflection of madness in the pools of black in his eyes.

"So why are you here?" Claire asked, tears beginning to roll down her face.

"To finish what I started."

Chloe was crying. Matt remained quiet. She leaned over, covering her son with her body. Claire shook her head. "No."

"It all started with him, Claire." Chuck's eyes were on Matt, his arm outstretched in a stiff line with his finger on the trigger. "And that's how it'll all end."

"You're not taking my son!" Claire lunged forward, swiping at Chuck's face, and she felt her nails break skin on his cheek right.

Chuck screamed but didn't fire his gun. Instead, he pistol-whipped Claire on the back of the head.

A throbbing ache radiated from the point of contact as Claire flattened to the carpet. Every few seconds, a stabbing pain split through the middle of her skull, voiding any attempts at lifting herself from the floor.

"Your family should have died after the creature took your son."

Spit sprayed over the back of Claire's neck from Chuck's words, and she slowly managed to turn around to look up at her kids in the chair. Both were crying now, clutching on to one another. "It's all right." She spoke softly. "Everything is going to be fin—AHH!"

Chuck kicked Claire in the ribs, and she rolled to her back. The next breath sent a thousand knife-like stabs into her side that traveled up like lightning toward the base of her skull.

"Stop it!" Matt flung all eighty pounds of his body toward Chuck, who knocked him away like a gnat buzzing around his head.

"NO!" Claire stood and then immediately fell back down, hard. She twisted her ankle in the process, and Chuck slammed his heel into her chest and she flattened to her back.

Chuck aimed the gun at her, which was better than it being on either Matt or Chloe. "You don't get a choice anymore. There is no other door, no other way out!" His lunacy heightened. "It doesn't end any other way." He raised his arm with the pistol high above his head, and the last thing Claire saw was his snarl as he knocked her unconscious.

* * *

Joy. Power. Hunger. All of it filtered through Owen's veins as he sprinted through the woods. The scent of blood filled his nose. He tasted the metallic liquid on his tongue. It was primal, sensational, overwhelming and addictive.

Never in his life had Owen felt more connected to the nature around him than he did at that moment. The world had a heartbeat, and with every pulse, he felt something new. A tree, mud, water, a leaf, a falling branch, a rush of wind, a bird taking flight, the patter of insect wings fluttling through the air. But amidst the life of the world, there was also death. And that was where the greatest flavors were derived.

Death awakened the beast and sent it into a frenzy, and Owen latched on to the experience. It was like an addictive poison with side effects of pain and misery. But to Bacalou, they tasted like candy.

Bacalou sprinted between the cypress trees, practically running on water, when a voice broke through that caused it to slow, and then stop.

Owen couldn't hear the whisper, but he felt the creature's reaction. It was like someone had pulled the leash on the beast. Its master had forced it still, and it whimpered like a distressed dog.

Another harsh yank, and this time Bacalou roared, sending Owen cowering. It snapped and howled, its anger growing wild. Owen shut his eyes and covered his ears, rocking back and forth like a child.

A force tugged at his chest, but Owen kept his eyes shut, and suddenly the world of death and misery and pain disappeared, and he was wet, and hot, and tired.

He slowly opened his eyes, finding himself on all fours. His hands and knees were sunk deep in the mud. His body trembled, and water dripped from his face and hair.

The sun had fallen, and a cloudless sky revealed the stars and moon through the branches of the trees.

"You enjoy it," Madame Crepaux said.

Owen jerked away from the sound of her voice. "Wha—" He coughed, choking on his own dry tongue. He'd never been so thirsty before. "What happened?"

"You already know," Madame Crepaux answered. "The creature resides inside of your soul now. It wants the same thing you want. The death of the heir of Charles Toussaint."

Owen shook his head. "No, that's…" The memories of the beast flooded across his mind. He remembered everything that it wanted when it took control. The death, the pain, the soullessness.

He looked to Madame Crepaux once more, this time noting the change in her appearance. Her voice was the same, but she was younger. Much younger. The wrinkles along her face had been replaced with the taut firmness of youth. The clothes hung to the curves of her body, and the golden flicker of her eyes had brightened. His expression of disbelief triggered her to smile.

"I was not always an old hag," Madame Crepaux said.

"How?" Owen asked.

"The same power that created Bacalou now flows through me," Madame Crepaux answered. "With the curse lifted from the house, I was finally able to retrieve Queen Samba's gris-gris." She glanced down to her hands, her eyes wide with wonder. "It is more powerful than I ever dreamed. She truly was a Queen of Voodoo."

Owen pulled his legs from the mud, and with the aid of a nearby tree, stood, his knees cracking together. "My family. I want to see them."

Madame Crepaux's face saddened. "We always seek those we love near the end." She walked closer, her footsteps soundless. Her hips swayed seductively, and her lips pouted outwards. "I know the pain that drives you. I know how much your family has been through." She stroked his cheek, and the touch radiated a warmth that spread through the rest of his body. "That pain will continue unless you face it."

Owen jerked his head away from Madame Crepaux's hand. "Face it?" He pointed to the ground. "I've been crawling up shit mountain for the past six months. I lost my job, my car, my home, and when I brought my family here to get away from all of that, I met you."

"You were brought here because that was the will of Bon Dieu."

"I came here because I needed a fucking job!" The veins along Owen's neck throbbed, and he stepped backward. "I came here because there was no place to go!" He flashed an angry, skeptical grimace. "There is no man in the sky, there is no great being controlling our destiny. There is us and the choices we make. That's it!"

"You have seen so much, and yet you still do not believe," Madame Crepaux said. "What is it that you don't under-stand? What is it that keeps you from seeing the truth?"

"My family!" Owen screamed the words, and then felt his body collapse. His knees smacked the mud with a thump, and then a sudden burst of tears flooded from him. "My family." He didn't want to believe what Madame Crepaux was saying because that meant that no matter how hard he tried, no matter what he did, his family would never be able to escape the pain that they had endured. Misfortune was written in their destiny. And wanted better for them.

Madame Crepaux knelt at his side and placed a hand on his shoulder, again providing that familiar warmth. "Many people find it difficult to put their faith into something greater than themselves. But you must understand something, Owen Cooley." She took his hand and cupped it between both of hers. "Your life is not your own. Your family is not your own. We are all born from a culmination of events that predated mankind itself." She leaned close, and Owen caught the sweet scent of her breath. "You are a good man, Owen Cooley. And Bon Dieu finds good men to help in his cause." She smiled. "He found me. And he led me to you. Let me help you. Please."

The rage inside Owen's heart calmed, and he sat there in the mud, letting this woman hold his hand, holding his whole life really, and chose to believe. "How can I be helped now?"

"I have found someone willing to trade his life for yours."

Owen shook his head, confused. "Who?"

"Your father-in-law."

"No." Owen stood, his legs wobbling like a newborn calf, turning his back to her as he stomped away. "I'm not putting Claire through that."

"His mind is nearly gone now," Madame Crepaux replied. "He knows of the risk, but I must have both parties' consent before I make the transfer."

"I'm not doing that to Claire!" Anger rattled his voice, and he continued his trek through the woods, unsure of where he would go, unsure of what he would do, and then Madame Crepaux suddenly appeared in front of him like an apparition.

"And what are you doing to her now?" Madame Crepaux asked. "She knows it is only a matter of time before the disease that cripples her father's mind takes him completely. She has accepted his life as over, but not yours."

"And what kind of man would I be if I let him do this?" Owen asked. "How do I live with myself?"

"But that's the point," Madame Crepaux answered. "You live. Your wife needs a husband. Your children need a father.

Let them have it." Madame Crepaux gripped him by the shoulders, squaring him up with herself. "We must act now, Owen Cooley. I can only keep Bacalou restrained for a short time before it takes over your body again. And if that happens, then I do no not if I will be able to bring you back again. What is your decision?"

The beast rumbled in the back of Owen's mind, its own desires clashing with Owen's. He remembered the power, the thrill, the intoxicating scent Bacalou drifted over Owen's senses. It drifted past his nose, luring him closer.

Owen closed his eyes, quieting Bacalou, trying to remember his own thoughts, his own desires. But the creature had embedded itself deep.

Inside Owen felt dark, lonely, afraid. But past the darkness and the stench of the dead, Owen saw a small beacon of light. The longer he focused on it the brighter it grew, and it wasn't long before it took shape.

It was Claire, and Matt and Chloe. They were at the dinner table in their home in Baltimore. Chloe had smeared spaghetti sauce all over her face and was giggling about the mess, which had sent the rest of the table into a flurry of laughter. Smiles. Happiness. Life.

Owen opened his eyes and saw the fleck of gold in Madame Crepaux's gaze, her hands still firmly gripping his shoulders.

"Even if I agree to this," Owen said. "How do I convince Bellingham that all of this was true?"

"He must witness what will happen. Him and as many of his deputies as he can spare." Madame Crepaux placed her hand against Owen's cheek. Her palm was warm and smooth against the rough stubble of beard that had grown in over the past few days. "It is almost over. And when it is done, your family will have a chance to rebuild."

After everything he'd been through, the small piece of

good news should have brought a smile, but Owen's face remained gaunt. He'd have to find a way to live with himself, and he hoped that Claire would find it in her heart to forgive him. Hell, he hoped he had it in his heart to forgive himself.

"We must go." Madame Crepaux interlaced her fingers with Owen's and tightened her grip. "Charles Toussaint grows restless, and in his restlessness, he grows more dangerous."

And as Owen pictured the death of the man who brought him here, the origin of so much of his family's pain, he prayed that Chuck's death would be painful. He prayed for that more than anything.

Owen sat in a chair on the far wall of Roger's hospital room. It was late, and Madame Crepaux had concealed them with darkness from the rest of the staff. Even when they entered, the nurses couldn't see him. He watched their movements through a black veil, still fighting the beast for control of his own mind.

He focused all his concentration on enduring the pain of keeping the beast at bay. Madame Crepaux's powers helped, but it was still a struggle. She needed time to prepare Roger's body.

"How much longer?" Owen asked, not bothering to keep his voice down as it too was concealed by her magic.

Madame Crepaux kept her focus on Roger, her hands glowing with light as she hovered them inches above Roger's head and heart. "Your father-in-law is weak. He must be strong for the transfer, or you will both die and the heir of Charles Toussaint will live."

Most of Owen's thoughts had been centered around Chuck Toussaint and his family and everything that had occurred over the past few days. His eyes drifted to Madame Crepaux's hands and shook his head in disbelief at what he saw. Magic. The stuff of fairy tales.

He thought about the man he'd attacked when Bacalou had taken control. Did he survive? If he didn't, it might not matter what happened next.

"Worrying will not help you now, Owen Cooley," Madame Crepaux said, her attention still focused on Roger. "It does nothing but waste your energy."

"When I was unemployed, I worried a lot," Owen said, staring at the white tiled floor. "I worried about putting food on the table. I worried about keeping a roof over my family's head. I worried about keeping the power and water turned on. I worried about bills, and payments, and making sure that my kids had what they needed." He rubbed his eyes, suddenly dry from his staring contest with the floor. "I'd probably give everything up to just have to worry about those things again."

Madame Crepaux stopped her procedure with Roger and quickly appeared in front of Owen, kneeling, that young, beautiful face staring up at him. She took his hands. They were warm, strong. They reminded him of Claire's hands.

"The world tests us when we are most vulnerable and weak," Madame Crepaux said. "It pushes us beyond our limits and what we're capable of." She shook her head. "It forces us to survive, but in that survival, they miss the most important element of life."

Owen was lost in those golden eyes. They were transcendent. It was like staring into the eyes of god. He squeezed her hand back, a yearning filling his soul that he didn't know he possessed. He wanted to know the answer. He wanted someone to lead him. He wanted something to believe in again. "And what is that?"

Madame Crepaux smiled. "Laughter, and joy, and the wild unknown of tomorrow." She pressed her finger into his chest right where his heart was, and that same warmth from her hands spread through his whole body. She leaned close enough to give him a kiss, and then stopped with only a sliver of space between their lips. "I knew a man like you once, Owen Cooley. When I looked like the young woman you now see. He shared the same burden that has rested on your shoulders. The enormity of it is overwhelming. But know that in this moment, even when it is darkest, there is still life. And it flows through you."

Owen closed his eyes. He pictured himself back in Baltimore, back with his family, back at his old job, back with his friends, remembering what it was like before all of this happened. Before the move, before he lost his job, before everything spiraled out of control.

But despite the concentration, and despite Madame Crepaux's words, he couldn't find that life inside of him anymore. All he saw now was Bacalou. It was attached to his soul, turning the joy of his memories to ash.

"I can't remember anything good," Owen said, staring down at his hands. Desperation dripped from him like sweat. It was repulsive, contagious, and when he stank of it when he was unemployed, no one would touch him with a ten-foot pole, so he hid it. He hid it with smiles, and jokes, and a faux-confidence that he knew would shatter from the slightest breeze of questioning. But he didn't hide here, not in front of her.

Madame Crepaux cupped his cheek. The warm sensation returned and he shut his eyes, leaning into her touch.

"It does not feel like it now, but you will remember those times sooner than you think."

Owen shook his head, his eyes still closed. "How do you know?"

"I don't," Madame Crepaux answered. "But I have faith."

Owen looked past Madame Crepaux and at Roger who still lay on the bed, sleeping, his mind broken in ways that Owen couldn't understand. He knew the old man was still inside somewhere in there, fighting to find his way back despite the disease.

Madame Crepaux appeared at his side. "I'm finished."

Owen picked up the old man's hand and held it in his own. "We do it here?"

"No," Madame Crepaux answered. "The house will have more power for me to draw on." She turned to Owen. "Are you ready?"

"No," Owen answered. "But I guess that's just part of the burden."

* * *

THE DULL ACHE that pulled Claire from unconsciousness was almost unnoticeable at first, but as the pain grew, so did her conscious mind. She opened her eyes, the imprinted patterns of the carpet zoomed so close she could see the individual fibers of the fabric.

The pain in her head sharpened as she pushed herself up, but the floor wobbled unevenly and she crashed back into the carpet with a heavy thump. For a moment Claire forgot where she was, what happened, but as the whimpering sobs broke through the raging storm of pain in her mind, it returned like a surging storm flood. "Chloe. Matt."

Claire lifted her head, blinking away the blind spots that plagued her vision, and got a hold of her bearings. She saw the bed, the chair, the TV stand, and then the small cut out of the sink and the closed bathroom door. She got her feet under her and used the bed to help keep herself steady.

The back of her skull throbbed, the pain worsening as she sat down. She patted the wound, and blood shimmered off her fingertips when she examined the damage. She examined the room, the walls and ceiling shifting like waves on a beach. She was alone. *Alone.*

Panic gripped her and she shot up from the mattress, stumbling forward and screaming. "Matt! Chloe! Matt!"

Claire's voice grew raspy and shrill, the veins along her neck throbbing and tense. She looked at the overturned furniture, the smashed lamp flickering on the ground, and then the closed bathroom door. She lunged for it, flinging it open, and saw Chloe tied, gagged, and bound in the bathtub.

"Chloe!" Claire rushed to her daughter's side and untied the ropes around her wrists, then removed the gag. "Sweetheart, are you all right?"

"He took Matt." Chloe sobbed, the skin around her eyes red and wet with tears. "He said he was going to hurt him." She twisted her face into a painful grimace and flung herself into her mother's arms.

Claire lifted her from the tub, focusing all her strength and coordination to not fall over as she rested Chloe on the bed. She brushed the matted and sweaty hair off her daughter's forehead and cupped her face. "Chloe, listen, I'm going to get help, okay? I need you to stay here, and if someone comes back that isn't me, I want you to hide."

Chloe nodded in response, and Claire didn't burden her already frightened daughter with overwhelming her with more details of stranger danger than she needed.

Night had fallen since she'd passed out, but a single parking lot light illuminated the police cruiser below and Claire extended her body over the railing off the balcony. "Help! Help me!"

The bodies in the squad car remained motionless. Claire hurried down the balcony, sprinting down the stairs, her voice hoarse and raw. "Help!" Her plea echoed through the night and she hurried down the staircase, her eyes locked onto the squad car below. The moment her feet touched the first floor, she broke out into a shambled sprint, her head still woozy from the vicious blow that knocked her unconscious.

Claire smacked her palm against the trunk of the police cruiser and pulled herself toward the window. She reached her hand for the shoulder of the deputy inside, but when she saw his face she jumped backward, her mouth agape with a breathless scream.

Thick mats of blood coated the heads of both officers, their bodies still held up by the seatbelts across their chests. She gagged from the putrid stench of blood and brain, turning away from the gruesome scene.

Claire spun around in the empty parking lot, the one street lamp burning a bright circle on the black pavement of the asphalt. All the windows in the motel were dark and empty, but the light in the front office still burned.

In a half limp, half walk, Claire stumbled toward the office with tears in her eyes. She searched the darkness, screaming Matt's name, but each bloodcurdling cry was answered only with silence.

Claire pushed open the door to the front office, and her cry was cut short by the dark patch of blood splatter on the back wall, and the limp outstretched hand she saw lying back behind the counter. She retreated outside, hand on her mouth, the flesh around her eyes twitching in terror.

She sprinted up the steps toward the room. With the room turned upside down and sheets and clothes flung everywhere, Claire clinched her fists at her sides, searching for her purse. "Chloe, do you see—"

The phone rang near the door beneath a pile of clothes. She flung the blouses and shorts away and unearthed the cell phone and answered immediately. "Hello?"

"Claire!" Owen's voice broke through clear and loud.

"Owen, Chuck has Matt!"

"What?"

Claire pursed her lips shut and then looked to Chloe, who

was still crying on the bed. She took hold of her daughter's hand and squeezed it tight. "What do we do?"

"Find the sheriff," Owen answered. "Tell him to come to the house on Cypress Lane. Tell him I want to turn myself in for everything that's happened."

Claire shook her head. "But… It's not true, right?" She clutched the phone tighter. "Owen, tell me it's not true."

A pause lingered before Owen answered. "Just tell him to come to the house. And you need to hurry. Do you have a car?"

Claire's mind wandered to the blood-stained police cruiser out front. "No."

"Tell the sheriff to send some deputies to pick you up," Owen said. "Go to the sheriff's station and stay there."

Claire pressed the back of her hand to her forehead and closed her eyes. She scrunched her face in preparation for tears but kept them at bay. "Okay."

"I love you, Claire."

She teared up. "I love you too." There was more she wanted to say, more she wanted to tell him, but she stopped herself. And with that, the call ended.

Claire lowered the phone, the few tears that fell suddenly multiplying like raindrops in a thunderstorm. Sobs rolled her shoulders forward and she buried her face in her palms, not looking up until she felt the heavy thump of Chloe on her leg as her daughter squeezed her tight.

Claire dropped to the floor and wrapped her arms around her little girl, and for a moment she let herself forget that she was a mother, a wife, and a daughter. In that moment she was afraid, and she had no idea what to do next.

"Mommy?" Chloe asked. "Mommy, are you okay?"

Claire wiped her eyes, nodding. "I'm fine, sweetheart." She kissed Chloe's cheek and then, with some effort, stood. She glanced down at her daughter, the five-year-old bundle of energy and art with her beautiful eyes and that inquisitive mind, and her strength returned.

Maybe Madame Crepaux had found someone to take Owen's place? She shuddered at the thought of whatever poor soul she'd managed to get and for a brief moment was filled with regret, but the pain was the price to keep her family whole.

he windows of the house were dark, and remnants of police tape were strewn about the outside. No cars. No lights. Everything was still and dead, but Chuck knew that was where it would all end.

A whimper sounded behind him, and he spun around and hushed the boy who was bound and gagged in the mud. Chuck had knocked him unconscious at the motel, and he had started to wake.

Chuck thought about beating him back to unconsciousness, but he wanted the boy alert for when Owen saw him. He wanted Owen to live the fear of his son through his boy's eyes.

Matt groaned through the dirty cloth rag. Mud speckled his cheeks, and the whites of his eyes shone brightly in the darkness. He rolled helplessly from side to side, tugging at the restraints on his wrists and ankles.

Chuck walked over and violently gripped the back of Matt's head and exposed the pale and puffy flesh of his jugular. He gave Matt a look up and down, and then grimaced. "I saw kids like you at my school growing up. Boys with fathers who cared. I could smell it on them like cologne." He gave another vicious tug at Matt's scalp, and Matt winced from the harsh angle of his neck. "It only made them weak though. Out of all the things my father did to me, at least I can say he didn't make me soft. Not like yours."

Chuck slammed Matt's head to the side and the boy smacked into the mud. His little chest heaved up and down in quick, panting breaths. Chuck stared at him in the sludge, rolling impotently from side to side.

"Daddy will come for you," Chuck said. "And then he'll watch you die." He hunched over and placed his hands on his knees, his face reddening from the rush of blood pumping into his skull. "And when you die, it'll be because your father let you. You hear me?" Chuck inched closer. "Your father let you die."

Absentmindedly, Chuck reached for the empty space where his pendulum once resided. When he grabbed nothing but air, he dropped his hand to his side and snarled. With one hand, he snatched the back of Matt's collar and dragged him through the mud, away from the house and deeper into the swamp. There was one more place he wanted to visit before the guests of honor arrived.

The trees thickened, the mud gave way to water, and the boy continued to struggle against the push the entire way. Chuck sent the tip of his boot into the boy's side, which elicited a crack and a guttural cry into Matt's dirty gag.

Sweat, mud, and swamp water speckled Chuck's body as he dragged Matt through the mud and water until he finally arrived at his family's gravesite. Moonlight brightened the headstones and the glass of the mausoleum.

Chuck tossed Matt near one of the graves, but the boy made nothing but gasping, wheezing noises. He looked on the brink of passing out again. "Don't move."

Chuck navigated the disrupted cemetery with hesitation, a place he hadn't visited since he stole the amulet off his grandfather's body. His father had told him that he didn't need to wear it, but the closer the return of Bacalou crept to the twenty-five-year mark, the more nervous he grew.

It was anxiousness worse than anything he experienced as a child. He couldn't sleep. Couldn't eat. He thought of nothing except the doom of the creature whose sole purpose was to kill him.

For Chuck, the necklace represented the one constant protection in his life, which he found oddly symbolic. What should have been the job of his father instead was a glowing stone. Emotionless, cold, hard, and unyielding. But in those ways, it was exactly like his real father.

It was almost comical when Chuck thought about it. All of the time and energy he put into pining for his father's affection and approval, and in the end it never added up to shit. And as he passed grave after open grave, he thought about the enormity of his family and all the people they'd killed throughout the years.

"We're fighters, Charles, champions!" his father would say. "We don't quit, we don't stop, and we never run. We face whatever is down the road like men! The world loves to break men. It's its favorite pastime. But the world will never break the Toussaints. You hear me, Charles? You come from a long line of tradition, and power, and success. Every Toussaint has done that, and god help me, I will do everything I can to make sure you're not the last. Are you ready for such a future, Charles? Or will you crumble like so many weak-minded fools?"

He was six when his father delivered that rousing speech. And what he remembered most was not what his father had said, but the way he looked when he said it. The reddened cheeks, the wiry muscles, the veins bulging from his father's neck. Out of everything, what he feared most was his own father.

Chuck stopped halfway to the mausoleum at one of the crumbled tombs. The headstone was new, as his father had only passed away a few years ago. He knew it was Owen that had done this damage, no doubt when he was searching for the pendulum. It must have been the old woman who told him about it. The man wasn't smart enough to figure it out on his own. It was why he picked him in the first place.

His father's coffin was exposed and Chuck had a fleeting impulse to open it. There was a part of him that wanted to see his father look weak. He was rarely sick, and even when he was, he pushed through it. In all the years he knew his father, Chuck never once saw him nap, ask for help, or help someone without getting something in return.

"Everything has a price, Charles. And it's best that you are the one setting the cost. Time is money, Chuckie."

Chuck stared down at the headstone, the engraved letters and dates still polished and clean, though a hint of green moss had started to form over the top.

"It's over, Dad." Despite the swirling pain in his gut, Chuck's voice remained steady. It was easier to face his father when there wasn't any chance for repercussions. He figured every man needed to repent to someone at the end, and he couldn't think of anyone else but his father.

"Everything our family built is going to crumble. The house, the factory, the money, it's all going away." Chuck glanced to the mausoleum and the old grave that rested by its side where he knew Charles Toussaint I was buried. "I didn't live up to the name. I didn't live up to what you wanted me to be." He turned back to his father's headstone, tears streaming down his face. "I wasn't the son you wanted. I know that." His voice cracked and he wiped the snot from his upper lip. "But you should know that you weren't the father I wanted. You were cold, and mean, and distant. Where you should have picked me up, you let me fall. Where you should have held my hand, you shoved me away. When you should have loved me, you gave me nothing but resentment."

Chuck clenched his fists and he trembled. All the hate, all the anger, all the pain that he felt as a child returned tenfold. Those memories that he'd spent so much time repressing and trying to forget flooded back in spades.

Chuck kicked his father's headstone, the heel of his shoe giving a muted thump against the dense concrete. He struck it again, harder. Then again, and again, and again, until a sharp pain radiated from his knee to his hip.

He hobbled back a few steps, tears still in his eyes, his cheeks red and wet, his hair glued to the front of his forehead in a smeared and sweaty mess. He raised his face to the sky, arms outstretched. "Can you hear me, Father? Do you see what's become of your only son? Do you? *Do you!*"

But instead of his father's roaring voice, instead of a flash of lightning or thunder answering him in the sky, there was only the light buzz of cicadas. There was no raising of the dead, no signals from the afterlife. Just like the fears of his childhood, he found the dead to be lifeless and final.

The tears dried, and a slow chuckle rolled from Chuck's tongue. It started quiet and soft, nothing but the gentle gyration of his shoulders giving away his humor, and then the laughter roared into the night as the tears on his face dried.

"I'll see you soon, Father," Chuck said, wiping his nose with his dirty sleeve. He turned away from the tombs of his family and trudged back to where he left Matt Cooley. He picked the boy off the ground, who was still wheezing from the boot to the ribs, and carried him toward the house. The house where it all started. And the house where it would all end.

* * *

BELLINGHAM RUBBED the knobby knuckles of his arthritic hands. They hurt tonight. More than usual. A light tremor appeared in his left pinky finger, vibrating violently without his consent as he sat in a chair close to the nurse's station on the operating wing of the hospital.

His deputy was still in surgery. It took them two hours to get back to the hospital after trudging back from that swamp. Luckily Deputy Hurt had the good sense to tag the location of the shack with GPS on his phone before they took off. They'd need to get back out there, analyze the body, make sure it matched up with what Owen Cooley was saying, which the sheriff thought it did.

Bellingham sat, hunched over. The past few days had worn him down. But what sucked the life out of him most was the fact that so much of it could have been prevented if he'd just listened to Owen Cooley in the first place.

Deputy Hurt saw the same thing that he did when Owen turned into that... thing. But how in the hell was he supposed to convince a judge what happened when there were two dead bodies involved? And if Lacroix didn't survive the operating table, that slim chance of Owen Cooley maintaining his freedom would drop to zero.

"Sheriff?" The nurse at the station poked her head up from her computer, her hand covering the mouthpiece of her phone. "You've got a call from one of your deputies."

Bellingham's knees cracked as he stood and hobbled over. A few flecks of dried mud broke off from his pant legs, and he grabbed the phone. "This is Bellingham."

"Sheriff, I've got Claire Cooley here with me."

Bellingham grunted. "Put her on."

"Um, Sheriff?" The deputy grunted and then cleared his throat. "There's more."

Without thinking about it, Bellingham grabbed hold of the edge of the nurse's desk for support. Whatever more he was about to hear wasn't good.

"The deputies you had watch over Mrs. Cooley were killed. Shot through the head in their squad car."

Color drained from Bellingham's cheeks, and his elbow thumped loudly on the desk as he stopped himself from falling. The floor spun, and he saw the nurse's lips move as she stood to check on him, but he couldn't hear what she was saying.

"Sheriff?"

"It was Chuck?" Bellingham asked, closing his eyes.

"Yes, sir."

A sickness formed like a pin-sized needle in the middle of his gut, and Bellingham reached for it absentmindedly. "Put Claire on."

Muffled voices and the sound of hands filtered through the speaker until Claire's voice sounded in his ear. "Sheriff, you have to get to the house."

"Are you all right?" Bellingham asked. It was the father in him. The woman was just about the same age as his oldest. And god knew that would have been his first question if he was speaking to his own daughter.

"He took Matt," Claire said. "You have to get to the house, Sheriff."

Bellingham shook his head and stepped away from the desk, stretching the cord of the phone. A sense of strength was returning, action and purpose pulling him from the pits of weakness. "On Cypress?"

"Owen will be there, and I know that's where Chuck is going."

"Why?"

"Chuck kept talking about how he was going to finish this, how he was going to make it to the end of the line. Sheriff, please." The strength cracked along with her voice. "Please, my family... we've been through enough."

"Claire—"

"You believe us, right?" Claire asked, a hopeful desperation in her tone. "After what you've seen, after everything that's happened, you have to believe us. We're not crazy, we're not making this up, we're telling the truth."

"It doesn't matter if I believe you. Once this goes to court, we need something more than just black magic and what we said we saw. We need evidence."

"And you'll find it at the house," Claire replied. "But you have to go now. You have to hurry. Please, Sheriff. I'm begging you."

Bellingham looked to the clock. It was almost midnight It'd been nearly two days since he'd slept. It was too long for a man his age. But the finish line was up ahead. He just needed to dig a little deeper. "All right, Claire. I'll take my men, but I want you and your daughter at the station. And that's not negotiable."

"Thank you, Sheriff."

"Put the deputy back on." Bellingham waited for the shuffle to happen over the phone and after he relayed the instructions to the deputy about what he wanted, he hung up. He tapped his forefinger on the nurse's desk. He turned to look at her, and her eyes were big and wide like a full moon. It made her look younger. That type of hopeful fear always made people look younger. Unless you were already old, like he was. "I want to know about Deputy Lacroix's status the moment he's out of surgery, understood?"

"Yes, sir."

"Good." Bellingham's boots clicked against the tile on his way out, and he grabbed the rest of his deputies in the waiting room. He left only one behind to monitor the situation with Lacroix. As he walked, more mud from the trek through the swamp speckled that white tile, leaving a trail of dirt.

Louisiana mud was strong stuff. Like concrete to most people. He remembered as a kid getting stuck in it once or twice. But as a child when he was immobile, he was never scared. It was all just a game back then. There weren't any real consequences. No, at the time it was only silliness.

It was funny how your mentality changed when you got older. Now getting stuck was a curse. It moved against progress. Forward, forward, always forward. Now when he looked down at the mud on his pants, the only thing he thought about was that he'd have to buy another pair. It always went back to money, didn't it? That reason we complained about something, or the justification for our lot in life.

Bellingham thought about those things as he climbed behind the wheel of his cruiser. They were peculiar thoughts, and somehow they frightened him. Times were changing. But Bellingham desperately hoped that he had enough strength left to help one family pull themselves from the mud.

The trip to the house on Cypress Lane was similar to the trip to Bacalou's world. A tugging sensation that pulled him through a tunnel of darkness after he touched Madame Crepaux's hand, and moments later he found himself in the living room of the old house.

Owen wobbled a few steps, his mind dizzy from the trip, but when he looked over at Roger, the old man had hunched over and thrown up his breakfast.

Madame Crepaux glided across the floor and toward the closed front door. "He is out there. In the swamp."

"Gah!" Owen buckled to his knees on the floor, a stabbing pain radiating from his chest and outward toward his limbs and the base of his skull. Bacalou was making a move, and Owen wasn't sure if he'd be able to keep the beast at bay for much longer.

Madame Crepaux placed a hand on his shoulder, and the pain lessened. "Hold on for just a little bit longer, Owen Cooley."

"Just hurry." Another flash of pain struck his chest, and he was pushed to his hands and knees. He arched his back and scrunched his face tight as he opened his mouth to cry out, but nothing but a breathless gasp escaped.

"Roger, come." Madame Crepaux helped the old man over to Owen's side, and Roger knelt. "Take his hand, and hold tight."

Sweat poured off Owen in buckets as Bacalou roared in angry defiance of Owen's control.

"Owen," Roger said, his voice eerily calm as he gave Owen's hand a squeeze. "Son, look at me."

Owen kept his eyes shut tight, the pressure at the front of his skull throbbing and aching throughout his entire body. Roger squeezed his hand again, and Owen forced his eyes open. He slowly turned to the old man and saw that his expression was still and calm. And all Owen could think about was the fact that in a few moments, he would be dead.

"Tell Claire that this wasn't her fault," Roger said. "Tell her that this was my decision and that this was the best way I could help my family." The strength on his face wavered, and his lower lip quivered. "You make sure she knows that. And you tell Matt that I'll always be with him, and you tell Chloe that I want her to draw a picture for me to keep." His hand finally shook as the last words left his mouth.

"Roger…" Owen struggled to hang on as Madame Crepaux placed her left hand on Owen's head and her right on Roger's head. But he couldn't think of anything to say. He couldn't find the words the man deserved. "Thank you."

"Bacalou!" Madame Crepaux's voice bellowed loudly throughout the room. "Hear me!"

Owen felt the creature fix its gaze toward Crepaux. A growing heat radiated from Crepaux's hand, and Owen saw the remnants of the light beaming from her palm spread onto the floor.

"Ooo-La-Cunna-Do-Eee-Way. Ooo-La-Cunna-Do-Eee-

Way. Ooo-La-Cunna-Do-Eee-Way. OOO-LA-CUNNA-DO-EEE-WAY!"

"GAAH!" Owen tensed, his muscles spasming as Bacalou roared inside of his mind. He clenched his hands tight into fists as the creature stirred, thrashing about in defiance. The heat worsened, the light brightened, and the pain intensified.

The incantation drudged up the creature's memories, and they swirled to the forefront of Owen's consciousness. Darkness, and the putrid stench of death drove the creature mad with desire.

Owen felt his hold over the beast slipping as Bacalou grew angrier and more defiant from Madame Crepaux's chanting that became faster and faster. Owen's eyes rolled back, and he seized on the hardwood. Just when Owen felt the darkness pull over him in finality, a bright burst of light blinded him and in one momentary instant, he felt his soul leave his body. Beneath him he saw the transference of Bacalou into Roger, the creature lusting in a crazed whirlwind for the hunt for its prey.

And then Owen was tugged back into himself and was returned to the pain and agony of his own flesh. A cavern formed in the spaces where Bacalou had resided. Owen trembled, his body feeling like nothing more than a shell that would collapse in on itself from his own weight.

A few beads of sweat dripped from the tip of his nose and collected on the ground like raindrops. Owen looked over to find that Roger was gone, and Madame Crepaux had suddenly moved toward the front window of the house.

Still shaking, Owen rolled to his side, his strength yet to return. "What—" He gulped. "What happened?"

"It's done." Madame Crepaux's reflection was in the window. Her expression was stoic and her voice a flat whisper. "Bacalou has taken Roger's body as a vessel."

Owen looked around the house. Nothing but their old

furniture was there. No trace of Roger had even been inside. He shook his head, confused. "It just left?"

"Bacalou has hunted the heir of the Toussaints for a very long time," Madame Crepaux answered, still staring out the window, her expression stoic. "It will kill the last Toussaint in its own way." A smile finally broke the façade. "And it will be a painful, dreadful affair."

Owen pushed himself off the floor and hobbled toward Madame Crepaux. He took her arm and spun her around to face him with surprising ease. "Matt. He still has my boy. The creature—"

"I know the answer you want to hear, Owen Cooley." Madame Crepaux's smile resembled that of a grandmother trying to soothe a young child. "But it's an answer that I do not have. And even if I did, I would not tell you."

Owen backed away from her, still shaking, clutching the walls for support so he wouldn't collapse from disbelief. "You told me that this would get my family back." His cheeks reddened with anger. "That's what you said it was all about, right? Life? And now you won't tell me if my own son will be able to keep his?"

"Owen, it is not wise to know to a future that hasn't been writ—"

"Don't give me that shit!" Owen slammed his fist into the wall, and it throbbed from the vicious hit. "That mystical Voodoo bullshit is all you've fed me since I've run into you. I want the truth, and I want it from you now!"

Madame Crepaux glided toward him, her demeanor still calm and cool. "Chuck Toussaint wants to hurt you before he goes away. He blames you for everything that has happened to him, and he wants you to feel the same gut-wrenching pain and anxiety that has plagued him his entire life. And he thinks killing your son will do that to you."

Owen nodded absentmindedly as he turned away from Madame Crepaux. "And what happens now?"

Madame Crepaux returned to the window and resumed her idling staring contest with the world outside. "We wait for Chuck Toussaint to find us."

* * *

CHUCK LINGERED at the swamp's edge, just before the start of the clearing of the field that led toward the house. He saw the light through the windows, and he heard the screaming. And not long after it was all done, he heard the familiar rattling of the creature's staff.

He looked back down to Matt, who lay motionless on the ground, his lips turning a light shade of blue. When he breathed, a rattling wheeze squeezed from his lungs.

Chuck yanked the boy to his feet. He kept the gun close and crouched low in the tall reeds on his way across the clearing, dragging the impotent Cooley boy behind him. His eyes were fixated on the house ahead of him. There were no windows on the side of the home he was approaching, but the lights he saw from earlier were coming from the front of the house, so he made his way toward the back door.

Another rattle echoed across the field, and Chuck froze. He crouched lower, barely anything viewable beyond the reeds. A chill crawled up his spine. He exhaled a puff of frosty air. He turned left, then right, then back toward the house, all the while the air around him freezing colder and colder.

Another rattle, and then another, the bones cracking together more violently the closer he moved toward the house. Without realizing it, Chuck had broken into a sprint, revealing himself from the tall grass on his path toward the back door, Matt's limp body still being dragged behind him.

The bones cracked and reached a crescendo as Chuck touched the handle of the back door. He was breathless as he entered but when he shut the door behind him, the rattling ended.

Silence fell in the house, and he dropped Matt on the floor, placing both hands on the pistol. With the commotion he made and after forgoing his stealth outside, there was no way that they didn't hear him enter.

Chuck scanned the dining room from the hallway. He passed a room on his left and poked his head inside, finding it empty. When he reached the end of the hallway, he edged himself to the corner, using the wall as cover.

"I know you're here!" Chuck screamed, his voice carrying across the room to the front of the house. He adjusted the grip of his pistol, his fingers peeling off in quick, sweaty jerks before he reset them. He kept waiting for Madame Crepaux to come out of nowhere, but a part of him knew that she wouldn't interfere with the creature's game. Not now. Not when it was so close to the end.

"I've got your boy!" Chuck spoke the words mockingly and smiled at the thought of Owen's torture. Death had come for both men tonight. And Chuck was Owen's Grim Reaper. "You come out now, or I blow his brains out." Chuck placed the tip of the gun against Matt's skull, not even looking down at the boy. If he had, he would have seen the pale blue of his lips had spread to the rest of his face. "Now, Owen!"

And then, with his hands in the air, Owen stepped into the dining room from the kitchen. His complexion was pale white, his skin almost glowing in the darkness. His face was gaunt, his eyes tired. Chuck had expected fire and brimstone, but instead what he saw was a despondent father offering his plea to a mad man.

"It won't prove anything," Owen said, shuffling his feet toward Chuck, his hands still up, but lowering from fatigue.

"And it won't change what'll happen to you." He stopped halfway. "It's out of me. It's hunting you."

"It's been hunting me my entire life," Chuck said, the gun barrel still pressed firmly against Matt's head. "Even when it wasn't." Chuck tossed Matt to the floor in front of him and then aimed the pistol at the boy. Matt remained motionless on the floor. His chest rose and fell quickly from the short gasping breaths.

Owen cried. "Please." His lips quivered and his body trembled. He was no longer a man on the verge of collapse. He had already fallen.

"You know, I hated my father. Couldn't stand him. He was a soulless piece of shit that tormented me, maybe even more so than the creature whose sole purpose was to kill me." Chuck stepped forward, gun still aimed at Matt's head. "But I'm not weak. Not like he thought I was. Not like you."

Owen dropped to his knees, still crying. "P-Please, I—, I—"

And as Owen's voice cut out, Chuck blinked, thinking that his vision had blurred as Owen's figure slowly dissolved into what looked like black smoke. Owen's eyes flashed and flickered with specks of gold, and before Chuck could make the connection, a force viciously knocked him from behind.

On the ground, Chuck saw the angered face of the real Owen Cooley, who hammered his fists against Chuck's body. The witch had tricked him.

Owen pinned the wrist with the pistol to the ground and with his free right hand pummeled Chuck's ribcage until he couldn't hold the gun any longer.

The pistol clanged against the floor with a dead, heavy smack, and Owen gripped Chuck's throat with both hands. He squeezed, cutting off the airflow, and Chuck smacked impotently at Owen's arms as the room darkened and suddenly flushed with cold.

The wail of sirens flashed outside as Chuck and Owen grappled on the floor.

"Owen!" Madame Crepaux's voice thundered in the room as black water, thick and goopy like tar, dripped from the ceiling and rose from beneath the floor. "He is for Bacalou to take! Not you."

Car doors slammed out front, and the hurried pace of footsteps flooded into the living room and down the hall toward the kitchen.

Dark black blotches began to fill Chuck's vision, and his head grew heavy as Owen continued to choke him. But out of his peripheral, he managed to see the officers with their guns flooding into the room, their attention half on the fight between himself and Owen and the black goo that covered the floor.

"Owen, let him go!" Bellingham aimed his service pistol at Owen, his finger on the trigger. "Now!"

"He tried to kill my family. Tried to kill me. Took my boy." Owen's eyes remained fixated on Chuck's, his gaze intensified and crazed. "Why shouldn't I kill him?"

"I'm giving you to the count of three, Owen!" Bellingham stepped closer, and more deputies filed into the dining room. The count was over twelve now. "One!"

Owen squeezed harder, cutting off the last of Chuck's air. "Two!"

Chuck's hands fell to his sides, the strength to fight back no longer in his arsenal. His eyelids fluttered open and close. He heard the mumbled shouts of the officers, and Owen's response, but the world blurred. And suddenly he saw a hand appear on Owen's shoulder, and the voce around his neck cease.

Chuck gasped, sucking in air as he saw Madame Crepaux pulling Owen back. He coughed and gagged, splashing in the shallow black water as more dripped from above. His throat was raw, and the muscles around his neck were tender. He looked up to Madame Crepaux, who stared down at him with contempt.

"Feel good about yourself?" Chuck asked, his voice raspy.

Madame Crepaux shook her head. "I did this for a good woman who did nothing but help people. I did this because it is people like you who walk this Earth and think of it as disposable. I did this because what your family did was nothing but hurt and exploit everyone around them." And then the contempt in her eyes transformed into pity. "You were not born evil, but you let evil influence your every move, and it consumed your soul. And after all of that debt, your collector has finally arrived."

She stepped away, and Chuck was left on the floor alone, where Bellingham and his deputies had their pistols aimed at him.

Chuck propped himself up on his elbows and then rolled to his side, hacking and still trying to catch his breath. Black water dripped from his shirt and elbows with a light drip, drip, drip.

"You think those guns scare me?" Chuck said, his eyes wild, his face reddening despite the drop in temperature. Most of the deputies were shaking, everyone's breath puffing icy air into the room. He pushed himself to his hands and knees and laughed, the humor thick with desperation. "Go on. Shoot me."

A tremor rippled the water and shook the house. It was deep, like a bass drum at a concert held at an arena. Another tremor. Another ripple. The spaces between the heavy beats grew faster, like something or someone was gaining speed.

Chuck pushed himself from his knees as the water bubbled behind Madame Crepaux. They started small, like soda bubbles, but grew larger, and bursting with mucky pops that sprayed the black goo farther over the spread.

And then the water grew still. The tremors stopped and noise was sucked from the room. Chuck shivered and puffed another breath of icy droplets. A rattle. Those bones. His eyes bulged from his skull and he scrambled backward until he slammed into the wall.

"NO!"

Another rattle. Black matted hair rose from the black water in the center of the room.

"NO!" Chuck pushed himself harder against the wall, as if he could squeeze himself between the tiny cracks between the wood.

Black water dripped from Bacalou's body, fully emerged from the darkness. It opened its mouth, those jagged and exposed teeth sharp and dripping with the same black goo that reached to Chuck's ankles.

Bacalou extended its claws, its wide stumpy feet vibrating the floor with every step. He roared, its breath the stench of death.

And despite all the talk of wanting to face his demons, and all the buildup of trying to come to terms with the lack of his father's love for him and how his dad had never made him weak, Chuck screamed at the top of lungs as he scurried backwards on all fours. "NO! Please! NO!"

Owen pulled Matt off to the side, clutching his son with both arms and shielding him from the stand-off between man and beast.

Chuck ran over to the pistol he'd dropped on his retreat, and when he reached for it, Bacalou lunged and knocked it from his hand. "Please, no!" Chuck smacked into the back wall, with nowhere else to run.

"Queen Samba's curse has finally come to an end," Madame Crepaux said, still standing back as the creature roared in ecstasy. "And so have you."

Tears streamed down Chuck's face, and he whimpered

pathetically as Bacalou came within inches. The creature stared down at Chuck with those wide black eyes just staring at him, and as Chuck stared into the darkness, into the face of death, his life flashed before his eyes.

But they were only memories of fear and pain. All the words of his father came back to him, all of the stares from the kids in the halls at school, and all of the self-doubt that he filled himself with. It was an onslaught of shame and embarrassment. And as those last few tears froze on his cheeks from Bacalou's cold, death-like presence, the creature looked as though it was relieved that it had finally come to the end. And in the creature's relief, Chuck felt a sense of ease in those last moments. Right up until Bacalou rammed the claws from its left hand through Chuck's chest.

"GAH!" Blood spurted from Chuck's mouth, and blood seeped from the wounds on his chest as Bacalou lifted the impaled heir of his foe into the air. The blood that covered his shirt started off red, and then transformed into the same black that covered the floor and rained from the ceiling.

Bacalou's eyes glowed white, and then the creature roared again, flinging some spittle over Chuck's face, and then jammed its second pair of claws into Chuck's lower abdomen, which elicited a second wail from the creature and a second animalistic howl from Chuck.

More blood, more pain, more death, it all oozed from Bacalou and Chuck's union. The creature's eyes glowed brighter, and it opened its mouth wide.

"Open fire!" Bellingham pulled the trigger first, and after that first thunderous crack bellowed from his pistol, a cacophony of gunshots followed from his deputies.

Bullets ricocheted off Bacalou's hide impotently, but the creature turned with its black eyes and roared, a stench of death and maggots filling into the air as the officers continued to shoot.

"NO!" Madame Crepaux thrust her hands out, and a powerful wave of air thrust the sheriff and his deputies backward violently into the wall. The similar golden glow from her eyes also radiated from her hands and pinned the officers where they lay. "You must see now! You must see the truth." She turned her head back around, her arms remaining outstretched, and locked eyes with Bacalou. "Show them."

Chuck's body spasmed, his head flinging forward, and his limp arms rocking forward then back in a harsh jerk. A force tugged at something deep within Chuck's body. It was like his insides were being ripped out. The pain was tremendous, and as the pull from within grew stronger, he noticed that he was moving. Not him necessarily, but a part of him. It was the part of him that was alive, the part of him that comprised all of the emotions and happiness and life of his past, his present, and his future. It was his soul.

And as Chuck's soul was pulled from his body, he looked back and cried at the sight of his mortal self, and suddenly he was set ablaze with fire, skin melting, hair burning, the smell and taste of burnt flesh filling the room.

Chuck watched himself burn and his soul be consumed into the creature's black heart. He caught one brief glimpse of Owen Cooley, who was still rocking his boy in his arms, praying that he would survive. And as if to prove he should be damned, Chuck Toussaint wished that the boy would die right there in front of his father. And with that, he was gone.

Bacalou removed its claws from Chuck's dead body and let it collapse to the floor. Its eyes still glowed white, and it roared. It was a victorious and righteous cry. And as the creature turned, the black water on the floor receded, and the ooze dripping from the ceiling ended.

Madame Crepaux approached the creature, smiling, tears streaming down her face that looked as golden as the flecks in her eyes. "Queen, you are free."

The beast wailed, and black smoke sprouted from its head, shoulders, chest, legs, and stomach. It swirled into the ceiling, dissipating into nothing. And as Bacalou's body evaporated, it slowly exposed light. Beautiful, white light with flashes of green.

Bellingham and his officers gawked at the sight, their guns limp in their hands at their sides. And then, as the officers approached the light, drawn to it like moths to a flame, Owen rocked his boy, clutching him close to his chest, checking his breathing and sobbing lightly to himself. He saw the blue lips, the pale face, and the fluttering eyes. His son was fading in and out of consciousness. "Stay with me, Matt."

His son answered with a rattling gasp. His eyes rolled back into his head and his mouth went slack.

"No," Owen said, gently grazing Matt's lips with his fingers. "Stay with me, son. Come on." He gave Matt a little shake, but there was no more wheezing, no more movement. Just still coldness. "God, no." Owen sobbed. Tears burst from his eyes, and he wept. "God, please, no." He lowered his head and gently placed his forehead against his son's. "Not now. Don't take him from me now."

Suddenly, and almost as mysteriously as the coldness appeared, it thawed, and the light approached both Owen and Matt.

Owen lifted his head, the light shimmering down from the dismantled creature. He blinked, unsure of the mirage as the light took the shape of a woman. She had thick black hair, wild and untamed, and she possessed the sharpest green eyes that Owen had ever seen.

"You have suffered much." Her voice drifted softly, floating through the air as the light around her took shape into a womanly form. "I have caused much of that suffering."

She lowered her green eyes to Matt. "His soul, it is leaving him."

"Save him," Owen said, his eyes bulging with the pleading mercy of a father. "Take me if you have to. Just please, save him."

The woman moved closer and reached down to lift Owen's chin. She smiled. "The love of a father can do much in this world. It can make a son's memory live on even after he's gone. Our children never leave us, not even in the next world."

Owen's lower lip quivered. "I don't know what the next world has in store for me." More tears broke loose from his eyes. "But I know my son deserves better."

The woman nodded and then pressed her palm against Matt's head. She closed her eyes and lifted her face toward the ceiling. She hummed, low and deep, and vibrations channeled through Matt's body and Owen's arms. He felt the tremor, then a warmth radiated from his son.

The light illuminated through Matt's skin, and Owen's boy glowed like moonlight. It was beautiful and translucent. And just as the light faded and the woman removed her hand from Matt's head, there was silence.

Owen's world, his future, his own life paused for the next few moments. He watched his son for any movements, any sign, any chance that he was going to come out of this alive. And just when those moments stretched to the point of despair, Matt gasped for breath.

"Matt? Matt, can you hear me?" He ran his fingers through his boy's hair and clutched him tightly. And as Matt opened his eyes, Owen burst into tears.

"Sacrifices do not go unnoticed," the woman said, and then turned to Madame Crepaux. "You never lost faith, and for that, I thank you." She gave a light bow.

Madame Crepaux immediately dropped to her knees. "I

do not deserve such honor." She bowed until her head touched the floor.

Queen Samba lifted Crepaux's chin. "You deserve that, and much more."

"Take me with you." Madame Crepaux latched onto the Queen in longing. "I beg you."

"You still have work to do here, my child." Queen Samba looked around the walls of her old house, basking in the glow of nostalgia. "My gris-gris is now yours. It will serve you well." She turned to the officers, every single one of their jaws slack save the sheriff. "You are men of law. I am a woman of nature and earth. It is rare the pair see eye to eye, but I believe we serve the same cause."

And as Queen Samba spoke her last words, the brilliant light started to dissipate and spread out into the air. The last to leave was her face, and when all that remained was her brilliant green eyes, the light finally ended.

ONE WEEK LATER

*T*he black lace veil that hung from Claire's head provided a distorted view of the inside of the car as well as the scenery they passed. Her hands rested in her lap, and a dull throb suddenly radiated from them. She glanced down and discovered that her hands were clenched tight into fists. She uncurled her fingers and the aching subsided.

"Mommy? Are we almost there?" Chloe asked, looking up from her seat right next to her mother.

Claire kissed the top of her head. "Almost, bug." She looked to Matt, who sat on the other side of his sister. His face was glued to the passing buildings outside the cab's window. "Matt, are you all right?"

"Yeah." The answer was short, quiet. It was the response he gave for most things these days. Yeah, okay, fine, or no were about all she could muster from him.

Claire did her best to control her breathing. She closed her eyes, trying to calm that growing ball of anxiousness nesting in the pit of her stomach. It randomly ballooned to the rest of her body without her consent throughout the day. But she couldn't lose it where they were going. Not today.

She glanced out the window of the car from the backseat. The sky was blue and it was beautifully sunny outside. A fact that she thought her dad would have appreciated.

Chloe leaned up against Claire's arm. It had been a long twelve hours. Between the mess with the courts and Owen still in jail, she had to coordinate this little trip back to Baltimore herself. And while there wasn't a body to bury, she wasn't about to have her father's headstone rest in a state or a town that he never really knew. Louisiana wasn't their home. And that's where she needed to go. That's where he would have wanted to go.

The cab's brakes squealed to a stop and the cabbie's eyes appeared in the rearview mirror. "We're here."

Claire reached for her purse. "Matt, you take your sister out to the sidewalk. And hold hands. I need to pay the fare."

"That's all right," the cabbie said.

Claire waved him off, rummaging through the cavernous purse until she found her wallet. "No, it's fine, I—"

"Ma'am."

Claire looked up, finding that the cabbie had turned around.

"I'm very sorry for your loss. I wish you and your family the best."

It could have been the fact that she was burying her father, or the fact that she hadn't slept in over a week, or maybe it was just the simple gesture from a stranger to help make her life easier, but Claire Cooley had never been so glad to be home and so thankful to find a piece of kindness amidst all the struggle. "Thank you."

The cabbie nodded, and Claire joined Matt and Chloe on the sidewalk. She wiped her eyes as the cab drove off and then reached for her children's hands. "All right, guys. Let's go."

The cemetery was a small plot of land on Baltimore's west side. It was the same cemetery where her mother was buried, and there was already a spot reserved for her father right next door. Her parents had picked the location without her knowing, and her father had already taken care of and paid for most of the arrangements after he discovered he had Alzheimer's. But that was her dad, always thinking ahead, always trying to make the hard stuff easier for her to deal with.

Claire navigated her way through the headstones, her heart pounding harder and faster in her chest the closer she moved to the plot of land. She gripped Matt's hand tighter and as if the boy knew what it meant, he squeezed back and she stopped.

"It's okay, Mom," Matt said. "We're all here."

The strength of her reserve finally broke as her lips creased tight across her mouth and her eyes watered. "Yeah. I know, sweetheart." But that wasn't the truth. Not everyone was here. And while she knew that her oldest child, her only son, would do his best to take up the mantle of "the man of the house" while his father was away, it wasn't the same without Owen.

She wanted to be taken care of. She wanted her husband at her side as she grieved the loss of her father. After everything that happened, was that really too much to ask? Was that stretching the credit of her pain too far? She didn't think so, but life never cared about what you wanted. It gave you what it had, and right now this was it.

Claire took a few breaths, the snot rattling violently in her nose, and then she walked forward. Her steps were slower, and she kept her eyes glued to the pair of headstones at the end of the row. One had been weathered a little bit, but the other was unmistakably brand new.

Both Chloe and Matt stared at the fresh piece of stone, and Claire knelt to get a better look at the engraving. The name and years of life were all neatly and professionally carved, and in quotes was the phrase her father had requested in his will.

Keep hold of hope even when it's dark.

Claire covered her mouth and stifled a whimper. She collapsed forward on her hands and clutched the dirt as both Matt and Chloe came rushing to her side. She couldn't fight back the grief any longer and she cried, sobbing loudly and wildly as she clutched her children tight.

Her father wasn't supposed to die like this. This wasn't how she pictured the end. But in a way, she was grateful that he didn't have to suffer anymore. She knew the burden the disease had placed on him. He was an intelligent man, a man with pride and dignity. Alzheimer's had stripped those things from Roger Templeton.

"I hope you found your peace, Dad." Claire wiped her eyes, and Matt pulled a tissue out of her purse, handing it over to his mother. "I love you, and I'll always miss you. Every day."

"Me too, Grandpa," Chloe said, and then blew the head-stone a kiss.

"Yeah," Matt said. "Me too."

They sat there for a while in silence, just holding onto one another. Claire knew that she needed to get back to Ocoee. Things needed to be taken care of for Owen's trial, and she needed to coordinate with that prick of an attorney of his. But for the time being, for the next twenty minutes, she let herself forget about that. She closed her eyes and let the memories of her father flood her mind. They were all good ones, which she was thankful for, and for a moment, it was as though all was right with the world. She had her kids, she was back home, and the sun was shining.

* * *

THREE MONTHS **Later**

That house at the end of the dirt road on Cypress Lane could barely be seen from the road. The branches of the cypress trees that stretched over the road swayed in a rare afternoon breeze that offered a reprieve from the late summer heat.

A moving truck sat alone at the end of the drive, and every few minutes a man would exit the house and haul another box out of the back. The boxes were large, and small, and after that, furniture was moved inside. Mostly bedframes and mattresses, still covered in brand-new plastic from the store.

Madame Crepaux stood in the doorway between the kitchen and the dining room, watching the beds being carried up to the second-floor bedrooms, and then she drifted her eyes down to the boxes that contained all of her books and bottles and elixirs.

"All right, Miss." The movers exited the room that once belonged to Matt Cooley and wiped their brows, the inside of the house just as hot as the weather outside. "That's everything out of the truck." He descended the steps and pointed to the cluster of boxes that littered the floor. "You need any of these taken upstairs?"

"No," Madame Crepaux answered. "Thank you."

"All right then." The mover had a ring of sweat around his collar, which he plucked at. He fanned himself and grimaced from the heat. "Is your A/C not working? My brother and I can take a look at it if it's not."

"I enjoy the heat." Madame Crepaux flashed a pretty

smile, and the two men smiled nervously in return. She'd hired out of town movers, and neither men knew of her reputation in Ocoee.

"All right then," he said. "Have a good rest of your day." He tipped the front of his ball cap, and he and his brother walked toward the front door, glancing around at the house on their way out. The truck rumbled as they started the engine, and the noise faded as they drove away.

Once alone, Madame Crepaux closed her eyes. The open windows and doors welcomed the sounds of nature. Frogs, birds, insects, all humming in the orchestra of life. It had been a long time since this house had experienced those sounds.

She opened her eyes and glided through the dining room, up the staircase, and then back toward the room that belonged to Matt Cooley. She knew that Bacalou was gone, and she knew that the Queen had vanished into the next life, but still her steps were hesitant.

Recent history had a way of clinging to the present like a morning dew. It would eventually give way to the heat of the day, evaporated and forgotten. But in those first few hours, after the events when the wounds and memories were still fresh, the world was still fragile.

Crepaux lingered at the doorway to Matt's room. Inside were two beds with a table next to each bedside. The mattresses were bare of sheets, which were packed somewhere in the boxes downstairs. She drifted her eyes from ceiling to floor and from left to right.

"It will be as it was, Queen Samba." Madame Crepaux spoke softly, almost as if she were whispering a prayer. "The sick will come to be healed, and I will use everything that you have taught me. This will be a house of life again." She crossed the threshold of the doorway and stopped at the window.

The treetops of the swamp swayed back and forth from the breeze, which Madame Crepaux caught from the open window. Clear blue skies allowed the warmth of the sun to beat against her cheeks, and she smiled.

After nearly two centuries of closed doors and barred windows, and death and misery, the house that had taken so much was finally ready to give back. Wrongs had been righted. And with a mind that had already lived a lifetime in a rejuvenated body, Madame Crepaux felt hope rise within her. It was the hope of tomorrow. It was the hope of change. It was a hope emerged from the ashes of pain. And that kind of hope always burned so much brighter and stronger than anything else.

* * *

AT THREE O'CLOCK in the afternoon on Sunday, no traffic ran through Main Street in Ocoee, Louisiana. Which wasn't an irregularity, but after the media circus of the past three months, Sheriff Bellingham was glad to be done with it.

The shine and sexy of the trial had worn off in the public eyes, and the audience had moved on to newer and more exciting things.

But while the public had moved on, Bellingham was still dealing with the aftermath of the trial and subsequent events. And today was the final piece of that puzzle.

Charles Toussaint VII had no heirs, and there were no other branches left in the family tree. Chuck's will had stated that in the event of his death that all of his wealth would go to his first ex-wife. Bellingham had met the woman last month when she came to collect what she had been bequeathed. Their interaction was short, and Bellingham could tell that underneath the business-like demeanor, she was hurting.

Even after a marriage dissolves, love still lingers. It's a residue that never breaks down, only grows smaller and weaker as time passes. Bellingham had met her once before, years ago before Chuck had taken over the family business. She was a lovely woman, too sweet for Chuck.

She had remarried and lived on the West Coast, with no desire to keep anything of her late husband's. She sold everything. The house, cars, and the factory.

It was a blow to the whole town, because the moment she sold it off, the people who bought it started stripping it down for parts. Today, the factory doors were finally closing for good.

Bellingham drove over with the chain and lock, choosing to do it by himself instead of sending a deputy. The mass exodus of the town had already started, people moving to either New Orleans or Houston in search of work. The factory had kept people employed for a long time, and despite the Toussaints' violent history, Bellingham thought that had to be worth something.

The outside of the factory looked the same as Bellingham shifted his cruiser into park. The parking lot was empty, and the usual noise and commotion from inside had stopped, but its shell hadn't changed. Bellingham had heard that some of the equipment had been shipped to China. He supposed that was where the work was though. He doubted anyone from Ocoee would be able to get work there.

The chains rattled defiantly as Bellingham pulled them from the passenger seat. He wrapped them around the door handles and then snapped the lock into place. The doors buckled as Bellingham tugged at the handle to make sure they didn't open too far, and he found a gap just big enough for a few roaches to slip through. He let go, satisfied.

Sweat collected quickly on his face and stains formed in tiny blotches under his arms. The only remnant of the building's purpose was the sign that ran across the top of the roof. Toussaint Auto. That sign had been here longer than the sheriff had been alive.

With the factory closed, it was like the town's motor had been turned off and then ripped out. He wasn't sure if the town would survive, but he wouldn't be here long enough to find out. After nearly forty years in law enforcement, tomorrow was his last day. And not by choice.

With the trial and debacle that unfolded the only way for Bellingham to help Owen was to admit that the department had screwed up the investigation. And when he said the department, he meant himself.

Part of the deal for Owen's release from his prison time was that Bellingham be publicly fired for his incompetence on the job. He'd be lying if he said it didn't sting. But he figured it was a small price to pay for putting a man and his family through so much. After all, if he had just listened to Owen in the first place, then a lot of people might still be alive.

He knew that the knowledge of what happened here would haunt him at night. After long days of doing nothing but fishing and drinking can after can of Miller, he'd lay down in bed next to his wife and try and calm the voices of doubt. He figured he'd be able to silence them most of the time, but he knew there would be nights where the voices would be too loud to drown out.

It was all in his head of course; a self-inflicted torture for a man who had done his best to always do the right thing. Just like the chains he put on that door to keep it locked, he put chains on himself to keep the bad locked away in its little corner.

At least he was able to do one thing right after all of it was over. The fact that Owen Cooley was no longer in jail would offer some solace. And while Bellingham wasn't able to re-employ all of Ocoee, he was glad that he was able to put in a good word to his friends out west.

Owen was still a young man, with enough time to heal after what happened. There would always be a scar, but a scar was better than bleeding.

* * *

Sparks flew from a welding torch outside the hull of a large tanker anchored at the dock. The welder hung from the side of the ship, hovering fifty feet in the air as the waters from the bay lapped against the ship's hull below. Sweat glistened on the back of his neck that had burnt to a nice shade of red.

The welder skillfully ran the torch down the side of a panel, the heat melding the new metal panel into place. The line was straight, the soldering skillful, and once the job was finished you could barely tell there was anything done at all.

The flame in the torch cut out, and Owen lifted the welding mask. He wiped his forehead, smearing a grey ash across his skin. He reached for a thermos of water and sipped from it greedily, the cool liquid running down the sides of his mouth. He splashed the rest over his face and set it down. Just before he re-donned the welding mask, the whistle in the shipyard blew, and the workers topside hollered down.

Owen descended the ship in the elevator with the rest of the crew that worked topside. He kept his head down, avoiding a few of the glares that he'd received since he started working. So far no one had said more than two words to him. But he didn't care. He just wanted to do his job and go home at the end of the day.

Owen lugged his welder suit and lunch pail out to the rusted truck he managed to buy for a thousand dollars when they first moved out here. Another three hundred dollars got it running, and while it siphoned gas like a fish breathes water, it got him to work on time.

Owen's muscles groaned in thanks as he sat behind the wheel. He squeezed his hands into fists a few times, his body out of practice from the physical labor that the job required. But three months locked in a jail cell had a way of wearing you down.

Traffic bottlenecked on the interstate, another wreck backing up cars for at least a mile. It added another thirty minutes to his commute, and when Owen turned down the street to his family's new neighborhood, he offered a wave to the elderly woman across the street from him as he pulled into his driveway.

The door hinges groaned as Owen stepped out and turned toward Mrs. Delver. "How's that stove working now?"

Mrs. Delver waved back, nodding and rocking in her old front porch chair. "Just fine, Owen, just fine. Your family coming to the block party this Saturday?" She gave her eyebrows a hopeful raise, craning her neck forward.

"We'll see. Have a good night." Owen turned before the old woman could answer and walked the path to the front door, which needed a new coat of paint. The whole house could use a new coat of paint.

He stepped inside, Mrs. Delver's words echoing in the back of his mind. He already knew what the answer would be. It was a no. Despite the hospitality of the neighbors and being as far away from Ocoee, Louisiana as they could possibly get, it would take some time before they could get back to anything normal.

"Claire?" Owen dropped off his work gear in the front closet by the door. The house was dead quiet, and he stepped through the kitchen, finding it empty. "Claire, you home?"

A dull smack echoed through the walls, and Owen spun

JAMES HUNT

toward the back of the house where the noise originated. He slowly made his way toward the back door. Another smack. Voices drifted inside from the backyard. A ball passed by the tiny window in the door. Another smack, this one louder as Owen reached for the doorknob.

A fresh evening breeze drifted through the open door as the baseball was swallowed up in Matt's glove. It was the first time in nearly four months that he'd seen his boy smile.

"Hey, Dad!"

The screen door swung shut as Owen stepped onto the lawn. "Hey." He smiled back, then glanced to Claire, who had a glove on her hand and a shimmering gleam of sweat on her forehead. The evening sun highlighted her hair and eyes. Even in that ratty old shirt she wore with her hair in a pony tail and no make-up on her face, she was still just as beautiful as when they met.

"They were getting a little dusty." Claire pounded her fist into the mitt. "Thought we'd give them some air."

"Yeah," Matt replied, smiling and tossing the ball in his hand. "They were suffocating in those boxes."

"I bet." Owen spotted Chloe in the corner of the yard. She was sprawled on her back over a blanket with a book in her hand. "And what are you doing over there, bug?"

"Shh!" Chloe didn't even look away from the page. "I'm trying to concentrate, please."

Owen raised an eyebrow at Claire as she caught another ball from Matt. "Anything you'd like to share?"

"We went to the library today," Claire said, heaving the ball back toward Matt with bullseye accuracy. "Our daughter has discovered the art in the Louvre."

"The Louvre?" Owen laughed.

"Shh!" Chloe said, this time eyeing her father from her leisurely place on the blanket. "There isn't anything funny about learning and appreciating the classics."

Owen shook his head as Chloe returned to the book and turned the page. "Where on earth does she learn to say things like that?"

"TV," Matt and Claire answered simultaneously.

Matt beelined a fast ball and connected with Claire's glove in a pop akin to a firecracker. Claire winced and immediately removed her hand from the glove. "All right, Mom's gotta take a break." She tossed the glove to Owen, ball still tucked away inside. "I'll let your dad take over." Claire kissed his lips and then smacked him hard on the ass on her way up the steps to the screen door. "Go get 'em, slugger!"

Owen hopped across the lawn with a light spring in his step that he hadn't felt in... well, he couldn't even remember the last time that he did. He slipped the glove on and lobbed the ball to his boy, which triggered another wide grin across his face. Owen rotated his shoulder. "Little stiff."

"I guess the gloves aren't the only things with a little dust on them," Matt said, laughing as he threw the ball to his dad.

Ball smacked into glove. "Was that an old man joke?" He tossed the ball back with a little more pepper on it and tried to hide the wince from another shot of pain in his shoulder.

Matt laughed, gobbling the ball up just before it got past him. He spun around in a circle and then flung the ball back wildly, but Owen snatched it at the last second. "Maybe it was."

"Well," Owen said, glancing at the ball as he tossed it back and forth between his hand and glove. "This old man still has a few things that he can teach you." He chucked the ball back and smiled as Matt caught it.

And the pair played catch for a while, Matt talking about his day, and Chloe chiming in every once in a while but never looking away from her book. It was the most vocal Matt had been since they moved out here.

The back door swung open, and Claire wiped her hands

on a towel that hung over her shoulder. "All right, dinner's ready. Chloe, bring in that blanket."

Their five-year-old groaned as she rolled to her side and pushed herself up on all fours. She kept a finger in place from where she left off then bunched up the blanket that was half her size. Matt came over to help, and she kissed his cheek.

"You're a doll," she said.

Owen laughed and removed his glove. He watched his kids pass their mother inside, and then he looked to the sun which had finally dipped below the horizon. Nothing but pinks and oranges and light blues swirled in the sky. He wondered if anything like that was painted in The Louvre.

"Hey."

Owen jumped a little, Claire suddenly at his side.

"You all right?"

He pulled her close and kissed her. It brought up a passion and desire that neither of them had felt in a long time. They'd made love a few times after Owen was released from jail, but it always felt mechanical, more out of necessity than want. Their bodies were hungry, starving for one another. But in those moments of starvation you rarely tasted the food, instead you only filled the hunger.

But here, now, in their back yard after a long day's work and coming home to find his family smiling and feeling normal for the first time in months, Owen wanted to taste again. He wanted to let life run through his veins. He'd tasted enough death to last him a lifetime.

Owen finally pulled back, but Claire lingered with her lips still in the same position as when he kissed them. With her eyes closed, she inhaled. "Wow." She opened her eyes. "Hi stranger."

"Hi." Owen kissed her once more. "What's for dinner?"

Made in the USA
Middletown, DE
13 August 2019